D0053641

RAGS & BONES

RAGS & BONES

New Twists on Timeless Tales

Edited by Melissa Marr and Tim Pratt

LITTLE, BROWN AND COMPANY
NEW YORK   BOSTON

Compilation copyright © 2013 by Melissa Marr and Tim Pratt
"That the Machine May Progress Eternally" copyright © 2013 by Carrie Ryan. "Losing Her Divinity" copyright © 2013 by Garth Nix. "The Sleeper and the Spindle" copyright © 2013 by Neil Gaiman. "The Cold Corner" copyright © 2013 by Tim Pratt. "Millcara" copyright © 2013 by Holly Black. "When First We Were Gods" copyright © 2013 by Rick Yancey. "Sirocco" copyright © 2013 by Margaret Stohl. "Awakened" copyright © 2013 by Melissa Marr. "New Chicago" copyright © 2013 by Kelley Armstrong. "The Soul Collector" copyright © 2013 by Kami Garcia. "Without Faith, Without Law, Without Joy" copyright © 2013 by Saladin Ahmed. "Uncaged" copyright © 2013 by Gene Wolfe. Illustrations © 2013 by Charles Vess

Little, Brown and Company

Hachette Book Group
237 Park Avenue, New York, NY 10017
Visit our website at www.lb-teens.com

Little, Brown and Company is a division of Hachette Book Group, Inc.
The Little, Brown name and logo are trademarks of Hachette Book Group, Inc.

The publisher is not responsible for websites (or their content) that are not owned by the publisher.

First Edition: October 2013

Library of Congress Cataloging-in-Publication Data

Marr, Melissa.
Rags and bones : new twists on timeless tales / edited by Melissa Marr and Tim Pratt. — First edition.
volume cm
ISBN 978-0-316-21294-6 (hardcover edition) — ISBN 978-0-316-21292-2 (e-book edition)
1. Paranormal fiction. 2. Short stories, American. 3. Fairy tales—Adaptations. 4. Science fiction. [1. Short stories. 2. Supernatural—Fiction. 3. Fairy tales—Adaptations. 4. Science fiction.] I. Pratt, Tim, 1976– II. Title.
PZ5.M328Rag 2013   [Fic]—dc23   2012045583

10 9 8 7 6 5 4 3 2 1

RRD-C   *5 2 5 0 2 0 0 1   1 2 / 1 3*

Printed in the United States of America

For Neil,

whose remarks led to this anthology.
You are now and have been a wonderful inspiration,
beloved friend, and good/bad influence.

— M. M.

For Mom and Dad,

who gave me a house full of books to grow up in.

— T. P.

TABLE OF CONTENTS

Introduction

The editors' lives had overlaps before we knew each other. Tim studied creative writing in North Carolina and then went on to edit and write; Melissa studied literature at another North Carolina university, and then went on to be a university literature teacher for twelve years before writing. By the time Melissa began to write, she had found Tim's short stories; he also published her first story. Along the way, they became friends with a mutual love of short stories, literature, and science fiction and fantasy. This anthology was born from that mutual love—and a strange retelling of *Heart of Darkness* in the form of a children's cartoon that Tim wrote.

The anthology also sprung from remarks Neil Gaiman made one night in New York about retelling tales, in particular about retelling a specific fairy tale. Whether he remembers that the tale in question was the same one he retold in this collection, we don't know. One of us sort of hopes it was all a grand coincidence. That's what happens with writers: the art we encounter swirls and combines and evolves inside our minds. Those of us who love literature, old tales, folk tales, fairy tales, and half-remembered stories keep them all in some strange simmering pot and ladle out bits into our own new stories. We return again and again to old loves and old obsessions, or wrestle with the troubling and problematic aspects of stories we adored when we were young.

The two of us thought it would be fun to ask some of our favorite writers to return to those best-beloved old stories, intentionally this time rather than in the usual subconscious ways. We asked them to choose stories that had moved them, influenced them, and fascinated them, boil those stories down to the rags and bones, and make something new from their fundamental essences. The results are wonderful. You don't need to be familiar with the original sources of inspiration to appreciate these tales, but if these stories send you in search of their literary ancestors, you aren't likely to be disappointed by what you find.

In a story that grew far beyond anyone's expectations, Rick Yancey takes Nathaniel Hawthorne's "The Birth-Mark" into a distant future where our fear of science and the mystery of love mingle in fabulously disturbing ways. Carrie Ryan leads us into a different future—one where we have gone underground and rely on technology even more than we do in the real world. Kelley Armstrong also takes on the future, but in her hands, it is not technology but magic that drives the story—magic and brotherly love. In all three—both horror and science fiction—human foibles are the true heart of the stories.

But not only do the stories in *Rags & Bones* reflect the literary influences of the authors, they also reflect personal interests and influence. Margaret Stohl drafted her tale while on the set of the film adaptation of her co-authored series—and tied her tale into an area she visits for her writing. *Beautiful Creatures* co-author Kami Garcia crafted a story that makes use of her background as a fighter and as a teacher in underfunded areas.

Both stories reflect the authors' stores of knowledge and experience, but develop in delightfully dark and unexpected ways.

The structures and styles chosen for the stories offer interesting variety as well. Garth Nix offers an unreliable narrator who tells his own story—or a version of it—inspired by Rudyard Kipling's overly ambitious characters. Holly Black imagines the vampire Carmilla from the eponymous story by Sheridan Le Fanu as an immortal, but still modern, teenager fighting her own nature, written in the form of a desperate confessional outpouring. Saladin Ahmed gives a voice to the maligned and caricatured Saracens from *The Faerie Queene*, harnessing the imagery and rhythms of that proto-epic-fantasy for his own purposes. Gene Wolfe looks beyond the end of a William B. Seabrook tale of savagery and inhumanity to speculate on the disturbing consequences. Several of the other authors tried narrative styles different from their normal approaches, and in every case, the resulting story is one we are thrilled to share with you.

The editors also included stories of their own in the collection. Without telling the other, both turned to the American South in their stories: North Carolina native Tim Pratt adds a touch of Southern lit to a Henry James story and Melissa Marr takes a story from traditional Southern lit and tangles it in a Scottish/Orcadian influence.

We hope you enjoy the results.

—*Melissa Marr and Tim Pratt*

That the Machine May Progress Eternally

Carrie Ryan

It isn't until he's nearing the bottom of the ladder that Tavil realizes his sister hasn't followed him. He stares up the narrow tunnel to the surface expecting to see her there, but instead he finds nothing except darkness capped by a wash of stars.

"Pria!" When he calls her name, his voice echoes unnaturally from the metal walls surrounding him. He isn't used to this claustrophobic nature of sound; where he lives there's space for noises to unfold and stretch.

His sister doesn't respond. Doesn't even pop her head over the lip of the tunnel to taunt him or let him see her face. Tavil hesitates, wondering if he should go back or if Pria's merely lost her nerve. He glances down. Not far below him a harsh light glows, illuminating where his feet curl around the lowest rung. Only a small drop and he will be fully inside the Underneath. A humming sort of buzz reverberates everywhere until it seems to settle within his bones, rattling even the individual corpuscles in his veins.

How easily the sound lures him, the very nature of its mechanicalness entrancing. It is like a heartbeat, as if this world is itself alive and not just the components nestled within. This thought both repels and awes Tavil. By its very nature—or more aptly by its lack of nature—the underground domain of the Machine is abhorrent. This is an unquestionable fact in Tavil's world.

And that's what makes it alluring. Because Tavil doesn't believe in the unquestionable. He wants to see the Machine for himself before its inevitable demise.

He releases the rung of the ladder and lets himself drop into the artificial light. As he does, a monster of metal screams toward him, forcing him to dive against the wall. He flattens his body and sucks in a breath. Even so, the distance between his chest and the side of the carriage is less than a hand's width and his shirt flutters in the buffeting wind that clatters with a *WHOMP WHOMP WHOMP* until the thing is finally past. It roars around a curve, following a set of rails into the distance. In its wake is a kind of perfect silence broken only by the constant hum of the Machine and the pant of Tavil's breathing.

Tavil's body trembles, every bit of him almost on fire from the fear. He doesn't know when he closed his eyes, but it was after he'd seen a face peering at him. It had been through a glass window as the train sped past and it had been only a glimpse. Whether the creature had been male or female, Tavil couldn't say, but he was pretty sure it had been a human. Its body was puffy and white, its head bald except for a few wisps of hair, and its mouth open in surprise, fleshy pink gums gleaming where teeth should have been.

The image is enough for Tavil to feel he understands this buried world and he is ready to leave. But when he turns, the hole he'd climbed through no longer exists. In its place is a smooth expanse of white tile, a continuation of the unending pattern throughout the tunnel. The broken scraps of debris that had littered the base of the hole are gone as well.

And this is when he feels the truth of where he is: so deep underground that the climb down made the muscles in his legs and arms quiver. There are not enough kinds of measurements for the amount of earthen weight between him and the surface. Between the stale yellow air of the Underneath and the freshness of fog. Between the constant artificial light and the shifting time of darkness.

He is trapped. Brutally so. As if in a casket, in a grave, in a tomb. He claws at the tiles, not caring when his nails break and his fingertips smear the white walls with blood. He screams, not caring if someone hears; hoping they do and will cast him out like the Homeless.

"Help me!" he cries. "Help!" In the space between panicked sobs he thinks he hears an echo beyond the tiles. A whisper down the hidden ventilation shaft. A call for help like his own. He pauses to listen. There is a scraping and his heart slams in his chest thinking that it is Pria come at last to rescue him.

He is standing, staring up at where the tunnel to the surface used to be, his face sodden with tears and his body heaving with ragged breaths, when the worms arrive. He doesn't notice them until one is wrapped around his legs, pulling tight. As he falls he catches glimpses of their long white mechanical bodies and then his head strikes the ground and there is only darkness.

He wakes on a bed in a small room with a floor shaped like the cell of a honeycomb. A chair is pushed against one of the far walls and between it and the bed sits a square table with a gargantuan book resting on top. Tavil pushes up on his elbow and swings his legs around until he's sitting. He stares at the cover of the book, tilting his head until he can read the title: *Book of the*

Machine. The pages inside are thin and whispery, almost transparent, so that when he holds his face up close to one he can make out the movement of his fingers across the other side. The pages are covered with series of numbers and words so tiny that his eyes burn trying to focus.

The light in the room isn't bright, but neither is it dim, and Tavil searches for its source but finds nothing. The light just *is*. The same as the humming felt by every aspect of his body, vibrating almost from the inside out. When Tavil stands, the hairs on the very top of his head skim the ceiling, making him feel as though he should constantly duck. It takes only a few strides for him to reach the other side of the room, which has begun to feel more like a cage. Why else would its dimensions be so perfectly confining?

He wonders if perhaps he is in a cell or some sort of jail, if this is his punishment for trespassing. If so, how long will he be trapped underground? Just like before, the thought of the weight of dirt resting between him and the surface causes his chest to tighten and his skin to prickle. He plucks frantically at his shirt and pants, neither of which are the ones he was wearing when he climbed down the ladder.

As he spins, his eyes scouring one wall after another, all he finds are endless rows and columns of buttons except for one blank expanse, which he takes to be the door. He throws himself against it, but it will not open and the seams along the hinges are too tight for him to wedge his fingers into them. What he needs is a weapon, so he flings the book to the floor, grabs the table, and heaves it at the door.

It isn't enough. He tries to lift the chair, but there's some sort of mechanical motor embedded in its base and it's too heavy to move easily. As a last resort he reaches for the book and, in a frenzy, hurls it across the room. When it strikes the wall by the door the covers bend back and the insides explode. Delicate pages fill the air like the petals from an apple tree on a breezy spring morning.

The door swings open and pages drift free, floating lazily through the opening into whatever lies beyond. The success shocks Tavil and makes him catch his breath in such a way that the blood returns to his hands and his heart ceases its screaming. He rises and steps forward, shoulders hunched so his hair won't brush against the ceiling. The spine of the massive book left a mark where it struck the wall, just below a button. He rubs the hem of his shirt between his fingers, drying them of sweat, and after licking his lips he presses the button.

The sides of the door swing together again, sealing him inside. He presses it again and the doors open, the movement creating a soft *swiff* of breeze that unsettles the papers scattered around his feet.

Tavil peers outside. A tunnel stretches out in front of him, curving gently away as it veers into the distance. There is nothing particularly unique about the tunnel. Its walls are the same color as his room (white), though unlike his room they are bereft of buttons. The ceiling is a bit higher, so Tavil can stretch to his full height. The hum still throbs, and the air tastes old, as though it has been through too many lungs before entering his own.

He crosses the threshold and begins to walk. To where he has no idea. For what purpose is simply the necessity of movement and the desire for escape. He cannot stay here where the walls are too close and there is no room to breathe. The more he thinks about the tightness surrounding him, the more frantic he becomes.

His heart no longer listens to his command to be calm and it roars inside his chest. Likewise his mind sends out panicked signals: *I am trapped. I am trapped. I am trapped.* Tavil tries to override the message but his body is inconsolable: it sweats, it numbs, it shivers.

There is only one thing for it: Tavil must get back to the surface. Now. He must see the sky, hear the silence, taste air that hasn't been stripped apart by some machine. But as he runs, the corridor only continues to curve away, hiding any hope of a destination.

He passes other doors set along the sides and he imagines other people trapped in buttoned-up rooms like his own. The doors are all closed, hiding their occupants, shielding them from even the existence of a world mere feet away from their own.

Shielding them from him.

Tavil wonders if they can hear the way he screams. The raggedness of his breathing. His fists hammering, hammering, waiting for someone to open their door and help him.

But there is nothing until he rounds the curve and is faced not with the endless monotony of before but with the novelty of an open door. He approaches it carefully and stares across the threshold. It's a mirror of his own but without the bed, only a chair in the middle with a table next to it, the massive book perched on top.

It is empty. He turns to move on when something catches his eye: a mark on the wall, just inside the door, beneath a button. The mark is familiar to him. He knows it because he made it, moments ago when he threw the book at the door.

The book that had exploded spewing paper across the floor and out into the tunnel. All of it is gone now, cleaned away. The book replaced. Nothing remains of his panicked tantrum except for the mark on the wall and the small tremors in his chest, the remnants of alarm drifting away through his system.

Calmer now, Tavil stoops into his room but leaves the door open to give the impression of space. Of an exit to this tomb. He sits in the chair, his body almost instantly relaxing as it sinks into a plush softness that seems to wrap and hold his body in a soothing comfort.

There are buttons arrayed along the arms and he presses one, squawking in alarm when the chair jerks forward and rolls across the room. Never in his life has Tavil moved by any means other than his own: first crawling, then walking, then running and climbing. The sensation of being carried by something that churns with a motor instead of beating with a heart feels wrong, and when he can't find a way to stop the mechanical chair he's forced to climb over the back of it to escape being pinned against the wall.

Even though it has met an immovable obstacle, the little motor in the chair continues to whir, adding a new frequency of humming to the air. It grates against Tavil, causing his teeth to ache as he stands in the middle of the room clenching his jaw.

He turns to the book on the table, flipping open the cover so forcefully the pages flutter. He presses his hand flat against them, not caring that the sweat of his palm dampens the page, running the text together in an almost blur. Then he begins to read.

Tavil sits in his chair in the middle of his tiny room, the door now closed. Thanks to the Book of the Machine, he has learned how to order food (delivered immediately on its own table that rises from the floor with a touch of a button); how to change the lighting (a toggle switch on the wall); how to turn on music (a separate toggle switch). He knows how to summon a tub full of hot or cold waterish liquid, a toilet, a sink, or even his bed—all of which rise from the floor with the push of the proper button.

His chair is set to warm and cradle him as he faces one of the many walls and holds the massive book spread open on his lap. He has been reading about communication through the Machine and has turned off the isolation knob, but still the room is silent. No one knows Tavil in the Underneath. No one has need to contact him.

And so he traces his finger along the thin pages of the book, mumbling to himself as he reads, and then he presses a button and across the far wall a round blue disk drops from the ceiling and bursts into color.

So much has surprised Tavil in so many ways this day that even this marvel can hardly elicit a gasp of fear. Instead his blood blooms with a sort of curiosity as he sits forward, the colors resolving into images that give the appearance of looking out a window aboveground. He stands and walks slowly forward until he can trace his fingers across the flat plane, the color from the glass glowing against his flesh but dissipating the moment he removes his hand from contact.

It is a wonder of a world perfectly wrought, and he recognizes it instantly. The dusty landscape capped by brown-black clumps of dried weeds, stretches of sharp-edged stones meandering along the surface like scars, the gray fog hovering in the distance. The stones are all that is left of a great building that once existed long ago. Tavil knows of it because he's been told stories: of how this was the last structure to stand against an enemy—before the Underneath, before the Machine, before men attempted to defeat the sun. He has seen the ruins himself once before, when he journeyed with his sister to view the sea for the first time.

At the images Tavil feels something hard and immovable begin to grow in his chest. It crushes the air from his lungs and presses against his ribs, this feeling that he is *wrong*. Where he is, the air he breathes, the chair by which he stands, and the buttons over which his fingers hover...all of it wrong.

That place through the screen, that is the truth and he should fear to be parted from it for so long. His legs feel weak, and he sits. The book slips from his numbed fingers to land on the floor with a thud. It touches the ground for only an instant before the floor lifts it again to a height where Tavil merely has to slide it back onto his lap with no effort exerted on his own part.

And then something moves onto the screen: a wheeled carriage carrying a human-shaped creature unlike any Tavil has laid eyes on before except through the window on the train. This one is mannish, his body round and draped in a tunic that hides most, but not all, of his wobbling white flesh. A respirator masks his face, covering from his chin to just below his eyes and strapped over his bald head.

He is speaking. Tavil knows this only because the man's jowls bunch and sway. Tavil touches a button, and the sound soars around him.

"...against an inner rebellion of those who'd once lived within these walls and in other structures surrounding the castle."

"That's not even close to correct," Tavil mumbles to himself, the noise floating a bit in the air of his room before settling around him. The history of the ruins isn't one of rebellion, but of protection: a town defending itself against the onslaught of another.

The man on the screen hesitates and adjusts his mask. This squeezes the several layers of skin trapped under his chin even more, so that his flesh bulges out from his neck. He clears his throat and continues.

"The remnants of which are, of course, still scattered through the Seven Hills of Wessex, which leads to the idea that..."

Tavil barks with a sort of indignant laughter while the man prattles on. "*Eight* Hills," he calls to the screen.

Again, the man pauses and fiddles with the straps of the respirator. His breathing is wispy and echoes against the chambers of his mask. Tavil hears someone cough and then a grumble, the sound filling his room from some unknown source in the same way as his light.

This is how Tavil understands his mistake: that as he hears so also can he be heard. He fumbles for his book, intending to shuffle through the pages to learn which button will silence anything he might say.

But his task is cut short when the lecturer continues, seeming to speak directly to him, though Tavil feels this must not be possible. "I assure you, that the hills number seven is not a firsthand idea. It is beyond fact at this point."

Tavil sputters. "That's absurd! All you have to do is look around and count. It's not like they're not obvious!" Someone hisses as others begin to murmur, but he ignores them. He stands before the screen tapping it with his fingers as though the lecturer can see where he points as he counts out the hills. "There's one with the crag, two next to it where the top is sheared off to the west."

He's forced to talk louder and louder as the chatter emanating from the walls begins to grow overwhelming. They bark against the prospect of using observation to determine any sort of information, arguing that doing so adds an improper color, a bias skewed toward any idea that has not come down through intermediaries.

Tavil shouts over them all. "Three is just behind—it can sometimes be hard to see in the mist but right now it's clear and four—"

And then one voice—a woman's—breaks through the rest, clearer than the others: "Tell them *nothing* about the surface."

This stops Tavil, his finger hovering just over the screen. He takes a step back. "Who said that?"

He's met with the roar of attendees from the lecture, their words and arguments now grown indistinct.

"Who said that?" he demands again.

Some kind of feeling tickles along the back of his neck and he catches his breath to listen. It is the same instinct he learned to heed on the surface, with the wilds of the remaining world around him. He shakes his head against the humming in the walls, the voices in the air, but they continue to overwhelm any sense of his surroundings. He pounds the button by the door and it springs open. He stands and listens. Behind him is the chatter from the lecture, and in front is the long, curving tunnel.

He starts to walk, letting his frustrations burn through energy, opening his senses to this dry mechanical world. Ahead of him he hears a new noise, the whir of a machine different from the one humming in the walls. He speeds up but the sound eludes him and so he begins to run.

It always seems to be just around the next corner. Sometimes he'll catch a glimpse of something darting, and he pushes himself faster until he comes tearing around the same unending bend and there in front of him a wheeled carriage sits.

A woman steps from the carriage. She is unlike the man

from the screen or the person Tavil saw on the train. While she is still of a roundish shape, she is tall, able to carry herself on her legs, and her long dark hair swings as she moves. She steps through an open door.

"Wait!" he calls out.

But then as the doors begin to close she turns to almost face him. He knows, without her having to utter a word, that it is the woman who issued the warning.

Tavil stumbles when he sees that she, like him, is of the surface. Her skin has seen the sun, of that there is no doubt—it is written across her cheeks in the form of freckles. In her hands she carries the massive book. When she sees Tavil running for her, her eyes flare slightly. She does not move or make any effort to stop the doors from closing.

And then she is gone and Tavil is left pounding on the door. There are so many questions he needs to ask her.

He notices a button and he presses it until the door swings open again and he is faced with nothing but an empty white box. He storms inside, looking for any trace of the woman but finding only more buttons—columns of them racing up the wall.

He pushes one and a small red light blinks in its center. The doors close, he feels something twist in his stomach, a sensation of growing heavier, and then the doors open again and he is facing the tunnel. Only this one is different; there is no wheeled vehicle sitting in front of him.

He has moved to another level. He listens for sounds of the woman, but there is nothing. He moves back into the box and presses another button. He repeats this again and again but there is no trace of her. No trace of another living being at all. And then he has touched the last button and the doors open and he is someplace new.

Long platforms stretch out away from him and from them branch more platforms that lead to the decks of several massive airships. Their bloated hulls curve toward the heavy domed ceiling, where the stretch of white tiles is marred by a large circular opening that presumably leads to the surface far above. Tavil is familiar with the hulking ships, but he has only ever seen them from a distance as they rise out of the tunnels from the Underneath and sail off toward the horizon. Their cabins have always been shuttered, but now they are not and Tavil can see inside.

Each is a mirror of his own room below: a chair, a table, walls crowded with buttons. Almost all are empty, and it is the rare window through which Tavil glimpses the bulbous flesh of another human being.

They are all headed to the surface, and just thinking the word makes him realize that he can almost taste how the air on this level is different. As if each airship brings a bit of the world above back with it as it arrives.

A fierce yearning spreads through Tavil, a desire to abandon this mechanical world and return home to his sister. He strides along the platform, choosing a ship at random and climbing toward it. At the top he's met by a woman with an officious demeanor.

She looks at him oddly, and her voice holds a note of suspicion. Her eyes slide away from him as she states, "Please present your Egression-permit."

When Tavil has no response, she glances at him. "I'd simply like to get to the surface," he finally tells her.

An expression of horror crosses her face at his request but she quickly controls it. "This is the airship to Courland."

That tight feeling Tavil experienced the first moment he realized he was trapped underground begins to crawl along his arms. Perhaps it is the taste of the surface on the back of his tongue or the knowledge that he has finally found a way out of the labyrinthine Machine, but he is unable to hold back the sensation of being buried alive.

He swallows again and again though his mouth is dry. "Please," he begs. "I need to get to the surface." In an attempt to gain the woman's sympathy, he places his hand on her arm.

She recoils instantly, disgust roiling her features at the physical contact. "You forget yourself!" Her words bite at the air, and Tavil takes several steps back. He can see her pulse pound furiously in her neck.

She says nothing more, refuses to even look at him. He waits, hopeful, but is finally forced to retrace his steps to the small white box and count the buttons back down to his level, where he wanders until he comes upon an open door with a mark along the wall where it was struck by his book.

Everything in his room is as it was except the image on the screen is of a different blob of flesh sitting in a carriage in a different landscape. That, and the air is filled with the sound of chimes. Buttons flash along one wall. When he presses one, a voice issues forth asking if perhaps he'd attended the lecture on the Brisbane school of music or a discussion on Plewis's theory of the French Revolution as informed by Graubert.

Even as he stands, doing absolutely nothing, the bells continue to chime, and the voices issue forth. They ask to share ideas; they ask his thoughts on a recent lecture; they talk about the recent scent added to the bathwater and whether he prefers the new platters used to hold the food.

Tavil sits in his chair and he listens, searching for that voice that had warned him, "Tell them nothing about the surface," and yet he never hears it. He thinks about this warning, trying to understand what it means and why it was issued. To tell him to say nothing is to imply both that there is something he *could* tell and that something should be kept secret.

But what could that be? He can think of nothing special about the surface: food is scarce, machinery is a distant memory used only as a cautionary tale, life is not about sitting but moving and doing for oneself and the community. It is about existing *with* nature rather than opposed.

And so, after a while, his curiosity overwhelms him and he issues a question of his own to those voices on the other side of the buttons along his walls. "Tell me about the surface," he asks. He hopes he has tread close enough to the female voice's warning that perhaps she might chastise him again and in doing so he'll be able to communicate with her directly.

If she heard his question, she is silent, but others are not. Instantly, he is inundated with responses: the surface is frozen, it is dry, it is cracked, it is broken, it is uninhabitable. It is irrelevant. It is where they render dissenters Homeless, the worst conceivable punishment.

What he hears is all incorrect, but he cannot understand the purpose of the misinformation. Those living aboveground have always been aware of the Machine, the great cities below the surface, and why should the reverse not also be true?

Why do they not know of the small communities scattered in the hills, people living with the land rather than below it? How can they not know that it's possible to survive aboveground where they don't need the Machine to feed and clothe, to teach and communicate? Perhaps it wasn't easier aboveground, but it was honest and sustainable.

Though he has learned how to isolate himself to stop the unceasing communications now inundating his room, he chooses not to. Instead, he presses the buttons to call for his bed and to dim the lights, and then, in the darkness, he listens to the chatter, trying to understand.

During the night, while Tavil sleeps, the conversations have shifted to other topics. He wakes to a discussion on the historical significance of indoor plumbing. Voices respond to one another rapid fire, citing various lectures they've heard as sources.

He turns the isolation knob, at first seeking solitude, but then he is faced with nothing but the humming of the Machine around him. He calls back the voices for company.

As he listens he reads the Book of the Machine, searching until he finds the information on Egression-permits. Immediately he presses the proper button to apply for one and is rejected almost instantly. The Book informs him he is allowed one application per day, and so he waits.

His ninety-seventh day underground is the first that he forgets to apply for an Egression-permit. He doesn't realize this until the next morning, and he presses the button immediately and almost as quickly receives his rejection. He experiences only a moment of disappointment before turning to the walls and his buttons.

He has already planned his day: a lecture on the lakes of Sumatra followed by a discussion of such, and then he has promised several correspondents to listen to their ideas and give his thoughts on them. At first he found such invitations tedious and pointless and only indulged them out of boredom.

However, as time passes he begins to gain a bit of a reputation in the cities Underneath for a perspective almost wholly intermediary. Because the only information Tavil knows first-hand relates to life on the surface, which he refuses to ever discuss, anything he knows beyond that must necessarily come through intermediaries. He learns nothing about anything directly; rather, he learns only what others have thought about those things.

Because of this reputation, Tavil finds his time more and more sought after. So much so that gradually, as the months collect upon themselves and turn into years, he spends less time outside his room, walking along the tunnels, looking for the woman with skin like his, searching for a way to the surface.

More and more his days are spent moving only between his bed and his chair until, in the distance of time, his legs grow soft and his body rounded. Rarely anymore does he think of his sister left behind at the mouth of the ventilation shaft so long ago. When memories of life aboveground do enter his consciousness, he shudders at the thought of the wasteful expanse. At the bugs, the variance of temperature and light, the struggle of daily necessities like preparing food and eliminating waste.

In these moments he's reminded of just how much comfort the Machine gives; how much easier it is to exist in his little room where all needs can be met with the touch of a button.

Sometimes, however, in a fit of nostalgia, he'll decide to strike out and explore like he did during his first days underground. He'll wheel his chair to the door and call for the carriage, grumbling over having to walk the distance between the two. He'll take the lift to the top floor, where he'll call for another carriage, and he'll let it carry him along the platforms so he can stare up at the airships, wrinkling his nose at the stench they bring.

He'll think about his first trip here so many years ago, and the sensation of placing his hand on the ship attendant's arm, and he'll shudder in revulsion and embarrassment. How unenlightened he'd been to seek physical contact! To seek anything of necessity or desire outside of the Machine!

As often as not he'll bring the Book of the Machine along with him on these jaunts, finding himself unsettled and anxious when he can't place his hands on its cover and murmur, "Blessed is the Machine," in an echo of the words recently printed on the opening page. Besides, to not constantly carry the Book is to invite suspicion of being anti-Mechanism, which carries a punishment of Homelessness.

Out of a sense of dwindling obligation Tavil continues to apply for an Egression-permit. Sometimes a week or a month will go by and he'll have forgotten, but then some small thing will trigger a reminder—a lecture on the Seven Hills of Wessex or mention of an airship route being terminated—and he'll promptly press the button to submit his application.

Thus he's surprised when, one day, rather than the expected and usual rejection, he is approved. As evidence of the approval, a button by the door begins to glow with a green light—if he were to press it his door would open, a car would gather him and deliver him to the top level, a mask would be presented to him, and a narrow door would open to a vestibule leading to the surface.

Tavil doesn't move. Instead, he sits in his chair, the voices of his friends drowning the humming of the Machine, and tries to understand what to do with this new information.

The thought of going aboveground appalls Tavil. It has been

years since he was there last, with his sister at night hovering around the tunnel to the Underneath. Would he even be able to find his way to the village again? Would anyone recognize him anymore? He closes his eyes and imagines what it would be like to go back: all that space, the silence, the gray fog that dampens everything it touches.

His heart races at the thought of it, his muscles going rigid. Without the walls of his room, what's to keep his body—his mind and his soul—contained? What use is the world of the surface to him anymore?

There would be no one to clothe him, feed him; no buttons to press for light and music, his bath and his bed. Everything civilized exists in the Machine now, he thinks to himself.

In his agitation he reaches for the Book of the Machine, finding an instant peace as the weight of it settles in his hands. He presses the button indicating how unwell he feels and an apparatus drops from the ceiling to check his pulse, his temperature, his blood pressure, his respirations. A table rises from the floor with a cup perched on top, and he takes the proffered medicine without thought.

He calls for his bed and turns his isolation knob. In the dark silence he listens to the Machine hum around him: everywhere, like a womb. He stares at the green button by the door until he can stand it no longer, and he turns to his other side and falls asleep with the secure knowledge that the Machine will care for him, the Machine will tend to him, the Machine will always protect him until the day it grants him euthanasia so another may take his place.

For weeks the green button glows by Tavil's door. Whether the room is dark or light, whether he is present or not, whether he is awake or asleep. It becomes like a persistent itch that he can't reach and he's reminded of what it was like to sleep aboveground where, no matter how hard he tried, the beds would always fill with grit that dug into his skin, arresting comfortable slumber.

Here his sheets are always perfectly crisp, and not once in his years underground has he found a speck of dirt in his bed. Dirt doesn't exist Underneath; there is no need for it.

And yet, every time he thinks to cancel his Egression-permit, he finds an excuse to delay the action. He tells himself he is merely too busy today, but perhaps tomorrow will be different.

Once he even goes so far as to open his door and summon the car, but the gulf between his doorway and the carriage is too great—the idea of that much movement too taxing. He retreats to his chair and his buttons, his correspondents and his lectures.

Life continues in the Machine the way it always has; the green button fades into the background in the same way as the mark by the door where it was once struck by the large book. Tavil has learned to ignore these things because to think of what he did to the Book of the Machine—hurling it across the room and causing it to break apart—makes him shudder. How profane he had once been! How barbaric!

Eventually the decision regarding the Egression-permit is made for him. The Central Committee of the Machine has decided there is no need to go to the surface as there is nothing new to learn from it. It revokes all outstanding permits, and that is that. The green light in the button dims and extinguishes, and Tavil smiles almost wistfully, thinking for a moment how nice it might have been to see his sister again, before beginning his lecture on the Seven Hills of Wessex.

Tavil is asleep when he hears the noise. It intrudes in his dreams because of its novelty—a sound that doesn't exist in the Machine. He sits up in bed. There is no need to press the button for light because over the past weeks something has changed in the Machine. His room is in a perpetual shade of twilight no matter how often he presses the button or complains to the Central Committee.

Still the noise persists. Laboriously, he heaves himself into his chair and causes it to motor across the room to the source of the noise: the door.

Someone is knocking on the other side as if trying to secure his attention. A light sweat breaks across his forehead and in the folds of his arms at the thought of another person endeavoring to initiate face-to-face communication.

He contemplates ignoring the knock and calling for a bath instead to wash away the offending perspiration. But the bathing liquid has been a bit tepid and a touch malodorous for his liking lately.

Throughout all these thoughts, the sound persists, gratingly so, and he fumbles for the buttons, forgetting for a moment which is the one to activate the door, as it has been so long since he used it last.

The door parts, and Tavil is faced with a woman. He sees no carriage waiting in the corridor, and he is exhausted just thinking of the energy she must have expended bringing herself to his room. She stands just across the threshold and, though much time has passed, he recognizes her: long hair that sways with her subtle movements, legs strong enough to carry her for as long as she could want, dark spots spread across a face browned from the sun.

She is the one from the surface. An expression of disgust shifts across her features as she takes in his appearance. When she speaks, Tavil is jolted back to that moment on his initial day Underneath when she issued her first, and only, warning: *Tell them nothing about the surface.*

He struggles to remember what to do in a situation such as this. Whether there is some sort of greeting he is supposed to give, a gesture he should offer. Unable to come up with anything, he merely sits in his chair and stares.

"The Machine is stopping," she tells him.

The statement jolts Tavil, sending a tremor of alarm through him. He reaches for the Book of the Machine, needing the comfort of its weight, but he has left it behind on the table by his bed. His fingers fumble in agitation, searching for something to occupy them.

"To say such a thing is blasphemous," he informs her.

"No matter," she says. "I have friends in other cities—they've seen the signs. It's only a matter of time now."

Tavil doesn't want to believe her. "Impossible. No lecturer has touched on such an idea. Besides, the Machine is omnipotent—it cannot stop."

Her upper lip curls. "Even so, the Machine was made by men and has escaped the bounds of men's understanding. There is no one left who knows enough of the whole to repair it."

Tavil scoffs. "The Machine will fix itself."

She shakes her head. "It will not. The power station is failing and soon enough everything else will follow. Those left Underneath will suffocate. Now is the time to escape to the surface—it's the only chance to survive."

Drops of sweat drip along Tavil's cheeks, his desire to reach for his Book so powerful he is almost shaking. The woman's words begin to penetrate deeper into his consciousness, attaching themselves to recent events to give them significance and meaning. All the little ticks and hiccups in the operation of day-to-day life that never occurred before and have been so subtle and pervasive as to be ignorable: buttons not responding as usual, lags in repairs, shudders sometimes felt within the walls.

All of it supporting the same conclusion the woman has drawn. "Why are you telling me this?" Tavil asks her.

The woman drops into a squat so that she is facing him head-on. "You're from the surface, like me. There are more of us down here—we're the only ones who know how to live aboveground. We're the ones with the best hope outside the Machine."

She reaches forward. "Come with us," she says as she grasps his hand in hers.

At her physical touch Tavil recoils, jamming the button to move his chair away from her. "You forget yourself!" He rubs his hand against his tunic as if he can somehow erase the feeling of her flesh resting on his own.

Shaking her head, the woman straightens. "You'll die if you stay down here."

In response, Tavil presses the button to close the door, sealing himself back into his sanctuary. He wheels to the center of his room but doesn't disengage the isolation knob. Instead he stares at his hand, remembering the feel of the woman.

There's a part of him, a small part, that used to know how to climb trees and walk for miles through the grassed plains, that knows the woman speaks the truth and accepts it. It explains the lights, the bathing liquid, why his favorite music sometimes pauses and gasps as it never has before. There have been delays when he presses the button for food, and his bed has twice now risen from the floor with its sheets still tossed about and wrinkled as if he'd just awoken.

When he was a child, his parents and theirs before them predicted that the cities of the Machine could not continue forever. They spoke of ancestors who'd been rendered Homeless, cast out of the Underneath after a rebellion, and who had thereafter chosen to live a natural, honest life on the surface. According to them, technology was a bane rather than a blessing; it rendered men decadent and complacent.

And Tavil had believed them. He'd abhorred those who lived underground and awaited the day their constant quest for comfort would cause them to collapse in on themselves. It's why he'd snuck down the tunnel that night so long ago. To see the Underneath for himself, before its inevitable end, so he would have firsthand knowledge of the Machine to pass on to future generations as a warning to never allow life to sink to such depths again.

But his parents had been wrong. He'd been wrong. Underneath is progress, evolution. It is life at its most advanced— existence for the pure pursuit of ideas and the cleansing of the human soul!

He reaches for the Book of the Machine and lifts it to his lips. "Oh, Machine," he murmurs, kissing the cover. Holding the Book is tangible proof of the truth he'd been denied as a child on the surface: that there is power greater than himself.

The thought comforts him, causes his trembling to cease and the sweat gathered along the remaining wisps of his hair to dry. He closes his eyes to feel the hum of the Machine around him, caring for him and protecting him. He is a part of it now, irrevocably so.

So be it if it fails—this marvelous Machine of progress. He has known of this inevitability from the moment he released the final rung of the ladder and fell into its depths. He will not abandon it now, will not return to that old life of strain and sacrifice.

It is too much to ask of him. He would rather live his last moments below the surface, ensconced in the Machine, than spend eternity aboveground away from its comforting hum.

Even until the end, Tavil's faith in the Machine is absolute. He has his rituals, and he adheres to them faithfully: repeating the mantra of the Machine as the first and last words he speaks each day, kissing the cover of the Book three times before opening it and after setting it down, ensuring it never touches the floor or that its spine faces the door.

Some of these are habits he developed on his own over time, others are shared by the larger community of believers. Even as the medic system fails, the lifts cease their function, the bathing liquid turns foul, and the beds no longer rise from the floor, those Underneath continue their devotion.

If anything, this causes Tavil's idolization of the Book to intensify as it remains proof of the Machine's supremacy.

And then the communication system collapses, the last throes of their dying world. Tavil knows that many around him have left their rooms to gather in the tunnels and along the airship platforms. Unlike him, they did not know of the inevitability of this day; they had not been expecting and waiting.

They had not known their fate as he has.

The idea of joining one of these groups repulses him. He rubs his hand against his tunic, remembering the last time he came into physical contact with another human being. The woman from the surface, who'd warned him of this day and asked him to eschew what he believed for the chance at a life he did not want, who'd offered him a false salvation from a world he so embraces.

In these final moments, Tavil thinks of his sister, Pria, left behind on the surface. He pictures her face framed by the stars as he'd last seen her before climbing down the ladder into the Underneath. What a life she must have led, constantly wrenched by the needs of the human body: for food, for shelter, for the constant touch of others. No time for her soul, any moments of quiet contemplation necessarily rare.

His life would have unfolded similarly had they never seen the geyser of air pouring from the ground and found the shallow hollow where a man from the Underneath flailed about around an old ventilation shaft. Had Tavil never decided to take the unexpected opportunity to see the world of the Machine for himself.

What a waste his life would have been had he stayed aboveground.

Tavil sits in the chair in the middle of his room. The motor in its base ceased working yesterday and so he hasn't moved since. Though the lights have cut out, Tavil still turns the pages of the Book, feeling the thinness of the paper with his fingers. He does not need to see to know what is written on them; he memorized his favorite passages ages ago.

When the Machine stops, there is nothing. The walls cease their vibration, the constant hum finally stills. Tavil mumbles lines from the Book to himself, clinging to the comfort of his eternal adoration of this marvelous Machine.

Otherwise the world would be too silent.

When I first read "The Machine Stops" I thought of it as a fairly straightforward postapocalyptic story: the Earth's surface becomes uninhabitable, which forces mankind underground to live in cities where every aspect of existence is controlled by the Machine. However, the more I reread the story and considered it, the more I came to see it as a work of genius.

Not only is it a thought-provoking meditation on the role of technology in our lives, it is also a graceful portrayal of faith and how easy it is to become so focused on worship of a *thing*—on a representation of the belief—that one can lose sight of belief itself. In the story, E. M. Forster leads his characters toward a very deliberate conclusion in which they ultimately understand, and accept, their fallacy. This is what I wanted to explore in my own story.

There is a moment in "The Machine Stops" when one of the characters makes his way to the surface through an old ventilation shaft and later recalls: "I thought I saw something dark move across the bottom of the dell, and vanish into the shaft." This is where my story begins: What if that dark shape were a man from the surface, and what would happen to him if he became trapped in the Machine?

The King of Elfland's Daughter (1924). The Irish writer Lord Dunsany wrote over sixty books, including short story collections, mysteries, plays, essays, an autobiography, and several novels, of which, unquestionably, *The King of Elfland's Daughter* is his best. Evocative and wildly inventive, his prose has influenced many writers, including H. P. Lovecraft and Jack Vance. I know when I began reading this novel, I was forever and completely enthralled by Dunsany's language. For years afterward, every bit of writing I put my hand to was not-so-very-subtly influenced by his lyricism.

Here the reader finds Alveric, the prince of the Vale of Earl, who is sent by his father, the king, into Elfland so that when he returns it will be with some bit of magic that will enrich the lives of the mundane people who live within the fields we know. The witch, Zironderel, gifts the prince with a magic sword made from lightning bolts gathered from under cabbages in her garden, on the high land where the thunder rolls. In due course, after winning through adventure after adventure, he does return with the Elf King's daughter, Lirazel, and soon everyone in his kingdom will know the coming of too much magic into their lives.

The King of Elfland's Daughter

Losing Her Divinity

Garth Nix

It was a year ago, or slightly more, as I recall. I was coming back from Orthaon, I had been there to discuss the printing works at the original monastery, they had a very old press and, though it worked well enough, it had been designed to be driven by slaves, and since the most recent emancipation a number of the mechanical encouraging elements needed to be removed, quite a difficult task as the original drawings for the machine were long lost and some parts of it were very obscure.

What? Oh no, I was not present as a mechanician, I was there to write an account of the reworking, I thought it might prove to be of some interest, for one of the city gazettes, or perhaps as a selection in a book that I have begun, observations of curious machines, sorceries, and the like.

You might yourself make an interesting dozen pages, Master Puppet. I have heard of you, of course. Read about you, too, unless I miss my guess. That is to say, I have read about a certain sorcerous puppet who bears a striking similarity, in the works of Rorgulet and in Prysme's *Annals*—oh, of course, Sir Hereward, you would rate at least as many pages, I should think. But you desire discretion, and I respect that. No, no, I *will* be discreet, I do not write about *everything*. Yes, I am aware of the likely consequences, so there is no need for that, good knight...please, allow me to withdraw my throat a little from that...it looks exceedingly sharp. Really? Every morning, without fail, one hundred times each side, and then the strop? I had no idea. I do not treat my razor so well, though perhaps it gets less shall we say...use... no, no, I am getting on with it. Have patience. You should know that I am not a man who can be spurred by threats.

As I said I was coming back from Orthaon, traveling on the Scheduled Unstoppable Cartway, in the third carriage, as I do not like the smell of the mokleks. Speaking of razors, what a job it must be to shave a moklek, though I have heard it said it is required only once, and the handlers rub in a grease that inhibits the regrowth. Done at the same time as the unkindest cut of all, though nothing needed there to prevent the regrowth, of course. It is interesting that the wild mammoths treat the occasional escaped moklek well, as if it were a cousin who had fallen on unfortunate circumstances. Better than many of us treat our cousins, as I can attest.

Yes. I was on the cartway, in the third carriage, through choice, not primarily through lack of funds, though it is true both fare and luxury reduce from the front. We had stopped, as is common, despite the name of the conveyance. My compartment was empty, save for myself, and though the afternoon light was dim, I had been correcting some pages that the dunderheaded typesetter of the *Regulshim Trumpet-Zwound* had messed up, a piece on the recent trouble with the nephew of the Archimandrite of Fulwek and his attempt to...ouch!

I told you I need no such encouragement, and it would have been a very short digression. You might even have learned something. As I was saying, the light suddenly grew much brighter. I thought the sun had come out from behind the skulking clouds that had bedeviled us all day, but in fact it was a lesser and much closer source of illumination, a veritable glow that came from the face of a remarkably beautiful woman who had stepped up to the door of my compartment and was looking in through the window. A very good window; they know how to make a fine glass in Orthaon, no bubbles or obscuration, so I saw her clear.

"Pray stay there, for a moment!" I called out, because the light was extremely helpful, and the proofs were such a mess and set quite small, and there was this one footnote I couldn't quite read. But she ignored me, opening the door and entering the compartment. Rather annoyingly, she also dimmed the radiance that emitted not only from her beautiful face, but from her exposed skin. Of which there was quite a lot, as she was clad only in the silken garment that is called a rhuskin in these regions, but is also known as a coob-jam or attanousse, I am sure you know it, a very long, broad piece of silk wound around the breast and tied at the front and back so that the trailing pieces provide a form of open tabard covering the nethers, save when a wind blows or the wearer attempts a sudden movement, as in entering the compartment of a carriage on the Scheduled Unstoppable Cartway.

She had very fine legs. I may have admired them for a moment or two, before she interrupted the direction of my thoughts, which I must confess were running along the lines of the two of us being alone in the compartment, and the interior blinds, which could be drawn, and why such a beautiful, shining woman would intrude upon my compartment in particular, even though of course it is not entirely unusual that beautiful women throw themselves upon...why do you chuckle, Sir Knight? Not all women favor height and splendid mustaches, and the obvious phallic overcompensation and fascination with swords...and yes, daggers like that one, which I do not want thrust through my hand, thank you. This hand that has written a hundred... well, ninety books...and has many more to write! Thank you, Master Puppet. I would be grateful if you could keep your...your comrade contained.

So. She was in the compartment, beautiful, illuminated, and semi-naked. Obviously a sorceress of some kind, I presumed, or a priestess, perhaps of Daje-Onkh-Arboth, they tend to be lit up in a similar fashion. I had no idea then what she actually was, you understand.

She smiled at me, winked, and sat down on the cushions opposite.

"Tell them you haven't seen me, and put me in your pocket," she said, very sultry and promising. "It shall be to your advantage."

"Tell who—" I started to ask, but she shrank away before my very eyes, and in a matter of moments there was no longer a shining woman on the cushion, but a small figurine of jade, or some similar greenstone, no taller than my thumb. Now, as you can plainly see, I am a man of the world who has seen a great deal more than most, but never anything like that. I picked up the figure, and was further surprised to find it very cold, as cold as a scoop of ice from the coolth-vendors you may have seen along the street here, offering their wares to chill a drink or a feversome brow.

I put her in my pocket, the deep inner one of my outer coat, where I keep a selection of pencils, an inkstone, and other odds and ends of the writer's trade. It was none too soon, for there was a commotion outside only a few seconds later, with a great clattering of armor and the usual unnecessary shouting of military folk, the roar of battle mounts and the like, all of which I understood immediately to be the sudden arrival of some force bent on intercepting the conveyance, which meant more stopping and greater delay. I was not pleased, I tell you, and even less so when two rude troopers flung open the compartment door, waved a pistol and a sword in my face, and by means of emphatic gestures and strange, throat-deep grunts, demanded that I alight.

Naturally, I refused, pointing out to them that there were numerous treaties guaranteeing the inviolate nature of the Unstoppable Cartway, and that by interfering with it they were risking war with no less than three city-states, and the Kingdom of Aruth, admittedly a great distance away at the terminus, and not only these polities but also the parent company of the Cartway, which they might not know was the Exuberant Order of Holy Commerce, well known for its mercenary company business, in addition to its monopoly on Hrurian nutmeg, the original source of the order's wealth, which by curious chance—

Your interruptions, sir, delay matters far more than my minor educational digressions. Yet I protest in vain, as in fact occurred with these other soldiers. After they had dragged me out quite forcibly, I ascertained that in fact they were deaf-mutes, directed solely by a sign language that I did not know, involving numerous finger flicks from their officer. This fellow, from his ill-fitting gun-metal cuirass and the crushed plumes of his helmet, was clearly more priest than soldier, the armor worn over robes of an aquamarine hue flecked with silver bristles, here and there showing silver buttons that were embossed with the heads of two women, one gazing left, the other right, and apparently sharing the same neck. I did not immediately recognize this outfit, but then there are many gods in the Tollukheem Valley, some with multiple orders of followers.

"Have you seen Her?" asked the officer, the capital "H" readily apparent in his speech.

"Who?" I asked.

"The Goddess," said the officer. The capital "G" was also very evident.

"What goddess?"

"Our Goddess. Pikgnil-Yuddra the Radiant One."

I must admit that upon hearing this description the jade figurine felt suddenly very much heavier in my pocket, and I felt a similar chill around my heart. But I gave no sign of this, nor of the slight unease that was beginning to spread in the region of my bowels.

"Am I to understand you have lost a goddess?" I said to the officer, with a yawn. "I am afraid I have never heard of your Pikgnil-Yuddra. Now, I trust you will not be delaying the Cartway for very long?"

"Pikgnil-Yuddra the Radiant," corrected the officer, with a frown. "You are very ignorant, for our Goddess is the light that does not fail, the illuminatrix of the city of Shrivet, and verily for leagues and leagues about the city!"

"Shrivet…Shrivet…" I pondered aloud. "But that is at least a hundred leagues from here. I take it the illumination does not extend that far? I believe here we fall under the aegis of the god of Therelle, the molerat-digger Gnawtish-Gnawtish?"

I made the molerat godlet up, of course, for my own amusement. That part of the world is so infested with little godlets that no one could know them all, and as the soldiers were from Shrivet, which was indeed a great distance away, they would have no clue.

"Other gods do not concern us," said the officer. "Only our own. She must be here somewhere, we were only an hour at most behind her chariot."

"Chariot?" I asked. I looked around, hoping to see it, for I was naturally curious about what style of chariot a luminous goddess might drive, and what manner of locomotion might propel it, or beasts draw it.

"Crashed half a league back," said the officer. "But near the track of this...this..."

He gestured at the carriages of the Cartway, and the ten mokleks harnessed in line, with their mahouts standing by their heads and the guards in the howdahs watching the temple soldiers search with surprising equanimity or possibly cowardice—certainly they had made no attempt to intervene. There were more guards by the rear carriage, and the conductor-major herself, but they were even more relaxed, offering wine to another priestly officer.

"It is called the Unstoppable Cartway," I said. "Though clearly it is neither unstoppable nor do the mokleks draw carts, but luxurious carriages. I believe in its infancy, carts were drawn, carrying a regular cargo of foodstuffs from Durlal to Orthaon, and manufactured goods on the return—"

The officer was, as might have been expected, uninterested in learning more. He interrupted me most rudely.

"Have you seen the Goddess?"

"I don't know," I countered. "I am traveling alone in my compartment, a blessed luxury, but I confess I have looked out the window from time to time, and upon several occasions have seen women."

"You would not mistake her for a mortal woman," snapped

the officer. "She is bright with virtue, her light constant, a shining star to guide correct behavior."

"No, I can't say I've seen anyone like that," I said. By this point I had noticed that while everyone had been rousted from their compartments, there were no individual searches taking place and the general ambience had become more relaxed as the Goddess was not found within the carriages. There seemed only a small chance that the jade figurine would be found upon my person, and I must confess that I was intrigued by this search for a goddess, even more than I was interested in her physical charm.

"Does your Goddess regularly take…ah…unscheduled journeys?"

"Pikgnil-Yuddra the Radiant does not leave the city ever," said the officer firmly. "Only Yuddra-Pikgnil the Darkness may leave the city."

I confess that a slight frown may have moved across my brow at this point. Discussing godlets with their priests is often fraught with difficulty, and this search for a goddess who had not left, or who possibly had, but under a different name, was very much in keeping with the tradition of godlets who did not at all correspond to their priesthood's teachings or texts.

"I'm not sure I follow," I said. "You are searching a hundred leagues from Shrivet for a goddess who does not leave the city ever, and there is another goddess who does leave the city but you are not searching for her?"

"They are the twin Goddesses of Day and Night," said the officer. "Pikgnil-Yuddra the Radiant may not leave the city, and Yuddra-Pikgnil the Darkness may not enter, save at certain festivals. A week ago, the temple was discovered to be empty, the warders slain, the bounds broken, and Pikgnil-Yuddra the Radiant was no longer housed there."

"So it is Pikgnil-Yuddra the Radiant you are looking for?"

"We seek the Goddess in both aspects," said the officer. "For it may be the doing of Yuddra-Pikgnil the Darkness that has unhoused Pikgnil-Yuddra the Radiant, in their eternal struggle for the souls of the people of our city."

"I see," I said, though to be accurate, the only thing I saw was yet another idiotic priest, a member of a hierarchy that was preserving their authority by drawing upon the power of an imprisoned extra-dimensional intrusion that had become anthropomorphized by long association with mortals. Yes, unlike the great majority of the deluded people who populate this world, I do not think of them as gods or godlets. Indeed, it has been theorized that should a mortal here be somehow introduced to some other plane of existence, there they too would have the powers and attributes seen here as godlike. But I speak to those who know far more than I, if indeed you are as I believe you to be, agents of that ancient treaty—ah, you are a barbarian, Sir Knight, to so interrupt civilized discourse in the interest of what you like to call the bare facts. I will continue.

Suffice to say that after some show of searching and questioning, the priestly soldiers departed and the Cartway continued. Shortly after the cries of the mahouts had ceased and the mokleks had stretched out to their full shamble, our conveyance traveling at a remarkable speed only slightly slower than a battlemount's lope, I felt a stirring in my coat pocket. Reaching in, I withdrew the jade figurine and set it upon the seat at my side, whereupon a few moments later it once again became an alluring woman, or rather goddess, though this time she kept her radiance dimmed to the extent that she merely glowed with the luster one finds inside the better kind of oyster shell, one likely to provide a pearl.

"So, you are a runaway goddess, to wit, one Pikgnil-Yuddra the Radiant," I said conversationally as she rearranged her rhuskin, not for modesty, I might add, but rather to show off those beautiful limbs to even greater advantage.

"Don't be silly," she said. "I am, of course, Yuddra-Pikgnil the Darkness. But you can call me Yuddra."

"I am slightly confused," I replied. "The priest-officer said that it was your, ahem, counterpart—"

"Sister," corrected Yuddra. "You might say we are twins."

"Your sister, then, who had become unhoused and traveling. Also, if you are the Darkness, why are you illuminated?"

"There is no difference between us," replied Yuddra, stretching her arms up toward the padded ceiling—padded these last twelve years, I might add, since the unfortunate overturning of a carriage that was inhabited by the Prince-Incipient of Enthemo, resulting in his crown being forced down over his ears, the ceiling back then being considerably harder—a stretch that made me catch my breath, I confess. I reached out to her, and to my extreme disappointment, found my hand passing through the waist I had hoped to encircle, Yuddra proving no more substantial than a wisp of steam.

"There is no difference between us," repeated Yuddra. "In fact, we have swapped roles many times over the past millennia. Sometimes I stay in the temple, sometimes Pikgnil does."

"But now you are both wandering," I said, essaying to lift her hand to plant a courteous kiss, but with the same result as my previous attempt. "Out of your temple, far from your power, and pursued by your priesthood. What has brought you to this pass?"

She smiled at me and leaned in close, with just as much effect as if she were normal flesh and blood, perhaps even more so, given that the tantalization of not being able to touch is well known as an erotic accentuator, one employed to great effect in the theater of . . . yes, yes, you know what I'm talking about, I'm sure, puppet excepted.

"Just such a matter as now concerns us both," she said. "I am jade and air, and have always been so, save for brief periods of corporeality. My sister, as always, is the same, and both of us . . . want more."

"So you are able to assume a fleshly form?" I asked, this being the chief part of her speech that I had taken in. "For some short time?"

"Yes," said Yuddra. "But it is difficult. Pikgnil and I want to permanently assume mortal form, so that we may experience in full the experiences we have heretofore only . . . tasted."

"What do you require to assume a mortal form?" I asked, being driven by curiosity as always. "For those short periods, I mean."

"Blood," said Yuddra, and smiled again, showing her delicate, finely pointed teeth. "Mortal blood. A few clavelins might grant me an hour, but where to find a willing donor? It must be given freely, you see."

A clavelin? A small bottle, about so tall, so round, commonly used here for young wine. Not an excessive amount and, though I am no barber-surgeon, I knew that a man could lose more blood than that without fear of faintness.

"I should be happy to oblige Your Divinity," I said. Long caution caused me to add, "Two clavelins of blood and no more, I can happily spare, and indeed I would welcome a charming and *touchable* companion to lessen the drear of this journey."

She smiled again and agreed that such a diversion would be pleasant, that in fact a great part of her desire to assume a permanent mortal form was to engage in just such activities as I suggested, but on a more regular basis. I must confess that I had expected her to use those sharp teeth to draw my blood in the manner of those creatures some call the vampire, but rather she had me use my penknife to make a cut on my hand, and allow blood to drip into the saucer of one of the teacups provided by the Cartway, along with the samovar that had been bubbling away since Orthaon. As I let the drops of blood fall, Yuddra licked the liquid from the saucer, very daintily, after the fashion of a cat. As she consumed the blood, I saw her grow more corporeal, the pearly light fading and her skin becoming... real, I suppose, though still extraordinarily beautiful.

I shall draw the shades on the window of this retelling, as I drew the actual shades in the carriage. Suffice to say that time passed all too quickly, and far too soon I found her growing once again incorporeal, though there was a curious pleasure to be derived when she was neither truly there nor entirely not. I believe she also found the time well spent, Sir Knight, so you can wipe that small smirk from your face. I have studied the works of the great lover Hiristo of Glaucus, and practiced much therein, up to page one hundred and seventy-seven, and there is a young widow who resides near me who has agreed that we shall together essay the matter of pages one hundred and seventy-eight to eighty-four—

Yes! I am getting on with it. The blinds were drawn up, the Goddess sat opposite, the sun shone in, and we had got another dozen leagues closer to Durlal. I made a cup of tea, the black leaf from the Kaz coast, not the green from Jinqu, and made further inquiries of Yuddra, if indeed she was that sister.

"So you wish to no longer be a goddess, but to become permanently mortal?"

"I do," said Yuddra, eyeing my steaming cup of tea with a wolfish, hungry look. "I have not, for example, ever tasted that drink you have. There are so many tastes, so many experiences that are beyond the purely energistic to savor, as I would do!"

"But tell me, how is it that you will become mortal?" I asked. "Surely not by the imbibing of blood, for if two clavelins amounts to but an hour, then the supply required to maintain corporeality would be...monstrous, and not likely to be freely given."

She laughed and tossed her head back.

"Pikgnil has found a way, or so she said in her last missive. I am to meet her at Halleck's Cross, and then we are to make our way to...but perhaps I should not tell you, for despite our embraces, I fear you are not entirely sympathetic to my cause."

There she glanced at the ring I wear, which, as you see, shows the sign of the compass, the mark of my order. I was a little surprised that she should be so worldly as to recognize the sign, and beyond that, have some understanding of the strictures, yet only a little, else she would have understood that I would have no wish to stand in the way of a god who desired mortality, believing as I do that we mortals must be paramount over gods, that it is our works that will endure, when the last godlet is thrust back to whence it came. I believe this is a more extreme view than you share yourselves, for I understand you have fooled yourselves with definitions, gods deemed beneficial or trivial, and gods malevolent and harmful, to be destroyed or banished. We consider them all a pest, to be gotten rid of at any opportunity. Though use may be made of them first, of course.

"It is true I do not care for gods," I told her. "But as you wish to become mortal, I shall consider you a mortal and not my enemy. Provided your aim does not require the desanguination of many people by trickery, for example."

"No, it does not involve blood," said Yuddra. She shifted near the window, and looked out. "I think we near Halleck's Cross and here I must leave you. Please, do not speak of our tryst, indeed even of our meeting, for we must remain free of the temple, and they have many spies and paid informants."

"I will not speak of it, nor write of it," I said. "I hope that one day we might meet again, when you are but a mortal woman and not a fleeing goddess. Should you wish to, my house in Durlal is easily found, it has a roof of yellow tiles, the only such in the street of the Waterbear."

There is little more to tell of that first encounter. As we drew up at Halleck's Cross, she turned once more into that cold jade figurine and, at her instruction, I carried her from the platform and across the street, depositing her in the branches of the ancient harkamon tree that marks some ancient battle. I turned back after I crossed the street, and saw a cloaked and hooded figure swoop upon the tree, take up the figurine, and be gone, a person that though shrouded, I reckoned to be the sister goddess.

And that, I presumed, was that. A curious encounter, a brief and no less curious tryst, and an odd tale that I had promised not to tell. I had work to do, pages to be corrected, stories to be written. I soon forgot Pikgnil-Yuddra the Radiant and Yuddra-Pikgnil the Darkness, save in some half-remembered dreams, in which the two of them happened to come by...ah...such dreams are sweet, though sadly oft ill-remembered...

Please! I continue. Yes, I did see the Goddess again, as I am sure you know or you would not be here, taking up time I had allocated to write a denunciation of the guild of parodists' most recent stupidity. I saw her a few days ago I think…What? It is not easy to be exact when one works as much at night as in the day. Very well, it was last night, but already this one is almost at the dawn, so it is not so far to say two days ago.

I was working here, in my study, sitting in this very chair. I heard a faint knock at that door, though no visitor had been announced and indeed my goblin had long gone to bed and so would not have answered the front door in any case. Having some respectable number of enemies, I took up the pistol from the drawer, that same pistol you have confiscated, Sir Knight, though I know not the reason, any more than you should take my paper knife, for all it looks like a dagger. I assure you the sharpness is required to swiftly slit a signature of this rough paper I use for notes, that my neighborly printer sells me very cheap as being offcuts and remainders. A blunt knife will tear and rip, and is no use at all.

"Come in," I called out, my voice steady, for all that my finger was upon the trigger and my heart beat a little more rapidly than was usual.

The door opened slowly, and a bent figure entered, to all appearances some aged crone, so covered in shawls and scarves that I could not make out a face at all, until she shuffled closer and straightened, so that the light of my lamp fell upon her face. An aged and withered face, a woman twice my age or more but yet…there was something familiar there. Her eyes were bright, and younger, and I knew her.

It was Pikgnil-Yuddra, or her sister. No longer radiant, no longer young, rather greatly aged and very clearly mortal.

"You know me, then?" she croaked. Her voice still retained

something of her former self, but her appearance astounded me. It was no more than a year since we had met on the Cartway.

"Yuddra-Pikgnil the Darkness," I said quietly, but inside I felt a new excitement, for I suspected there was a story here such as few might ever hear, a story that having heard, I might then remake in writing and call my own.

"Yes. I was once Yuddra-Pikgnil the Darkness," said the old woman, and creaking, she sat where you sit now, Sir Puppet, and set her bag, a shabby cloak-bag of boiled leather, upon the seat you occupy, Sir Knight. "And you once expressed a desire to see me again, and so I have come."

I was a trifle alarmed by this, sensing some undercurrent of permanent residence being suggested, but that could be dealt with later, I felt. The important matter was the story, the story was the thing!

"But tell me, how have you come to be as you are now?" I asked. "What of your sister? Where did you go?"

"After Halleck's Cross," said the old woman. She looked past me as she spoke, her old eyes seeing things that were not there, at least not for me to see. "Where did we not go? It was my sister's plan, she was the one who had thought upon it longest, and it was she who found the way. Not the blood drinking, for that would not answer, not for very long. If we could have drunk blood taken forcefully, that would have been a different road, and we did try that, when we were very young. But it did not work, and we could not discover why it did not work, save that it was a stricture of our making, when first we came.

"We tried other things, sought wisdom from sorcerers and priests, wizards and wise folk. None of them could help us. In the end it was Pikgnil who found the answer, a decade or more ago, when she was being me, outside the temple, wandering in search of how we might escape our godhood.

"There is a place far to the northwest, beyond Keriman and the Weary Hills, beyond even Fort Largin and the Rorgrim Fastness, up in the mountains beyond the Valley of the Hargrou, just below the peaks where the Diminished Folk dwell. A place called Verkil-na-Verekil, a ruined city, yet where some mortals still live, eking out their simple lives.

"Pikgnil had found an ancient text that spoke of Verkil-na-Verekil, of the city before it was ruined, of the king who ruled there, and of his crown. It was his crown that interested us, for the text spoke of its singular property, that it could make a man a god...or..."

She smiled, her teeth no longer white and shining, but gray with age, and broken at the edges.

"Or make a god a man.

"It was a long way to Verkil-na-Verekil, a difficult way, for our powers were greatly reduced with every league we traveled from Shrivet, the locus of our extension from the otherworld. By the time we passed Rorgrim Fastness and began to climb into the mountains, I could not take the jade shape, and it took both of us together to conjure some little light. Worse than that, we were fading, our energistic presences weakening. It became doubtful that we could even reach Verkil-na-Verekil, it might be simply too far...but we resolved to press on. We did not know what would happen if we did overextend ourselves, whether our existence would be terminated, or the stretched energistic threads that led back to the temple would contract, and we would find ourselves once again imprisoned in Shrivet. By then, we did not fear termination and should we end up back in the temple, we would simply try again. So we pressed on.

"We did reach Verkil-na-Verekil in the end, albeit as thinly painted caricatures, little more than half-caught reflections in a mirror...which in some ways was helpful, for the people there were still loyal to ancient ideals, and guarded the ruins well, some of them armed with weapons that could slay even such as we were...yet thin as shadows, we slipped past them, and went deep into the ruins and there, in the deep of the mountain, yes, we did find the crown."

She fell silent then, her eyes downcast, her ancient hands trembling with the import of what she told.

"Go on," I said. "You found the crown...Did you put it on?"

"Pikgnil put it on," whispered the old woman. "Even as she raised it to her head, I felt a presentiment of doom and the flash of a long-forgotten memory. I screamed at her to wait, but she would not wait."

"It made her mortal?" I asked.

"Yes. It made her mortal, with the full weight of all our years," said the woman who had been a god. "I saw her turn to flesh, and smile in triumph, and then the smile twisted, fear shone in her eyes as that flesh sank upon her bones, the smile became a rictus grin, and then she decayed before my eyes, turned to charnel meat and thence to bare, fleshless bones, and I felt the magic flow from the crown, and I too became mortal and my shadowed shape took flesh, and I remembered that long ago, when we first burst out upon this world, we were one, a single thing, and it was called Pikgnilyuddra, that only became two as the centuries passed and the priests wove stories that shaped us, the twins of day and night...and all of those thousands of years we had been upon this earth, all of them came pouring into me from the crown!

"I lunged forward and slapped the crown from the skull that

wore it…saving some scant few years of life, but too late, for I am as you see me now. Mortal but ancient, too old for the simplest pleasures that I hoped to taste, too old even for those who guarded the crown to consider an enemy, so that they let me by, thinking me only a crazed old biddy of their own people. And so I came, in many weary steps and by weary ways, to Durlal. I remembered a scribbler, who I had some fondness for, and so here I am and here I would rest, before I go on to Shrivet and my rightful place."

So there you have it. I gave her some supper, a bed, a cloak. In the morning I added some money to her purse, enough for the fifth carriage on the Cartway to Orthaon, and from there she would have an easy way to Shrivet.

That is all I can tell you. I suppose you would catch her easily if you took the next Cartway, she won't have gotten far from Orthaon. I presume you do wish to catch her, that she must be… tidied up, the books made correct? Even if she is no longer a rogue goddess, but mortal, still your business, if as I presume your business is indeed the dispatch of such unhoused and irregular godlets?

Other business? What other business could we possibly have? I have told you everything. Yuddra was here, she left, she is no longer a god. I am a busy man, I have much to write, look at this desk—

The bag? Her bag? Yes, I did mention a bag, boiled leather, with bronze clasps. I have no idea what was…Why are you putting on those armbands? What does the writing on them mean? It is no text that I recognize. I do not like this, though you are guests in my house I think I shall leave, at once!

Ah, that hurt, and is quite unnecessary. Yes, I shall sit quietly, though I do not like your mumbling, it smacks of priestly doings and, as you know, I am by reason of principle opposed to priests and gods.

Mister Fitz, you unnerve me, as a puppet you are alarming enough, but if that is what I think it is, sorcery is forbidden within this precinct, and there is no need for it, none at all.

What are you doing, Sir Knight? That is a particularly ancient casket, most precious, where I store my old manuscripts, there is no occasion to open it and in any case I have lost the key. Though now I think of it, perhaps the key is in the pocket of my other coat, which I left at the Dawn-Greeter's Club after some revels the other day. You know of the club, I'm sure, frequented by night workers, particularly printers and the like. I shall just slip over there and fetch my coat, and the key—

How now! There's no need, you might have merely asked me to take my seat again. I shall not get the key, then, and so your curiosity about my old parchments and scribblings will not be answered. Why should I shield my eyes? I shall do no—

I see, or rather, I see with some difficulty. That was a most remarkably bright flash, Master Puppet. As I mentioned, that is...or was...a very ancient casket, and melting the lock off will have damaged its value considerably. I fear I must ask you to pay for it, a matter of at least ten, no a dozen, guilders of this city, none of your sham coin. And I must forbid you to ransack my papers...yes, I have laid an old cloak upon them to keep out the damp. I must suppose that the smell is from some vellum that has grown a noxious mold, or an inadequately scraped calfskin, I write upon various materials. I am in the middle of an important piece now as it happens, and so must require solitude to continue, please...

A corpse? An old woman's corpse? I have no conception how that might have gotten there. You are playing some complex joke upon me, perhaps? I shall call for the Watch! Help! Help! Help! Heeeelp!

I presume from the lack of muffling, smothering, or other restraint that you have already paid off the Watch? Such foresight indicates men...a man and a puppet...attuned to pecuniary advantage. I have some wealth, and would happily pay a suitable sum so that this matter may remain confidential. Shall we say twenty guilders? No? Fifty, then? A hundred guilders! It is all that I have, take it and leave me...

The bag under her feet? With bronze clasps? As you can see, untouched by me. I didn't kill her, she just died in her sleep, she was old. I put her in the casket for now, to avoid trouble. Her bag likewise, see, the crown is there. I hid it so that it could not be used by others who might be tempted!

What? Of course I didn't wear the crown! How dare you make such a suggestion. I wear the compass, I am on the square. "Men before gods" is my creed. Such a crown is worthless to a true man. Take it, and go, and I shall not swear a complaint against you. It is against my beliefs, but I shall not stop another from becoming a god, clearly I cannot stop you in any case.

You do not want to become a god, Sir Knight? And you, Master Puppet, with your sorcerous needle, what are you doing? Yes, yes, this time I shall shield my eyes, but that crown is valuable in itself...

I should not have believed it if I had not seen it myself. To destroy such a beautiful thing, even though it be tainted with... with evil magic. But I presume that completes your business here. Allow me to show you to the door, and I trust that we shall not meet again.

Another needle, Master Puppet? What can you need with another needle? The crown is destroyed, the old goddess is dead, all is right with the world, or will be once I am finally left alone!

What? I told you I would never put on the crown. How can you see signs of...I don't understand...energistic tendrils... unlawful protrusion of entities...it is all Khokidlian to me, pure nonsense, so upsetting in fact that I need a drink. I will fetch a bottle and we might share it as a stirrup cup for your departure... ah...that really did hurt and was quite, quite unnecessary. We are all friends here, are we not?

Yes, I confess, I am a curious fellow. I collect oddments, ancient jewelry, that sort of thing. Perhaps I did just touch the crown to my forehead, but nothing happened, nothing much, and anyway, how could you know? I tell you I am not a godlet, I am just a man, I will cause no trouble, I am just a—

Like a lot of people, I first encountered Rudyard Kipling's "The Man Who Would Be King" in its filmic form. I liked the John Huston–directed movie a lot. I suspect I would like anything that teamed Michael Caine and Sean Connery together, but having them in a really good film based on a great story was even better. When Tim and Melissa first suggested the *Rags & Bones* concept to me, Kipling was one of the authors I immediately thought I might like to pay my respects to with an homage. Possibly because I worked in a bookstore when Kipling's books first entered the public domain and thus they are inextricably linked in my mind: I still have nightmares about the sudden influx of dozens of new editions of *The Jungle Book*.

Once I had the idea of revisiting "The Man Who Would Be King," I thought about the two central characters. Who would my buddies be, my Peachy Carnehan and Daniel Dravot? It wasn't a great leap from there to decide I would use my existing duo, Sir Hereward and his puppet companion, Mister Fitz. The other main character is, of course, Kipling himself, who in the original narrates the story in the first person. Possibly because I'd recently been rereading a text from my university days (the story collection *Points of View*, edited by James Moffett and Kenneth R. McElheny), I decided to twist this somewhat and write the story as a dramatic monologue, with the writer character "overheard" as he tells the story of two wayward goddesses and we, the reader, also apprehend what is happening as he narrates both past and present.

The Sleeper and the Spindle

Neil Gaiman

It was the closest kingdom to the queen's, as the crow flies, but not even the crows flew it. The high mountain range that served as the border between the two kingdoms discouraged crows as much as it discouraged people, and it was considered unpassable.

More than one enterprising merchant, on each side of the mountains, had commissioned folk to hunt for the mountain pass that would, if it were there, have made a rich man or woman of anyone who controlled it. The silks of Dorimar could have been in Kanselaire in weeks, in months, not years. But there was no such pass to be found and so, although the two kingdoms shared a common border, no travelers crossed from one kingdom to the next.

Even the dwarfs, who were tough, and hardy, and composed of magic as much as of flesh and blood, could not go over the mountain range.

This was not a problem for the dwarfs. They did not go over the mountain range. They went under it.

Three dwarfs were traveling as swiftly as one through the dark paths beneath the mountains.

"Hurry! Hurry!" said the dwarf in the rear. "We have to buy

her the finest silken cloth in Dorimar. If we do not hurry, perhaps it will be sold, and we will be forced to buy her the second-finest cloth."

"We know! We know!" said the dwarf in the front. "And we shall buy her a case to carry the cloth back in, so it will remain perfectly clean and untouched by dust."

The dwarf in the middle said nothing. He was holding his stone tightly, not dropping it or losing it, and was concentrating on nothing else but this. The stone was a ruby, rough-hewn from the rock and the size of a hen's egg. It would be worth a kingdom when cut and set, and would be easily exchanged for the finest silks of Dorimar.

It had not occurred to the dwarfs to give the young queen anything they had dug themselves from beneath the earth. That would have been too easy, too routine. It's the distance that makes a gift magical, so the dwarfs believed.

The queen woke early that morning.

"A week from today," she said aloud. "A week from today, I shall be married."

She wondered how she would feel to be a married woman.

It seemed both unlikely and extremely final. It would be the end of her life, she decided, if life was a time of choices. In a week from now she would have no choices. She would reign over her people. She would have children. Perhaps she would die in childbirth, perhaps she would die as an old woman, or in battle. But the path to her death, heartbeat by heartbeat, would be inevitable.

She could hear the carpenters in the meadows beneath the castle, building the seats that would allow her people to watch her marry. Each hammer blow sounded like a dull pounding of a huge heart.

The three dwarfs scrambled out of a hole in the side of the riverbank, and clambered up into the meadow, one, two, three. They climbed to the top of a granite outcrop, stretched, kicked, jumped, and stretched themselves once more. Then they sprinted north, toward the cluster of low buildings that made the village of Giff, and in particular to the village inn.

The innkeeper was their friend: they had brought him a bottle of Kanselaire wine—deep red, sweet and rich, and nothing like the sharp, pale wines of those parts—as they always did. He would feed them, and send them on their way, and advise them.

The innkeeper, chest as huge as his barrels, with a beard as bushy and as orange as a fox's brush, was in the taproom. It was early in the morning, and on the dwarfs' previous visits at that time of day the room had been empty, but now there must have been thirty people in that place, and not a one of them looked happy.

The dwarfs, who had expected to sidle into an empty taproom, found all eyes upon them.

"Goodmaster Foxen," said the tallest dwarf to the innkeeper.

"Lads," said the innkeeper, who thought that the dwarfs were boys, for all that they were four, perhaps five times his age, "I know you travel the mountain passes. We need to get out of here."

"What's happening?" said the smallest of the dwarfs.

"Sleep!" said the sot by the window.

"Plague!" said a finely dressed woman.

"Doom!" exclaimed a tinker, his saucepans rattling as he spoke. "Doom is coming!"

"We travel to the capital," said the tallest dwarf, who was no bigger than a child, and had no beard. "Is there plague in the capital?"

"It is not plague," said the sot by the window, whose beard was long and gray, and stained yellow with beer and wine. "It is sleep, I tell you."

"How can sleep be a plague?" asked the smallest dwarf, who was also beardless.

"A witch!" said the sot.

"A bad fairy," corrected a fat-faced man.

"She was an enchantress, as I heard it," interposed the pot-girl.

"Whatever she was," said the sot, "she was not invited to a birthing celebration."

"That's all tosh," said the tinker. "She would have cursed the princess whether she'd been invited to the naming-day party or not. She was one of those forest witches, driven to the margins a thousand years ago, and a bad lot. She cursed the babe at birth, such that when the girl was eighteen she would prick her finger and sleep forever."

The fat-faced man wiped his forehead. He was sweating, although it was not warm. "As I heard it, she was going to die, but another fairy, a good one this time, commuted her magical death sentence to one of sleep. Magical sleep," he added.

"So," said the sot. "She pricked her finger on something-or-other. And she fell asleep. And the other people in the castle—the lord and the lady, the butcher, baker, milkmaid, lady-in-waiting—all of them slept, as she slept. None of them have aged a day since they closed their eyes."

"There were roses," said the pot-girl. "Roses that grew up around the castle. And the forest grew thicker, until it became impassable. This was, what, a hundred years ago?"

"Sixty. Perhaps eighty," said a woman who had not spoken until now. "I know, because my aunt Letitia remembered it happening, when she was a girl, and she was no more than seventy when she died of the bloody flux, and that was only five years ago come Summer's End."

"...and brave men," continued the pot-girl. "Aye, and brave women too, they say, have attempted to travel to the Forest of Acaire, to the castle at its heart, to wake the princess, and, in waking her, to wake all the sleepers, but each and every one of those heroes ended their lives lost in the forest, murdered by bandits, or impaled upon the thorns of the rosebushes that encircle the castle—"

"Wake her how?" asked the middle-sized dwarf, hand still clutching his rock, for he thought in essentials.

"The usual method," said the pot-girl, and she blushed. "Or so the tales have it."

"Right," said the tallest dwarf, who was also beardless. "So, bowl of cold water poured on the face and a cry of 'Wakey! Wakey!'?"

"A kiss," said the sot. "But nobody has ever got that close. They've been trying for sixty years or more. They say the witch—"

"Fairy," said the fat man.

"Enchantress," corrected the pot-girl.

"Whatever she is," said the sot. "She's still there. That's what they say. If you get that close. If you make it through the roses, she'll be waiting for you. She's old as the hills, evil as a snake, all malevolence and magic and death."

The smallest dwarf tipped his head on one side. "So, there's a sleeping woman in a castle, and perhaps a witch or fairy there with her. Why is there also a plague?"

"Over the last year," said the fat-faced man. "It started a year ago, in the north, beyond the capital. I heard about it first from travelers coming from Stede, which is near the Forest of Acaire."

"People fell asleep in the towns," said the pot-girl.

"Lots of people fall asleep," said the tallest dwarf. Dwarfs sleep rarely: twice a year at most, for several weeks at a time, but he had slept enough in his long lifetime that he did not regard sleep as anything special or unusual.

"They fall asleep whatever they are doing, and they do not wake up," said the sot. "Look at us. We fled the towns to come here. We have brothers and sisters, wives and children, sleeping now in their houses or cowsheds, at their workbenches. All of us."

"It is moving faster and faster," said the thin, red-haired woman who had not spoken previously. "Now it covers a mile, perhaps two miles, each day."

"It will be here tomorrow," said the sot, and he drained his flagon, then gestured to the innkeeper to fill it once more. "There is nowhere for us to go to escape it. Tomorrow, everything here will be asleep. Some of us have resolved to escape into drunkenness before the sleep takes us."

"What is there to be afraid of in sleep?" asked the smallest dwarf. "It's just sleep. We all do it."

"Go and look," said the sot. He threw back his head, and drank as much as he could from his flagon. Then he looked back at them, with eyes unfocused, as if he were surprised to still see them there. "Well, go on. Go and look for yourselves." He swallowed the remaining drink, then he laid his head upon the table.

They went and looked.

"Asleep?" asked the queen. "Explain yourselves. How so, asleep?"

The dwarf stood upon the table so he could look her in the

eye. "Asleep," he repeated. "Sometimes crumpled upon the ground. Sometimes standing. They sleep in their smithies, at their awls, on milking stools. The animals sleep in the fields. Birds, too, slept, and we saw them in trees or dead and broken in fields where they had fallen from the sky."

The queen wore a wedding gown, blindingly white, whiter than the snow, as white as her skin. Around her, attendants, maids of honor, dressmakers, and milliners clustered and fussed.

"And why did you three also not fall asleep?"

The dwarf shrugged. He had a russet-brown beard that had always made the queen think of an angry hedgehog attached to the lower portion of his face. "Dwarfs are magical things. This sleep is a magical thing also. I felt sleepy, mind."

"And then?"

She was the queen, and she was questioning him as if they were alone. Her attendants began removing her gown, taking it away, folding and wrapping it, so the final laces and ribbons could be attached to it, so it would be perfect.

Tomorrow was the queen's wedding day. Everything needed to be perfect.

"By the time we returned to Foxen's inn they were all asleep, every man jack-and-jill of them. It is expanding, the zone of the spell, a few miles every day. We think it is expanding faster with each day that passes."

The mountains that separated the two lands were impossibly high, but not wide. The queen could count the miles. She pushed one pale hand through her raven-black hair, and she looked most serious.

"What do you think, then?" she asked the dwarf. "If I went there. Would I sleep, as they did?"

He scratched his arse, unself-consciously. "You slept for a

year," he said. "And then you woke again, none the worse for it. If any of the bigguns can stay awake there, it's you."

Outside, the townsfolk were hanging bunting in the streets and decorating their doors and windows with white flowers. Silverware had been polished and protesting children had been forced into tubs of lukewarm water (the oldest child always got the first dunk and the hottest, cleanest water) and then scrubbed with rough flannels until their faces were raw and red; they were then ducked under the water, and the backs of their ears were washed as well.

"I am afraid," said the queen, "that there will be no wedding tomorrow."

She called for a map of the kingdom, identified the villages closest to the mountains, and sent messengers to tell the inhabitants to evacuate to the coast or risk royal displeasure.

She called for her first minister and informed him that he would be responsible for the kingdom in her absence, and that he should do his best neither to lose it nor to break it.

She called for her fiancé and told him not to take on so, and that they would still soon be married, even if he was but a prince and she already a queen, and she chucked him beneath his pretty chin and kissed him until he smiled.

She called for her mail shirt.

She called for her sword.

She called for provisions, and for her horse, and then she rode out of the palace, toward the east.

It was a full day's ride before she saw, ghostly and distant, like clouds against the sky, the shape of the mountains that bordered the edge of her kingdom.

The dwarfs were waiting for her, at the last inn in the foothills of the mountains, and they led her down deep into the tunnels, the way that the dwarfs travel. She had lived with them, when she was little more than a child, and she was not afraid.

The dwarfs did not speak to her as they walked the deep paths, except, on more than one occasion, to say, "Mind your head."

"Have you noticed," asked the shortest of the dwarfs, "something unusual?" They had names, the dwarfs, but human beings were not permitted to know what they were, such things being sacred.

The queen had once a name, but nowadays people only ever called her Your Majesty. Names are in short supply in this telling.

"I have noticed many unusual things," said the tallest of the dwarfs.

They were in Goodmaster Foxen's inn.

"Have you noticed, that even among all the sleepers, there is something that does not sleep?"

"I have not," said the second tallest, scratching his beard. "For each of them is just as we left him or her. Head down, drowsing, scarcely breathing enough to disturb the cobwebs that now festoon them..."

"The cobweb spinners do not sleep," said the tallest dwarf.

It was the truth. Industrious spiders had threaded their webs from finger to face, from beard to table. There was a modest web between the deep cleavage of the pot-girl's breasts. There was a thick cobweb that stained the sot's beard gray. The webs shook and swayed in the draft of air from the open door.

"I wonder," said one of the dwarfs, "whether they will starve and die, or whether there is some magical source of energy that gives them the ability to sleep for a long time."

"I would presume the latter," said the queen. "If, as you say, the original spell was cast by a witch, seventy years ago, and those who were there sleep even now, like Red-beard beneath his hill, then obviously they have not starved or aged or died."

The dwarfs nodded. "You are very wise," said a dwarf. "You always were wise."

The queen made a sound of horror and of surprise.

"That man," she said, pointing. "He looked at me."

It was the fat-faced man. He had moved slowly, tearing the webbing and moving his face so that he was facing her. He had turned toward her, yes, but he had not opened his eyes.

"People move in their sleep," said the smallest dwarf.

"Yes," said the queen. "They do. But not like that. That was too slow, too stretched, too *meant*."

"Or perhaps you imagined it," said a dwarf.

The rest of the sleeping heads in that place moved slowly, in a stretched way, as if they meant to move. Now each of the sleeping faces was facing the queen.

"You did not imagine it," said the same dwarf. He was the one with the red-brown beard. "But they are only looking at you with their eyes closed. That is not a bad thing."

The lips of the sleepers moved in unison. No voices, only the whisper of breath through sleeping lips.

"Did they just say what I thought they said?" asked the shortest dwarf.

"They said, 'Mama. It is my birthday,'" said the queen, and she shivered.

They rode no horses. The horses they passed all slept, standing in fields, and could not be woken.

The queen walked fast. The dwarfs walked twice as fast as she did, in order to keep up.

The queen found herself yawning.

"Bend over, toward me," said the tallest dwarf. She did so. The dwarf slapped her around the face. "Best to stay awake," he said, cheerfully.

"I only yawned," said the queen.

"How long, do you think, to the castle?" asked the smallest dwarf.

"If I remember my tales and my maps correctly," said the queen, "the Forest of Acaire is about seventy miles from here. Three days' march." And then she said, "I will need to sleep tonight. I cannot walk for another three days."

"Sleep, then," said the dwarfs. "We will wake you at sunrise."

She went to sleep that night in a hayrick, in a meadow, with the dwarfs around her, wondering if she would ever wake to see another morning.

The castle in the Forest of Acaire was a gray, blocky thing, all grown over with climbing roses. They tumbled down into the moat and grew almost as high as the tallest tower. Each year the roses grew out farther: close to the stone of the castle there were only dead, brown stems and creepers, with old thorns sharp as knives. Fifteen feet away the plants were green and the blossoming roses grew thickly. The climbing roses, living and dead, were a brown skeleton, splashed with color, that rendered the gray fastness less precise.

The trees in the Forest of Acaire were pressed thickly together, and the forest floor was dark. A century before, it had been a forest only in name: it had been hunting lands, a royal park, home to deer and wild boar and birds beyond counting. Now the forest was a dense tangle, and the old paths through the forest were overgrown and forgotten.

The fair-haired girl in the high tower slept.

All the people in the castle slept. Each of them was fast asleep, excepting only one.

The old woman's hair was gray, streaked with white, and was so sparse her scalp showed. She hobbled, angrily, through the castle, leaning on her stick, as if she were driven only by hatred, slamming doors, talking to herself as she walked. "Up the blooming stairs and past the blinking cook and what are you cooking now, eh, great lard-arse, nothing in your pots and pans but dust and more dust, and all you ever ruddy do is snore."

Into the kitchen garden, neatly tended. The old woman picked rampion and rocket, and she pulled a large turnip from the ground.

Eighty years before, the palace had held five hundred chickens; the pigeon coop had been home to hundreds of fat white doves; rabbits had run, white-tailed, across the greenery of the grass square inside the castle walls, and fish had swum in the moat and the pond: carp and trout and perch. There remained now only three chickens. All the sleeping fish had been netted and carried out of the water. There were no more rabbits, no more doves.

She had killed her first horse sixty years back, and eaten as much of it as she could before the flesh went rainbow-colored and the carcass began to stink and crawl with blueflies and maggots. Now she butchered the larger mammals only in midwinter, when nothing rotted and she could hack and sear frozen chunks of the animal's corpse until the spring thaw.

The old woman passed a mother, asleep, with a baby dozing at her breast. She dusted them, absently, as she passed and made certain that the baby's sleepy mouth remained on the nipple.

She ate her meal of turnips and greens in silence.

It was the first great grand city they had come to. The city gates were high and impregnably thick, but they were open wide.

The three dwarfs were all for going around it, for they were uncomfortable in cities, distrusted houses and streets as unnatural things, but they followed their queen.

Once in the city, the sheer numbers of people made them uncomfortable. There were sleeping riders on sleeping horses, sleeping cabmen up on still carriages that held sleeping passengers, sleeping children clutching their toys and hoops and the whips for their spinning tops; sleeping flower women at their stalls of brown, rotten, dried flowers; even sleeping fishmongers beside their marble slabs. The slabs were covered with the remains of stinking fish, and they were crawling with maggots. The rustle and movement of the maggots was the only movement and noise the queen and the dwarfs encountered.

"We should not be here," grumbled the dwarf with the angry brown beard.

"This road is more direct than any other road we could follow," said the queen. "Also it leads to the bridge. The other roads would force us to ford the river."

The queen's temper was equable. She went to sleep at night, and she woke in the morning, and the sleeping sickness had not touched her.

The maggots' rustlings, and, from time to time, the gentle snores and shifts of the sleepers, were all that they heard as they made their way through the city. And then a small child, asleep on a step, said, loudly and clearly, "Are you spinning? Can I see?"

"Did you hear that?" asked the queen.

The tallest dwarf said only, "Look! The sleepers are waking!"

He was wrong. They were not waking.

The sleepers were standing, however. They were pushing themselves slowly to their feet, and taking hesitant, awkward, sleeping steps. They were sleepwalkers, trailing gauze cobwebs behind them. Always, there were cobwebs being spun.

"How many people, human people I mean, live in a city?" asked the smallest dwarf.

"It varies," said the queen. "In our kingdom, no more than twenty, perhaps thirty thousand people. This seems bigger than our cities. I would think fifty thousand people. Or more. Why?"

"Because," said the dwarf, "they appear to all be coming after us."

Sleeping people are not fast. They stumble; they stagger; they move like children wading through rivers of treacle, like old people whose feet are weighed down by thick, wet mud.

The sleepers moved toward the dwarfs and the queen. They were easy for the dwarfs to outrun, easy for the queen to outwalk. And yet, and yet, there were so many of them. Each street they came to was filled with sleepers, cobweb-shrouded, eyes tightly closed or eyes open and rolled back in their heads showing only the whites, all of them shuffling sleepily forward.

The queen turned and ran down an alleyway and the dwarfs ran with her.

"This is not honorable," said a dwarf. "We should stay and fight."

"There is no honor," gasped the queen, "in fighting an opponent who has no idea that you are even there. No honor in fighting someone who is dreaming of fishing or of gardens or of long-dead lovers."

"What would they do if they caught us?" asked the dwarf beside her.

"Do you wish to find out?" asked the queen.

"No," admitted the dwarf.

They ran, and they ran, and they did not stop from running until they had left the city by the far gates, and had crossed the bridge that spanned the river.

A woodcutter, asleep by the bole of a tree half-felled half a century before, and now grown into an arch, opened his mouth as the queen and the dwarfs passed and said, "So I hold the spindle in one hand, and the yarn in the other? My, the tip of the spindle looks so very sharp!"

Three bandits, asleep in the middle of what remained of the trail, their limbs crooked as if they had fallen asleep while hiding in a tree above and had tumbled, without waking, to the ground below, said, in unison, without waking, "My mother has forbidden me to spin."

One of them, a huge man, fat as a bear in autumn, seized the queen's ankle as she came close to him. The smallest dwarf did not hesitate: he lopped the hand off with his ax, and the queen pulled the man's fingers away, one by one, until the hand fell on the leaf mold.

"Let me just spin a little thread," said the three bandits as they slept, with one voice, while the blood oozed indolently onto the ground from the stump of the fat man's arm. "I would be so happy if only you would let me spin a little thread."

* * *

The old woman had not climbed the tallest tower in a dozen years, and even she could not have told you why she felt impelled to make the attempt on this day. It was a laborious climb, and each step took its toll on her knees and on her hips. She walked up the curving stone stairwell, each small shuffling step she took an agony. There were no railings there, nothing to make the steep steps easier. She leaned on her stick, sometimes, to catch her breath, and then she kept climbing.

She used the stick on the webs, too: thick cobwebs hung and covered the stairs, and the old woman shook her stick at them, pulling the webs apart, leaving spiders scurrying for the walls.

The climb was long, and arduous, but eventually she reached the tower room.

There was nothing in the room but a spindle and a stool, beside one slitted window, and a bed in the center of the round room. The bed was opulent: unfaded crimson and gold cloth was visible beneath the dusty netting that covered it and protected its sleeping occupant from the world.

The spindle sat on the ground, beside the stool, where it had fallen seventy years before.

The old woman pushed at the netting with her stick, and dust filled the air. She stared at the sleeper on the bed.

The girl's hair was the golden yellow of meadow flowers. Her lips were the pink of the roses that climbed the palace walls. She had not seen daylight in a long time, but her skin was creamy, neither pallid nor unhealthy.

Her chest rose and fell, almost imperceptibly, in the semidarkness.

The old woman reached down and picked up the spindle. She

said, aloud, "If I drove this spindle through your blooming heart, then you'd not be so pretty-pretty, would you? Eh? Would you?"

She walked toward the sleeping girl in the dusty white dress. Then she lowered her hand. "No. I can't. I wish to all the gods I could."

All of her senses were fading with age, but she thought she heard voices from the forest. Long ago she had seen them come, the princes and the heroes, and watched them perish, impaled upon the thorns of the roses, but it had been a long time since anyone, hero or otherwise, had reached as far as the castle.

"Eh," she said aloud, as she said so much aloud, for who was to hear her? "Even if they come, they'll die screaming on the blinking thorns. There's nothing they can do—that anyone can do. Nothing at all."

They felt the castle long before they saw it: felt it as a wave of sleep that pushed them away. If they walked toward it their heads fogged, their minds frayed, their spirits fell, their thoughts clouded. The moment they turned away they woke up into the world, felt brighter, saner, wiser.

The queen and the dwarfs pushed deeper into the mental fog.

Sometimes a dwarf would yawn and stumble. Each time the other dwarfs would take him by the arms and march him forward, struggling and muttering, until his mind returned.

The queen stayed awake, although the forest was filled with people she knew could not be there. They walked beside her on the path. Sometimes they spoke to her.

"Let us now discuss how diplomacy is affected by matters of natural philosophy," said her father.

"My sisters ruled the world," said her stepmother, dragging her iron shoes along the forest path. They glowed a dull orange, yet none of the dry leaves burned where the shoes touched them. "The mortal folk rose up against us, they cast us down. And so we waited, in crevices, in places they do not see us. And now, they adore me. Even you, my stepdaughter. Even you adore me."

"You are so beautiful," said her mother, who had died so very long ago. "Like a crimson rose fallen in the snow."

Sometimes wolves ran beside them, pounding dust and leaves up from the forest floor, although the passage of the wolves did not disturb the huge cobwebs that hung like veils across the path. Also, sometimes the wolves ran through the trunks of trees and off into the darkness.

The queen liked the wolves, and was sad when one of the dwarfs began shouting, saying that the spiders were bigger than pigs, and the wolves vanished from her head and from the world. (It was not so. They were only spiders, of a regular size, used to spinning their webs undisturbed by time and by travelers.)

The drawbridge across the moat was down, and they crossed it, although everything seemed to be pushing them away. They could not enter the castle, however: thick thorns filled the gateway, and fresh growth was covered with roses.

The queen saw the remains of men in the thorns: skeletons in armor and skeletons unarmored. Some of the skeletons were high on the sides of the castle, and the queen wondered if they had climbed up, seeking an entry, and died there, or if they had died on the ground and been carried upward as the roses grew.

She came to no conclusions. Either way was possible.

And then her world was warm and comfortable, and she

became certain that closing her eyes for only a handful of moments would not be harmful. Who would mind?

"Help me," croaked the queen.

The dwarf with the brown beard pulled a thorn from the rosebush nearest to him, jabbed it hard into the queen's thumb, and pulled it out again. A drop of deep blood dripped onto the flagstones of the gateway.

"Ow!" said the queen. And then, "Thank you!"

They stared at the thick barrier of thorns, the dwarfs and the queen. She reached out and picked a rose from the thorn-creeper nearest her and bound it into her hair.

"We could tunnel our way in," said the dwarfs. "Go under the moat and into the foundations and up. Only take us a couple of days."

The queen pondered. Her thumb hurt, and she was pleased her thumb hurt. She said, "This began here eighty or so years ago. It began slowly. It spread only recently. It is spreading faster and faster. We do not know if the sleepers can ever wake. We do not know anything, save that we may not actually have another two days."

She eyed the dense tangle of thorns, living and dead, decades of dried, dead plants, their thorns as sharp in death as ever they were when alive. She walked along the wall until she reached a skeleton, and she pulled the rotted cloth from its shoulders, and felt it as she did so. It was dry, yes. It would make good kindling.

"Who has the tinder box?" she asked.

The old thorns burned so hot and so fast. In fifteen minutes orange flames snaked upward: they seemed, for a moment, to engulf the building, and then they were gone, leaving just blackened stone. The remaining thorns, those strong enough to have withstood the heat, were easily cut through by the queen's sword, and were hauled away and tossed into the moat.

The four travelers went into the castle.

The old woman peered out of the slitted window at the flames below her. Smoke drifted in through the window, but neither the flames nor the roses reached the highest tower. She knew that the castle was being attacked, and she would have hidden in the tower room had there been anywhere to hide, had the sleeper not been on the bed.

She swore, and began, laboriously, to walk down the steps, one at a time. She intended to make it down as far as the castle's battlements, where she could make it to the far side of the building, to the cellars. She could hide there. She knew the building better than anybody. She was slow, but she was cunning, and she could wait. Oh, she could wait.

She heard their calls rising up the stairwell. "This way!" "Up here!" "It feels worse this way. Come on! Quickly!" She turned around, then did her best to hurry upward, but her legs moved no faster than they had when she was climbing earlier that day. They caught her just as she reached the top of the steps, three men, no higher than her hips, closely followed by a young woman in travel-stained clothes, with the blackest hair the old woman had ever seen.

The young woman said, "Seize her," in a tone of casual command.

The little men took her stick. "She's stronger than she looks," said one of them, his head still ringing from the blow she had got in with the stick before he had taken it. They walked her back into the round tower room.

"The fire?" said the old woman, who had not talked to anyone who could answer her for six decades. "Was anyone killed in the fire? Did you see the king or the queen?"

The young woman shrugged. "I don't think so. The sleepers we passed were all inside, and the walls are thick. Who are you?"

Names. Names. The old woman squinted, then she shook her head. She was herself, and the name she had been born with had been eaten by time and lack of use.

"Where is the princess?"

The old woman just stared at her.

"And why are you awake?"

She said nothing. They spoke urgently to one another then, the little men and the queen. "Is she a witch? There's a magic about her, but I do not think it's of her making."

"Guard her," said the queen. "If she is a witch, that stick might be important. Keep it from her."

"Eh? It's my blooming stick," said the old woman. "I think it was my father's. But he had no more use for it."

The queen ignored her. She walked to the bed, pulled down the silk netting. The sleeper's face stared blindly up at them.

"So this is where it began," said one of the little men.

"On her birthday," said another.

"Well," said the third. "Somebody's got to do the honors."

"I shall," said the queen, gently. She lowered her face to the sleeping woman's. She touched the pink lips to her own carmine lips and she kissed the sleeping girl long and hard.

"Did it work?" asked a dwarf.

"I do not know," said the queen. "But I feel for her, poor thing. Sleeping her life away."

"You slept for a year in the same witch-sleep," said the dwarf. "You did not starve. You did not rot."

The figure on the bed stirred, as if she were having a bad dream from which she was fighting to wake herself.

The queen ignored her. She had noticed something on the floor beside the bed. She reached down and picked it up. "Now this," she said. "This smells of magic."

"There's magic all through this," said the smallest dwarf.

"No, *this*," said the queen. She showed him the wooden spindle, the base half wound around with yarn. "*This* smells of magic."

"It was here, in this ruddy room," said the old woman, suddenly. "And I was little more than a girl. I had never gone so far before, but I climbed all the steps, and I went up and up and round and round until I came to the topmost room. I saw that bed, the one you see, although there was nobody in it. There was only an old woman I didn't know, sitting on the stool, spinning wool into yarn with her spindle. I had never seen a spindle before. She asked if I would like a go. She took the wool in her hand and gave me the spindle to hold. And then she held my thumb and pressed it against the point of the spindle until blood flowed, and she touched the blooming blood to the thread. And then she said..."

A voice interrupted her.

A young voice it was, a girl's voice, but still sleep-thickened. "I said, now I take your sleep from you, girl, just as I take from you your ability to harm me in my sleep, for someone needs to be awake while I sleep. Your family, your friends, your world will sleep too. And then I lay down on the bed, and I slept, and they slept, and as each of them slept I stole a little of their life, a little of their dreams, and as I slept I took back my youth and my beauty and my power. I slept and I grew strong. I undid the ravages of time and I built myself a world of sleeping slaves."

She was sitting up in the bed. She looked so beautiful, and so very young.

The queen looked at the girl and saw what she was searching for: the same look that she had seen, long ago, in her stepmother's eyes, and she knew what manner of creature this girl was.

"We had been led to believe," said the tallest dwarf, "that when you woke, the rest of the world would wake with you."

"Why ever would you think that?" asked the golden-haired girl, all childlike and innocent (ah, but her eyes! Her eyes were so old). "I like them asleep. They are more...*biddable*." She stopped for a moment. Then she smiled. "Even now they come for you. I have called them here."

"It's a high tower," said the queen. "And sleeping people do not move fast. We still have a little time to talk, your darkness."

"Who are you? Why would we talk? Why do you know to address me that way?" The girl climbed off the bed and stretched deliciously, pushing each fingertip out before running her fingertips through her golden hair. She smiled, and it was as if the sun shone into that dim room. "The little people will stop where they are, now. I do not like them. And you, girl. You will sleep too."

"No," said the queen.

She hefted the spindle. The yarn wrapped around it was black with age and with time.

The dwarfs stopped where they stood, and they swayed, and closed their eyes.

The queen said, "It's always the same with your kind. You need youth and you need beauty. You used your own up so long ago, and now you find ever-more-complex ways of obtaining them. And you always want power."

They were almost nose to nose now, and the fair-haired girl seemed so much younger than the queen.

"Why don't you just go to sleep?" asked the girl, and she smiled guilelessly, just as the queen's stepmother had smiled when she wanted something. There was a noise on the stairs, far below them.

"I slept for a year in a glass coffin," said the queen. "And the woman who put me there was much more powerful and dangerous than you will ever be."

"More powerful than I am?" The girl seemed amused. "I have a million sleepers under my control. With every moment that I slept I grew in power, and the circle of dreams grows faster and faster with every passing day. I have my youth—so much youth! I have my beauty. No weapon can harm me. Nobody alive is more powerful than I am."

She stopped and stared at the queen.

"You are not of our blood," she said. "But you have some of the skill." She smiled, the smile of an innocent girl who has woken on a spring morning. "Ruling the world will not be easy. Nor will maintaining order among those of the Sisterhood who have survived into this degenerate age. I will need someone to be my eyes and ears, to administer justice, to attend to things when I am otherwise engaged. I will stay at the center of the web. You will not rule with me, but beneath me, but you will still rule, and rule continents, not just a tiny kingdom." She reached out a hand and stroked the queen's pale skin, which, in the dim light of that room, seemed almost as white as snow.

The queen said nothing.

"Love me," said the girl. "All will love me, and you, who woke me, you must love me most of all."

The queen felt something stirring in her heart. She remembered her stepmother, then. Her stepmother had liked to be adored. Learning how to be strong, to feel her own emotions and not another's, had been hard; but once you learned the trick of it, you did not forget. And she did not wish to rule continents.

The girl smiled at her with eyes the color of the morning sky.

The queen did not smile. She reached out her hand. "Here," she said. "This is not mine."

She passed the spindle to the old woman beside her. The old woman hefted it, thoughtfully. She began to unwrap the yarn from the spindle with arthritic fingers. "This was my blooming, bollocking life," she said. "This thread was my life..."

"It *was* your life. You gave it to me," said the sleeper, irritably. "And it has gone on much too long."

The tip of the spindle was still sharp after so many decades.

The old woman, who had once, long, long ago, been a princess, held the yarn tightly in her left hand, and she thrust the point of the spindle at the golden-haired girl's breast.

The girl looked down as a trickle of red blood ran down her breast and stained her white dress crimson.

"No weapon can harm me," she said, and her girlish voice was petulant. "Not anymore. Look. It's only a scratch."

"It's not a weapon," said the queen, who understood what had happened. "It's your own magic. And a scratch is all that was needed."

The girl's blood soaked into the thread that had once been wrapped about the spindle, the thread that ran from the spindle to the raw wool in the old woman's left hand.

The girl looked down at the blood staining her dress, and at the blood on the thread, and she said only, "It was just a prick of the skin, nothing more." She seemed confused.

The noise on the stairs was getting louder. A slow, irregular shuffling, as if a hundred sleepwalkers were coming up a stone spiral staircase with their eyes closed.

The room was small, and there was nowhere to hide, and the room's windows were two narrow slits in the stones.

The old woman, who had not slept in so many decades, she who had once been a princess, said, "You took my blinking dreams. You took my sleep. Now, that's enough of all that." She was a very old woman: her fingers were gnarled, like the roots of a hawthorn bush. Her nose was long, and her eyelids drooped, but there was a look in her eyes in that moment that was the look of someone young.

The old woman swayed, and then she staggered, and she would have fallen to the floor if the queen had not caught her first.

The queen carried the old woman to the bed, marveling at how little she weighed, and placed her on the crimson counterpane. The old woman's chest rose and fell.

The noise on the stairs was louder now. Then a silence, followed, suddenly, by a hubbub, as if a hundred people were talking at once, all surprised and angry and confused.

The beautiful girl said, "But—" and now there was nothing girlish or beautiful about her. Her face fell and became less shapely. She reached down to the smallest dwarf, pulled his hand ax from his belt. She fumbled with the ax, held it up threateningly, with hands all wrinkled and worn.

The queen drew her sword (the blade's edge was notched and damaged from the thorns) but instead of striking, she took a step backward.

"Listen! They are waking up," she said. "They are all waking up. Tell me again about the youth you stole from them. Tell me again about your beauty and your power. Tell me again how clever you were, your darkness."

When the people reached the tower room, they saw an old woman asleep on a bed, and they saw the queen, standing tall, and beside her, the dwarfs, who were shaking their heads, or scratching them.

They saw something else on the floor also: a tumble of bones, a hank of hair as fine and as white as fresh-spun cobwebs, a tracery of gray rags across it, and over all of it, an oily dust.

"Take care of her," said the queen, pointing with the dark wooden spindle at the old woman on the bed. "She saved your lives."

She left, then, with the dwarfs. None of the people in that room or on the steps dared to stop them or would ever understand what had happened.

A mile or so from the castle, in a clearing in the Forest of Acaire, the queen and the dwarfs lit a fire of dry twigs, and in it they burned the thread and the fiber. The smallest dwarf chopped the spindle into fragments of black wood with his ax, and they burned them too. The wood chips gave off a noxious smoke as they burned, which made the queen cough, and the smell of old magic was heavy in the air.

Afterward, they buried the charred wooden fragments beneath a rowan tree.

By evening they were on the outskirts of the forest, and had reached a cleared track. They could see a village across the hill, and smoke rising from the village chimneys.

"So," said the dwarf with the beard. "If we head due west, we can be at the mountains by the end of the week, and we'll have you back in your palace in Kanselaire within ten days."

"Yes," said the queen.

"And your wedding will be late, but it will happen soon after your return, and the people will celebrate, and there will be joy unbounded through the kingdom."

"Yes," said the queen. She said nothing, but sat on the moss beneath an oak tree and tasted the stillness, heartbeat by heartbeat.

There are choices, she thought, when she had sat long enough. *There are always choices.*

She made her choice.

The queen began to walk, and the dwarfs followed her.

"You *do* know we're heading east, don't you?" said one of the dwarfs.

"Oh yes," said the queen.

"Well, *that's* all right then," said the dwarf.

They walked to the east, all four of them, away from the sunset and the lands they knew, and into the night.

Author's Note . . . .

The first book I remember owning was a picture book about a mermaid. The first book I loved was an illustrated "Snow White." The illustrations were, to my three-year-old self, beautiful, and the story was gripping, terrifying, and it ended perfectly. Years later I retold it as something very dark, and that version of the story seems to be making its own way in the world.

As a young journalist, I was assigned to read a small pile of "sex and shopping" blockbusters and write about them. I noticed, with a small amount of surprise, that the plots were all fairy-tale plots. I remember constructing, as an exercise, a high-tech, contemporary version of "Sleeping Beauty." I did not write it—I was not that cynical—but Sleeping Beauty has hovered at the edges of my mind ever since.

When Melissa and Tim asked me to visit a story I had loved, I thought of so many authors I have loved, so many stories. And then I asked if I could go back to the Sleeping Beauty In The Wood, and felt very lucky when they said yes.

Kai Lung's Golden Hours (1922). English author Ernest Bramah wrote several collections of stories that feature his droll story-teller, Kai Lung, beginning with *The Wallet of Kai Lung* and followed by *Kai Lung's Golden Hours*, and then by *Kai Lung Unrolls His Mat* and *Kai Lung Beneath the Mulberry Tree*. They are all set in a China created entirely from Bramah's own imagination (since he never once even visited the country), a misty land-scape rife with sly dragons, ferocious bandits, wily mandarins, and beguiling maidens continually placed into dramatic circum-stances that always offer his titular hero yet another chance to spin a tale studded with small delights and exquisite language.

On first reading, I simply fell head over heels into Bramah's world, and my imagination still patiently treads its subtle paths.

Kai Lung's Golden Hours

The Cold Corner

Tim Pratt

I left home five years ago, and haven't been back since—so why do I still think of it as home at all?

After almost a week spent driving across the country on I-40 East, I cut north on Highway 202, and within an hour reached the outskirts of my hometown, Cold Corners. The only corners are in the endless rectangular fields of soybeans and tobacco, and with triple-digit heat and 90 percent humidity in summer, it's hardly "cold," so I don't know where it got the name. (Local wisdom contends the name is a corruption of some Cherokee word meaning "fertile land," but I'm willing to bet that's pure Carolina invention.)

I thought about pulling off to the gravel shoulder and calling David to let him know I'd arrived safely, but decided against it. When he threw all my clothes, my best saucepan, and my knife bag out the window of our—technically his—condo in Oakland, that was probably his way of saying "Don't call me, I'll call you." His flair for the dramatic was one of the things I'd loved about him, when he wasn't being dramatic at *me*. David was my first real boyfriend after culinary school, and I'd been dumb enough to think it was forever. Dumb enough to think I could go more than a couple of years without screwing it up, anyway.

The closer I got to Cold Corners, the less eager I was to finish the trip. I decided not to go up to the "big house"—once owned by my grandparents, now home to my older brother, Jimmy, his wife, and nephews and nieces I hadn't seen in years—right away. I wonder, if I *had* gone to their house first, taken my place as the younger child, slipped into those old patterns, put up with the teasing and sympathy for my televised failure for a few days, then slunk back to California... would I have ever truly found my way home again?

I tell people the only thing I miss about home is the food, and that much is true. I got to town at lunchtime, more or less, and thought I'd be able to face the prospect of Jimmy, Mom, Dad, and the extended F if I got a bite to eat first. After a week of greased-up fast food and limp pizza delivered to motel rooms, I was hungry for something real—being picky is an occupational hazard of being a chef—and the prospect of Eastern Carolina barbecue sounded like a gateway to heaven.

You can't get it on the West Coast. Oh, there are places that serve "Carolina-style" barbecue, but at best it's an approximation, carob when you want chocolate. In North Carolina alone, there are two distinct styles of barbecue, though both start with slow-cooking a pig in a pit full of burning hickory chips: there's the One True Barbecue, with vinegar-and-red-pepper sauce, favored in Eastern North Carolina, and the heretical Lexington-style barbecue more common in the western half of the state, with its hideous gloppy tomato-based sauce.

I pulled up in the weedy gravel parking lot outside Willard's B-B-Q, a Cold Corners institution renowned far and wide for the lightness and perfection of its hush puppies and the skill of its pitmaster. What a great title for a cook—the best I've ever had is "executive chef," and that doesn't come close. (Of course, just then, I didn't have any job title at all, unless you count "recently fired for trying to punch a customer.")

There were no cars or pickups in the lot, which was beyond bizarre—it should have been packed, even on a Tuesday. For a heart-stopping moment I looked up at the faded sign (depicting the inevitable smiling pig wearing a chef's toque) and worried that Willard's had closed...but then I saw movement inside the greasy windows and climbed out of my car.

Summer in North Carolina. Stepping out of the air-conditioning was like having a sheet sopping with warm water wrapped around my face. A sudden, brutal pang of homesickness for the East Bay hit me. I remembered the place in the hills where David and I used to sit and watch the cool fog roll in over the bay below, but I couldn't see a way back there that ended in anything but pity or pain.

I hit the button on my key chain to lock the car, then felt stupid. When I was a kid, people barely locked their houses here, let alone their cars. Then I remembered some of my brother's recent e-mails complaining about tweakers and thieves, and left it locked. My friends in Oakland used to joke about how I was a simple country boy too trusting to make it in the big city, but I bet meth heads made up a bigger percentage of the population in my hometown than they did in the East Bay. I'd lost at least two of my innumerable second cousins in home meth-lab accidents.

I pushed through the front door of Willard's into a dim space full of empty square tables draped in red-and-white-checked plastic tablecloths. A couple of ceiling fans whirred away like the propellers of ancient planes, swirling the hot air around.

"You driving one of them hybrids?" the brassy blonde leaning on the counter said, and I braced myself for contempt and sneers as I nodded, but she just said, "The way gas prices are going, I oughta get one of those myself. The pitmaster drives a van rigged to run on biodiesel, and he ain't bought gas in years—just strains out the hush puppy and french fry oil and uses that. What can I getcha?"

The menu was chalked up on a board behind the counter, and looked like it hadn't been changed since the last time I'd been there, at least half a decade before. "I'll take the number two plate and an iced tea." No need to specify sweet tea; that was the only way they did it at Willard's.

"Sit down anywhere. It'll be right out." She sauntered back to the kitchen.

I took a table near the counter, and like all the other tables, it held a glass bottle of hot sauce, a squeeze bottle of sweeter barbecue sauce, a cage of sugar packets in case your tea wasn't sweet enough (hard to imagine), and a roll of paper towels in lieu of napkins, the latter an innovation I considered suggesting to the owner of my restaurant back home, before I remembered he'd fired me. It seems unfair to get fired for something you did when you were so drunk you barely remember it, but that's life.

I pulled out my phone—I'd finally turned off the keyword alert that told me every time my name was mentioned online, but I still occasionally, morbidly, checked the social media sites to see what people were saying about me—but there was no signal. I didn't have time to be annoyed before the waitress was back with a red plastic oval tray that held a heaping scoop of barbecue ("pulled pork" as the rest of the world calls it), a white bread roll, and a wax-paper-lined basket of hush puppies.

The food was...well, I'm a cook, not a food writer, but it was like eating my own childhood memories. The barbecue was cooked to perfection, seasoned just right, spicy and vinegar-astringent sauce combining ideally with the meltingly delicious fat in the pork. The hush puppies were perfect, too: oblongs of deep-fried cornbread, just a little crunchy on the outside, sweet and fluffy inside. The tea was sweet enough to make me want to schedule a cleaning at the dentist, but even that tasted like home.

I ate with single-minded intensity, then leaned back in my chair and belched quietly to myself. The waitress squinted at me from the cash register. "You look real familiar to me," she said. "You always had blond hair?"

"Oh. No, but if you recognize me it's probably because—I've been on TV lately. That reality cooking show, *Stand the Heat.*"

She did not seem awed by my fleeting celebrity. She frowned, and I revised my estimate of her age from thirties to forties. "Had to cancel the cable a while back," she said. "Never seen it. Did you win?"

I shook my head. "Came in fourth. Got cut right before the finale. That episode just aired last week." I think I kept all the bitterness out of my voice. There were three finalists. Even the two who didn't win would get perks: money, bragging rights, invites back for a future all-star show. They were good chefs, and one of them had even been a friend—a summer-camp kind of friend, though, and we hadn't kept in touch since we stopped living in the same New York town house—but I didn't believe any of them were better than me. I'd been a front-runner, and I knew it, winning lots of the weekly competitions...but one fish bone in one fillet served to one flamboyantly vicious guest judge had ended my run.

"Too bad," she said. "Still, fourth place ain't bad. I never came in fourth place at anything. Maybe I saw you in a magazine or something, though I swear...Huh. I've always wondered about those shows—is it all real, or is it fake, like pro wrestling?"

I hesitated, unsure how to answer the question, even though I'd been asked its equivalent many times. "It's...the contests are real, the games and competitions, though they cut out a lot of the boring stuff to make it seem more fast-paced and exciting. But when you watch the shows, the stuff you see people say, a lot of that's *encouraged*, if not exactly scripted. And..." I tried to think of a way to say what I meant. "The me on-screen isn't the real me. I don't think I'm that cocky, for one thing, and they really tried to play up the fact that I come from the South—I swear they showed every time I said 'y'all,' four or five times at least. The producers turn you into a character."

In fact, the bizarre falseness of reality TV had knocked me off balance in my own life, causing me to question all sorts of assumed truths—was I the person my friends thought I was, hotshot chef and grinning joker, or was that just another character I was playing, or a character they needed me to play? Who was the *real* real me? My anxiety over that question had led me to make some lousy decisions and burn way too many bridges. This road trip was supposed to help me settle the question of who I was and what I wanted, but it wasn't working so far.

I could tell I'd lost the waitress—at least, I thought so, until she said, "I reckon we all have to play different parts for different people. Sometimes I think the only time we can really be ourselves is when we're all alone with nobody to disappoint."

I laughed and said that was true. I left a generous tip on the table, then went up to the counter and paid the bill—I was stuffed, and the whole meal cost less than a happy-hour cocktail at a decent restaurant back in Oakland. "Is Junior out back?" I asked, leaning on the counter across from her.

She raised an eyebrow. "You know Junior?"

"I used to live around here. Even worked here at the restaurant one summer in high school, just running the fryer. My first real cooking job." Junior was the owner and pitmaster, and he'd been in his fifties back then, a big man who got up long before dawn to start cooking the day's pigs, and who always smelled of fragrant smoke.

"Well, ain't that something!" she said. "We should hang your picture on the wall, you being on TV and all. I hate to be the bearer of bad news, honey...but Junior passed on last year. Wasn't a heart attack, either—everybody always thinks it was the food—it was cancer." She pronounced it almost like "CAIN-sir," and I wondered if I'd pick up my old accent again while I was in town, the way unwrapped butter will pick up the flavor of onions or garlic sitting next to it on the counter.

"Oh, I'm sorry to hear that. He was..." Kind of a son-of-a-bitch, really, bossy and short-tempered and a perfectionist, but then, lots of chefs were like that, and he *was* a chef, even if a very specialized one. "He was something else," I said at last.

"He left the restaurant to his assistant," she went on. "None of his kids wanted to get into the family business, and he knew they'd just sell the place, so he gave it to TJ instead. Lord, there was a fuss about that! But it's all settled down now. Did you know TJ?"

"No, I don't think so, but that's funny—I'm a TJ too." Terrence James Brydon, and even though everyone called me Terry nowadays, to my family I'd always be TJ.

"Small world. Where you living now?"

"Oakland, California." Even though, on the show, they always put "San Francisco, CA" underneath my name on the screen. Irritated the shit out of me. Some of the best, most innovative cooking is happening in the East Bay, where newer chefs can actually afford to open restaurants—some of them, anyway. I couldn't afford it, hence my attempt to make money by going on the show, my brush with temporary fame, and all the unpleasantness that followed. And also hence my decision to accept this year's invitation to the family reunion, because three thousand miles away from my new life seemed like a good place to be.

"California," she said, and didn't add the perfunctory "land of fruits and nuts." For which I was grateful, since I was just the kind of fruit and nut people thought of when they said that. Part of why I'd gotten on the show was because the producers liked the idea of a six-foot-three, former-high-school-football-playing, Southern-food-specializing gay chef. (I'm not even gay—I'm bi, but reality show producers like bisexual contestants only when they're cute women.) "What brings you back here?" she asked, and seemed genuinely interested.

"Family reunion." I dredged up a grin. "You can't get good banana pudding on the West Coast." The closest I'd come was a gourmet small-batch banana-pudding-flavored ice pop.

"I believe it. Have a good day, now, and come back and see us before you head west."

"I'll do my best." I didn't tell her I'd walk across the surface of Mercury for another meal at Willard's. After all, people who lived here could come by anytime they wanted. Barbecue was as everyday here as good burritos are back on the West Coast. I just thanked her and went outside, the bell over the door jingling above me.

I paused for a moment, the heat enfolding me like a monster's embrace. The air seemed wavy, distorted like flawed glass—like the heat shimmers you see over blacktop. I wiped sweat out of my eyes. Though the idea of my air-conditioned car was tempting, I decided to trudge around back to see the pit. Open-pit barbecuing is an endangered species even in North Carolina, with old restaurants closing down and not many new ones opening, and even though I was sure nothing had changed since my brief stint as a fry cook, I wanted to take a look at the setup while I still could.

Before I made it around the corner, though, I saw something that made me stop dead. A man wearing soot-stained overalls came toward me from behind the restaurant, mopping at his neck and brow with a filthy white cloth.

I stared at him, because he was *me*. Same mole just below the right eye. Same crooked nose from when it got broken and set not quite right during a game back in high school. He was wearing smudged glasses, and he outweighed me by twenty or thirty pounds (most of it beer belly), but the only other real difference was his greasy flyaway brown hair—and mine had looked the same until I buzzed it short and dyed it blond.

I took a step backward, but he didn't look a bit surprised at meeting his doppelganger. "Huh," he said. "Never thought we'd see you around here again." His accent was thick, far more so than mine, which had mellowed a lot after a few years out of state. My native Californian (ex) boyfriend David used to laugh whenever my dad or brother called and asked for me, because he could barely even understand their hellos.

What do you do when you're faced with *yourself*, or at least some *version* of yourself? David was doing a lit degree in grad school (on his rich parents' dime), and he told me once that the writer Jorge Luis Borges claimed to have met a younger version of himself in a park, and had a pleasant conversation with his counterpart while sitting on a bench.

But I'm no Borges. And this other Terry—this TJ—wasn't a younger me, some fry cook unstuck in time, but a me my own age, early twenties, but living another life. Time travel, I could just about comprehend, but *this*?

I ran, faster than I ever ran in an attempt to score a touchdown or catch a bus. I jumped into my car and tore out of the parking lot, watching myself diminish in the rearview mirror.

By the time I got to the big house, I'd stopped shaking and had convinced myself I'd just seen someone who looked a little like me and freaked out. I blamed days on the road with no company but my own, compounded by the collected stresses of getting a little bit famous, getting a lot drunk, doing stupid things, going from semi-celebrity chef to unemployed, and getting dumped by my boyfriend and kicked out of the house, not to mention the cognitive dissonance of returning home for the first time since I left at eighteen.

I pulled up in front of the big house, next to a dusty station wagon (hers) and a gleaming, pristine black half-ton pickup (his). Before I'd even gotten out of the car, the screen door on the front porch banged open and a stream of nephews and nieces flowed out. I'm a fairly terrible uncle—I could tell you all their names, I think, but not which kid each name belonged to—but I'm not utterly hopeless: I had a bag of gifts for them, with a snow globe containing the Golden Gate Bridge, a collapsible miniature telescope, a little puzzle that had something to do with spherical magnets, and other gimcrackery that would fall apart under their zealous attention, but would delight them in the meantime.

Once I'd distracted the pack with presents, I made my way up the porch, into the embrace of my older brother, Jimmy, who had a farmer's tan (he's a contractor), a sloping potbelly, thin-, ning hair, and a grin as wide as the world. He's a dozen years older than me, because I was a "bonus baby"—in other words, the accidental surprise my parents hadn't *meant* to have, though they did their best to never let me suspect it. Jimmy hugged me hard, but not hard enough to crush the inevitable pack of cigarettes tucked into his shirt pocket. His wife, Emily, fluttered in the background, blond and insubstantial, cooing noises of welcome. She looked exactly the same as she had at their wedding (I was a groomsman, sweating like only a twelve-year-old in a borrowed suit can): like a rare and fragile bird, though I knew she was a lot tougher than she seemed.

Before long I was settled in a rocker on the porch beside my brother, each of us holding a beer, looking out across the long fields, the wife and children off somewhere else, and it was like I'd just been here yesterday.

"So why come back this year?" Jimmy said. "We've invited you for every reunion, and you always said you were too busy. So, what—sixth time's the charm?"

I shook my head. "Things back in Oakland just got ... weird."

Jimmy grunted. "My brother, Chef Hollywood."

I snorted. "Being on TV is a pain in the ass. My boss liked it—a lot of people came into the restaurant when the show started—and he gave me a raise to make sure I wouldn't leave. But getting recognized on the street is just weird, and having people come into the restaurant, not because they heard the food was good, but because they wanted to get a look at me…" I shook my head. "And then, I don't know, some of the attention, maybe it went to my head, got me in a little trouble…"

One night I'd gotten very drunk—I'm a chef, and we drink, as a rule, but this was orders of magnitude beyond my tolerance, with admirers buying me round after round, and this one guy, maybe twenty years old and adorable, paid me a lot of attention. One thing led to another. My boyfriend, David, found out, and that was it. We were over. The funny thing was, David and I had an open relationship, and were both known to see people on the side. But we also had rules: check in with your partner before getting intimate with someone new, and always practice safe sex, and…I failed on both counts.

I was so upset I kept on getting drunk, right on through my next shift, and when some asshole at table four started yelling about how overrated I was, how my food looked pretty on TV but tasted like shit, I came wading out of the kitchen and tried to hit him. I was so messed up I didn't even connect, just knocked the table over and fell on the floor. That spared me an assault and battery charge, but not my job.

I wasn't sure I wanted to tell Jimmy all that, especially about David dumping me. He knew I wasn't straight, of course—at this point, everyone with a TV did, but I'd come out to my family when I was seventeen. My parents took it in stride; they live in the very buckle of the Bible Belt, and if pressed I'm sure they'd say they were Christian, but they'd never been churchgoers. My mom sort of suggested that if I liked women *too*, I might as well just find a nice girl and marry her, nobody'd ever know the difference, but she didn't press the point. When my brother found out

I'd been involved with other men, he just nodded and absorbed it—like the desert absorbing a spoonful of water—and we never spoke of it again. So I just said, "I acted like a real asshole, and pissed off a lot of my friends, got in trouble at work, and it seemed like a good idea to get away for a while, and come home, and try to remember who I really am."

Jimmy nodded like that made sense. He's a good brother.

I wasn't willing to go into my interpersonal breakdowns with him, but maybe he *could* set my mind at ease about something else—the mysterious pitmaster TJ. Maybe he was some cousin I'd forgotten, which would explain the family resemblance. I said, "I stopped by Willard's on the way in—"

Jimmy whistled. "That's a shame, ain't it? When Junior passed, his kids thought they'd sell the place and make a pile of money, but nobody wanted to buy it. I guess it's hard to find anybody who wants to get up before dawn to cook pigs every day. I hate seeing the place all closed up, though, the windows broke, and all that graffiti the meth heads scrawled on the walls...End of an era. We can run over to the White Swan later if you want, they do a good barbecue plate, even if it's not pit-cooked."

My belly was still full of Willard's pulled pork, and even after two swigs of beer, I could taste the last residue of the hush puppies in my mouth. Was Jimmy messing with me? For what possible reason? If Willard's was closed...what did that mean? Was I having a nervous breakdown?

I put my beer down gently. "I, ah...It's been a long trip. I think I could use a nap."

Jimmy nodded. "Sure. I don't know why you had to drive the whole way—you could've flown in, rented a car in Raleigh."

"I just wanted some time to think." Which was true, though

in point of fact, I wasn't sure I'd had any thoughts worth thinking in those long days on the road. The problem is, no matter how far or fast you drive, you can't leave *yourself* behind. And if you can't feel at home in your own head, where can you?

"We've got one of the spare rooms made up for you. You're lucky—tomorrow night we're going to have a full house, people staying over, sleeping on every couch and cot and bit of floor, and you've got a bed to yourself. We're gonna have to stack cousins around you like cordwood." He grinned. "I hope you're ready to get stared at and whispered about tomorrow. Prodigal son and celebrity all rolled up into one."

"I can't wait," I said.

I'd expected to sleep until dinnertime or so, but when I woke up blinking in that stale room that smelled of mothballs, it was full dark, which that time of year meant it must be past nine p.m. I fumbled for my phone and saw it was closer to two in the morning. I groaned and rolled out of bed, switching on the lamp by the bed. My belly rumbled unpleasantly, and I slipped out, going down the hallway in my socks, past family photographs that had hung on the walls since my grandparents were alive. Jimmy and his wife hadn't altered the decor much, so it was still all done in Country Cluttered.

I went downstairs, avoiding the creaking step with my ancient instincts, and into the kitchen, where a single light burned above the stove, as always. I poked my head into the fridge, which was absolutely packed with food ready for tomorrow, or prepped to be popped into the oven according to a byzantine schedule devised by the wives. Most of what I'd learned about the logistics of meal prep had come from getting underfoot in Southern kitchens during the holidays, when hordes of women worked with clockwork precision to turn out their respective specialties, all ready to hit the table at the same time: chicken pastry, baked macaroni and cheese, candied yams, fried chicken, collard greens, green bean casserole, black-eyed peas, banana pudding, two dozen kinds of pie…

I didn't dare disturb that shrine to Southern cookery, so I sat at the table and ate a bowl of kids' cereal and topped it off with an apple so improbably large and red that there was no way in hell it was organic. After I finished eating I thought for a moment, then scribbled a note to leave on the kitchen table—couldn't sleep, went for a drive, home by morning—and went outside.

Willard's was shuttered and graffiti-covered, and when I peered in the shattered windows, there were no chairs or tables, just heaps of unidentifiable trash and empty beer cans. I went around back, to the pit and the smokehouse, and found just a dirty hole in the ground next to a tin-roofed shack, all looking entirely unlovely in the moonlight.

Okay, then. I was going crazy. Fair enough. Good to know.

After that, I drove around some old familiar roads, past the high school where I'd been a minor football hero, through the half-empty remnants of our main street, and around the grave-yard, whose underground population vastly outnumbered that of the living in Cold Corners.

Eventually I drove over the long bridge that spanned the river, and the air went all blurry for a moment—or, more likely, my exhausted eyes watered.

I slowed down, and on the far side of the river saw my first sign of light and life in that postmidnight world: a long low wooden building near the bank of the river, with a dirt lot packed astonishingly full for the late hour: pickups, motorcycles, station wagons, sedans, SUVs...everything but a hybrid like mine. Some little country bar, the kind I'd brazened my way into often enough as a teenager, armed with a fake ID and the certain knowledge that I'd always been big for my age. I thought, *I could go for a drink*, and turned into the lot.

I sat in my idling car, staring at the sign above the door, illuminated now by the wash of my headlights.

It said TJ'S PLACE.

The door banged open and a man staggered out, lifting his hand in front of his face to shield himself from the glare of my headlights. But before his hand rose, I saw enough of his face to recognize him easily. He was dressed in a flannel lumberjack shirt with the sleeves ripped off, grease-stained jeans, and a dirty baseball cap—all things I'd never wear—but his face was familiar enough. I saw it every day in the mirror.

He lowered his hand, squinted, and gave a hesitant wave.

I reversed out of the lot, making my little hybrid's tires squeal, and roared back toward the big house. Once I'd flown across the bridge, I forced myself to slow down, because I knew the local cops love nothing better than pulling over speeders with out-of-state plates.

And I was a bit terrified that if I did get pulled over, the smirking cop would be wearing my face.

I did sleep, a little—a thin sort of sleep, just before dawn. I woke after a couple of confused hours to the smell of frying bacon and went downstairs, where an epic breakfast was under way:

yellow heaps of scrambled eggs, fluffy as clouds; fried slices of ham; scratch biscuits and sausage gravy. The nieces and nephews were arrayed around the big kitchen table, devastating the food set before them, while my brother and sister-in-law leaned companionably against the sink, sipping mugs of coffee. "Domestic bliss" is a funny phrase to use in a room where between three and five children (it was hard to count with them in motion) are making colossal amounts of noise, but nevertheless, it fit.

I poured myself a cup of coffee and joined my brother and sister-in-law. "Sorry I slept so long. I was more wiped out than I thought."

"Mom and Dad stopped by for dinner last night," Jimmy said, and I winced. He laughed. "It's all right, they'll be along to see you soon enough. Mom did peek in on you when you were sleeping, though, just like she did when you were a little boy."

I watched the kids demolish their breakfasts. "I should have helped cook. I feel bad."

"Nah," Jimmy said. "You'd just get underfoot. You could whip up some pork brains and eggs if you want. Emily won't make 'em."

I mimed gagging. Our grandmother had loved brains and eggs for breakfast. I'm hardly squeamish—I've cooked my share of kidneys and sweetbreads and made feasts of offal, and I've been known to defend chitlins and pickled pig's feet to certain chefs of my acquaintance, but just the thought of those grayish brains mixed with yellow scrambled eggs has been enough to turn my stomach since childhood.

"You can help fry up the chicken for lunch, I reckon," Jimmy went on. "None of that 'fried chicken three ways' business you did on the show, please, if you can restrain yourself."

"Buttermilk fried chicken, Korean crispy chicken, and Middle Eastern style," I said, grinning. "That dish won me the car I've got parked out in front of your house, you know."

"I don't believe Aunt Helen has ever even *heard* of turmeric," Emily said. "Or coriander either."

"She'd call it terrorist chicken if you put it on her plate," Jimmy said. "She's real proud of you anyway, though. I imagine she'll be along in a couple hours. She always comes early. Lots to do before then. Give me a hand setting up, little bro?"

I finished my coffee and got to work. We set up long folding tables underneath the spreading branches of the ancient oak trees in back of the house, where the shade would protect us from the worst of the day's heat. We shook out plastic tablecloths and set up folding chairs, giving me flashbacks to catering jobs I'd taken during cooking school. As we worked, I glanced at Jimmy and said, "You know of a bar down by the river? Right close to the water, just on the other side of the bridge?"

"Doesn't ring a bell," he said. "There used to be a pool hall down there, but I believe it burned down four, five years ago. Why?"

"Oh, I thought I saw a place when I was out driving last night, that's all. So much has changed around here, I'm just trying to get my head around the way things are now."

"Ha. Sure. I know the real reason. The reunion hasn't even started yet, and you *already* need a drink. Ain't that right?"

"You got me there," I said.

"We'll crack a couple beers after noon," he said, and winked. "Any earlier and Emily gives me this *look*. You aren't married, so you can't understand, but ninety-nine percent of making it work is avoiding doing things that get you *that look*." He suddenly took an intense interest in the mechanism of the folding chair in his hand. "Mom told me about your, ah, friend, that y'all broke up, and I just wanted to say, I'm real sorry to hear that."

I don't think I've ever been more touched by anything in my life. I knew better than to spoil the moment by showing him how much it meant to me, so I just waved it away and said, "Plenty of fish in the sea."

"Just don't let Aunt Helen hear you're single. She knows every single girl in the nearest five counties, and she'll start planning your wedding before you've finished saying hello to 'em."

"If you need me later," I said, "I'll just be hiding under this table here."

But I didn't hide. My parents got there around noon, and Mom and I did the big hugs, the it's-been-too-longs. Dad shook my hand solemnly. He's always been a formal guy, and after a two-minute conversation we'd pretty much caught up as well as we were going to. More people started trickling in soon after that, and the trickle became a flood by around three p.m. By four, there were at least a hundred members of the Brydon family tree and associated branches milling inside and outside the big house. Several packs of feral children roamed wild among the fields, countless half-familiar faces grinned at me, and I got my cheeks kissed far more often than a man of twenty-three years ever should.

Oh, a few of the second cousins pointedly refused to talk to me—being openly queer *and* Californian was too much for them—but most of the relatives were willing to ignore my moral failings, and a few made a great show of being especially liberal-minded and asking after my *boy*friend, which was a twist of the knife I could have done without, even though they meant well.

Aunt Helen was one of those, much to my surprise. (She's not really my aunt, technically—she's something like my grandmother's second cousin—but where I come from every female relative over a certain age is an aunt, and yes, you pronounce it "ant," like the bugs that ruin picnics.)

When the memory-lane walking and inevitable sympathies over my failure to win on *Stand the Heat* got to be too much, I holed up in the kitchen for a while, helping Emily and a rotating cast of Brydon women handle the cooking. They were willing enough to accommodate my presence, giving me trivial tasks, though traditionally men do not pass the kitchen's threshold during our family's high holy days. I was able to lose myself, as always, in the rhythms of preparing food. Eventually, though, the pies were being taken outside, and the puddings, and the cakes, and the lemon squares, and the divinity fudge, and there were no more excuses to hide away.

I strolled outside with a can of beer in my hand, listening to the sound of a hundred separate conversations, the clang of horseshoes hitting a metal post, and the trash talk of some of the teenage boys playing basketball against a hoop set up beside the barn (which hadn't held livestock in a generation, but was full of all manner of broken mechanical junk).

I ambled out under the tall trees, feeling nearly at peace. I was among my people. They ate what I liked to eat. They had the proper degree of reverence for college basketball. Their accents were the ones I heard spoken in my dreams; the one I still took on myself, after a few drinks. Sure, I wasn't really one of them anymore, but they were a part of me—maybe even a bigger part than I liked to admit.

Clearly, I decided, seeing these doppelgangers—these other

versions of myself—was indicative of some kind of identity crisis. I'd gone through a lot of upheavals and changes recently, and I hadn't entirely figured out what it all meant. My brain was trying to make sense of all the changes I'd gone through, that was all. Coming home, remembering who I *used* to be, was just a little too much for my brain to bear, too many aspects of myself coming into conflict, so I'd gotten a little sleep-deprived and let my imagination get away from me.

Maybe I was done with California. I wasn't necessarily ready to come back *here*—I couldn't see myself taking over Willard's and becoming a pitmaster, vision of myself doing exactly that notwithstanding—but it did occur to me that I'd spent five years desperately running away from my hometown. Trying to avoid the life I'd seen so many of my old friends fall into: knocking up a seventeen-year-old girlfriend, dropping out of high school, marrying too young, getting a job at the turkey plant—

I walked past a pecan tree, the air shimmered, and there I was: another me, sitting on a folding chair beside a woman with hair the color of fresh-mown hay, both of them cooing over a baby in my—in *his*—lap. I knew the girl, too. Kelly White. My senior prom date, still pretty enough to be the obvious date for a football star.

We'd made out, and more, in the back of the car I borrowed from Jimmy after the dance, and we'd dated on and off that last summer, but then I'd gone off to college on a football scholarship for a semester, before dropping out to go to culinary school, and we'd never even talked since—

This other me, this *father* me, wearing a polo shirt and steel-rimmed glasses (unlike my own contact lenses), looked up. He frowned. "You're here?" he said, handing the baby to his wife.

She didn't appear to notice my existence at all. "We never thought we'd see *you* again."

I closed my eyes. Without opening them, I said, "I do not understand what's happening."

"Huh." His voice was closer—he must have walked toward me. I still didn't open my eyes to look. "I guess it has been, what . . . over a dozen years, since you saw the rest of us?"

I had a flash of memory—vague and secondhand, like the memory of someone else's account of a dream. Walking into a field, the air filled with heat shimmers, and other kids, ten-year-olds, standing in clumps and chatting, and apart from different clothes and haircuts they all looked exactly the same—

"Go to the bar," the other me said kindly.

"What bar?" I whispered.

"Don't do that. You pulled right up into the parking lot last night. We all saw you. Just go."

I turned, eyes closed, and walked ten or fifteen steps before I opened my eyes and looked back. No me. No Kelly. No baby.

I didn't say anything to anyone, just went to my car, navigated around the dozens of other vehicles parked on every available scrap of the property, and set off toward the river.

The air shimmered as I crossed the bridge, and there was TJ's Place. The parking lot wasn't as full as it had been last night, just a handful of cars. I parked on the gravel, far away from the front door, and approached the bar slowly, like I was stalking prey.

I pushed inside, and it was pure honky-tonk: board floor, beer signs on the walls, dust in the corners, a couple of pool tables, a bunch of mismatched chairs, and a scuffed-up bar along the back wall.

"They say you can't go home again," a voice slurred, and I looked to my right, where a version of me—except maybe thirty pounds lighter, skeleton-thin—sat gazing into a mug of beer next to an untouched basket of onion rings, shiny with grease. "But here you are."

Two other Terrys were playing pool. One of them—he had an outlandish mustache—tipped the rim of his trucker hat with one finger in greeting. The other, leaner and dressed in a wife-beater, was focused on lining up a shot and didn't pay me any mind at all.

I went toward the bar and slid onto a stool. The me behind the counter wore a black T-shirt, tight, that showed off his biceps. I had the brief and horrible thought, *He's pretty cute*, and shook it off. I hope I'm not *that* narcissistic.

"Just tell me," I said, when he sauntered over toward me. "Is this hell? Or purgatory, or something?"

"Nah. That'd be kind of a disappointment, wouldn't it?" He shook his head. "You went far away. Clear to California. A couple of us went to Australia, New Zealand. One to Japan, teaching English as a second language, ended up staying over there. You're the only one to go so far away and then come *back*." The bartender drew a beer and slid it in front of me.

"The only one," I repeated.

"Sure," the bartender said. "You don't remember? You were at the big gathering when we were ten years old, I'm sure of that. You missed the one when we were fifteen—a few of us missed that one, there was an away game that day, a lot of us played ball. And of course, by the time of the eighteen-year reunion, you were gone."

"I used to pretend," I said slowly. "That I had . . . a brother, an identical twin, I mean, except . . . wait, that's not right—"

The bartender drew himself a beer too, and took a sip. "Aunt Helen used to say I was the only little boy who ever had *himself* for an imaginary friend."

I remembered then. Being a little kid, pretending, and . . . "Playing with myself—shit, that sounds wrong—"

"We make that joke all the time," the bartender said. "We've always been able to see each other, hear each other, and every once in a while, we get together. Some of us who went to college have theories about why, about how it works. Science and all that. The ones who got religion have theories, too, and their ideas are totally different." He shrugged. "I don't know if we're ghosts or projections from alternate dimensions. Doesn't much matter to me. What we are is family. Most of us—at least, a lot of us—stayed close to home, and so we run into each other a lot. We started having reunions every year when we turned eighteen, most of us living away from home, with a little more autonomy. We started comparing notes, using each other to test things out. What would happen if I dated *that* girl, or bought *that* truck. Eventually I thought, hell, I'll open this bar, a place we can all get together, anytime. Guaranteed clientele. Best decision I ever made."

"I've been wanting to open my own place for years," I said. "How'd you afford it?"

He grinned. "I have investors. The fellas all clear out on weekends, when I open to the public. Officially, the bar is closed for private functions every other day of the week. My friends think I named the bar like I did because I've got a big ego—TJ's Place. I never tell them, it's just a description. It's a place for TJ. All of us."

"How many of us are there?" I asked.

He leaned on the bar and looked thoughtfully across the room. "About two dozen regulars." He pointed to a row of photographs behind the bar, without turning to look. "Those are some who've died. Two in Iraq, one in Afghanistan. Oh, that one on the end, he's not dead, he went into pro football. Rode the bench in Baltimore for a few seasons, only played in about three games when injuries took out the starters, but, hell, it's something. Most of us who tried that path just blew out our knees in college. Those guys ran into each other sometimes, in college—a bunch of them got the same scholarships. We have to split them up when we all play flag football at our get-togethers, so they don't form one team and crush the rest of us. Not many of us took your path, as far as I know. That's probably why you never ran into any of the rest of us out in California."

"I...I don't understand what this *means*..."

The bartender nodded. "Sure. None of us do. Doesn't have to mean a lot, I guess. Except, you're never alone. What's that old saying? Home's the place where they can't turn you away?"

"Home is the place where, when you have to go there, they have to take you in," the drunk by the door slurred. I turned to look at him. He grinned, showing the gaps of lost teeth. "Robert Frost, 'The Death of the Hired Man,' 1915."

"We might have a picture of that one up on the wall soon, too," the bartender said, nodding toward the drunk. "If he goes on the way he's been. He was a schoolteacher for a year, but being new he got laid off after the budget cuts, and nowadays...he's a cook, too. But he cooks meth, and he snorts up a lot of his own profits. We've tried to help him out, but..." He sighed. "Some of us don't want help."

I swiveled back on my stool, unwilling to see a vision of

myself fallen so much farther than I'd ever feared possible. "But...does all this mean I'm not *real*, or that I'm the figment of somebody's imagination, or..."

"I think *I'm* the real original TJ, for what it's worth," the bartender said. "Of course, so do most of the rest of us. I think I'm definitely one of the most *plausible* ones. But you? Moving to California, telling everybody you like to sleep with men—I mean, most of us keep that to ourselves—getting on TV? Unfucking-likely." He took another sip of beer. "Still, here you are."

"Are...any of us...happy?" Something like this, a miracle—no matter how prosaic the bartender found it—had to have *some* meaning, didn't it? Had to provide some kind of revelation?

"Happy?" he said. "Sure. Off and on, anyway. And some of us are miserable. About like anybody, I guess. All our lives...it seems amazing, I know, to think of them all lined up next to each other, all those possible worlds, rubbing up together. But every one of our lives is just a *life*, man."

I drank my beer. It was one of my favorite kinds, a pale ale. I wasn't surprised.

The bartender tilted his head. "So, TJ—or, wait, you're one of the ones who likes Terry, right? How long are you in town for?"

I blinked. "I don't know. I told Jimmy I was just going to stay a couple of days, but...I don't know what I'd go back to, really. I was hoping to start my own restaurant, but I didn't win the big prize money, and the whole idea of trying to make my own way, it's just *exhausting*."

He chuckled. "Oh, we could probably work something out. Those investors I mentioned? They're other versions of *me*. Some of us do all right, and we're always willing to chip in to help each other out. The logistics get tricky—we have to convert our cash to gold or something, can't risk bills from one world having the same serial numbers as bills in another, they'd think you were counterfeiting. But we've done it before."

I opened my mouth, then closed it. Silent partners? With *myself*?

"That's...incredibly generous. But I'm not even sure opening a restuarant is what I want to do. It's what I'm *supposed* to want..." I shook my head, and was surprised by tears welling up in my eyes. I stared hard at the scarred wood of the bar before me. "I don't even know who the hell I am anymore, you know?"

"Oh, yeah. I definitely know. But we're here for you, brother. We missed you, too. And anything we can do to help..."

"I don't know what you could do. If I can't figure out my shit on my own, I'm not sure how having even *more* of me around would help. If I had a little time, to get my head together, to figure out what I want to do, who I want to *be*..."

The bartender grinned. "Tell you what. Sometimes, in extreme cases, we've been known to switch places. Strictly temporary—unless everybody agrees they want to make it permanent. You can step out of your own path, and walk on another's for a while. Get a taste of another TJ's life, or take a vacation from life entirely. Say one of us needs a break, and another one needs a change...we help each other out. Like I said, you're an outlier, you've got a pretty rare path. I'm sure we could find a TJ who'd want to take your life for a spin for a while. Give you some breathing room in the meantime. And lots of us know how to cook."

I lifted my head. "Really? Would I have to, like, take someone else's place, or..."

A shake of the head. "Not necessarily. Unless you want to.

One of us could just say he's going camping, or taking a solo hike up the Appalachian Trail, or going on a fishing trip, and disappear into your life for a couple of weeks. Even if they act a little funny around your friends, that's all right—you're in a weird place right now, right?"

I frowned, thinking of horror stories, doubles and body snatchers, and the bartender must have seen something on my face, because he snorted.

"You think someone might steal your life? Really? Is it all *that* great?"

"No," I admitted. "I fucked it up pretty good."

"There you go. We wouldn't put up with that kind of identity theft bullshit, anyway. We've had to cast some of us out before, for crimes against the self, though we hate to do it. We don't put up with nonsense."

"So you'd do that, one of you—one of *me*—just out of kindness?"

He nodded. "We're family. What else is family for? And it doesn't get much closer than this. Every one of us who makes bad decisions...hell, we *all* know it could have happened to any of us. There but for the grace of good luck. If you decide to step off your path, and want to hide away, you can stay here for a while. There's a room in back with a cot, you can use the kitchen, there's even a shower I got some of the guys who went into contracting to install."

I looked around at the tables and chairs, the jukebox in the corner, vintage tin signs on the walls. Running a restaurant sounded pretty daunting. But I could work in one. I didn't know much, but I sure knew my way around a kitchen. Maybe if I didn't have to do anything for a while but pay attention to what I had in front of me on the grill or the chopping block, things would sort themselves out in my head. And if I got stuck, there were people around here I could ask for advice. People who knew me at least as well as I knew myself.

I took another sip of beer. "Have you, ah…ever thought about selling food here? I mean, something besides onion rings and greaseburgers? Because, maybe…"

The bartender snorted again. "Ha. Well. I guess you know what kind of food my regulars like, don't you?"

He reached out to shake my hand, and I was home at last.

"The Jolly Corner" by Henry James is—to simplify—the story of a man who comes home after a long time away and meets the ghost of the person he *might* have become, if he'd never moved away. It's a haunting and thought-provoking story, and has always appealed to my obsession with those turning-point moments in life, when you could have become someone other than the person you are: chance meetings that transformed your romantic or working life, opportunities seized or allowed to slip away, literal and figurative roads taken, or not. It seemed to me that, if it were possible to meet the ghosts of our possible lives, there wouldn't be just one ghost—there would be dozens, scores, maybe hundreds, sharing some essential qualities, but radically different in other respects.

And who's to say this life, the one I'm living right now, isn't really just the ghost of some other, vastly different existence?

Oh, and while I'm no chef, I am a North Carolina boy who lives in the East Bay nowadays. Willard's B-B-Q is inspired by the legendary Wilber's Barbecue in Goldsboro, North Carolina, home of the One True Barbecue. Stop by if you're ever in town.

Millcara

Holly Black

Wake up. Wake up. You have to wake up.

I want to say that I never meant for it to happen, but I *never ever* mean for it to happen and it always *does* happen and I keep on doing it, so what does that say about me? Mother told me that keeping going when other folks don't is the difference between them that succeed in this world and them that lie down in a ditch to die, but I don't know if I can keep going if you're not with me.

Remember when we dreamed about each other? When you were only a little girl, you dreamed that I came into your room and got into bed with you and pressed my mouth against your neck. And I dreamed it too—the exact same thing, waking up in your room, not sure how I got there and climbing into bed with you. I remember how warm and lovely it was right up until you started screaming. That has to mean something. That has to mean that our souls were destined for one another, that fate wants us to be something more to each other than—

WAKE UP.

Wakeupwakeupwakeupwakeup.

Even if you wake up and hate me.

And yes, I admit it, Mother has a scam. Your father suspected as much in the end and your uncle too. They were right—right about everything, except how much we really were friends, best friends just like we swore, just like we smeared in blood on one another's dirty palms, just like we whispered against one another's skin. But it's true that Mother does get into car accidents in front of rich families with daughters about my age. Usually fathers and daughters on their own. The accidents aren't the easiest to plan—she has to find a park where she knows the family goes for walks in early summer evenings. (We grow overheated and lethargic when the sun is high in the sky, so Mother knows our best performances will be at night.) Then she has to arrange to have the car break down suddenly—with an engine fire if possible, conjured with sleight of hand and a little spilled gasoline.

I should add that these are never her cars. She borrows them or steals them and, as you might guess, abandons them once I am securely in the hands of my new family.

But things will be different now. It will be just the two of us and we'll make up new games. We'll be sisters, just like any two girls with the same blood in their veins. We'll be sisters and more than sisters. We'll run through museums, mocking and applauding, until the security guards chase us. We'll pretend to be statues on the street and scare people by moving. We'll be bold and brave and do things no one has thought of before and we'll do them always together.

I'll make a deal with you, how about that? I'll tell you the rest of it. Everything, Laura. The ugly parts too. And in return you'll get up, won't you, sleepyhead? I will tempt you with coffee and bagels and my own mouth on yours, breathing you back to life.

So here it is, all the truth:

The plan is supposed to play out exactly like it did, except for the ending. Immediately after the car accident, Mother always springs out in great distress, pointing to the father of the family, just as she did to your father: "Help me, sir, please, my child is still in the car! I don't know what to do! No, no ambulance. Just help me get her some air."

She says that once people are singled out of a crowd, they almost always do what they're asked. Isn't that odd? It's like magic, like how people thought that if a witch knew your name, she could make you do whatever she wanted.

If only that were true, I'd *make* you wake up.

My part in the plan is to go very limp when I'm picked up, and then seem to awaken at the ministrations of father and daughter. I am to blink up into their eyes and charm them with my pliant and sweet nature. I am so very grateful! Mother is so very beautiful! She weeps a single crystal tear! Then Mother has to deal with something about the car and *oh*—your apartment or house or villa or chalet is so close by that you want to take her dear daughter there? Well, how kind and unexpected!

They never see Mother again. She comes back for me eventually, but by then I'm creeping away like a thief in the night.

It usually goes just as it did with your family:

- First, I explain that I don't know her cell phone number. It's a new cell phone, her last one was stolen and she changed the number. I cry prettily over how stupid I am. (You might think me vain to say this, but I practice; real crying is so often ugly.)
- I am very charming. Again, please don't think me vain; I have had a long time to become charming. I can speak to your father in French and I have perfect man-

ners. I always wash the dishes after dinner. I remain poised on the brink of adolescence; I will never reach thirteen. On the first night, I faint dramatically, so as to show I was dealing bravely with my pain. The fainting embarrasses me very much. I forget myself and speak more French as I come around, half in a delirium. Everyone likes a little blonde girl with wide eyes begging their pardon *en français*.

•   When your family begins to press about my family, I drop hints of an overbearing and very rich European father and a nasty divorce.

•   Just as everyone is sure Mother has abandoned me entirely, she calls. She's in the hospital and she's so very sorry to inconvenience the family. She should be out soon, but she's not supposed to use her phone and if it wouldn't be too much trouble, could I stay there tonight and maybe tomorrow? Your father shouldn't agree, but he does. When he puts down the phone, he's embarrassed he's agreed, but he has.

•   Then, finally, days later, my mysterious European father calls. Mother is irresponsible and dangerous, he says, and his daughter has made such a fast friend in yours that it would be a shame to part them. He offers a decent chunk of money (five thousand dollars!) to let me stay for the rest of the summer. Otherwise, he will send me a plane ticket and I can fly home by myself—I'm certainly old enough and so what if flying frightens me. (Father's role has been acted out by a variety of players and his exact country of origin changes with the accent that each person can fake the best.)

It doesn't work every time, but you'd be surprised how often it does. Fathers raising little girls on their own are away a lot and they don't like their daughters to be all by themselves in their vast apartments. They trust their staff, but not like they trust the aristocratic and slightly naïve daughter of a rich European. And it's summer after all, hot sticky summer, when all the rules are different.

Remember how it was when I came home with you? I rode up in your building's chrome elevator, watching your face reflected in the metal. You were so incredibly beautiful that I think I lost my heart to you in that moment. Your windblown tangle of honey-dark hair and eyes the color of tree sap, liquid and luminous, made me feel faint wanting only to be closer to you, to press my clammy hand in yours. You saw me looking and smiled a tiny smile. It felt like passing notes right under the nose of the teacher.

When we got to your apartment, with big windows looking down on the park and air-conditioning so cold that the hairs rose on your arms, you took me right to your room. I sat on your bed, pretending to still be weak from the accident, leaning my head against the comforter and inhaling the smell of you, of strawberry shampoo and Hello Kitty perfume. You docked your iPod and played a song I had never heard before, one with a girl wailing about the wretchedness of her love. I asked about the books on your shelves, ones I'd never seen before, about black holes, astrophysics, and one by Carl Sagan called *The Demon-Haunted World: Science as a Candle in the Dark* that made me shudder with the dread of discovery.

"I want to see space someday," you said. "It's the last great mystery, other than what's at the bottom of the ocean. Either way, I'm going to wear a suit like Iron Man's and see things no one has ever seen before."

See, I remember it word for word. I remember everything.

"I think there are mysteries everywhere," I told you. "If you're looking for them."

You snorted, but you didn't look displeased. "Like what?"

"I'll show you," I promised. "Tomorrow."

"It better not be one of those mysteries like 'why do people sneeze when they're exposed to a burst of sunlight?'"

"Is that true?" I asked, fascinated, my bragging forgotten.

Your father ordered in Thai food and we ate it at the raw-edged Nakashima dining table next to the wall of windows. I never have much appetite, so I pushed my pad thai around and listened to you and your father talk. He was quiet, but unexpectedly funny in the way only quiet people can be and too polite to ask me all the questions I could see swimming in his eyes. But you asked me about what pets I had, whether there were horses at my private school, what Broadway shows Mother and I had seen, what books I loved, what television shows I watched and whether there were different shows in Europe that were better than American television. I talked and talked and talked. When I looked out at the city, sparkling in the early evening, my heart swelled with giddy joy.

Then I cleared the table and washed the dishes, over your protests, slumping to the floor just as I was about to put down the drying cloth. It was a really good performance. You let me lie down in your bed and rested next to me, taking my temperature by pressing your wrist to my brow, like some grown-up must have once done for you. Then you read to me, softly, from a book of fairy tales that you said were silly, but good for the sick. I didn't tell you that I didn't think they were silly at all. Later that night, my mother called and charmed your father with her distress.

The next day, I said I had to go out to get a few things, but really I went to a storage unit in Midtown and brought back my own clothes in Bergdorf shopping bags.

And from then, everything was perfect. Lying in front of the big flat-screen, watching cartoons in the mornings; giggling over adding powdered cocoa to the milk in our cereal; passing gum back and forth by blowing huge bubbles and pressing them together until they stuck and one of us took the whole thing, tasting each other's spit in our mouths. Walking through the park with iced coffees, pressing the cups against one another's bare skin to surprise one of us into a shriek; trying on counterfeit McQueen scarves and short plastic skirts on Canal Street; and meeting up with your friends to see movies in deliciously cold theaters where we shared slushies that stained our mouths ruby red.

And then your cousin Bertha got sick and died within a week of her first symptom. I bet you're thinking about that, thinking about how I'd go down to her apartment on the eleventh floor on Wednesdays to watch that show about aliens that you thought was stupid. I bet you're thinking about how it was a Thursday morning when she collapsed.

I know what you're thinking, but let me explain.

Have you ever felt that when you were around a particular someone you were smarter and funnier and more beautiful? That all your charm and her charm ricocheted back and forth until it amplified itself to almost impossible heights? That's what it's like. Both of you are radiant, glowing with it. Her cheeks are rosy and her eyes are bright as flames. No one could resist her and I can't either. The thought of being without her is painful, impossible.

At the sound of her voice, you come alive. You feel it like the cresting of some dark wave out at sea. Her heart leaps and yours leaps with it. Then she's gone.

They die so fast sometimes. An afternoon of giggling. A weekend of sleepovers and secrets. A night of whispered confessions.

But could you really give up feeling that way? Could you give up the giddy joy of being so in tune with another that you can finish one another's thoughts? Could you give up being understood and being surprised and being made into a wholly finer version of yourself?

And you don't understand that when they're fading, when they're sick, I don't feel smug or pleased, I feel panicked. I feel like I am being left behind by the one person in the world I would most hate to lose.

And in that moment, they see me for what I am and despise me.

After Bertha died, things were different. Your aunt spent hours crying to your father, pacing the room, raving about how she had brought this on herself. How your uncle's work was dangerous and that it had always been only a matter of time before they struck at him. He was flying in from Chicago for the funeral, although your aunt told him that his daughter's memory would be best served if he stayed away.

I asked you what she meant once, but you said you didn't know.

I think you lied about that, but I don't blame you. You probably didn't want to scare me. You probably thought that your aunt was being silly and that I was superstitious enough to believe it.

I should have seen the danger, but I was too busy being tangled up in your world, listening to your sorrows and making your joys my own.

Remember that museum exhibit about vampires? It was at the very beginning of my stay, when we were still tentative with one another. How it made us laugh! They had the original cape that Bela Lugosi wore on the set of *Dracula* and the flowing gray nightgown dresses of his brides. There was a picture of his house in the Hollywood Hills with bright pink bougainvillea spilling down one side and his chihuahuas, which he called the Children of the Night. Then there was the picture of the dashing Lord Byron and the tale of how, after he broke his friend Polidori's heart, Polidori modeled the villainous Lord Ruthven in his book, *The Vampyre*, after the poet.

"Do you think they did it?" you asked.

"*Did it?* You mean Lord Byron and Polidori?" I asked. Lord Byron was handsome enough, but whatever magnetism had caused lover after lover to drown in his eyes was missing in the stillness of the portrait. His lip could not rise ever so slightly, tempting you to believe that you could cause him to truly smile if only you worked hard enough at it. "Maybe. Or maybe Polidori just pined away, loving Byron from afar."

"Have *you* ever been in love?" you asked me. Do you remember that?

"Yes," I told you. And I was. Of course I was. I still am.

"Did you tell the person?" You were watching me, as though my answer mattered.

"I'm shy," I said.

"You should leave a note," you advised me. "Can you imagine if Polidori left a note for Byron: I LIIIIIIIKE YOU. IF YOU

LIKE ME, CHECK THE BOX AND PASS NOTE TO SHELLEY."

I felt light-headed. You dragged me on.

Then we saw a series of photos with cards explaining how certain chemicals found in certain soils preserve a corpse and can even give it the appearance of life, how hair and nails grew after death, and how, at one time, people who suffered from something called catalepsy were accidentally buried alive. They'd seem dead, but they could still see and hear everything. Sometimes they'd start moving in their coffins, trying to scrabble their way out before the tons of dirt above crashed down and suffocated them. It was awful, awful, awful. We walked past the drawings illustrating the bloody and broken nails of those bodies. Then more drawings, these of how some dead were buried upside down, so the newly animated corpse would dig itself deeper into the earth instead of climbing out of its grave.

Thinking about a vampire tunneling deeper and deeper, I felt as though I could no longer breathe. It was too easy to think of dirt surrounding me on all sides, pressing down on my chest, cold and heavy. I sank to the floor of the exhibit and you had to sit there beside me while I explained in my own tangled way.

Then you took me to the bathroom and made me sit on the sink and press damp paper towels against my neck until I felt better.

You promised me that when I died, you would make sure my parents cremated me. You would insist that I should have what I wanted, you said fiercely, as passionate as I have ever heard you. I would never wake up alone and afraid, choking on grave dirt—not if you had anything to do with it.

I didn't have the heart to tell you that it was not fear that had made me weak and mewling, but memory.

On the way out, we stopped at the gift shop. You pointed and laughed at the fake widow's peaks, the contact lenses that turned eyes red, and the glitter body gel. We picked out twin amulets with tiny crystals forming the shape of eyes. They were supposed to protect us from evil. I loved to see it sparkling at the hollow of your throat. I wanted to believe in it, to believe it could really protect you from me, but three days after Bertha died and two days before her funeral, you fell ill.

"There is a sharp pain here," you told the doctor, touching just above the small swell of your breast. "I had a dream where a great catlike creature crouched over me, so I must be feverish. I feel so cold that my teeth are chattering. But I'm not nearly as sick as Millcara."

I lay beside you on the bed, sick with fear, sick with dread and with remorse, playing sick as I always did and hating myself for it. I blinked up at the doctor. "I'll be fine. Just please help Laura."

The doctor laughed at our devotion to one another. I decided that I hated him.

I heard him whispering to your father that it might be psychoemotional distress of some sort, but since the two of them had the same symptoms he was going to order an EKG, just to be sure there was no infection of the lining of the heart. And later, I heard your father on the phone with Mother, asking her about insurance cards and telling her that he was so sorry not to have taken better care of me.

And we missed the funeral, of course, lying in your bed, watching *Wizards of Waverly Place* on television. You had come to the part of your illness where you were constantly thirsty. You drank gallons of orange juice, big bottles of Pellegrino, one after the other, mugs of tea, and glasses and glasses of water right from the unfiltered tap. You said you could taste the metal of the pipes in it and the minerals and the darting of the little killifishes in the river it came from.

"Wouldn't that be amazing if it was true, Millcara?" you wanted to know. "If I could really taste the past? If I could taste the dust on the moon and know everything there was to know about it—or if I could really take a bite from the sun and lick the rings of Saturn? Did you know that black holes sing? They do. So if it's possible to hear the universe then maybe it's possible to taste it too." Your eyes shone with fever.

That was when I made my decision. There would never be anyone like you again. You must not die.

I waited until after midnight, when you were asleep, and snuck out, a jacket over my pajamas and flip-flops on my feet. I loitered around an apartment lobby across town, until a girl came down to get her mail. I asked her if she was bored. She said she was. I told her I knew a game. She followed me to the stairway, where I eventually left her.

When I got back to your apartment, I tried to creep in, but your father was awake, sitting at the kitchen table with your uncle. His leather duffel was on the floor and they had a bottle of some amber liquor on the table along with empty glasses in front of them.

"Millcara, where were you?" your father asked, sounding cold and mean and not at all normal.

Your uncle turned around. And I saw in his suddenly narrowed eyes that he knew me—knew what I was as no one but my victims has ever done. I backed up involuntarily. He half-stood before he remembered himself and sank back into his chair.

But a moment after it happened, I thought I must have imagined it. It must be guilt, I told myself, my own body slow with satiation, guilty at being caught creeping home from a prowl.

"I'm sorry," I said. "I'm not sure what happened. I woke in the bodega on the corner, but I couldn't remember why I'd gone there. I think I was sleepwalking. I had the milk case open and was just staring at the bottles."

Your father stood up and led me back to your room. "Please, you and Laura have to rest. I know that Bertha's death rattled you both. The doctor thinks that your both getting ill like you did might be a reaction to stress—but I can't have you going out in the middle of the night, do you understand? Your parents aren't here and I have to trust you to be responsible."

"I hate funerals," I said with utter sincerity. "I hate them."

He put both his hands on my shoulders and regarded me with a kind of fond exasperation. "Go to bed and we'll see how you're feeling in the morning." He smelled like booze and his eyes were red-rimmed, swollen with crying.

I crept into your room, your uncle's eyes on me. Once I was inside, I turned the lock and slid under your covers, reaching for your hand and twining your fingers in mine. Your breath was hot on my cheek and I was so happy for the steady rise and fall of your chest. I settled against you, closing my eyes and letting your languid warmth enter my limbs.

A few moments later, you whispered against my neck, "Most of the universe is made of dark matter, but no one can see it. Can you see it?"

I shook my head. I wasn't sure what you meant, but it might just have been more fever talk.

"Will it hurt?" you asked, your mouth moving against my skin, making me shiver.

"Will *what* hurt?" My heart was pounding now, sleep very far away.

"Dying," you said.

I wanted to tell you it wouldn't hurt at all, your heartbeats slowing, counting down to the thudding moment of final forever stopping, the gulp of one last breath. I wanted to tell you that, but I didn't want to lie. And that was all over anyway, I'd promised myself. I was never going to—not ever again.

The next morning, you were much better. You put on clothes and ate breakfast with your father. I slept late, huddled under the covers, the scent of you in my nose. My stomach hurt from feeding too much and too quickly the night before in the stairwell.

Then you came in, jumping on the bed. "Look," you said. "Wake up and look at this."

See, when *you* told *me* to wake up, I did. I woke up right away for you and you better wake up for me. Right now, please. Please-pleaseplease. Morning is coming, the sun is racing toward us, and your uncle will wake with it.

But then what you wanted was for me to look at a black-and-white photograph your uncle had given you. In it, a woman was sitting on a chair and a girl leaned in from the arm. They were at a New Year's Eve party in 1924—the year was marked on a centerpiece in glittering numbers. Confetti-covered tables and a band played blurrily on the stage behind them. The woman was wearing a shimmering beaded dress, her short black hair in finger waves and a necklace of eighteenth-century ivory theater tickets around her throat. The little girl had on a frothy lace dress that made her look younger than she was and a long strand of pearls. They both held champagne coupes in their hands. The little girl was me, of course, and the woman was Mother.

"She looks just like you," you said.

Hazy with sleep, I nearly told you it was a picture from a costume party, before I realized how ridiculous that would sound. Maybe your uncle hoped that I would be stupid enough to do something suspicious. I'm sure he tried to warn you about me, at least insofar as he thought he could without sounding crazy. No one as reasonable as your father would believe the little girl snuggled up against his daughter was a fiend. And you, Laura, you loved me, didn't you? You love me still. You have to—I won't be able to do what Mother says and keep going on if you don't.

"Wow," I said. "She really does. But like a younger me—and that dress is ridiculous."

"I wish there were still parties like that," you said.

At the party, dizzy with too much champagne, I'd met a boy a year younger than I was. We'd sat under one of the tables, like it was a play fort. He stabbed his fork into the swollen ankles of a society dame who stopped near it and told me all about his new puppy. Boys are loud and wild and gross lots of the time, but that night, I liked him. I think he died three days later.

I knew then that your uncle knew even more about me and Mother than I'd guessed when I'd seen the way he looked at me. He did not just suspect my nature—he knew of my history and of Mother's. He had come here hunting me. He knew what I had done to his daughter.

I had never been hunted before, although Mother had spoken in dark whispers of suspicious men, and a need for care.

"I'm going to take a shower," I told you, and escaped into the attached bathroom with a sundress clutched in my hand.

There, under the cold spray, as I watched my strange form, I knew I had to leave you. At the thought, I felt such a fierce possessiveness overtake me that I wanted nothing more than to run back to your bedroom, throw my arms around you, and draw you down to me. Without you, the hours of my days would pass in an agony of nervous terror that you would replace me in your heart. You would share your confidences with another, finding some new beloved friend to tell your stories about quasars and the Marianas Trench being the very deepest part of the ocean. I could not imagine there was a girl in the world who would not hang on your every word, who would not give anything to lie beside you as you slept, her breath mingling with yours.

In that state, I found my phone, unused and barely charged. I called Mother and in a voice tight with panic, told her about your uncle.

"He gave Laura a picture of us—an old picture—but he hasn't said anything to her. I heard his ex-wife say that it was his fault that Bertha was dead. I think she believes her daughter was killed in revenge for his hunting of—of things such as we are. I don't know what he means to do, but I just want him gone."

"Laura? Bertha?" Mother asked. "There are too many names. Slow down, I can't follow the story."

"Laura's the girl you left me with," I said, which seemed such a poor explanation for what you were to me. And I feared for you—Mother can be gluttonous and families can bring out an envious cruelty in her.

"I'm coming right now," she said. "Be ready to leave when I get there. Tell them your mother is taking you shopping and that she hopes she can take everyone to dinner later."

For a moment, the fiction seemed so normal that I could pretend it was true. We went to lunch and dinner with the mothers of your other friends all the time—they ordered salads and martinis and told us funny stories about when they were girls.

But what she meant was that we were going to run—to

another city, another string of fast friendships, and the emptiness of longing.

"Okay," I said in a whisper, wishing I hadn't called her. Your father liked me, after all. If he thought that your uncle meant to hurt me, surely he wouldn't allow it. No one believed in monsters anymore.

But summer would end, it would drag on into the chill of fall and I would lose you to school and to your sprint toward adolescence. I would stay forever as I am, my breasts two mosquito bites, my baby teeth never fully lost, my body forever hairless under my arms and between my legs. Only my hair and nails grow, longer and longer, forever and ever.

"Stay with the girl and her father," Mother said. "Don't let yourself be alone anywhere the uncle can corner you. Where are you now?"

"In Laura's room," I told her.

"Go into the kitchen and stay there."

I turned off my phone and tucked it into the pocket of my sundress. I could feel the other me, the night me, turning underneath my skin restlessly, but I shoved it down into the shadows and went out into the other room.

You sat at the kitchen island, a glass of water resting by your left hand. There were dark circles under your eyes and you appeared very pale, but you were smiling all the same. You spoke to me, and even though I was so scared that I do not know if I made any sense I managed to cross the room to sit beside you.

Because as I began to move, I saw that you weren't alone in the apartment.

Sitting at the dining table, your uncle had a steak knife in his hand and was using it to carve a long stick.

Eventually, I dared to ask, "Where's your dad?"

"He went out to get some bagels. I told him I was hungry and he was so happy that he wanted us to have a big brunch. Lox. Whitefish. Bialys."

"You hungry, Millcara?" your uncle asked, and his tone was taunting.

I looked a question at you, but you only shrugged in answer. The grieving are expected to act strange and everyone else is expected to ignore them.

I thought about Bertha, who'd been nothing like the man sitting on the other side of the room—a man with the glassy, bloodshot eyes of someone who hadn't slept in days. Bertha was nerdy and nice, full of life, obsessed with posting GIFs of her favorite TV shows to her blog and downloading British television. She'd been my friend and I'd drunk up all her strength until there was nothing left, and I hated that she was gone. All those things shouldn't have been possible to be true at the same time, but they were.

I looked at your uncle and I felt all the shame of my fiendish self, doomed to be ever separate from the world. And the bright sun coming through the windows made my head pound. I thought longingly of the shadows of your bedroom, of hiding under the covers of your bed like the child I would never truly be again.

In that instant, all I wanted was my mother.

The doorbell rang, and you jumped off your stool to answer it. Even though you were still sick you must have been tired of being cooped up inside, languishing in your bed. You wanted to move.

"Hello, Laura," Mother said, as though she remembered you. "I've come to take Millcara shopping. Is she ready?"

Even though I am not quite a child, I have always been child enough to need her, to see her as children see their mothers, as safe harbor, as a wonderful and indestructible sanctuary. I never could grow past that need.

Her face was what I saw, coming in with the light, on the first day of my new life. Hair black as the shadows that became my home, lips curved in a politely charming smile. She had saved me then and she would save me now.

Those are the things I thought in those moments.

Your uncle was on his feet, striding toward her. And in that split second, I saw the mistake she was making. She didn't remember you and she didn't remember your father, so when she saw a man in the apartment, she made an assumption.

"Thank you so much for taking care of my daughter." She took a step forward, past him, disregarding him on her way to me. She was always good at passing things off, my mother, acting as if everything she did was perfectly ordinary and that she expected the whole world to go along with her wishes.

Her eyes went to me, bright and clear.

I heard her gasp, a small soft sound, and I saw her eyes change. I had not seen his hand move.

Nobody knows better than I that death can come swift, and quiet, and ordinary as a knock on the door. But not for us, Mother had always said. Never for us.

She crumpled around the stick he had shoved into her back, sagging forward, and fell on her face. I heard you suppressing a cry, but I could not look at you. I could look only at her shining hair spread out on the rug, and at his cold face and the stake in his hand.

His work was not quite done.

But you raced past him, grabbing me and pushing me toward the door. And I ran, ran through the carpeted hallway, racing down the stairway, down twenty-eight floors to dash across the marble foyer, past the security man at the front desk and out onto the street. I ran for the park, running until I found a cool, dark place. I shook uncontrollably. I felt lost, so utterly and completely lost that I couldn't even really think anything but animal thoughts. My other, darker self took over for days.

When I came to myself, I thought of you.

And that is why I crept back into your room, all these weeks later. Seeing you was a balm to my heart: your eyes closed, your hair spread over your pillow like a halo of gold, your mouth as red as poppies and your skin—

Then your eyes opened.

I slid away from you, but you only smiled.

"I heard footsteps," you whispered. "I kept my eyes closed, so you wouldn't know I heard."

I just stared at you, dumbfounded, my happiness that you were still my friend, still my Laura, making me feel as though I were drunk.

You sat up, nightgown puddling in your lap as you pushed away the sheets. "Are we going to run away?"

"Yes," I told you, barely able to say more than that. I forced myself to go on. "But you can't come with me the way you are. Do you understand?"

"Just do it," you said, leaning forward and shutting my mouth with your own. "Don't explain. If you explain, I'll be afraid."

You told me it was okay, so wake up. WAKE UP.

Wake up, because we can do anything now. We can dive in your deep seas and walk across the sands of your moon.

Wake up, so I can show you all the mysteries I promised you.

Wake up, so we can drink secrets together.

Wake up. I love you. The stars are shining down on us. The taste of you is still in my mouth. The sun is coming. Wake up and run through the streets with me, run through the world with me. Wakeupwakeupwakeup.

I can't remember how old I was when I first read Joseph Sheridan Le Fanu's Gothic novella, *Carmilla*. I couldn't have been older than thirteen, because that was the year I obsessively researched vampires for the footnote-filled paper that would allow me to graduate from middle school and enter high school. In my memory, *Carmilla* is just always there, a defining piece of my inner vampire mythos. In rereading it recently, I was struck by how much it read like a dark, hothouse fairy tale. I absolutely adore the language—all the hot lips and languid, gloating eyes—that made me fall in love with vampires in the first place. I always wondered what the story would have been like from Carmilla's point of view, though, so in this story, I decided to try to puzzle it out.

Figures of Earth (1921). Richmond, Virginia–based author James Branch Cabell wrote his exquisitely crafted, imaginative tales during the age of Faulkner, Hemingway, and Fitzgerald. So it is little wonder, then, that mainstream popularity came his way only once, when his novel *Jurgen* was brought before the Supreme Court on charges of obscenity and for a time his name was indeed on every reader's lips. But his sophisticated, mildly erotic adventures filled with mysterious wizards and gods that steadily give way to yet more great and powerful gods were never the stuff of popular taste, and so his writing has been relegated to the obscure and the antiquarian. But this tale of the pig-keeper and very reluctant hero Manuel is a colorful romp touching on all the finer points of chivalry and heroism. Falling into and out of beds and bedrooms and high adventures and quests at every opportunity, Manuel molds, as his mother has told him to do, a fine figure of himself from every available material at his disposal.

To this day, so many years later, Cabell's implacable insistence that no one ever truly understands the will of their god(s) or the worlds that they have created, tempers my every thought as well as gifts me with a knowing, ironic smile, fully displayed at any of my grandiose ideas.

·Figures of Earth·

When First We Were Gods

Rick Yancey

Many lifetimes later, as he boarded the last ferry to Titan, Beneficent Page recalled the first and only time he fell in love.

Beneficent was married at the time to a woman named Courteous Spool, of the New New York Spools, a very prominent and powerful family whose patriarch, Omniscient Spool, served as chairman of the Conduct Review Committee, *the* most powerful position in the Republic of North America, more powerful than the president herself, since this committee was responsible for reviewing lifetime accomplishments, transgressions, and applications for Transfer. To get on Omniscient's bad side could literally cost you your life.

So the marriage was, at least from the Page family's perspective, an excellent match. Courteous was, by virtue of being the youngest, the favorite of Omniscient's seventy-six daughters.

Though it was Beneficent's sixteenth marriage, it was Courteous's first. She had been in love before, countless times, and had actually planned several weddings, always to call them off days—or sometimes minutes—before the ceremony. It became somewhat of a joke among the First and Foremost Families (the 3Fs): "So who is Courteous going to marry this year?" the 3Fs would snarkily ask each other. If Courteous had been the daughter of anyone else, this latest invitation would have been deleted with a roll of the eye and a cynical snicker. "Courteous actually saying 'I do'? *Riiiiiiiight.*"

But Courteous Spool wasn't the daughter of just anybody else. She was the daughter—the *favorite* daughter—of the chairman of the Conduct Review Committee. So when the invitation dropped into their cogboxes, trips and parties were canceled, schedules rearranged, Transfers postponed—or moved up, if possible—and even some labors induced or pregnancies terminated, because, though the odds were slim it would actually happen, you weren't going to miss the wedding of three centuries over something as commonplace as giving birth.

It would be a lavish affair, even by Spool standards. Omniscient's goal was to make the celebration so over-the-top outrageous that his daughter would be too mortified to call it off: seven hundred guests; more than a hundred performers, including the world-famous Amarillo Gladiators from Waco, who staged fights to the death with a variety of archaic and unusual weapons, including, in one memorable performance, a handbag full of bricks and a bullwhip festooned with sewing needles (the handbag won); exotic dishes prepared by the finest chefs in the world; door prizes that included a free Transfer regardless of your Conduct Review (jokingly called "Omniscient's Get Out of Jail Free card"); and all to take place at the most exclusive venue of all—the Gingrich Memorial Gardens on Moon Base Alpha. The lunar colony was only a few decades old in those days and most of the 3Fs looked at it as wildly exotic, the ultimate vacation spot, a nice place to visit but not somewhere you'd want to live.

Three days before the Big Day, Courteous went shopping

with her mother and her oldest sister, Genuine. It was her third visit to her favorite Transfer boutique in a week and a bad sign, in her mother's opinion. Perfectionism in the age of immortality is a recipe for disaster, and Courteous was a perfectionist. Her look for the ceremony had to be *just right*, as the ceremony itself had to be *just right*, as every potential mate had had to be *just right*. Of course, nothing is ever *just right*, even when death is discarded.

"What do you think about this one?" she asked her mother and sister, pausing before the display case.

"Five nine and a half," Genuine said, consulting the monitor beside the nude body suspended in the tank. "And ten pounds heavier. Your dress won't fit."

"I'll get a new dress," Courteous said. "I'm not crazy about it anyway."

"Courteous," her mother said. "You *love* that dress. It's a Tiffanplouf original!"

"It's too old-fashioned. No one does translucent gowns anymore."

"I did last year," Genuine pointed out.

"Exactly," Courteous said.

"The wedding is in three days," her mother put in. "It's too late to design a new dress."

"Then we put it off for another week," Courteous said with a casual shrug.

Her mother and Genuine exchanged knowing looks. They had witnessed this nearly a dozen times before: the piling up of excuses as the Big Day approached until the Big Day simply never came.

They continued down the row of display cases. "What about

this one?" Genuine said, stopping before a fetching seventeen-year-old inanimate. "Look how delicate her features are! And that little nose is to *die* for."

"She's the right height, too," Mother Spool noted. "And weight. The Tiffanplouf would fit *perfectly*."

"Unless it doesn't," said Courteous. "And if it doesn't, then we *will* have to postpone it."

"Well, there's only one way to make certain it fits," Genuine snapped. "Don't Transfer before the wedding! Who does that?" She turned to Courteous's mother for support. "I mean, who Transfers three days before their wedding?"

"*I* never did. Not in twenty-six marriages."

"She has a good point, Courteous," her sister said. "Maybe you're stuck in perpetual engagements because you're thinking your first will be the only wedding you'll ever have."

"Maybe it will be," Courteous shot back defiantly. "Maybe if I get this one *just right*, I'll never have to go through it again!"

"Well, I hope you don't, because after going through *this* seventeen times with you, I can't take any more."

After viewing another six rows of options and debating the merits of dozens of different looks (this one's face was "too long. I want to go with something heart-shaped and pixyish," that one's proportions were off, waist too long, legs too short, or vice versa), Courteous returned to her first choice, the tall one with the striking green eyes. Green, she explained, was Beneficent's favorite color.

"That's a good point," her flustered mother said, thinking what the designer at Tiffanplouf's was going to say when they informed him the dress would have to be totally redesigned in less than twenty-four hours. "Beneficent is expecting *this*," pointing at Courteous's present body, "not *that*," pointing at the tall, green-eyed inanimate floating behind the glass. "What if he doesn't like it?"

"It's *my* wedding," Courteous replied testily. "I suppose I can wear whatever look I want. If Beneficent doesn't like it, I can always change into something more to his fancy afterward, but I will *never* pick a look simply to please a man!"

Her mother sighed. Her strategy had completely backfired. Courteous's mind was made up: she was switching from a five-foot-six-inch body into one four inches taller and ten pounds heavier. Her mother linked up with the designer while Courteous completed her order and the Transfer agent prepped her new look. She was still televersing when Courteous was taken into the private room for the final upload to her master file. The designer's curses and threats of quitting thundered inside Mrs. Spool's head—thank goodness only she could hear them!—as Courteous handed the agent her psyche-card. Mrs. Spool would have missed the switchover entirely if Genuine hadn't found her at the last second, huddled in a corner of the boutique, pressing her hands over her ears in a futile attempt to muffle the outraged roars of the couturier.

"I have to go," she whispered. "She's about to switch."

She will not *switch!* the designer screeched inside her head. And then, remembering whose wife he was televersing with: *All right, but I make no promises. No promises! She may have to settle for something* off-the-rack!

"We're going to miss it," Genuine worried as they hurried to the Transfer room.

"Oh, they know we're here. They'll wait for us."

She was right, of course. Rarely was even the most routine Transfer done without some family member present—there was always the chance, no matter how remote, that something might go wrong in the switchover—and rarer still was any member of the Spool clan switched without a loved one there to murmur the obligatory, conditional good-bye.

Which Courteous's mother did, ending with the quote spoken at all proper Transfers:

"May you wake safely upon that far shore
When night is through
May you find no everlasting sleep
When breaks the Eternal Dawn!"

A final kiss. A final upload from Courteous's psyche-card to the master file. And then the first shot to put her to sleep. Her latest purchase rolled into the room, dressed now, hair carefully arranged, beautiful green eyes blank and staring sightlessly at the ceiling, the mind empty, a cup waiting to be filled with the trillion bits of data that was Courteous Spool. The download into her new look lasted a little over a minute. The pupils dilated, the body spasmed as circuits came alive, and the tall girl was whisked out of the room for full cognitive testing, but not before she looked up into her mother's face—a face not much older than her own—and smiled.

For a few minutes, there were two Courteous Spools in the world, the shorter, brown-eyed one and the taller, green-eyed one. Then, after the neurological and physical tests were completed to confirm the Transfer was a success, a second shot was administered to the first Courteous, or the *redundancy*, as it was called. This second shot stopped her heart.

She was dead.

And alive. In a body picked out just for her wedding. A body whose eyes were Beneficent's favorite color. A copy of a copy of a copy of a copy of a copy of a copy of a copy of the original, the one her mother had given birth to several lifetimes ago, but still Courteous.

"I don't know," she mused the next morning, examining her newest self in the mirror. "The faces always look a little different inside the display case. This nose didn't look so narrow and the cheekbones are a little *too* prominent, I think. Should I try to find another?"

She was leaving for the moon in less than an hour. There was no time to find another look and, at any rate, you were allowed only one Transfer every five years—it's time-consuming and expensive to grow inanimate human beings. But that particular rule just happened to be enforced by the Conduct Review Committee, which just happened to be chaired by one Omniscient Spool, who just happened to be the father of the green-eyed beauty standing in front of the mirror, who just happened to be his favorite daughter. If she wanted another look, she would get one.

Courteous turned to her personal assistant—her *persist*, in the parlance of the 3Fs—a pretty young girl named Georgiana, whose family had faithfully served Courteous for ten generations, and asked her opinion.

"I think it's beautiful," Georgiana said. "Much better than the last look."

"I'm not comparing it to the last look," Courteous said impatiently. She paused as a message from her mother dropped into her cogbox. The shrill voice rang annoyingly inside her head: *Forty-five minutes to takeoff, dear! Tick-tock, tick-tock!* "What would be the point of *that*? Tell me the truth; you won't hurt my feelings."

"No new look is perfect," Georgiana said carefully. "Those

eyes are the perfect shade of green, though. They'll go wonderfully with your gown."

"Oh, Georgiana," Courteous sighed, pinching her new nose and then pushing on the tip to flare the nostrils. "I envy you *finitissium* sometimes, I really do. You get just one body, and you never have to go through this *agony*."

"One body…and one lifetime," Georgiana murmured. Only 3Fs could spit on death's grave. The vast majority of people still lived finite lives—hence the slightly condescending and contemptuous name for them: *finitissium*, the finite ones. The day would come when Georgiana would be too old and feeble to properly care for Courteous. She would be sent off to live out the remainder of her days at the Retired Persists' Home and replaced with someone younger—hopefully someone from her own family, a granddaughter, perhaps, if she was lucky enough to have one. Being a persist was a choice job, if you could get it. Private quarters in the high-security family compound, not some shack in the sprawling slums that ringed the city, surrounded by open sewers and reeking garbage, preyed upon by the vicious gangs that ruled the ghetto. The job came with free health care, including vision and dental. And an education, if you wanted one. Georgiana was very proud of the fact that she was the first in her family to read and write. She also spoke a bit of Courtesian, much to her mistress's delight and the only reason she spoke it—to delight her: As long as she kept Courteous happy, her job was safe.

"Why am I going through it, Georgiana?" Courteous asked. "To please my father? To shut up those idiots who laugh at me? To save my family the embarrassment of yet another aborted wedding? I'm only four hundred and ninety-eight years old."

Staring at her eighteen-year-old face in the mirror. "Maybe I'm too young to get married."

"Do you love him?" Georgiana asked quietly.

"Love who? Oh, Beneficent. Well, of course I do. As much as I loved the others I thought I was going to marry."

"Then that's why you're going through it."

"It all just seems so *pointless*. Do you know how many times my father has been married? Forty-four. Forty-four times, Georgiana! People change spouses more often than they clean out their closets. And every time they say, 'This is the one. This is the person I'm going to spend eternity with.' Then forty or fifty years go by and you're just sick of each other, utterly *sick*, and it's on to the next 'true love.' My question is what good is eternity if you are eternally falling in and out of love? Joy. Despair. Desire. Revulsion. Excitement. Boredom. They should do away with marriage altogether, in my opinion. It makes you only *more* dissatisfied and lonely."

"But there's always a chance, isn't there?" Georgiana asked.

"A chance for what?"

"That someday you *will* find the one to spend eternity with."

Courteous thought about that for a long moment.

"Oh, what do you know?" she said finally. "You're mortal, and only a mortal can afford to be romantic. When we conquered death, we murdered love."

Even as those harsh words came out, there was a part of her that rebelled at the thought. Endless life increased the probability of everything, including the most improbable thing of all: a love that lasts longer than the stars. Perhaps Beneficent *was* the one of whom she would never tire, whose life she would share until the sun had burned all its fuel and died. How long would their love endure? A billion years? Ten billion? Until the universe was black and cold, until the final flaring out of the last star?

Georgiana sat down beside her, stroked her silky auburn hair, and said simply, "I believe in love."

Blinking back tears, Courteous whispered, "In spite of life eternal?"

"In spite of life eternal," her persist answered. "And because of it."

Two days later, Courteous married Beneficent Page.

Looking back three billion years later, Beneficent could not say how he happened to fall in love for the first and only time, the *why* of it always eluded him, but he could remember to the hour when it happened.

It was a little after seven o'clock on an early morning in May, four years into his marriage. He had risen at dawn, as was his habit, leaving Courteous to sleep in while he enjoyed a few moments of solitude on the balcony, where he could drink his coffee and stream the morning news into his cogbox with no distractions except the spectacular sunrise over the river. The golden light sparkled on the dark water and shimmered in the smoke rising lazily from the cooking fires of the tenements that spread out for miles below him.

It was his favorite part of the day. Just his coffee, the pleasant banter of the announcers echoing inside his head, the glorious sunrise, and himself: Beneficent enjoyed being alone. His own company he found perfectly agreeable. If the world had been a slightly different place and he slightly less ambitious, he might have never married, not Courteous and not the fifteen who came before her. He didn't love Courteous, any more than he had loved his former wives. He found her to be, like nearly every one of the 3Fs, shallow, vain, petty, and almost unbearably boring. But the world was what it was and his ambition was what it was, and now he had arrived, if not at the pinnacle, then at least within striking distance of it: He was the husband of the favorite daughter of the most powerful man on the planet. All that remained was a child. A child would seal his place in Omniscient's unofficial court, no matter what came of the marriage.

Sitting with his back to the door, he did not see her approach. Her fragrance announced her presence, a delicate floral scent popular among the *finitissium*, one that would, over the coming millennia, remind him of that moment when he realized he was in love.

"I thought you might like some muffins. Fresh from the oven," Georgiana said. She placed the platter beside his coffee.

The air smelled of smoke and perfume. The golden morning light caressed her lovely young face, unmarred, as one day it surely would be, by the ravages of time.

"Hmmm, blueberry, my favorite. Thank you, Georgiana," he murmured. He reached for a hot muffin, and the little finger of her right hand brushed against his left. With that accidental contact, that meaningless touch, something long dormant stirred inside him. Something larger than he, something even older than he, something that had been since the foundations of the earth. Something that he had never experienced before and never would again, not in three billion years. He tried to push it down, brush it aside, but it was far more powerful than he. He tried to ignore it as he bit into the warm muffin, a strange and thrilling sense of vertigo, which he blamed on the strong coffee, but it had already gripped him and not even the passage of three billion years could loosen its hold.

"Would you like to join me?" he asked, casually waving toward the empty chair beside him. He shut down his cogbox to silence the morning program in his head. Suddenly, he found the announcers' voices extremely irritating.

"Thank you, Mr. Page, but Mrs. Page will be rising soon and…"

"She won't be up for hours, we both know that. I can't remember a day when Courteous rose before noon. Please, Georgiana. I have no one to enjoy the sunrise with."

The persist had little choice but to join him. She sat with her knees pressed together, not looking at him, but across the water at the smoky glow of the tenement fires. She had extended family down there, though she had not seen them in several years. She was afraid to visit. She was young and pretty and well fed. She might be targeted by a gang for her nice clothes, robbed, beaten, perhaps raped.

"Have a muffin," Beneficent said.

"I had one already," she confessed.

"I know. I see a bit of crumb on your lip. May I?"

He reached toward her—she was very careful not to pull back or flinch—and gently brushed the crumb away with his thumb. The first touch was accidental; this second touch was not.

"Tell me something, Georgiana. How long has your family been with Courteous?"

"Almost two hundred years," Georgiana answered.

"And what do you think of her?"

"I care for Mrs. Page very much."

"No doubt, but I wonder if there might be some, for lack of a better word, *resentment*, too?"

"Oh no. Why would I resent her?"

"I would think resentment would be quite common for your people."

"To tell you the truth, Mr. Page, sometimes I..." She took a deep breath. It was a very dangerous thing to say. "Sometimes I actually feel sorry for her."

"Really? And why should someone like you feel pity for someone like her?"

She did not answer right away. Watching the smoke and the light that lit up the smoke, knees pressed together, refusing to look at him, she finally said, "When I was very small my mother told me a very old story, about a covetous man who wanted everything he saw, so when he died he was cursed with eternal hunger and thirst and imprisoned in a pool of water with a handful of delicious fruit hanging above him. Every time he bent to drink, the water receded, and every time he reached for the fruit, the fruit was pulled away."

"And that story reminds you of Courteous?"

"It reminds me of... many people."

"But we all drink to our fill," he argued. "We all eat till we can eat no more. Well, actually, ours is the feast that never ends." He popped the remainder of the warm muffin into his mouth, delighting in its rich, moist texture. "For example, tomorrow I am off to hunt great whites off the coast of Australia, armed with nothing but a bowie knife. The odds are extremely likely that I will be eaten alive. Yet I will wake the next day as whole and healthy as I am right now."

"In a different body," she pointed out. "And with no memory of what happened."

"Well," he said with a laugh. "I don't think being eaten alive is something I'd *want* to remember."

"I don't see the thrill in doing something dangerous if there is nothing to lose."

"Funny you should say that. I've often thought the same about love."

There was an awkward silence. Now why did I bring up love? he wondered. It was an odd transition, from being eaten alive by sharks to love. As the millennia passed, however, it seemed less odd and more prescient.

"Love or sharks, does it matter?" she asked. "Isn't all of it pointless if..."

"Yes, Georgiana? If...what?"

She lowered her eyes. "If you cannot fail."

He might have told her that he *had* failed. That he was a dismal failure when it came to love, if never having loved meant failure. For a shocking instant, he felt as if he might cry. He had not cried in...what? Five hundred years or more? When was the last time he had cried? He had no memory of it, but that did not mean much. The memory could belong to a lost day, like the one that would be sacrificed if he lost his duel with the sharks, for example. Your memory was only as complete as the latest download to your psyche-card.

"Have you ever been in love, Georgiana?" he asked.

She shook her head. Refusing to look at him. It was that refusal, he realized after many centuries of introspection, that had done him in. If she had looked at him in that pivotal moment, the spell her touch had cast might have been broken. It might have satisfied his curiosity, convinced him that she was nothing more than an ordinary girl, a *finitissium* unworthy of his notice.

But she *did* refuse to look at him, and, even more than that first touch, it was the look withheld that doomed him.

"What a pity," he sighed. "I was hoping you could tell me what it feels like."

"But you love Mrs. Page," the girl protested, looking at him finally, but he did not see it; he had turned away.

He left for Australia the following morning, without Courteous—she was absurdly, when you think about it, afraid of the ocean—and bagged four sharks on the first day, but on the next his luck ran out. A twenty-foot monster rocketed up from the deep, taking him by surprise, ripping his body to shreds before dragging the mangled corpse into the lightless depths. His persist returned home with his psyche-card, backed up the night before his last ill-fated dive, and within an hour of touching down, Beneficent had been downloaded into the new body he had reserved on the morning of his departure. He remembered nothing of his demise, of course. That distasteful memory had perished with the body that was slowly digesting in the guts of a dozen sea creatures, from the shark that had shredded him to the tiny bottom-feeders that scuttle across the floors of silent seas.

On the morning following his return, he was sitting on the balcony with his coffee, his cogbox on silent because just the thought of the announcers' voices was enough to set his teeth on edge, when he heard the door slide open behind him. He turned, smiling expectantly, certain that it was Georgiana with another plateful of muffins. It seemed more than just a few days since he had seen her.

"What?" Courteous asked. "Why do you look so surprised to see me?"

"I thought you were asleep," he answered easily.

His wife slid into the seat beside him. She was naked. The newborn light of day caressed her luminous flesh, her flawless skin. Beneficent sipped his coffee and looked away.

"You were smiling and now you're not," Courteous pointed out. "Do you find me hideous?"

"What an absurd thing to say."

"Tell me what kind of body you'd like and I'll switch."

"No, no. There is no need to switch, dear. I would love you no matter what look you wore."

"I don't like your teeth," she said.

"My teeth?"

"They're too long. Big as a horse's. Why did you choose something with such big teeth?"

He forced himself to laugh. "The better to eat you with, my dear!"

She wrinkled her nose. "It smells out here."

"It's the fires. I rather like it."

"I don't know how those people stand it."

"I suppose they have no choice."

"No, but *we* do." She stretched her bare arms over her head. "Let's go inside, and you can make love to me with those big teeth."

"Of course. Do you mind if I finish my coffee first?"

"We haven't made love since you came back from Australia. Is there something wrong?"

His coffee had gone ice cold. He sipped it anyway. A tiny sip. "No."

"I'm curious to see if your teeth are the only things overly large."

She rose from the chair. She was glorious, perfect, and he did not look at her. The door slid shut behind her. Beneficent turned up the volume of his cogbox to drown out his own thoughts. Several minutes later, the door opened again, and he closed his eyes. When he opened them, there was Georgiana, dressed in the drab gray uniform of a persist. He broke into a smile, though a small one. He was self-conscious now about the size of his new teeth.

"Georgiana! But where are my muffins?"

"Mrs. Page sent me to find you, sir."

"Why would she do that?" he wondered. "She knows where I am."

"She said you've either fallen off the balcony or got lost on your way to the bedroom."

Looking at her, he was struck by the contrast between her face and his wife's. Courteous was stunningly beautiful, possessing features only the daughter of a Spool could afford, a face that put Helen's to shame, and Georgiana's, though pretty, was so ordinary as to be homely next to hers. Why, then, did something bright and wonderful bloom inside him at the sight of that ordinary face?

"What shall I tell her, Mr. Page?"

"Georgiana, we've known one another nearly five years now. Please, call me Beneficent."

"Yes, sir," she replied with a slight stammer, lowering her eyes. He could see the fires down below reflecting in them. "Beneficent."

"Only when we're alone," he cautioned. "Never in Courteous's presence."

He handed her his empty cup. Trailed the tip of his finger along the back of her hand. She kept herself very still, eyes downcast, holding his empty cup.

"I've been thinking of you," he said softly.

"Of me?" She seemed shocked.

"Since the morning you brought me those delicious muffins.

In all my lifetimes, Georgiana, I swear to you I have never tasted anything more sumptuous, more…decadent than your muffins. Will you make them again for me? Tomorrow?"

"Yes, sir, Mr.…."

"Ah, ah."

"Beneficent."

"That's a good girl." He sighed. "Well, I suppose I must go see my wife now. Tell me something, Georgiana: What do you think of my new teeth?"

"Your teeth?"

"Do you think they're too large?"

She shrugged. "You can always switch if you don't like them."

"Of course, but I was asking if *you* liked them."

"Everyone's taste is different."

"You have no opinion, then?"

"It isn't my opinion that matters."

"It matters to me."

"Why?" Something like anger flashed in her eyes. "Why should my opinion matter to you or to anyone?"

"Dear Georgiana," he answered. "I may be immortal, but I am still human."

"I suppose that depends on the definition."

"Of immortality?"

"Of what is human." She moved at last toward the door, away from him. "And what is not."

Beneficent went inside and, finding Courteous waiting for him in their private quarters in all her unblemished perfection, made love to her, his cogbox blaring at full volume, not so much to drown out his own thoughts but to drown out Georgiana's parting words, *Of what is human . . . and what is not.*

Afterward, a quick shower and then a short tram ride to his job at the Research Center, the vast complex deep beneath the streets of New New York. Courteous's father had arranged an appointment for him to the prestigious Relocation Committee, which was charged with the enormous task of finding an Earth-like planet in the vastness of space to which the 3Fs could flee when the sun expired in a few billion years. The work was not terribly demanding, since *finitissium* technicians performed the bulk of it. Committee members, like Beneficent, mostly reviewed reports they couldn't understand, wrote—or had written for them—memoranda that few ever bothered to read, or, more often than not, played holographic games downloaded into their cogboxes. It was stultifyingly boring work, but serving on the Relocation Committee was considered a high honor and a stepping stone to the most powerful committee in the Republic, the Conduct Review Committee, Omniscient's committee, the committee that held in its hand the power of life itself and the one upon which Beneficent desperately wanted to sit.

Where he *would* be sitting, if not for one condition he had yet to meet. An unspoken but well-understood condition:

Four years into it, and the marriage had yet to produce offspring.

The bonds of holy matrimony were not terribly strong among the 3Fs. A marriage that lasted beyond four or five Transfers was uncommon; Beneficent was on his sixteenth marriage and Omniscient himself had been married more than forty times. Marriage doesn't last, the saying went, but children go on and on. Courteous's child—*his* child—would be a legitimate addition to the clan, and as its father Beneficent would be forever a link in the Spool dynastic chain. His marriage might—probably would—

end, but never the children from it. It was the only reason he had pursued Courteous. And, as long as they remained childless, he remained vulnerable.

He had broached the topic many times with her. It was the thing he talked about most. And it seemed the more he talked about it, the less she listened.

"I'm not ready," she would say. Or "In another decade or two. I'm still young. What's the rush?"

He dared not press too hard. She wasn't very bright, but she had siblings and aunts and uncles and cousins who were and who might, if they already hadn't, become suspicious that he had married her with less than honorable intentions.

He had lunch that day with an old chum from his boarding school days, Candid Sheet, who was in his two hundred and seventeenth year of service on the Research and Development Committee. He hadn't seen Candid in a while, so he had to reintroduce himself when they met in the restaurant.

"Well, I was going to ask how the shark hunting went, but now I don't need to," Candid remarked drily. "You're taller. I thought you never liked going over six-two."

"Courteous is five-nine and she wanted something at least six inches taller."

"I always stay within a half inch of my First Me," Candid said. "Why?"

"Because I'm cheap. I don't want to change out my entire wardrobe with every switch."

Lunch was a light affair: lobsters, porterhouses, creamed asparagus and fries, baked Alaska, and, ordered on a whim, a plate of blueberry muffins, which arrived during their postlunch cigars.

"Muffins?" Candid asked.

"I positively crave them." Beneficent took a big bite and was vaguely disappointed. They were not Georgiana's muffins, not by a long shot. "Tell me what you think about the teeth."

"What teeth?"

"These teeth."

"They're blue."

"That's from the muffin. I was talking about the size. Do you think they're too large?"

"Obviously someone thinks they are."

"Well, I just switched. I doubt Omniscient will grant a waiver based on the size of my teeth."

"He would if Courteous asked for one."

"I have a feeling she might."

"If she's interested, I have just the thing for oversize teeth. The prototype has just been approved for testing."

"What is it?"

"Simply marvelous is what it is! We developed it in conjunction with the Marriage Integrity Committee in an effort to strengthen and prolong fidelity. Basically the program accesses your visual cortex and overlays a holographic screen image over the face of your lover—or anyone's face, for that matter..."

"A holographic image of *what?*"

"Anyone you please! Say you've developed a little crush on a coworker or a friend or even some starlet in the televerse. It could be anyone. No need to risk divorce over a little crush. Simply execute the program and, *voilà*, the virtual face replaces your spouse's. Or, in your case, Courteous could overlay your current look with your prior appearance, and gone will be the offensive teeth."

"That *does* sound marvelous," Beneficent allowed.

"And the *most* marvelous part is only you can see it. Your partner need never know."

"She might like that," Beneficent said. "I do want her to be happy. We made love this morning, and I could tell the teeth bothered her, even though I was very careful to keep my mouth closed."

"I'll send her a copy of the prototype."

"No," Beneficent said, popping the last muffin into his mouth. "She'll think it's a virus and just delete it. Forward it to my cogbox, and I'll pass it along."

"This is just the beginning, Beneficent," his friend said, his eyes glowing at the prospect. "The second stage of human evolution is coming to an end. In another thousand years, we will be loosed from all corporal confinements. The third and final stage: pure conscious, pure being. The work of your committee will be scrapped—there will be no need to find a new Earth, and we will flee the dying solar system in a vessel the size of a tin cup."

Beneficent's heart quickened with something very much like fear.

"What do you mean?"

"Our entire existence will be virtual, a holographic construct of our own design, in which everything we desire will be ours to live and relive for all eternity. The end of pain, loss, heartbreak...and big teeth! The universe will expire, but we will not. We will lie forever in a paradise of our own making. We will be like true gods, then."

"My! That sounds..." Beneficent searched for the word. "Wonderful."

He tried out Candid's fidelity program that night. The

experience was disconcerting, bordering on the bizarre. The image kept slipping every time Courteous moved her head and there was a slight delay in reaction time. For example, Courteous's mouth would come open and, a millisecond later, the overlaid hologram of Georgiana's would follow suit. It was as if he were making love to both women—and neither of them. He found himself whispering to his wife, "Hold still, hold still." For when she held still, the image of Georgiana's face sprang to life in his visual cortex, the reproduction of it from his memory nearly perfect. His heart would leap exactly as if the woman in his arms actually *were* the woman of his dreams. *Hold still. Hold still.*

"Well, how did it go?" Candid asked him when they met again for lunch a few days later.

"She noticed a few glitches."

"For instance?"

Beneficent explained the shifting, the delay between the real expression and the hologram's. Candid suggested the problem might not lie in the program, but in whatever image Courteous was accessing. There might not be enough data.

"She might not remember your old self well enough. The hologram is only as good as the recollection."

"What does that mean?"

"It means the better she can remember a face, the better it will be holographically reproduced. Our studies have shown very poor results if one simply looks at a photograph or even a three-dimensional image. It's the living face that we best remember, smiling, laughing, frowning, talking, eating, what have you."

Beneficent said, "That might prove difficult."

"Because that face was eaten by a shark?"

"Perhaps she knows someone who has smaller, more attractive teeth. I'll ask her."

He did not, of course. Instead, he gave his persist a tiny holo-corder and instructed him to follow Georgiana anywhere she went outside the company of her mistress. On errands, at night in her quarters (if he could manage it without getting caught), on her off-day. He demanded daily uploads into his cogbox of the footage. At night, after Courteous had fallen asleep, he would creep out of bed and sit on the balcony, playing the footage over and over, trying to memorize every line, every detail of the girl's face, freezing on the close-ups and lingering over them for hours on end. He pinpointed every freckle, every blemish, calculated the precise angle of her smile. One night he even counted her eyelashes.

Hold still, hold still.

His results improved, but still were not perfect. He decided, if there was any hope of success, he must study Georgiana himself. It was very risky. He didn't dare stalk the girl, but made excuses to be around her more. He took a week off from work and whisked her and Courteous off to Paris for a four-day shopping spree. Then three weeks skiing in the Alps. And, of course, every morning he insisted Georgiana join him on the balcony for muffins and coffee.

Hold still, hold still! And the image would briefly fall perfectly into line and he could imagine it was Georgiana in his arms, her body beneath his, her sweet breath on his face and his upon hers, which was utterly *perfect*, down to the last eyelash, until Courteous moved or spoke, shattering the illusion.

"What is it?" she would demand. "Why do you seem so angry when we make love?"

"Not angry," he answered. "Self-conscious. The teeth thing."

"Really?" Courteous was becoming suspicious—who wouldn't? The urgent whispering, over and over, *hold still, hold still*, and the intense, disconcerting way he stared at her. She began turning off the light before their lovemaking, which ruined it for him; the program did not work in the dark.

And, because it didn't, something else didn't work either.

"I am so *sorry* I ever mentioned it," Courteous snapped after one particularly embarrassing session, when nothing they tried worked. "Those damned teeth. Tomorrow I'm speaking to Daddy about a waiver."

"I don't think it's the teeth," he confessed.

"Then what is it? What look do you want for me, Beneficent? I'll Transfer into it tomorrow."

"No, no. It isn't the look, darling. It's...well, it's been nearly five years now and there's still no...Well, it starts to feel a little, how do I say it? Pointless."

"*What* feels pointless?"

He laid his hand upon her bare stomach. "Just yesterday your father asked again. Just yesterday."

"And? Did you tell him he was asking the wrong person? Whichever one I may be in, it's my body. I will decide when to burden it with child."

"Perhaps that's the problem," he gently suggested. "It is not usually the kind of burden one takes on alone."

"You have children already, Beneficent," she reminded him. There were sixty-two of them from his prior marriages.

"But none with you, my love."

"And without a child, our union is pointless?"

"No, merely...imperfect."

He woke the next morning from a terrible nightmare. It began well enough. He and Georgiana were making love and in the middle of it she reached up and pulled off her entire face, revealing Courteous's face beneath the mask. *I know,* Courteous said to him in the dream. *I know.*

He felt he had no choice. He must confess his love to Georgiana, for he had come at last to the conclusion that there was no substitute for her, virtual or otherwise. Rising carefully so as not to disturb his wife, he tiptoed onto the balcony and waited for the dawn. He rehearsed what he would say when she arrived with the muffins. He would promise to be careful. He understood that, if they were caught, Georgiana could lose everything. Banishment to the ghetto, perhaps torture or worse. There was a law, rarely enforced but a law nevertheless, that stated carnal relations between 3Fs and the *finitissium* were punishable by death—for the *finitissium,* of course. He wouldn't put it past Courteous to push for the ultimate punishment.

"I can protect you," he planned to say. "If she discovers us, I'll find a place for you to hide, and I will visit you as often as I can. I cannot bear it any longer, Georgiana. I cannot bear the thought of being without you."

The sun rose. The golden light spread over the sprawling slum, kissed the dark surface of the river, crawled up the gleaming edifice atop which he waited.

He waited, and Georgiana never came.

At midmorning, he sprang up and staggered to the door in a panic. Something was wrong; he felt it to the bottom of his immortal being. The sum of four hundred lifetimes told him something was terribly wrong.

And he was right.

The door to her quarters was locked. He knocked softly, though did not dare call out her name. He hurried to the kitchen, but only the cook was there.

"Have you seen Georgiana this morning?" he asked.

No, the cook told him, he had not.

Back to his own quarters, where he found his marital bed empty. He looked up and saw Courteous sitting in the chair he had vacated, wrapped in a robe of flawless white, her long, bare legs, equally flawless, stretched out in front of her. He steadied himself with a few deep breaths before joining her.

"Good morning, my darling." With a kiss upon her perfect cheek.

"Beneficent. I thought you had gone to work."

"I'm not feeling very well today."

"Did you have a bad dream?"

"Why . . . no. Not that I can remember, why?"

"I thought I heard you cry out in your sleep. It's been happening quite a bit lately."

"Has it?"

She was sitting in the sun, he in the shade. She leaned her head toward him.

"Be a dear and rub my head, will you? I have a terrible headache."

He scooted his chair behind hers and gently rubbed her temples.

"Hmmmm. That feels delicious."

"Neither one of us has been feeling well lately," he said. "It's the doldrums. We can't afford to get into a rut, darling."

He was referring to the last terminal human malady: boredom. Extreme cases could be deadly, *permanently* deadly, since they might lead to suicide, the ultimate taboo in the age of immortality. Sibyls, they were called, after the myth. Sometimes the word was used as a verb, as in, "Did you hear about Gracious? She sibylled yesterday."

"Let's get away," he continued. "Have you ever been to Antarctica? It's the perfect time of year to visit."

"We just came back from the Alps," she reminded him.

"Antarctica is nothing like the Alps." He traced his fingers down her neck and began to massage her shoulders.

"I meant we just took a trip."

"I know it's rather primitive by your standards, but we'll spare no expense. We'll bring along the entire staff, your stylist included, that insufferable Carl or Kenneth or whatever his name is..."

"Kent, darling."

"Yes, Kent, even him, and Georgiana, of course..." He took a deep breath and asked, as if he'd just noticed, "but where is Georgiana this morning? I don't believe I've seen her."

"Georgiana? Oh, I dismissed her."

His fingers froze, but for an instant, and he said casually, "Oh, really? Dismissed her?" His mind was racing; his fingers were not. They slowly and lovingly caressed her perfect neck. "That's a surprise. I thought her family had been with you for two hundred years or more."

Courteous shrugged. Shrugged! A spasm went through his hands. He closed his eyes. *Hold still!*

"What...when precisely did you dismiss her?"

"Yesterday afternoon. I thought I told you."

"No. Or if you did, I've forgotten it. What was the cause?"

"I caught her stealing."

"Stealing?" His throat was tightening up. Breathe. Breathe!

"Or conspiring to steal. I confronted her, and she confessed. So I dismissed her."

"I see. Well. I didn't know her very well—hardly at all, actually—but thievery didn't strike me as part of her character."

"Oh, at your age you should know that the smallest sins are the hardest to hide."

"But now you're left without a persist. You should have told me before you sacked her. I could have procured another for you."

"Why do I need a persist, darling, when I have you?" she purred, rubbing her palms over the backs of his hands. "You will be my persist from now on, and wait on me hand and foot!"

"Nothing would bring me greater joy, my love," he said, and kissed her forehead. "Nothing at all."

He waited until the afternoon to escape, telling her he had a meeting down at the Research Center. On board the tram, he dropped a message tagged *urgent* into his persist's cogbox.

Meet me at my office. B. P.

"Georgiana is gone," Beneficent informed him the moment his personal assistant arrived. "I want her found."

"Have you dropped a message into her cogbox?" his persist asked.

"I don't have her address. And I can't ask Courteous for it, and do not ask me why I cannot ask. She is missing."

"Courteous?"

"Georgiana! Courteous dismissed her. Now, I know she has family in the East Quarter..."

"The East Quarter?" The persist's face bled of all color. The East Quarter was a notoriously dangerous section of the ghetto. Even Omniscient's private police, the dreaded CRC, the Captains of the Review Committee, refused to venture into the East Quarter after sunset.

"She shouldn't be too hard to find," Beneficent said. "A persist from the house of Spool hasn't been dismissed in any of their memories. It will be the talk of the ghetto. Follow the whispers to her front door."

"And once I find it? What would you have me do?"

"Bring her back to me, of course!"

"Bring her...?"

"Well, not *literally* to me. That wouldn't do. Bring her back here. Yes. Find her and bring her here and once she's here drop me a message. I'll find some excuse to come down. If not, stay here with her till morning. Don't let her out of your sight."

"And if she refuses?"

"What do you mean? What if she prefers squalor and disease and starvation to the lap of luxury? If she even bothers to ask, tell her you were sent by Candid Sheet, who is looking for a new persist for his wife."

"And what if I can't find her?"

"You are not to return until you do."

The persist was aghast. "I can't stay in the East Quarter past sunset! It would be suicide!"

"Here." Beneficent handed him a device slightly smaller than the palm of his hand. "If you find yourself in a tight spot, press the button."

"What happens when I press the button?"

"Anyone within a hundred feet will be neutralized."

"What will keep *me* from being neutralized?"

"The device itself. It insulates whoever's holding it. Make certain you don't use it anywhere near Georgiana!"

He pushed the man toward the door. The day was waning. "Hurry! And you better put on some sort of disguise. You're easy prey with that uniform on. Report to me immediately when you find her. Go!"

Beneficent had lived many lifetimes, but none seemed longer than the rest of that day. Or that night. For the sun drew low in the sky and the shadow of the tower stretched across the river and fell over the East Quarter, and the trash fires glowed a hellish red in the darkening day. Dinner with Courteous was a particular agony. To be forced to sit through seven courses, and afterward to join her for her favorite programs inside the televerse, insipid melodramas about the insipid lives of the insipid 3Fs in which nothing really mattered because there was no real risk, even the risk of a broken heart. And then, the worst of all, lying with her in the utter dark, a blind man groping in a lightless void, where her lightest caress was scorchingly painful. After midnight now, and still no word. What has happened? Where could his persist be? Where could *she* be? Dropping an urgent message into his missing persist's cogbox: *Where are you? Reply at once!* And hearing nothing, nothing at all. Tuning into the breaking-news stream, because surely, if his persist had used the device, word of it would leak out, even from the no-man's-land of the East Quarter. But there was nothing, nothing. And then, with less than an hour till dawn, actually considering going into the ghetto himself. Not to find his missing persist, damn him, but to find her.

He slept not at all that night—missing the auto-backup to his psyche-card, but that hardly mattered to him—and he rose with the sun. His eyes were red and swollen, as if he had cried his way through the night. He ordered up some coffee and waited for it on the balcony, watching the sunrise. Another message to his persist, and more silence in reply.

The door slid open behind him. He smelled coffee.

And muffins.

"Georgiana . . . ?" He wondered if he might be hallucinating. How could she be standing there in that same drab uniform, holding a plate of muffins, as if nothing had happened? How was it possible?

She placed the tray on the table, set down his cup. When she leaned over, he could smell her perfume, and his head swam.

"Beneficent?" she asked. "Is something the matter?"

"I thought...Courteous said...Georgiana, where have you been?"

"In the kitchen, making muffins. Oh, you mean yesterday? Mrs. Page gave me the day off. I was visiting my grandmother at the Retired Persists' Home."

"You were visiting...?"

"Didn't Mrs. Page tell you?"

"Of course. I must have forgotten." He made an attempt to pick up a muffin. His hand was shaking violently.

"Is everything all right, Beneficent?"

"Well, yes. Everything is fine, Georgiana. Everything is..."

He could not go on. With any of it. He hurled the crushed pastry over the railing and cried out, "I thought I had lost you! Never do that to me again, do you understand? I cannot bear it, Georgiana. I cannot bear it!"

Before she could escape, he threw his arms around her and pressed his face against the rough material of her uniform. Startled, she pushed against his shoulders, trying to free herself, but he had locked his hands behind her back.

"Mr. Page! Beneficent! What are you doing?"

"I love you. I have loved you for a very long time, and I don't know what to *do* about it. I've never loved anyone, not in six hundred years, Georgiana, and never will again, not in six billion or six *trillion*. If I lost you, I would destroy my psyche-card and throw myself off this balcony—I would pull a sibyl, I swear I would! It would be better to die than live a single day without you."

Pressing his face against her uniform, staining it with his tears.

"You cannot love me, Mr. Page."

"Exactly the problem!"

"No. I mean, you *cannot*. I am a *finitissium*."

"I don't care if you're a turtle! It doesn't matter to me."

"It matters to me."

He gasped. Her words weakened his grip and she broke free. Holding up her hands, as if to say *Stop! No farther!*

"You're in love with someone else," he said. It was not a question.

"There is no one else."

"Then why does it . . . ?"

She shook her head. "There *is* no one else," she said. "Only you."

She fell into his arms, her face shining in the first light of the finite sun, and he told her he knew her down to the last eyelash and she smiled as if she understood.

What had Courteous said? *The smallest of sins are the hardest to hide.* No wonder he had missed it.

The body of his persist was recovered in a steaming trench of raw sewage three days later. His throat had been slashed from ear to ear. The loss raised several uncomfortable questions in the minds of the CRC investigators, questions they shared with Beneficent. Why was his persist in the East Quarter after dark? How had he come into the possession of a neural neutralizer? Beneficent confessed ignorance on both matters, except to say his neutralizer was missing and he had long suspected his persist was addicted to metacoke, a deadly habit that Beneficent nevertheless tolerated because it greatly increased the man's energy and efficiency. He supposed the poor fellow had gone to the Quarter to fuel his habit. Beyond that, he knew as much as they did. The file was closed that day. Beneficent was, after all, the husband of Omniscient Spool's favorite daughter.

Beneficent met Georgiana that afternoon in a little cottage at the western edge of the Spool compound. Years ago, the cottage had been a guesthouse, then converted into a gardener's shed, then finally abandoned. They made love on a pile of old blankets in an atmosphere of moist earth and old fertilizer.

"Is it safe?" he had asked her.

"You know it isn't," she answered as they tore off each other's clothes.

Afterward, he held her in his arms, her head resting on his chest, and he watched the dust motes spin in the afternoon sunlight streaming through the cracks between the rotting boards. He thought of the CRC pulling his persist's bloated corpse from the trench reeking of human waste. The image had been mass broadcast, and he had inadvertently opened the message in his cogbox. He deleted it immediately, but it was too late, he had seen it.

Rot. Decay. He saw it everywhere lately, though it had surrounded him for generations. Even the beautiful flowers of the Spool gardens growing in abundance reminded him of the finiteness of all life—except his own. One day a strong wind would come and the walls of the old cottage would collapse. The wood would break down to its unrecognizable essence. Winter would come and the flowers would die. And the girl in his arms? She, too. She, too.

But he would go on and on. Young, ancient, blessed, cursed. The time was coming, as sure as the sun would one day swallow the Earth in its fiery maw, when every atom of her body, all seven billion billion billion of them, would be scattered and diffused. Nothing would remain but his memory of her, to torment him for eternity.

"What are you thinking about?" she asked. "Your heart is beating very fast."

"I'm wondering if she suspects."

"Of course she suspects. That's why she played that trick on you, told you I was sacked."

"She cannot find out, Georgiana. Where does she think you are?"

"I told her my brother was sick."

"I didn't know you had a brother."

"You don't know many things about me."

"I want to know everything. Your favorite color, what sort of music you like, what you dream about, the secret things you've never told anyone . . ."

"I don't have secrets. Well, just one, and that one you already know."

They could run away. Flee the city. It would be absurdly easy. There were still remote places in the world where they could hide. He could fake a suicide—the master files of all sibyls were erased, their psyche-cards destroyed. They could grow old together and, when they died, his atoms would scatter and mix with hers, like a flock of fourteen billion billion billion birds twirling in the sky.

"Well, there might be one more," she said.

"And that is? Come, you must tell me, Georgiana!"

"You won't like it."

"I don't care. Tell me."

"She will never give you a child."

He was shocked. "How do you know?"

"Because then you could divorce her. She knows the reason you married her. She's known since the beginning. 'He thinks I'm stupid. He thinks I don't know what he *really* wants.'"

The imitation was so dead-on, Beneficent laughed. "That was perfect. You sound just like her, emphasis, inflection, even your expression. Perfect!"

"I have spent my entire life in her company," Georgiana reminded him. "Nearly everyone has known her longer, but there is no one who knows her better. Because I am her persist: What does it matter what I know? And I will tell you one last thing I know, my love—she does not love you."

"Then why doesn't she leave me?"

"You really don't know? The answer is obvious. For the same reason she left so many before you at the altar. She is terrified of failure. Making a mistake, *admitting* she made a mistake— unthinkable! Now that she's taken the plunge, she will *never* admit defeat, and she will never allow you to force defeat upon her. As long as there is no child, you will stay, for it is the only thing you desire!"

"The only thing I *used to* desire."

He urged her onto her back and stared deeply into her eyes.

"Now tell me what *you* desire."

She looked away. "Don't make me say it. Please."

"I will hold you here until you say it, my darling, even if it takes a lifetime."

"A lifetime," she whispered. "Yes."

"A thousand lifetimes."

And she replied, breaking his heart, "A thousand? No."

The hours with her lasted no longer than a blink of her mortal eye. Those apart from her were longer than the age of the universe. He had never worked hard; now he hardly worked at all. He spent his days scheming, scouring the globe for a remote place in which they could hide, researching the law regarding the penalties in case they were caught, inventing plausible scenarios for a fake suicide. It struck him as exceedingly ironic that he served on a committee tasked with finding a new Eden before the sun blew up in their faces.

He managed to keep his plans from Georgiana for some time. He feared she might refuse. Not because she didn't love him, but because she also loved her family. If the truth came out, it would mean certain banishment to the ghetto, a sentence worse than death, their lives cut short by violence and disease and the slow suicide of despair. At some point, of course, he would have to tell her. He just didn't know when. Or how.

And then one day it slipped out.

Courteous was off on a weeklong shopping trip in Buenos Aires with her mother and twelve of her closest sisters. Beneficent gave the staff the week off, and they had the quarters entirely to themselves. For the first time, they had complete privacy. No schedule to keep. No facade to maintain. He had never known such feelings of freedom and release, and he was a man who enjoyed the ultimate freedom. He feasted upon her, day and night. He explored every inch of her lovely terrain. Drunk with love, he let down his guard and confessed his plans.

"You can't be serious," she said.

"I couldn't be more serious, my darling."

"Oh, Beneficent! My wonderful, mad, naïve, immortal lover. You know it could never work."

"But why? We've but to commit to it with all our hearts. The rest is mere logistics."

"It will never happen. You're too afraid of death."

He was stunned. He had expected her to bring up her family. She would refuse to sacrifice them upon the altar of their love.

"You're forgetting who you're talking to," he said.

"All of you are," she went on, speaking of the 3Fs. "It is the fruit you hunger for, the drink you thirst for."

"What you describe isn't fear but its opposite," he said.

"What does death bring, Beneficent?" she asked him.

He found himself shaking. Why was he shaking?

"Annihilation."

"No. It brings beauty."

"That's absurd."

"What is life without death, Beneficent? You of all people can answer that question. A never-ending orgy of emptiness that you stuff with meaningless activity. Everything is disposable, including your relationships—*especially* your relationships. Courteous understands that much at least. She wants to pretend it *matters*, that by killing death you have not killed all hope of love."

"But she doesn't love me. You said so yourself."

"Not *you*, Beneficent. Not love for any particular person. *Love.* There is no meaning, no beauty, no love without death. Don't you understand? That's why you're afraid. You hunger for something that only death can give you."

"No," he said, thinking it over. "I can't put into words why you're wrong, but I can say this: I love you. I know I love you. I will always love you, though I live ten billion years."

Her eyes welled with tears of pity. She touched his face. "That is the effect, not the cause, my love. We both know why you fell in love with a persist, a servant girl, a *finitissium*. I will pass like a spring rain, Beneficent. And you will go on."

He puzzled over her argument for many days. One rainy

afternoon he walked alone in Omniscient's gardens, amid the wildflowers and roses, and wondered how much of their beauty came from the fact that they would fade. Death was the horrible blemish they had managed to wipe clean from the human face. Now perfected, was that face hideous? By making it perfect, had they defiled it past all recognition? Was that what lay behind their obsession with "looks," disposable bodies with which they quickly grew dissatisfied, casting them aside as casually as an old coat? *In another thousand years, we will be loosed from all corporal confinements*, Candid had predicted. There would be nothing outside themselves but a "tin cup" floating in a lightless void. The pleasures of the flesh would exist only inside their own holographic constructs, in every way "real" but in no way actual. The ultimate freedom of life unending. The ultimate prison of unending life.

"Georgiana is right," he said to himself, to the roses and wildflowers, to the rain. "It *is* about death. Not my own, though. No, not mine!"

He turned on his heel and hurried back to his office. He had been looking at the problem from the wrong angle. He'd been selfish. It was not what he was willing to give up, but what was in his power to give. In less than an hour, he had settled upon the basics, the broad outline of a very narrow path that led the way out of his impossible dilemma.

As he told Georgiana: once the heart commits, the rest is logistics.

"I have something for you," he told her a week later. They were cuddling beneath a blanket in the old cottage. The year had grown old, the days cold, gray, and cheerless. Naked, she shivered against him.

He pressed an envelope tied with red ribbon into her hand.

"What is it?" she asked. He had never given her a present before.

"Open it and see."

She pulled out the small blue card and said, "Oh, no, Beneficent."

"Only in case something happens. I'm leaving for my anniversary trip in three days."

It had been his idea to celebrate the five-year mark of his marriage on the moon, the place where his vow to love Courteous for all eternity had been sealed.

"It's a very touching gesture, my love," Georgiana said. "But if something should happen, they will ask why your wife's persist has your psyche-card."

"It isn't my psyche-card."

Her eyes widened in the gloom. "Courteous's?"

"Yours."

She was speechless. What he said made no sense.

"Or it will be," he added nervously. Her silence unnerved him. "Once you've been downloaded onto it."

"You offer a gift that isn't yours to give," she said finally.

"Only if I'm caught."

"No," she said, pressing the card against his fist. "Take it back, Beneficent. I don't want it."

"It doesn't hurt, you know," he murmured, gently stroking her bare arm.

"I won't be downloaded onto a piece of plastic. Besides, what would be the point?"

"I have a friend who works on the Research and Development Committee. There's a program he's working on that can merge two psyches. Well, not a true merger. The donor psyche loses consciousness forever. The receiver retains his personality and memories, but incorporates those of the donor into himself."

"You would...take me into yourself?"

"In a manner of speaking. I don't mean now. I mean...I mean, just in case. When...when the time comes."

"You would make me immortal." Her eyes shone with wonder and love. "Hiding forever inside you."

"I told you once I wanted to know everything."

She threw her arms around his neck and kissed him, again and again, pressing her deliciously warm flesh against the length of his body and, oddly, he swore he could smell muffins.

That evening he and Courteous dined at the Olympus, which no one called the Olympus, but the Top, as in, "Let's meet at the Top." The restaurant sailed a thousand feet above the city, held aloft by a quantum envelope of antigravity, offering spectacular sunset views of the metropolis, where the 3Fs might dine like the gods, far removed from the petty mortal strife of the ghetto. The only thing missing was ambrosia, though the Top made up for it with twelve courses, a wine list unrivaled in the Western Hemisphere, and an after-dinner massage.

"To five wonderful years," Beneficent said, raising his glass.

"No, to persistence," Courteous said.

Persistence? Was that a play on words? He said, "That implies I had a choice whether to pursue you. But the truth is I couldn't give up even if I wanted to."

She set down her glass without drinking. "Then why did you?"

"I didn't. I haven't. What do you mean?"

"What is five years to us, Beneficent?" she demanded. "What is five hundred? Five thousand? A day. An hour. A blink of an eye. Look around you. Everything you see in this room, everything you see outside this room for as far as you can see it, all of it will be gone one day, but you and I will endure."

"Yes," he said. "We will endure."

"Why do we celebrate anniversaries and birthdays anyway? Why do we celebrate any benchmark when time no longer matters?"

"It isn't about time. It's about—"

"It's all about time," she snapped. "Time so abundant it has no value anymore. Once the most precious thing on earth, now the most worthless. It is as if we took a diamond and ground it into a lump of coal."

"My darling, you know where that kind of thinking leads. Remember what they teach us in school: Value the moment. Don't think too much about the future. Don't try to imagine yourself a thousand or ten thousand years from now. Imagine *now*."

"And what do *you* imagine when you imagine *now*, Beneficent?"

"I imagine you being happy."

"And I imagine you being honest."

Their first course arrived, gliding to their table upon a silver tray. Grilled flounder in a light cream sauce. The fish's eye stared back at Beneficent, blank, unblinking, dead.

"Are you enjoying her, Beneficent?" Casually, as if asking how he liked the fish. "Enjoying the *now* of her? Because, you know, the *then* will not be so pretty or exciting. Will you still be enjoying her in two hundred years, when you can hold the entirety of her being in the palm of your hand? She is a diamond now. What will you do when time has ground her to dust?"

He set down his fork and said quietly, "Do you want a divorce?"

She laughed. "Over *Georgiana*? That thing? Really, Beneficent, you're forgetting who you're talking to. You should be punished, I agree, but it would be an odd punishment that gave you exactly what you wanted!"

"You will dismiss her—for real this time."

"That would be a fitting punishment for *her*, but not for you. You were willing to sacrifice your own persist to rescue her, which makes me wonder what you would *not* risk. You might leave me, in any case, and I will not let you leave me, Beneficent. Do you understand? *I will not allow you to leave.*"

"And how will you stop me?"

"You know how I will stop you. What masochistic pleasure does it give you to hear me say it?"

"You'll report her to the CRC. She'll be tried for consorting and put to death."

"You really should thank me, Beneficent," Courteous said with a brilliant, beautiful smile. Her face was flawless, the face of Venus herself, and the most hideous thing Beneficent had ever seen. His stomach turned in revulsion.

"Thank you?" he choked, tasting the oily bile bubbling up the back of his throat.

"For keeping her as my persist. That way you may enjoy her until time is finished with her."

"Hmmm." He tried to appear calm, but his blood roared in his ears, his heart threatened to explode from his chest. "That seems a punishment even odder than divorce."

"Do you think so? She will fade bit by bit before your very eyes, hour by hour, day by day, year by year, the slow torture of time, her malicious lord, Beneficent, though not yours, not yours. *Your* torture will be to watch it—to watch and be powerless to stop it."

"Your punishment presumes that I love her," he pointed out coldly, or at least he hoped he sounded cold. *Hold still, hold still!*

"Your words confirm that you do."

She dismissed the subject then with a wave of her hand. His love for Georgiana held no more significance for her than the sun setting over the smoky horizon. Pretty in its way, spectacular even, but commonplace, an everyday occurrence.

"Now you said on the way to dinner that you had a surprise for me," she said. "Something to do with our anniversary. Tell me, Beneficent. I'm dying to know."

The second course arrived: a tomato bisque and rolls dripping in butter. Courteous tore off a piece of bread and dunked it into the rich soup, and the flesh of the bread turned scarlet.

"It's not something I can tell you," he said. "I must show you."

"I'd prefer that you just tell me."

"And I would prefer that I just show you."

Through the next ten courses, as all light bled from the sky, during the after-dinner massage, lying naked beside her on the white divans, the twinkling lights of the city shining through the glass floor, like, his mind insisted, a million diamonds, and then the shower afterward, lathering her perfect flesh, her quintessential form, he maintained his composure. They chatted about their pending celebration upon the moon. Gossiped about the latest scandal among the First and Foremost Families. Discussed the recent news, fresh from their cogboxes, of the fighting in Africa and the proposed union of the Republic of North America with the United States of Europe into one mega-state, the United Atlantic Republic. They boarded the private shuttle a little after midnight, sated in body and spirit.

"Where are we going?" Courteous asked, for it was clear they were not heading in the right direction. "Beneficent? Where are you taking me?"

"To show you the surprise."

He took her hand. Smiled reassuringly. Kissed her gently. The shuttle dropped into the unloading bay and then it was just a few steps to the tram, and then just a couple of stops to their destination.

"My Transfer boutique?" she asked. "Beneficent, what do you have up your sleeve?"

"Come and see," he said.

The Transfer agent was waiting for them behind the frosted-glass door, smiling, obsequious, giddy with excitement, a coconspirator in Courteous's anniversary surprise. Giggling, the agent led Courteous to the prep room, asked in a very dramatic voice, "Are you ready, darling?" and threw open the door. Courteous gasped.

Lying upon the padded table was the wedding look she had chosen over her mother's objections five years before. Tall with flashing green eyes, because green was Beneficent's favorite color.

"Well, what do you think?" Beneficent asked, beaming. "They've discontinued this look, but I managed to pull a few strings..."

"I found it," the agent said proudly. "Pulled it out of deep, deep storage. The last one!"

Courteous pursed her lips and said, "I don't want it."

"Oh, darling, please say that you will," Beneficent said. "It's perfect, don't you see? A new beginning—or rather, another chance at the same beginning." He turned to the agent. "A moment, please."

When they were alone, he took her hands in his and gazed imploringly into her eyes.

"My old look is waiting in the next room, my love," he whispered. "I'll switch, too, and it will be as if the last five years didn't happen."

"It's too soon," she whispered.

"Your father signed the waivers yesterday. Here." He dropped the documents into her cogbox.

"Father approved?"

"Courteous, you are right. Of course it was stupid—*is* stupid—of me to consort with that girl. It's not the thing I desire, but denied that desire I turned to her…"

"The thing you desire…" she echoed. "What do you desire, Beneficent?"

"You know what I desire. What sadistic pleasure does it give you to hear me say it?"

"You would have me believe you seduced Georgiana because I refused to bear you a child? It is *my* fault?"

"It is the fault of our curse, Courteous. The blemish upon our perfect face."

"Don't talk to me in riddles. I don't care about the waiver; I was never fond of that look."

"But I was," he said. "Courteous, you know there is no choice between her and you. How can there be? You said it yourself. She will pass; you will endure. I pledged to care for you for all eternity, and that I will. No mortal thing can ever come between us—how could it? No matter how much I think it can't or hope it won't, the flower fades, the rain passes, the sun winks out."

He fell to his knees before her, still clinging to her hands.

"Put on the look," he pleaded. "You may switch when we return, but for this, for me, for *us*, put it back on."

"Are you a wise man, Beneficent?" she asked, her eyes filling with tears. "Or are you a fool?"

But she allowed him to lift her onto the empty table. Beneficent summoned the Transfer agent. Handed him Courteous's blue psyche-card for the upload to her master file. Her eyelids fluttered; she was "saved." A final kiss and then, whispered so only he could hear, "I will do it, Beneficent. I will bear your child."

"I know, I know," he whispered back, stroking her perfect cheek. He spoke the obligatory words, *May you wake safely upon that far shore*...He stepped away from the table. The agent took his place. Unobserved, Beneficent removed her card from the slot and inserted an identical card.

She will pass; you will endure.

The agent administered the first shot, the one that stole away her consciousness. As she drifted into oblivion, she kissed Beneficent's hand, and said in a desperate voice, "Tell me it isn't pointless. Tell me that it's beautiful."

"It is not, and it is," he told her, but she had already fallen asleep.

"That was the most romantic thing I've ever seen in my *life*," the agent said, tears streaming down his cheeks. A moment later, his joy turned to confusion: the system was not responding to the Transfer command. His fingers danced over the touch screen, trying to track down the error.

"Is there a problem?" Beneficent asked.

"Incompatible data streams," the agent muttered. "The psyche-card isn't matching the master file..."

"But it matched on the upload," Beneficent said.

"I know! I've seen mismatches before on uploads—a damaged psyche-card or an input error—but never afterward."

He pulled the psyche-card from the slot to examine it for defects. Beneficent left his wife's unconscious body and stood behind the agent, peering over his shoulder.

"It can't be the card," Beneficent pointed out. "As you said, if the card was damaged it wouldn't have uploaded."

He pulled the blue card from the agent's grasp and slid it back into the slot.

"Download her."

"I'm not allowed," the agent protested. "The protocol is quite clear, Mr. Page. In the event of incompatibility with the master file..."

"Overwrite it."

The poor agent was taken aback. "Excuse me?"

"Overwrite the master file."

"Mr. Page, if I overwrite the master file with corrupted or incompatible data, the damage could be irreversible."

"I will take full responsibility."

The agent didn't quite know what to say. The proper procedure was to abort the Transfer, wake Courteous, and run a full system check to track down the error. With any other client, he might refuse, but this was not just any other client. This was a member of the first and foremost family of *all* the First and Foremost Families. Refusal could cost him his livelihood. Or worse, his *life*. But if he *didn't* refuse, if he overwrote the file and something terrible happened, he *still* would be held responsible for ignoring the protocol! He was in an impossible situation. His only prayer was Beneficent's same prayer: that the Transfer took without a hitch.

May you wake safely upon that far shore . . .

The eyelids of Courteous's new look—or her old one, since she had worn it before, on her wedding day—fluttered as the data flooded into its brain, igniting synapses, wiring the irreversible connections that made up the human map, mixing memory and desire, breeding lilacs, as the poet said, out of the dead land.

Both men held their breaths until it was done, and the green eyes came open, the pupils contracting in the sudden onslaught of light. Beneficent leaned over, so his face filled the entirety of her vision, so that all she could see was his reassuring smile.

"Hello, my love."

Her body convulsed upon the table, and Beneficent seized her flailing hands and held them tightly between his own, whispering urgently, "No, no, no. Don't be afraid. It's fine now, perfectly fine, it's done, you're here with me forever now, my precious one, my darling, my true love."

And he covered her new face with kisses, Georgiana's perfect, flawless face.

"Beneficent," Georgiana whispered hoarsely. "What have you done?"

"It is not about what I am willing to give up for you," he told her. "But what I can give *to* you."

Beneficent dropped a message into Georgiana's cogbox: *You are Courteous now! If he suspects anything, we're both doomed!*

"And how are we feeling?" the agent asked Georgiana, patting her bare arm.

"A little light-headed," she murmured, clutching her lover's hand.

"Hmmm-mmmm." The agent was studying her vitals on the monitors. Blood pressure and heart rate slightly elevated, but that was to be expected, brain activity normal. He ran quickly through the obligatory questions. What year was it? Who was the president of the Republic? What was her mother's maiden name? What was her earliest memory? She answered all fifty questions correctly—there was no one who knew her mistress better— hesitating on only one: What is the name of your persist?

The agent had her wiggle her toes, flex her fingers. He tested her reflexes, then helped her down from the table and ran the usual tests on balance, coordination, and basic neurological function. All the while, messages from Beneficent dropped into her cogbox. *You're doing marvelously! It's almost over. Be strong, my love.*

The agent was a bit baffled, but relieved. The Transfer was a complete success. He excused himself and wheeled Courteous into the adjoining room for the second shot, the one which would stop her heart. It could be disconcerting, to say the least, to watch the body you had just a moment before occupied die right before your eyes. In any other age, it would be called murder. In this age, it was called *termination of the redundancy*.

In this particular case, however, it *was* murder.

"You must stop him," Georgiana demanded.

"It's too late," he said.

She shoved him aside and started toward the door, but collapsed before she had taken two steps. A Transfer could be overwhelming, a disorienting existential disconnect, particularly the first and especially if you've had no warning, no chance to prepare yourself mentally. Beneficent lifted her into his arms and carried her back to the table.

"*Why?*" she asked weakly.

"Because I could not suffer you to die."

The Transfer agent returned to their room. Georgiana burst into inconsolable tears, but it was too late: Courteous was already on her way to the incinerator.

At Beneficent's request, the agent gave Georgiana a mild sedative. It was not an uncommon reaction, to grieve the passing of your former look. The *little death*, it was called.

He brought her back to their quarters in the white tower and laid her in his marital bed, drawing the covers over her shivering form, promising her she would feel better in the morning. Dawn was near. He went onto the balcony and waited.

He closed his eyes when the door behind him slid open. The smell of warm muffins. Her delicate scent. What had he said to Courteous? *The flower fades, the rain passes, the sun winks out.* Her cool hands pressed against his closed eyes and her soft voice murmured in his ear.

"Good morning, my love."

He grasped her wrists and stood up. She saw at once something in his expression. Love gives us eyes that see down to the marrow of our lover's bones.

"What is it, Beneficent?" she whispered.

"Nothing," he answered, gazing into the face of Georgiana's redundancy. He realized he was seeing this face for the last time, and his heart ached with a sudden rush of grief. *You're smashing the empty vase,* he told himself sternly, *the flower within endures!* Keeping a firm grip upon her wrists, he swung her toward the railing. She giggled nervously, a little unnerved and confused.

"A trifle," he said. "Not to be considered." And he kissed her one last time before hurling her over the railing.

Two days later, they departed for the moon to celebrate the anniversary of his marriage to his dead wife. It was understandably hard for Georgiana. Not only did she have to adjust to her new body, which can be hard enough, but she had to adjust while pretending to be her former mistress, mourning the untimely and tragic suicide of her persist, who also happened to be herself! Beneficent had justifiable concern for her mental health. The trip could not have come at the more perfect time. Just the two of them, away from all family and familiar surroundings, the ideal opportunity for her to recover and get used to her new body—and the mind-boggling reality of life eternal.

Their room had a glass dome for a ceiling, so when they made love they could see the Earth suspended like a glittering blue diamond in the star-encrusted sky. Their bodies, unfettered from Earth's heavier gravity, strangely insubstantial, as if their bones were hollow. She cried afterward and here even her tears were lighter and rolled as if in slow motion down her perfect cheeks.

"You lied to me," she accused him. "You said you would take me into yourself, not imprison me."

"Imprison you?" He was confused. "But I have freed you, Georgiana."

"You are a murderer, and I am the accessory to the crime."

"More like the motive, I would say."

She struck him across the cheek. The blow fell lightly, though, like her tears.

"What I have done, I have done," he said simply. "It was the only way."

He kissed away her tears. They did not taste the same as her old tears. He pushed that disconcerting thought away. *Not the vase, but the flower!* He looked deeply into her luminous green eyes, the color of the wet grass of Omniscient's garden, and, despite himself, saw a stranger there.

"If you don't like it, you can always choose another," he said.

"Another what?"

"Another look. I don't mind. It isn't the look I love, it's you, Georgiana. Why, you can even switch back if you like."

"Switch back? Switch back into *what*?"

"All they need is a sample from your former self. A strand of hair from your comb, for example. They can grow a replacement." His voice rose with his spirits. Of course! Why hadn't he thought of it before? "A replacement you can replace when it reaches a certain age so you will always be the Georgiana you always were!"

"And how will we explain *that*?" she demanded. "A 3F switching to a replica of her dead persist?"

"An expression of your love for her," he offered rather weakly. "A tribute to her lifelong devotion. A way to bring her back from the grave, as it were..."

"They will think I've lost my mind—or that *Courteous* has lost her mind, I should say. I don't think you understand the magnitude of your crimes, Beneficent. Not only did you murder her, but you have imprisoned me inside her body, inside her *life*, for now, for all *eternity*, I must live inside the fiction that I am her...Oh God, what have you done? Beneficent, what have you done?"

He decided it was a terrible mistake, putting Georgiana into a look Courteous had worn, particularly a look she had worn on her wedding day. It was too much for both of them; it raised his dead wife bodily so she stood between them, casting a blemish over the perfection of their love. Upon their return to New New York, he approached Omniscient and tactfully asked for another waiver, explaining that his favorite daughter had not liked her anniversary present as much as they both thought she would. He brought Georgiana back to the boutique to pick out a new look, something that would remind neither of them of Courteous. But that proved more difficult in practice than in theory, for some part of every sample reminded Georgiana of her dead mistress. The nose. The shape of the ears. The curve of the mouth. He grew frustrated, at one point blurting out, "Well, good God, there's going to be *some* resemblance. We're *human* after all—we can't transfer you into a dog!" They left without making a choice.

That night, he was unable to perform in bed, and he fled onto the balcony, his heart burdened with a sense of profound and utter despair. She followed him without even pausing to throw a robe over her faultless body and, when he saw her naked, he snarled at her to conceal herself. Her nakedness reminded him too much of Courteous, who had lacked all modesty.

"What shall I put on?" she shot back. "My old uniform? Would you like that, Beneficent? I'll put it back on, though it's much too small for me now, and I'll go down to the kitchen and make you some fresh muffins—is that what would please you?"

That was it, he thought. That *must* be it. He brought a few strands of her original hair to the Incubation Facility. While he waited for the new Georgiana to be grown, he spoke to her family and friends, or rather *Courteous's* family and friends, explaining that the reason she had not chosen a new persist was that she could not move past the loss of her old one. She had loved Georgiana like a sister. Well, just a little bit *more* than her actual sisters and half sisters, to be honest. Her psych-profile indicated it might help her through the mourning process if she switched into a replica of the poor girl for a few years. To his astonishment, everyone thought it was a marvelous idea, terribly touching and therapeutic at the same time. Somehow the news leaked, and stories about the plan began to appear in cogboxes and in the televerse. It became a national sensation. Never had the two worlds of 3Fs and *finitissium* collided in such a way. He managed to keep Georgiana out of the public eye, refusing all requests with the excuse that she was too overcome with grief to grant any interviews.

When the time came and she saw her new—that is, her *old*—body lying lifelessly upon the table in the Transfer room, Georgiana was overcome. The prospect did not feel like a return to her. To her it was the pool. It was the delicious fruit. And when she awoke and looked at Beneficent with the same eyes that had adored him in the old cottage, he did not appear the same, as if *he* had switched into a new body and this face before her was the face of a stranger. That night she dissolved into tears when he tried to make love to her. To her, it did not feel like lovemaking.

It felt like rape.

Beneficent assured her these feelings would pass. They had an eternity to grow used to each other again. Privately, he was not so sanguine. He, too, was deeply troubled. She was not, though he tried with every ounce of his ancient being to pretend otherwise, the same sweet persist he had fallen in love with twenty years before. He grew a little desperate, and one night while they made love activated the old program Candid had given him, generating a holographic image in his visual cortex of her former face, identical in every regard to her current one, overlaying the present with the past, and the past jerked and shifted and refused to hold still, and afterward he had a horrible dream of standing in a pool of crystal clear water, dying of thirst but unable to drink.

Her body grew old. She switched into a new one—that is, the *old* one—but the problem, for lack of a better word, persisted. She agreed, for both their sakes, to wear her old uniform when they were alone in their quarters. She even cooked his muffins and brought them to him on the balcony at sunrise. It was on one of these mornings, while she sat across from him silently watching the smoke from the cooking fires curl lazily into the temporal blue, that he looked over at her profile and recoiled in disgust. He set down his half-eaten muffin. It tasted like cardboard.

One day several thousand thereafter, he returned home from work to find her missing. No note. No message from her in his cogbox. He dropped a message into hers; they had reservations that evening at the Top, and he wondered where she might have gone. The message went unanswered. He dropped several more into the family's boxes: *Have you seen Courteous? We have a seven thirty at the Top.* No one had seen her all day. For a brief moment, he was filled with terror. Somehow they'd been found out. The CRC had taken her into custody. Any moment they would appear at his door. Arrest. Conviction. Oblivion. He tore apart their quarters, looking for any clue that might tell him where she had gone. He even dug through the trash, and that's where he found her psyche-card, shredded into a dozen pieces. While he stared with dumb horror at the shards of plastic in his hands, as if it had been waiting for the perfect time to drop, a message appeared in his cogbox:

My love. By the time you receive this . . .

He silenced her voice, flung the useless remains of her memory onto the floor, and raced from the room, into the elevator, onto the launch platform, into the hovercraft, across the darkening landscape, high above the petty mortal strife, his thought a single refrain, *Hold still, hold still!* He did not know where she was, but he knew where he must go.

He leapt out of the craft onto the wet grass of Omniscient's garden and tore down the path, between the undulated heads of a thousand flowers, toward the old cottage, where a crowd had already gathered, including members of the press and agents of the CRC. Courteous's mother and Genuine, her favorite sister, were there too, and when they saw him they pushed the crowd aside, making a path for him to the front door that hung precariously upon a single hinge. He stepped inside, knowing what he would find.

There is no meaning, no beauty, no love . . .

He fell to his knees before her lifeless body and, forgetting himself in that moment, cried out, "Georgiana! Georgiana, do not leave me!"

A hush fell over the onlookers, the witnesses she had arranged for her suicide to prove she was a Sibyl, to ensure her master file would be destroyed. Someone whispered, "He calls her Georgiana!" And another: "He's mad with grief, poor thing."

"Like *her*," a third said. "Didn't you hear? Courteous left a note: she simply could not go on without her darling Georgiana!"

"I *saved* you," Beneficent wailed. "I gave you eternal life! Don't go, Georgiana, don't go!"

But it was too late. She was gone. In truth, she had left him long ago. The moment he stole her mortality from her, his true love was gone.

Courteous had told him that time had no power or meaning anymore, and he prayed she was wrong, that with the passage of enough of it, the pain might fade, the memory of Georgiana would recede after a few thousand years into a sepia-toned, bittersweet, infinitesimally small point in his endless life, a life that expanded like the universe until objects dropped over the cosmic horizon, forever too far away to see. A few thousand years did pass, during which he remarried—several times—fathered hundreds of more children, even rose into the Conduct Review Committee, where he sat at the right hand of Courteous's father. Georgiana's death had bound him to the family as no offspring ever could.

Then a million years. And another. And another. Then a billion and a billion more on top of that. The sun ballooned in the sky, turned an angry red. Temperatures soared. The oceans began to evaporate. Their probes located another planet in a distant galaxy, nearly identical to Earth and much younger, a new home that would last a good six or seven billion years. The basecamp on one of Saturn's moons was completed, their last refuge before the final launch into deep space.

As he settled into his seat for the ferry ride to Titan, next to his new wife—they had been married only six hundred years—Beneficent looked out the window for his last view of Earth, a hellish landscape, lifeless, infused in crimson light, not a leaf or flower or stubborn weed left anywhere (the weeds were the last to die). He took his wife's perfect hand and closed his perfect eyes and sorted through his cogbox until he found the message he had been saving since, it seemed to him, the dawn of time. A time when the world was green and wildflowers bloomed in summer gardens and eternal life had yet to mar the perfect mortal face of his beloved. *My love. By the time you receive this . . .*

He had started to delete it innumerable times over the millennia. It wasn't the words so much that he dreaded to hear—he was sure he knew the gist of them—but the sound of her voice. He wasn't sure he could bear hearing it again. He had kept the message, though, because nothing else of her remained. Those seven billion billion billion atoms had diffused long ago across the vast surface of a dying world.

It seemed fitting to hear her voice now, before that world was gone. So he played the message as the seat beneath him shuddered and he began to rise above the shattered Earth, her voice filling the darkness inside his head, the lightless abyss between his immortal ears:

My love. By the time you receive this I will be gone. I will have taken back the precious thing that was taken from me. Do not grieve for me, beloved. And do not torture yourself with blame and guilt. Death is the yoke that frees me. From boredom and regret and envy, though the worst of these is envy. I am filled with it. I envy every living thing. I envy the trees. I envy the grass. I envy everything that grows or walks or crawls upon the face of the Earth. You would make me perfect by giving me eternal life, but, beloved, don't you understand it was your love that made me immortal? Your love that perfected me? And that it was the very fact that I would one day die that made me precious to you? Now that I am gone, your love will come back to you. It will, I pray, sustain you until the end of time, until the never-ending ends and the last star dies.

Beneficent dropped his reply into the void, where it fell for an eternity, unheard:

Tell me it isn't pointless. Tell me that it's beautiful.

A brilliant and eccentric (read "mad") scientist, aided by a physically grotesque assistant, takes it into his head to play God with dire consequences. *Frankenstein?* No. Nathaniel Hawthorne's "The Birth-Mark," a story published twenty years after Mary Shelley's Gothic masterpiece.

"The Birth-Mark" is certainly not the most famous Hawthorne story, and it doesn't even come close to being one of the best. But it has always appealed to me, despite its painfully dated melodrama and—to our twenty-first-century sensibilities—naïve fear of progress (read "science"). But as a piece of speculative fiction, as an example of the nineteenth century's fear and fascination with scientific progress, and as a tragic romance, I love it. The lead character, a stereotypical mad scientist type, is blinded not by ambition or pride, like many tragic figures—and in the end it isn't science or progress that dooms him—but love.

We look at scientists differently these days, but our fear of technology run amok lingers. It is, perhaps, even more pervasive now than in Hawthorne's day. So I thought it might be fun to take the underlying themes of "The Birth-Mark" and place them squarely in the middle of that fear, in a possible future where that fear might be fully realized. For we suspect—well, deep in our hearts we're pretty damn sure—that it isn't the scientists who are mad . . . it's science itself.

Sirocco

MARGARET STOHL

I. L'Incidente (The Accident)
If they had only found the body, Theo thought, *so much of this unpleasantness could have been avoided.*

Corpses, though unattractive, were a matter of indisputable fact. And facts, especially on the set of a decidedly B horror movie like *The Castle of Otranto*, were hard to come by—as hard to come by as truth, maybe, or your own trailer. Both of which were the topics of the day, especially after all the trouble.

The morning of the accident, now that Theo looked back on it, began like any other day. Or so he had told the *polizia*, when they had questioned him along with the rest of production. Theo had seen nothing, been nowhere near the set when it happened. In point of fact, he'd been sent home in disgrace only the night before, when he'd failed to produce the required twenty-four liters of fake blood for the severed hand shoot, and they'd had to wrap early.

The shame!

But that was last night. Today was a new day, and Theo had busied himself with *due* cappuccino, ordered at the same time and sprinkled with cocoa, alongside a flaky cornetto that only somewhat haphazardly contained pudding or not. These were carried outside, as usual, and eaten in hot silence, also as usual, at the small tables in front of the Jardinieri, the one café with an Internet point. Only the old woman had been there, the one with the still older hands and the ankles that looked like elephant legs, dry and cracking and firmly planted beneath her shapeless black shift. She nodded at Theo, he recalled, but didn't meet his eyes.

"Effing sirocco." That's what Theo had said, he remembered saying it, though aside from the Elephant Woman, there was no one there to tell. He hadn't had breakfast with anyone—not even with his father—since first coming on location to the small southeastern Italian town. The sirocco, the hot, gritty wind blown up from North Africa, had wrapped its fingers around Theo like a fist, carrying off the words the moment they left his mouth. Though he sat no more than fifty yards from the Adriatic Sea, there was no relief. Even the small medusas that lazed in the blue-lit waters had gone into hiding beneath the rocks. This particular wind's hold on Theodore Gray was miserable and total, like so many other things in his life.

What next?

Theo remembered it like flashbacks, like one of the dream sequences his father, Jerome Gray, the American director, *il regista americano,* was so fond of using.

Cue scene.

A boy running through the archway of the Porta Terra, stumbling over the cobblestone path leading into the Old City of Otranto.

Cue sound.

Shouting, in two languages. Italian for the shopkeepers, and English for the *americano.*

Cue crazy.

Frantic gesturing, hands flapping in the air like wings. Theo finally understood the vague message—that something was really, truly wrong. That something had finally *happened*.

The waitress finally tried to explain it to him, herself. "*Gli americani ottusi! Gli idioti di* Hollywood! *Hanno gettato una casa in mare!*"

Theo understood "stupid Americans"—he'd heard it often enough—and something about Hollywood, probably and deservedly equally stupid.

But that last part—tossing a house into the sea? Or a gelato into the house of sea? His Rosetta Stone Italian must be failing him.

The Elephant Woman shook her head, finally pointing up the hill toward the center of the Old City. When she spoke, her ivory teeth—capped in gold but rotting black—took on the air of some sort of ancient, evil treasure. "Go, boy. Castello Aragonese. There is trouble. *Americano* trouble." As if on cue, a gust of wind knocked a café table over, sending it rolling into the stone street, while a large black bird circled overhead, squawking. It was amazing, really, like a scene from a movie—possibly even the movie they had come to Otranto to shoot, themselves.

A black feather came floating down from the sky, and the Elephant Woman crossed herself. "*Il falco, un cattivo presagio.*"

"*Il falco?* The falcon?" Theo put down his cup.

"*Cattivo presagio,*" she repeated. "You say, *Inglese*, dark—dark omen." She kept speaking, but Theo couldn't hear, as the bells of the *cattedrale* had begun to chime.

Nine o'clock, on the hour.

After the bells faded into silence, only the sound of screaming hung in the air.

A *woman*.

Theo flinched.

Not just any woman.

A woman so famous for that particular scream, she'd made a career spanning forty years out of it. Pippa Lords-Stewart, star of stage and screen. Eclipsed only by Her Majesty's Own Sir Manfred Lords, Pippa's former husband and present costar of their current project—the first time they'd shared the screen in the decade since their infamous marriage more infamously ended. All of which meant more paparazzi than Theo had ever seen on one of his father's sets, which meant more coverage, which meant more money for the budget—or any money at all, as the case may be. Truthfully, Pippa and Sir Manny and their exquisitely rotten relationship—the sheer number of drinks either could toss at any given dinner went into the double digits—were the only reason Jerome Gray had managed to secure some slightly shady Bulgarian film financing at the last minute, once Germany had pulled out.

Nobody hated each other as well—or as wealthily—as they did.

But the woman could also scream like no one else, and that was Pippa screaming, Theo was sure of it. After the scene they'd shot on the roof of the Castello Aragonese last night—the one where Pippa, the lady of the castle, discovers the lifeless body of her son, who has been killed by a falling suit of armor—well, after seventeen takes, even a lowly production assistant like Theo would know that particular scream anywhere. A single close-up of the disembodied hand still wearing bloody armor had taken nearly an hour. "It's a freaking haunted castle. Get me more blood," his father had bellowed, between every take.

Twenty-four liters.

When it came to Jerome Gray and blood, there was never enough.

The only problem was, they weren't filming now—and yet Pippa was still screaming.

That one deduction sent Theo running through the Porta Terra, stumbling over the cobblestones like the shouting boy had before him, like the wind. He wound his way up through the alleyways of the Old City, past the shops, past the walls of weathered leather sandals and dried herbs and Puglian wine and ceramic bowls painted with olives or sailboats—past the clay tarantulas, the sign of the tarantella still danced in Salento—past the *cattedrale* itself, with the tombs and the crypts and the frescoes and the mosaic floor that looked as if it were built by a mad, drunk priest—until the Castello came into sight.

The Castello Aragonese, also known to production as the Castle of Otranto, and as thus the setting of his father's film of the same name, was the reason they were here for the hottest summer of Theo's seventeen years. His father had insisted a sound stage in Burbank wouldn't do, and Pippa agreed on this location when she'd heard Helen Mirren had bought a *masseria* in Puglia—which sounded very glamorous to Pippa, until she realized the word only meant "farmhouse," mosquitos and rocks and all.

And then there was the small matter of the castle itself, in reality. In hot, dusty reality. Squat and stone, the color of a carved brown potato and about as glamorous looking, it was perhaps not so much Gothic as medieval, and not so much preserved as abandoned. As far as security measures, there was only one key to the place, and only one surly Italian fellow (in the same dirty black rocker T-shirt, with the words "Pink Floyd" embossed in gold) named Dante allowed to wield it. Dante showed up most mornings, after he'd had a good two or three small coffees, to unchain the front gate and twist open the ancient iron bars. Dante locked the Castello again when he left for lunch and *sieste*—and since his *sieste* could sometimes last all the way until dinner, Jerome Gray had decided early on that production had no choice but to let themselves be locked in along with the gate. It had been Theo's job, then, to get the bar across the piazza to slide panini between the bars in the afternoons. Such was the glamour of life in the Castello.

Then came the transformation. The crew had spent hours adding carved foam pieces to every dusty wall, gluing silk cobwebs and synthetic ivy to every naturally webby, overgrown corner. The very real cannonballs that were still lodged throughout the place were sprayed a gleaming black over their disappointingly tan stone color, only to be scrubbed tan again when the scene had been wrapped. Stone the color of stone. Dust the color of dust. Mold the color of mold—and none of it the kind you see in the movies—that was the Castello. Really, Theo found it hard to imagine a novel had ever been written about the place at all.

A row of trailers had been set down in what once was the surrounding moat, now the home of wild fruit trees and tall grasses. The wind blew through them, rattling the grasses like maracas, sending the trailers shaking on their wheels. Still more trailers squatted along the sea wall behind the castle, where the battlements enclosing the town gave way to the rocky ocean itself. There was the props trailer, and the costume trailer. There was his father's trailer, where he watched the dailies and came out shouting into his headset (or into his water bottle, which had held many liquids though never, apparently, water) for the rest of the afternoon. There was Pippa's trailer, the one she shared with Sullen Matilda, her exceptionally dour assistant, who was only ever known to smile at Theo—a fact Theo found less not more encouraging. There was Sir Manny's trailer, and next to it, the one belonging to his equally sullen on-screen son, Conrad

James—that Conrad James, teen werewolf of the small screen and the oiled chest. (Oiled and shaved, as was pro forma for a twenty-six-year-old playing a teen wolf on a nonlupine "off" day.)

Only—

Theo stopped in his tracks, panting.

Only there wasn't Connie's trailer. Not where it was supposed to be.

There wasn't anything, only a gap in the row and a patch of blue-green sea.

And a line of production assistants as expendable as Theo himself, talking in clusters of tattoos and hipster bangs and cut-off jean shorts, smoking. "*—what with the wind, you couldn't hear a thing—*"

And Sir Manfred, wearing only half a head of hair extensions, screaming into a walkie-talkie, smoking. "*—it could have been me—*"

And Jerome Gray, Theo's father, talking to the *polizia* with both hands, smoking. "*—wind insurance? Who the hell needs wind insurance—*"

And Sullen Matilda, texting and smoking. "*—fofmfgf—*"

And Pippa, screaming and smoking. "Connie—Connie—."

That scream.

Conrad James.

Where was Connie?

By the time Theo reached the sea wall, he could see only the remnants of a white trailer, smashed upon the rocks a hundred feet below. A piece of white tin bobbed in the tides. A white door, with a red star upon it.

Conrad's trailer.

When Theo looked closer, he could see it was dripping red, staining the water and rocks beneath, just like the severed hand in the scene at the Castello the night before.

Less than a liter, by the look of it.

Effing movies.

There was no body, though. No body, and no Connie. Only red water and rocks, and a scattering of odd-looking black feathers, bobbing in the current.

That was the first problem.

That was how it all began.

II. La Maladizione (The Curse)

Within the hour, word had gotten out, and calls from the States came flooding in.

Production shut down. The cast sequestered themselves inside the small, warm darkness of the Bar Il Castello across the way, too afraid to enter their own trailers.

By lunchtime, the paparazzi posted blurry photos of the wreckage online at TopPop Italia.

By *sieste*, the *polizia* swarmed the Castello. The normally chained gates were taped off, surrounded by red-and-white-striped cones. There was no way in or out—and crowds of curious Italian tourists stood in the piazza, looking up at the large, stone potato-castle in front of them, wondering what all the fuss was about. Farther back, crowds of paparazzi sharpened their long, long lenses like so many teeth, like antennae.

An hour after that, the Guardia Costiera began dredging the harbor. It was the greatest spectacle Otranto had seen since plumbing first came to the region.

Bigger, even.

Inside the Castello bar, the cast put on a different sort of show, even if no one but Theo and the bartender were there to see it. "I've a mind to call the British ambassador. Those are my personal possessions. It's a matter of security." Sir Manny was unhappy because his cell phone was trapped inside the Castello, in the leather saddlebag he liked to sling over his director's chair.

"Security? Don't you mean insecurity?" Pippa rolled her eyes, tightening her clutch on her Coca-Cola Light. Theo wondered if she was going to throw it at him.

"Who's the one complaining about the paps getting their bad side up online, eh, darling?" Sir Manny narrowed his eyes.

Sullen Matilda glared back at him, sitting as she was between them. If drinks were thrown, she'd be the first casualty.

Theo decided not to wait to find out. Instead, he slipped outside, moving quickly past the production assistants who stood guard at the doorway.

He'd had enough drama for one morning.

It wasn't until Theo made his way to the shadows behind his father's trailer that he heard the shouting coming from inside.

"Don't answer that. Blocked number—that's Bulgaria, and I got nothing to say to Bulgaria." His father sounded frantic, and the phone only kept buzzing.

"Jerry. It's online already. Bulgaria knows. New York knows. LA probably knows." Diego, the Italian dialogue coach, answered in perfect English.

"What is there to know? If there's no body, there's no body. It can't be a murder if no one was murdered." His father sounded panicked.

"Tell that to the *polizia*, Jerry. They're shutting us down. You know that's what comes next." Diego was from Malie, the next town over, which meant he was the only person who knew anything about what the police or the town magistrates or the Italian film commission was actually going to do at any given time. "You know what they think, the whole castle's cursed. We shouldn't have come here. They shouldn't have let us film here, no matter how many euros crossed hands."

"You're acting like we bribed them." Jerome was shrill—the phones were still ringing.

"Because we did." Diego sounded relaxed. "You did, anyway."

"It's called business. I'm not in the mafia. And there's no curse, Diego. Unless you're talking about that fakakta plumbing."

Theo took a breath, climbing the steps to the trailer door. No one answered his knock, so he pushed his way inside, where his father and Diego sat at a small table, a bottle of some kind of gold-colored liquor between them.

"Jerome," Theo said, clearing his throat. He always called his father by his first name on set. Anything else, the director maintained, would have been weird. Theo thought this was weird, but his father ignored him—just as he did now.

Diego nodded at Theo, but he didn't stop talking. "You don't think it's cursed, Jerry, and I don't think it. But you have to ask— why have they kept the place closed down, all these years?"

Jerome poured himself another yellow drink. "Because it's Italy. Because no one got around to unlocking it. Why the hell do I care, so long as it's open tomorrow."

Diego shook his head. "No, Jerry. Because it's in the book. The book is about the castle—this cursed castle. And the curse is all anyone has on their mind since Connie..." His words trailed off.

"What curse?" The moment Theo said the words, his father looked at him like he'd popped some sort of peculiar bubble.

Diego pushed a tattered book toward Theo. "Hubris. Vanity.

Thinking the studio and our distributors are more important than a thousand years of local history."

Theo stared at the book. "That's all in this book?" The cracking black leather cover was embossed with fine gold print. He hadn't seen it in the trailer before. His father didn't usually read books, especially books as old as this one. *The Castle of Otranto*, by Horace Walpole. That's what the gold letters said, on the cover.

"Not in so many words," said Diego. "But see for yourself. The story of the castle is really the story of losing the castle."

Theo opened it to where one particular passage was underlined in red ink on the ivory page. He began to read.

"That the castle and lordship of Otranto should pass from the present family, whenever the real owner should be grown too large to inhabit it—"

"Too large?" Theo looked up, confused. "What does that mean?"

"It means, we're going to be driven out of the castle," Diego said, tapping the book.

"It doesn't say that." Jerome shoved the book out of Theo's hands.

"Why not? We're the largest cast and crew ever to come to Otranto," Diego offered unhelpfully.

"More like, it means the hundred thousand large we paid to use this dump wasn't large enough," snorted Jerome. "So now someone's screwing with us."

"Or the size of your ego," said Theo, looking at his father. "Extra-large."

Silence.

"I mean, our egos. You know. *Hollyweird*." Theo shoved the book away, but the damage had been done. It didn't happen very often, but on occasion his father heard him. So Theo kept talking. "Besides, if someone wants to start tossing people off cliffs—I mean, who's even the lord of the castle now, anyway?"

Jerome sighed. "I'd say it depends on how you look at it. I think the city owns the castle, but a threat's a threat. It could be meant for any one of us. Sir Manfred—he's literally a lord. Pippa—she's a lady."

"Not much of one," Theo pointed out.

Jerome smiled, softening toward his son. "Technically, anyway. And there's me."

"You are the boss man." Diego nodded. "Lord of the set."

"And Dante," Theo suggested, trying not to roll his eyes at Diego.

"Who?" Jerome furrowed his brow. He was still caught up in reconsidering his own lordly status, Theo imagined.

Diego sighed. "Dante. You know. The poor schmoe with the castle key."

"Who?" Jerome looked at him blankly.

Theo tried to help. "The guy with the key. He brings you your lunch, like, every day? His name's Dante."

"Sure. Dante, Diego, whatever." Jerome shrugged. Diego looked insulted. Theo tried not to laugh, but the obvious point hung in the air between them.

When it came to everyone involved with *The Castle of Otranto*, the movie—how could heads get any bigger?

More to the point, who *wouldn't* want to push any one of them off a cliff?

Theo shivered.

Jerome's phone buzzed again, and he picked it up. "Now fakakta Bulgaria is texting me. He's here."

"Here, here?" Now even Diego looked stressed.

"The cab stand, at Porta Terra." Jerome dropped the phone, pouring himself a tall, yellow drink. "Do me a favor, will you, Theo? Go get him."

Of course Theo would. He was a lowly PA. He'd have to do whatever Jerome said, even if he wasn't his father.

Which was how Theodore Gray came to meet Bulgaria for himself. Bulgaria—and the beautiful Isabella.

Because nobody told him Bulgaria had a daughter.

When Theo reached the Porta Terra, there was exactly one cab waiting at the stand—not a surprise, really, since there was exactly one cab company in all of Otranto—across from the pizza restaurant. This was only one of the reasons you ignored the people who said there was no tipping in Italy; you pissed off the one cab company in town, and you were never going to the airport again. Theo's father had learned that the hard way, which was why Diego had now been made to hire a car of his own.

This afternoon, the cab driver looked irritated, smoking while the engine ran. In the back, a man sat on the edge of his seat, his short, gray-suited legs dangling out the side. They didn't reach the ground.

Bulgaria.

A girl sat on a nearby bench, Indian-style, reading a book. An army backpack sat on the bench next to her. She was all kinds of hanging hair—in her face, down her back. It didn't seem to bother her; she blew the dark strands out of her face only when the wind blew them directly into her eyes.

Theo cleared his throat. "Hello?"

No response.

Neither the man nor the girl seemed to be in any kind of hurry, which apparently made the taxi driver rev the car's engine even more.

Theo took a tentative step closer. "Excuse me?" The girl still didn't look up. Neither did the man. Instead, he growled into the phone. "BS. It's all BS."

Theo tried again. "Sir?"

The man barked, "Don't tell me this isn't Jerome Gray playing the odds. He knows he has a crap production, and he's doing everything he can to shut it down and cash out before he hangs his own cash out on the line."

The girl finally looked up from her book and scowled. "Dad. Dad!" She turned to look at Theo. "Sorry. He's kind of a jerk. But I guess you're probably picking that up on your own."

"Me too."

"You're a jerk?"

"Yeah. No. My dad. I'm Theo."

"Isabella. Daughter of Jerk."

"Likewise. We must be related."

"Hope not."

The taxi driver revved the engine reproachfully.

Theo smiled, and Isabella smiled back, and he didn't say anything after that. He was too busy staring at what was, however improbably, the most beautiful creature he'd seen in seventeen years, let alone the last seven weeks.

Long black hair hung in straight lines—spiky black bangs—over pale skin and peach-colored lips. Strangely light eyes. Dark everything else.

She was like a Venus, Theo thought. She could have been in a thousand movies; she could have been a model...

"I hate this shit," she said, squirming uncomfortably.

In the front seat, the restless driver was squirming even more.

Theo was positively smitten. It was as if somewhere offscreen, rogue cherubs were staking him with every arrow in the prop trailer.

The short man in the taxi shouted louder, unaware of the relative significance of the moment. "But it's not his cash out there, it's mine—"

Theo and Isabella rolled their eyes, right at the very same moment. Friendships had been born for less, Theo thought.

Friendships, or something more.

The driver began to honk, one long blast after another. They'd been sitting at the Porta Terra for nearly a quarter of an hour now; enough was enough.

Then the man slid out of the car and onto the hot black pavement. He motioned to Theo. "Can you pay the guy, kid? Don't have anything smaller than a hundy—" He waved a fistful of euros in Theo's face.

Theo scavenged in his pocket, until he handed over every last euro to the angry driver. Bulgaria wouldn't be getting a cab to the airport anytime soon. Theo didn't care. It was funny. At least, he hoped Isabella thought so.

She did.

They laughed about it all the way back to the Palazzo Papaleo, the only hotel in town, Isabella hitching her backpack easily over her shoulder, while her father slipped on the hot stones in his patent leather loafers.

Connie may be missing, but the universe was kind, and all was right in the world.

"Are you crying?" Isabella leaned toward Theo, curiously, the moment the cobblestoned piazza of the *cattedrale* bumped into sight, just across from the hotel.

"It's the stupid sirocco; it's blown something into my eyes." Theo rubbed his sleeve into his eyelid. "Everything's fine, see?"

"I love the wind. It changes everything," Isabella said, pulling his sleeve away from his face. Then she smiled and ran toward the hotel, and Theo knew right then everything really would be all right.

Only the fact of the wind promised otherwise.

III. L'Investigazione (The Investigation)

The postcard-perfect sunset came and went, all peach and blue and geraniums and wrought iron and fuzzy orange stripes as it should be, before anyone came to meet Theo on the roof of the hotel.

He waited for Isabella, but it was only his father who finally appeared. It was disappointing, of course, but Theo was used to disappointment.

Jerome Gray slid into the chair across the table from Theo. He poured himself a glass of wine from the communal jug on the table—the sort Theo knew had been filled with basically a gas pump nozzle from the working vineyard nearest Galatina— without saying a word.

"So. Bulgaria." Jerome played with the bottom of his glass.

"Yeah?" Theo didn't look at his father.

"It would be helpful if you could entertain the daughter. Bulgaria and I, we have some tough conversations. Financials, that kind of thing."

Theo nodded.

"Because Bulgaria is a total dickwad," his father added. *He* couldn't let it go.

"Got it." *Takes one to know one.* So Theo thought. But still, he said nothing.

Jerome Gray drained his glass.

By the time Isabella and her father appeared at the rooftop restaurant of the hotel, the first jug was empty, and Theo's father was on his best behavior.

The wine had been flowing for hours. *Hours.* Better than the conversation, at least between the dickwads. Theo sighed. Though he had noticed his father not picking up his phone when it buzzed this time, either. "It's New York," Jerome had said. "I have nothing to say to New York, right?" Bulgaria had agreed. After that, Theo hadn't bothered listening.

Entertain her. That was what his father had said.

Entertain me. That was what the peach lips said. She didn't often touch her wineglass—neither one of them had needed to—but still, the dark red liquid reminded Theo of the red on the splintered trailer doors, dashed on the rocks of the harbor. He didn't feel sad, though. Not for Connie, not this time.

He was exhilarated.

Isabella smiled at him, sort of a smirk, while they both ignored the conversation around them.

"Do you even know what they're talking about?" She leaned forward, breathing the heady scent of muscat grape into his face. Theo felt like he was going to pass out.

"The movie, probably. Sixty million American dollars, most likely. All blown over the side of a cliff, as far as we know."

"All ruined by one dead guy." The words sounded sweet, any words would have. Even those.

"Exactly. At least, missing."

I love you. I mean, I think I love you. I'm going to love you. You're the most beautiful girl in the world.

"What?" She looked amused.

"Nothing." Theo looked at his plate of pasta, shaped like clumsy ears.

"Did you say something?"

"No." Theo shrugged. "Did you hear something?"

"I guess not."

"Do you want to get out of here?"

"Is that even a question?"

They were gone before either of their fathers noticed.

Theo first took Isabella's hand in the alley leading toward the Cattedrale di Otranto. Her fingers were cold and calm, while he felt warm and worried.

"It's beautiful," she breathed.

"You should see the inside. The mosaic floor. It's actually quite insane. Like, Zeus and Hera meet Adam and Eve insane." Theo smiled. "At least, insane by a monk's standards."

"Monks have very high standards." Isabella smiled back at him. "And you sound like you're pitching a movie."

Theo winced. "Speaking of which. Why are you here, I mean, with your father?"

"He always makes me meet him when he comes to Italy. I'm north of here, up in Viterbo for the year. My junior year. Intensive Latin and Italian. School Year Abroad."

"College?"

"High school." Theo felt a rush of relief; they were the same age, after all.

"I thought you guys were from Bulgaria? I mean, that's your dad, right?"

She shook her head. "We moved there when I was thirteen. Low-budget movie capital of the world. Before that it was strictly California. Sorry to disappoint you. I'm nothing too exotic."

I'm not disappointed. He didn't say it, but he realized it was true.

"Me, either."

They turned the corner and Theo found himself staring at a green wooden door. He stopped short. "That's Connie's place."

"Conrad? The one with the trailer that blew into the ocean? The dead guy?"

"Technically, he's missing. But yeah, you know. It's pretty crazy. The whole sirocco thing." Talking about it made Theo more uncomfortable than he wanted to admit. He was only seventeen; he'd never actually known a dead person until now.

Or missing, he reminded himself.

"If the guy's really dead, where are all the cops? Why isn't the place, like, roped off or something?" She looked excited.

"They think he was in his trailer, but they can't be sure. It's not like actors really live in their trailers, not when they're not on set. This is where Connie spends the nights—only no one's supposed to know that." Theo sighed. "When he's not in rehab, he isn't allowed to live on his own. It's part of his probation."

"What? What does that mean?"

"Let's just say, he's not the easiest person to insure. But when he showed up in town, he wouldn't stay where he was supposed to."

"And where was that?"

"With me. And my dad. On the other side of the *cattedrale.* But Connie had a fit, he wouldn't even move his bags in. We had to get him his own place. Off the books." Theo shifted, uncomfortably. "You probably shouldn't tell anyone."

"Let's check it out. Maybe he's here. Maybe he just passed out or something." Isabella's eyes gleamed at the idea.

"He didn't. My dad sent Diego over, first thing."

"Maybe Diego didn't look carefully enough." She started up the steps.

"Don't. We shouldn't." Theo didn't know why she'd even want to, but then somehow her wanting to made him want to, though he didn't—it was all so very confusing. "I mean, why?"

"Why not? Because he's a movie star. Because he's dead."

Keep her busy. Entertain her. That's what he'd said, his father.

"Okay. Yes. I guess. Just for a second."

They made their way up the rest of the stone steps—hundreds of years worn in the center, like everything else in Otranto—past the pots full of red geraniums. Conrad's door—painted a dark green, just like the exterior one—was closed, but when Theo pushed on it, it opened with a creak.

"Conrad?" Theo's voice sounded strained, like he was reading a line of dialogue from a particularly haunted scene. The one right before the hero gets the ax, he thought.

"No one's there," Isabella whispered.

"Maybe we should go." Theo tried not to sound relieved.

A woman poked her head out the door across the way. *"Buona sera—"*

It was her, the Elephant Woman. Theo's breakfast companion of many weeks now, the harbinger of all of Otranto's bad omens and *americano* doom.

And apparently, Connie's landlord.

"We really shouldn't be in here."

Theo looked uncomfortably around the small, square room—all white plaster walls and terra-cotta-tiled floors. He also tried not to look at the small wooden cross, nailed up over the bed, probably because of the heaps of unidentifiably illegal substances piled beneath it.

"Relax," said Isabella, picking up one of the plastic bags that composed Connie's stash. "What is this? Is that—a *beet*?"

"I don't know. Maybe a turnip? I wouldn't put it past him. He'd smoke Lindsay Lohan if you lit her on fire."

Isabella dropped the bag and walked outside to the portico. The harbor beyond the stone balcony looked only like the dark absence of lights; dated disco music floated over the water, from the dance club at the beach across the way.

Theo crept out after her. The balcony doors were wedged open, though every few minutes or so the wind blew them loose, slamming them into their wooden frames with a bang so startlingly loud, it sounded as if someone had been shot—no matter how many times you heard it. "It's just the wind," Theo said, though he didn't know who it was he was reassuring, not exactly.

"Right. Tell that to Connie. Poor guy." She laughed, but Theo didn't think it was so funny. Not when the poor guy's trailer was still in a thousand splintery pieces on the harbor rocks.

Had it been the wind? Really? Trailers were pretty heavy.

Isabella only kicked a wine bottle out of the way as she moved back to the door. "Poor, classy guy."

Theo picked the bottle up, righting it on the table inside the door. He followed her into the empty kitchen, where a green-and-white-checked oilcloth covered a square table. There was only a silver espresso kettle on the tiny stove, though Theo had gotten Connie coffee enough times to seriously doubt he'd ever managed to make it himself. He couldn't even manage to put sweetener in, not on his own.

"All right. We've seen enough. Let's get out of here."

Isabella hitched her bag more tightly to her shoulder. "Seriously? You know actors. This Connie guy's either dead—in which case he doesn't mind—or he's not—in which case he's probably such a power tool, you'd want to annoy him."

"Really?" Theo didn't. In fact, he was getting increasingly uncomfortable with the whole conversation.

"You have no idea." Isabella pointed to something beneath the bed. "Wait. Jackpot."

"His stash?"

"No. His laptop."

There it was, poking just one steel-cased corner out from under the crumpled laundry and the gossip magazines—mostly starring Connie himself.

Theo stepped between her and the bed. "Hold on. You can't just open his computer. He'll have it password protected. Some kind of alarm probably goes off at CAA every time you open that thing."

"Seriously? Are you always this much of a stiff?" She slid past him, yanking the laptop out from under the bed and flopping down next to it.

She flipped open the lid. "Okay. Password. Any ideas?"

"No. We're not doing this."

She ignored him. "It's not douchebag. So I'm stumped."

"Isabella." Theo gave up.

"It's not Spartacus, either. No intensive Latin here." She grinned.

Theo looked at the screen. "Some pet name for his girlfriend? Or his grandma. Or his car. Or maybe his—"

"Don't say it." Isabella shoved his shoulder.

"I was going to say dog." Theo shoved her back.

Isabella tapped her chin. "Or what about the name of his last movie? What was that?"

Theo was impressed. "Seriously? You really have to ask?"

"Hey, I've been in Italy, remember?" Isabella blushed. "And besides, I'm not really into movies."

"Just movie stars?" Theo raised an eyebrow.

"Okay. I'm into movies. I'm just not into douchebag movies."

Theo angled the keyboard in his direction and slowly began to type into the password box.

"TEEN_HAIRWOLF."

She groaned. "Really? That's even worse than I thought."

"Three hundred million at the box office. Bet you a hundred bucks, there's no way a guy like Connie would have wanted to type anything else."

The glowing white prompt flashed no more than three times before they found themselves staring at Connie's mailbox.

"I don't believe it. We're in."

Theo sprang up off the bed, pacing around the room. He didn't know what to do with himself. "We can't look at a dead guy's mail. Even if he's not a *dead* dead guy. Isn't that mail fraud or something? As in, a federal offense?"

Isabella clicked on the INBOX, nodding. "Probably worse than that, since we're not even in the country."

Theo tried not to look at the screen, but he couldn't seem to help himself. "Right. There might be all sorts of Italian laws."

Isabella clicked on NEW MAIL. "Except Italians don't have laws. They don't even bother to put money in their *Bancomats* on the weekend." She looked up. "Are you going to stop me or not?"

BANG—

The wind slammed the balcony door shut, so hard the walls

shook. Theo looked out at the moon in the glass of the door. It shone round and high, almost like in the *Teen Hairwolf* posters.

How many secrets could a guy like that have, anyway?

And he was missing, wasn't he?

It wasn't like the police weren't going to take all this stuff for themselves and sell it to the paparazzi, as soon as they found their way to Connie's apartment. Where he really lived.

Had lived.

It was only a matter of hours, really.

Minutes, even.

"Maybe just for a second."

One second turned into one hour. The Internet being what it was. The Internet, and secrets. .

Connie, it turned out, led a strangely uninteresting life online, at least for a minor movie star slash major drug addict.

The duller the e-mail, the more quickly Theo and Isabella flew through them—and the more they wanted to read. There was something gripping about every dull interaction with every dull ex-girlfriend, at least when they were reading them through the digital eyes of one possibly dead former star.

It was Theo who stopped everything.

All it took was one click on a particularly dull-looking attachment in an e-mail from Connie's agent at CAA.

Theo scrolled down the screen. "Wait a second. Look—that looks like some kind of insurance document."

"It is. It's a policy. See that word, right there. *Polizza. Polizza de Assicurazione.*" Isabella looked up at him. "It's absolutely an insurance policy."

Theo frowned. "Well, I guess the good news is that Connie

finally got insured. They were trying to get him bonded for, like, forever."

Isabella looked at him sideways. "What's the bad news?"

"Well, it sort of gives a motivation for somebody to kill him—I mean, doesn't it?" Theo didn't want to be the one to say it, but there. He had.

"You mean it's an insurance scam—like in the movies?" Theo didn't know why Isabella sounded so chipper about the whole thing.

"Yeah, except in the movies you usually find out they faked their own death. Instead of, you know, dying."

Isabella didn't respond. She just kept reading.

Theo tried again. "Oh my god. It's *Law & Order: Otranto*."

"Shh." Isabella quieted him. It seemed to Theo that she couldn't take her eyes off the screen.

"Isabella? You there?"

Only very slowly did she finally turn to Theo. "Why would a person like Connie want to fake his own death? He was making a lot of money just being Connie—wasn't he?"

Theo shrugged. "No question, that guy has a lot of outstanding debts. Probably buying smack from the Italian mafia, for all we know."

Isabella looked puzzled. "But he's not the beneficiary. Connie. He wasn't going to make any money from disappearing, not right now."

"So, maybe he's getting paid off. The Bulgarians might have had something to say about it..." Theo looked at her, embarrassed.

"Say it. You're talking about my father."

"I didn't say that."

"That's exactly what you said. And look, my Italian's not perfect, but that word there"—she pointed to a small line at the bottom of the screen—"*beneficario della politica.* The beneficiaries."

All Theo could see were two names, and he knew them both. He knew she did, too, but he left it to her to read them.

His heart was pounding in his ears—also like a *Law & Order: Otranto* episode. His heart was pounding, and all his witty comments blew out the window with the wind, toward the sea.

So the room stayed quiet, as long as neither one of them could think what to say next.

Because of the two names.

Two scanned signatures, on the dotted line.

The director, for one.

And the Bulgarian.

"It might not be them. I mean. They may not be involved." Theo said the words—finally, sadly, not even believing them himself.

"Or they might not *both* be involved." Isabella stood up, moving to the far window.

"What's that supposed to mean?" Theo bristled, in spite of everything.

She took a breath. "My father's a businessman. Your father's a film director. If someone were to sabotage his own production— well, one of those would have a lot better idea how to go about it than the other."

Theo ran his fingers through his spiky brown hair. "I can't believe you're saying that. I can't believe you're accusing the man. He's my father."

She looked like she wanted to slap him. "I can't believe you're *defending* him. What does that say about *my* father?"

Theo was incredulous. "I thought you hated your father?"

Isabella was furious. "I think you're confusing him with yours."

There it was.

Family ties had bound and gagged them both.

The room contracted around them with the impasse. They couldn't look at each other, but they couldn't seem to look away. The small space had only grown hotter and hotter with two more bodies and badly adapted technology—the outlet in the wall was, after all, practically smoking—inside.

This particular sirocco might as well be coming from inside the windows, rather than from the night sky beyond.

Then Theo caught something else. "Look at the e-mail attached to the policy. The time stamp. It's today. Why would someone send an e-mail about an insurance policy to a dead man?"

Isabella looked down at the screen, over his shoulder. "Unless he was a not-dead dead man?"

"According to the message, they're meeting tonight at the taxi stand."

She sniffed. "Of course they are. That's where your father meets people."

He raised an eyebrow. "People like your father, you mean." But the wheels were turning in Theo's head. "Fine. I'll go see for myself."

She flung her fingers into the air, just like an Italian, Theo thought. The gesture was endearing, even though she herself was—at this particular moment—not.

"What, you're going to march up to a criminal at an illicit rendezvous and demand an explanation?"

He shrugged. "Give me a little credit. I'm not going to march anywhere. Just spy. You can see the taxi stand from the piazza."

Isabella looked skeptical. "Not at night."

"Yes. From the roof of the Castello, you can. It's at the top of the hill—you can see the whole town from there."

"Fine."

"Fine."

"Midnight. That's what it says."

"Midnight."

"See you then."

"Same here."

They stood there in the dark heat, until Theo switched off the computer and yanked the plug out of the adapter in the wall.

When he looked back up, Isabella was gone.

The wind slammed the door, louder than a shot, faster than a bullet. It was enough to drive a normal person crazy.

This time, Theo didn't so much as flinch.

IV. *Il Castello (The Castle)*

Even the stones were hot beneath Theo's feet in the darkness. He could feel himself sweating as he reached the top of the hill, even if he couldn't see it. It didn't matter. He could feel it, the wind at his throat—its fingers around his neck.

He couldn't breathe without knowing it was there.

And I'm here, too.

He stared up at the Castello Aragonese. It may not have been all that impressive on its own, but the dark splotch of crumbling stone towers and cannonballs—twisting passageways and ancient turrets—blocked out even the moon, from where Theo stood.

How strange, he thought, to be standing here, in the middle of the night, in the center of the piazza, in the heart of town, in the heel of the boot—and facing—what?

For the first time, Theodore Gray had absolutely no idea.

Not about what had happened, not about what would happen. Not even about what was happening.

He didn't know if that was good or bad, but it was something. It was new.

"I didn't think you were going to make it." Isabella hung back in the shadows of the castle wall. It took a moment for Theo's eyes to adjust, but they did. She was dark and outlined in darkness. Something slight and shadowy, just like everything else around her.

He drew a breath. "I made it. This isn't a movie. In real life, people make it when they say they're going to make it."

"Not all people," she said, softly. .

"I do." He looked at her.

"And the wind doesn't push over trailers?" She looked like she was about to cry.

"No." Theo swallowed. "Not usually."

She looked away. "You sure, Theo? You want to do this? I mean, I don't blame you if you don't. It's a lot to handle. For either one of us."

Theo felt in his pocket for Dante's key—the only key to the castle, the one he'd had to drag out of Dante's hands in exchange for his brand-new phone. The deal had taken longer than he'd thought, and he almost hadn't made it all the way up the hill to the castle in time.

Standing here right now he almost wished he hadn't.

Theo pulled the key out now, looking at her. "Do I want to do this? I'm pretty sure I don't. Yet here we are."

Isabella nodded, taking the key out of his hand. "Well, then." She shoved the key into the lock. Rattled it, up and down. The chains fell, clanging, to the cobblestone ground beneath them.

Isabella threw her small body against the gate, and it creaked slowly open, just a few inches at a time.

It's ironic, Theo thought, how quickly some chains fall. While others—

She smiled at him. "After you."

A strangely hollow feeling overtook Theo, but when Isabella turned back to him, she didn't look especially like herself, either. It was like they'd both been cast in someone else's haunted, horrid ghost story.

"Do you hear something?" He stopped himself, his hand on the door.

She shrugged. "Some sort of bird, I think. Or an alley cat."

"It sounded like crying," said Theo.

"More like screaming," Isabella said, listening, her head crooked like a bird.

"We could go home," he said. "It's not too late."

But it was.

A horror movie, that was this story. *The Castle of Otranto.* *Of course.*

Wasn't that why he was here, for the longest, hottest summer of his seventeen years?

"Come on, then. What are you waiting for?" She tossed her hair and disappeared into the darkness, before his eyes.

He followed her into the night.

Inside the castle, it looked like oblivion—if oblivion looked like fog, Theo thought. Fog, billowing aimlessly toward nowhere in particular. That was how he'd become used to feeling; it was also how he felt, standing in the central courtyard of the Castello Aragonese.

Isabella didn't wait for him. She took off into the shadows, while Theo felt like his feet had been somehow glued into the very foundation of the Castello itself. Frozen in place.

He looked up at the soaring stone walls that rose into the

darkness around him. One floor, two, three, four—the many stairwells connecting the castle turrets to each other were largely hidden from sight now. He could see Isabella only from a distance now, a glimpse here and there as her T-shirt caught the moonlight on the stairs.

"Isabella! What are you doing? Come on, now—"

She didn't answer, and she didn't stop. She was heading for the castle roof, Theo knew that much. He recognized the path she was taking; he'd taken it himself, the night they shot the death scene, with Pippa and Sir Manny.

With Connie, and all the blood.

Fake blood, he reminded himself. *No use freaking out about it now.*

Then he started up the stairs after her.

He wasn't scared.

He kept his eyes on his feet for no particular reason, other than that it was difficult to go up the stairs in the pitch-dark.

Thinking this, he stopped and drew a lighter from his pocket, flicking it open.

The small splotch of light spluttered into an unsteady, pale glow.

I'm not scared.

"Isabella, wait!"

I'm not.

That's what he thought, when he mounted the final stair to the Castello roof.

That's what he thought, when he passed the dark *falconieri*, the small alcove where the falcon trainer usually slept, when a scene called for birds on set.

That's what he thought, when he saw Isabella standing on the edge of the stone roof, holding on to a thin, iron rail that rose from the blocky floor like a silver antenna.

That's what he thought when the wind whipped her long black skirt, fanning her hair out into the sky behind her.

"Oh my god. Come here," she said, without turning to Theo. "Come see. You have to see."

He took a step closer, like someone in a dream, in a trance. "What, Isabella? What are you saying?"

He reached out for her hand, and she took it, twisting her head toward him.

Bringing her lips to his.

She kissed him, sweetly, as if no one in the world existed, except the two of them—not even the two of them.

I love you, he thought. *I love you, and you're real, and I'm not scared. My father's not down there, and neither is yours. Connie isn't dead, and I'm not here, and we're on a train*, he thought. *We're on a train to Rome.*

We've escaped.

That's what he was thinking as he stepped up next to her, a giant black bird circling in the air around them.

We can escape.

That's what he was thinking as she took his arm, silver in the moonlight, and the black feathers blew in the wind, surrounding them.

We—

V. Il Falconieri (The Falconer)

In the distance, a bird shrieked. It sounded like a scream, like a child crying. It didn't matter; the sirocco wind took the sound away—that sound, and every other sound the moonlight and the midnight hid between them.

No one was listening.

Not anymore.

The boy from the café and the girl from the train lay unconscious on the cobblestone, far beneath the parapet. Only a few black feathers to break their fall.

No one noticed.

Not yet.

No one except the Elephant Woman, who stood on the blood-stained rocks near the harbor, below the castle, below the empty trailers, below the deserted set.

Holding out her hand, waiting for the black-feathered creature to return.

He had done well, Dante, her faithful. He was the lord of the castle, not anyone else. By sunrise, he would lose his feathers and his true shape, and return to his human form once again. Just as he had been for hundreds of years now.

They would go now, the *americani*. The two of them would be left alone—as they should be. That was their birthright, just as it had been her mother's, and her grandmother's, and her grandmother's grandmother before that. They alone were the Keepers of the Castello, Keepers of the Curse.

The Castello Aragonese would be locked again, and soon. It would never belong to anyone but the two of them, not really.

"Dante! Dante, bravo ragazzo! Bravo!"

When she smiled, her teeth were ivory and gold.

AUTHOR'S NOTE . . . .

The first time I read Horace Walpole's *The Castle of Otranto*, I was a graduate student. The second time, I was on my way to the real Castle of Otranto itself, as part of an artists' colony for the month of June. The Castello Aragonese, as it is locally known, is the only castle in the ancient, walled city of Otranto, a truly quirky town in a largely rural part of Italy known as Salento, or Puglia. This land, with its ancient shrines and churches and rocky sea caves and mysterious Stonehenge-like dolmen, is an old, old place—a mystical place, where things start and grow, where anything can happen, and where the sun colors everything it touches with a kind of earthy truth. As Otranto was where I began to write what would become my first completed novel, I now regard *The Castle of Otranto* as not just the first Gothic novel, but as the cousin of my own Gothic first novel. In the preceding pages, my Otranto has been recast for a modern setting, inspired by not just Walpole's Otranto, but by a love of all things Gothic and Southern Gothic, a recent brush with the world of film production, and, of course, four blissful summers at the Castello Aragonese itself. So, in that ancient southeastern light, I leave you with my modern spaghetti Gothic, "Sirocco."

The Shaving of Shagpat by George Meredith (1856). When the publication in 1704 of Antoine Galland's translation of *The Arabian Nights* proved immensely popular, it was followed by more collections (*Turkish Tales* in 1707 and *Persian Tales* in 1714), which proved to be just as commercially successful, and the exotic oriental fantasy was here to stay. Meredith himself became a prolific author of serious contemporary love stories and of sonnets, but it is for his first book that anyone interested in fantasy literature remembers him. He was twenty-five when he wrote it, a newlywed with a young child, and was perhaps hoping to catch the coattails of the boom in orientalism that so captivated the Western world. Whatever his hopes were, the novel flopped badly, and it quickly made its way to the remainder stalls, and Meredith never wrote another fantasy. His tale, though, is lovely, teeming with colorful supernatural events and monstrous jinn, lush with oriental scenery and vivid characters. The adventure gives us a heroic barber who seeks to follow the seemingly helpful advice of the sorceress Noorna bin Noorka, and shave the celebrated and revered Shagpat, the son of Shimpoor, the son of Shoolpi, the son of Shullum, "a veritable miracle of hairiness." There is a profusion of "jeweled cities far," and enormous armies that raise the desert into crimson dust, withered crones with joints as sharp as a grasshopper's, and a lofty mountain "by day a peak of gold, and by night a point of solitary silver." Through it all, Meredith's ironic wit is a pure delight, rewarding the reader's time with a singular vision of a world that never actually existed.

The Shaving of Shagpat

Awakened

Melissa Marr

Tonight, unlike every other night I have walked on the shore, a man stands on the beach near my hiding place. I can't pass him. He lifts his hands, palms open, and holds them out to his sides to show me that he is harmless. If he weren't looking at me so fixedly, I might believe him, but I don't think I should trust this one.

He is young, maybe nineteen, and fit. In the water, I could escape him, but we are standing on the sand. He has dark trousers and a black shirt; the only lightness is his pale blond hair. I hadn't seen it, hadn't seen him, until I was almost upon the crevice. Until this moment, until him, I'd been singing along with the steady rising and falling of the waves as they stretched toward the sand and fell short. Now I stand bare under moon and sky on a beach, and this stranger stares at me with a look of hunger.

No, I do not believe he is harmless at all.

"I won't hurt you," he lies.

Something in his voice feels like it wants to be truth, but I shiver all the same. I hadn't expected anyone to be on the beach at this hour, and I'm not sure what to do about the man who stands watching me with such intensity that I want to flee. Men do not look at you like that without wanting something, and in their wanting, they often hurt. My mother told me that truth long before I ever set foot on the shore. It is why I am careful when I come here.

Waves lap around my ankles as I try to think of a solution. I wish I could jump into the water and escape, but I am bound by rules as old as the ebb and flow of the water at my feet. I cannot leave without the very thing that he is preventing me from reaching. The best I can do is to avoid looking at the shadows of the crevice and hope he has no idea what I am.

"Are you alone?" he asks. His gaze leaves me then, sliding away. The moon is only half full, but it is enough to cast the light he needs. The beach has few barriers, nothing to hide others. It takes only a moment for him to determine that I am isolated, that I am trapped.

As his gaze returns, traveling over the whole of me as if to weigh and measure my flesh, words feel too complicated. *Everything* feels complicated. He is waiting for my answer, so I nod to indicate that I am alone, confirming what he already has discerned, showing him that I am truthful and good. Maybe that will spare me. Maybe goodness will make him turn away. Still, I tug my hair forward, hiding myself as best I can. Dreadlocks don't cover me as truly as untangled hair might, but I am in the waters too much to have any other sort of hair. The thick tendrils drape over my shoulders like so many ropes hiding my bareness.

"I'm Leo," he says, and then he walks over to the shadows and eliminates any chance I had of escape. He pulls the carefully folded skin from the crevice where I had hidden it. He is careful, knowingly handling it as if it were a living thing. It is, of course, but I do not expect land-dwellers to know that. Not now. Not in this country.

Then he walks away, his arms laden with the part of me that

I'd hoped he wouldn't see, and I have no choice but to follow. He who holds it, holds me. It is as an anchor, and I am tethered. The sea would swallow me whole if I tried to return with my other-self still here on land. I'm trapped more truly than if I were in a cage. This man, Leo, has my soul in his hands.

"That's mine," I say. "Please give it back."

"No." He stops then, turns, and looks at me. "Since I have it, you are mine." He strokes the skin in his arms as he stares at me. "Tell me your name."

"Eden," I say. "I'm called Eden."

"Let's go home, Eden."

I cannot go *home*. Instead, I have to obey him. It is the order of things, and so I walk away from my home. "Yes, Leo."

He smiles, trying to appear kind, pretending he means me no harm. Hate ripples through me like the waves during a storm as he leads me farther onto land. It's not an unfamiliar feeling. I hate many of the humans who spill their refuse into my sea, who leave their rubbish on the sands, who desecrate my world with their noise and filth.

I whimper at the weight of loss, at the freedom that might never be mine again.

His gaze falls to my bare feet. "Would you like me to carry you?"

"No," I manage to say. He *is* carrying part of me and that is the reason I am trying not to weep. I cannot say anything to change this: while he keeps my skin in his possession, I, too, am a possession. I am bound to obey the words he speaks, trapped under his whim and will.

Leo is quiet as we walk. I study him and find that he is strangely beautiful in that way that the very assured often are. He's taller than me, but he looks to be only a bit older. He's young and handsome. In times long gone, he would've been the sort of man a selchie felt lucky to have as a captor, but I never expected to be a captive. I believed that they had forgotten how to ensnare us. When a selchie woman's skin is found, she has no choice. Many husbands could be unsightly or brutish, but a selchie must follow, must stay, where her skin is kept. Once one of *them* takes your other-skin, your soul, into his arms, you are his.

I want to weep; I want to run from him. I can't do either. All I can do is wait and hope that he will slip, that he will do one of the two things that will set me free. If he strikes me three times in anger or if he allows me to have possession of my other-skin, I can return to the sea. I hope that he does not know the truths, that his ignorance will lead to my escape, that I will be whole again one day, that I will not lose myself in captivity. I know my history, but most of the land-dwellers have forgotten that we are here. Their ignorance is our safety.

But I am following a boy who owns me now, and I think that he was watching for me tonight. Those of us who live in the waters look much like the land-dwelling—at least when we are wearing only this skin. He glances at me, and I know that he sees only the part of me that looks like I belong on land. Other men have looked at me that way. I've walked on shore, and I've known men. None of them knew that there was another shape to me. They saw only *this* skin.

Leo knows more, and so I am trapped. The sea calls out, beckoning as waves do, but Leo leads me away. There is nothing more I can do.

Yet.

He says nothing more as he takes me to his home, a house that sits on an otherwise empty stretch of beach. It's a large squatting thing, a building of so many rooms that I become lost and sit weeping in the darkness until Leo finds me. After he chides me for foolishness, he leads me back to the room that he's assigned me. He does not want me to share his room. This, I think, is for his own reasons, not as a kindness to me.

As he stands just inside the doorway, he kisses me. It's a soft peck upon the top of my salt-heavy hair. "Silly girl," he says, but there is affection in his words.

Perhaps all will be well. Perhaps I will be able to convince him to free me.

Over the next few days, I realize that Leo can be kind. I am grateful for this. There are moments when I don't feel as if the world around me is too bright, too harsh, too alien. They are few, but they are present. He tries to make me smile, and sometimes I do.

Leo's home is comfortable in a way that invites silence: the carpets are thick; the counters are polished; the furniture is heavy with age and importance; and the staff is ever present with mute efficiency. I am lonely here, but before I am allowed to be out among Leo's friends, I must learn the right words—as well as the right forks.

Time passes as I learn all I must in order to be what Leo wants. He has already told me that the two most important qualities—beauty and obedience—are well met. He tells me that he'd watched for me, selected *me* especially, because of my looks. I understand from the way he stares at me so intently that I am expected to be pleased by his words, and because of what he's stolen, I cannot disobey him. I murmur, "Thank you."

"You'll be perfect, Eden." He beams at me. "Once you learn, you'll be the wife I should have, and you'll never leave me. Everything will be perfect. We'll be happy, you'll see."

I dip my head meekly as he likes. I have already learned

quickly that he is happiest when I show him modesty and obedience. "I will try."

"My father never uses this house," Leo says. "He's away in Europe all the time. No one will know about you until we're ready. You can stay here and keep up your lessons when I go back to university, and then in a couple of years we'll be married. I'll come to you on every break."

I keep my gaze down to hide my fear of such a life. I want passion, true love some day in the distant future with a man who is so overcome with love that he'll accept me for who and what I am. I want a man who did not trap me, who will not keep me in a cage. There is no happiness inside a cage, no matter how gilded.

The man in front of me breaks my heart as he stares happily at me. When he grows tired of smiling at me, Leo motions to the table. "Which one would you use for the salad?"

I select a fork. I know this answer, have learned these useless things because it is his desire that I do so. His desire rules me now.

"For lobster?" he prompts.

I stare at the utensils arranged in front of me. Nothing seems right, and this question hadn't been in the last drill. It is a trick. I look at him, hoping my anger is better hidden than it feels. "The staff will bring that...utensil."

Leo nods, and at first, I think that he hasn't heard the pause in my words or the fury in my mouth. Then he frowns, and I see that even if he doesn't know what it was, he has heard something. He gives me a tight smile that already I am coming to understand means that I will be punished, and he asks, "Did you practice the phrases in the folder?"

"Yes, Leo."

He watches me for a moment, and then he sighs and tells me, "I don't think there will be enough time to walk tonight, Eden. You'll need to practice more. We can try again when I get back from my swim."

"Yes, Leo," I say quietly, careful not to let him see my envy that he still swims in the sea every day while I am trapped on the shore. Even when we walk on the beach, I am not allowed to swim. I am permitted to watch him, but I am not allowed to touch the sea without his hand holding me fast.

And so the days pass. We practice all the things I am to learn. Leo explains my new life, what I should and—more important—should not do. I learn how to appear as if I belong in his world, how to eat at his table and sit at his side. I dress in the clothes he's brought for me (because I am not yet allowed to go to stores with him), and I try very hard not to cry as he cuts off all of my hair. The thick twisted locks fall to the floor with soft thumps, and I am left with close-shorn hair.

"It'll grow longer," Leo assures me. "You'll brush it every morning and night, so you don't have nasty dreadlocks. Nice girls have long, shiny hair."

As I have done from the first moment he lifted my soul in his hands, I again keep my anger in silence. I know that my silences and downcast gazes please him, so too do the words "What do you think?" I have learned already to use these as I have learned to use the right utensils and phrases.

And he rewards me with smiles and soft kisses on my cheek or forehead. He tells me that he loves me, and I smile at him. He wants me to say the words, but he does not demand it. I will say them one day. I will lie to him, and he will trust me then. He is a child in this, wanting love so desperately that he has caged me here and trains me like a pet. I will bide my time.

Already I can find the magic combination of words and gazes that result in walks at the edge of the water. It's a bittersweet temptation to be so close to the waves, but Leo holds tightly to my hands. I wonder if he knows, too, that there is a third choice for my freedom. I am not yet so desperate that I will ask the sea to consume me, but even if I were, I'd have to escape his grasp to do so, and as the weeks pass, my strength fades. The tight muscles I had from diving and swimming are softer now. I worry that even if I had my other-skin, I wouldn't have the strength to reach deep enough waters for the current to pull me under.

Leo kisses my eyes when they start to fill with tears and promises, "You'll be happy with me, Eden. I'll *make* you happy."

And I smile at him and lie, "Yes, Leo."

Weeks pass in that way, but I can't tell how many. I know only that the summer is ending, and that Leo will soon leave me. He seems nervous, repeating the orders to the staff as if he hasn't told them the selfsame words every day of late. They know that I am not to cross the threshold without supervision, that the doors must be kept locked, and that—although I am allowed to spend hours on the wide deck overlooking the sea—I must not be allowed to be there alone.

It is the last night before Leo leaves. We are both barefoot on the sand tonight, and Leo allows me to walk in the water. It is only as deep as my ankles, but it is my home and he is allowing me to be caressed by the waves. For that, I am grateful.

"I will only be gone a few months," he repeats yet again. "I'll call you every night."

We have practiced using the telephone, so I know how to take his calls when he is gone. I will answer and listen; I will report to him on what I have read while he is away.

"Maybe in the spring, you could visit me," he offers.

He seems to think this will please me, so I smile and say, "Thank you."

Leo likes that. He seems happy, and as we stand on the beach, he leans closer and kisses me. His lips don't part, and I am not sure if I'm grateful for that or not. I know well what happens between a man and a woman. One cannot avoid such knowledge in the sea, and I think I would take comfort in that here on the beach. I don't want Leo, but I want to be happier.

I open my lips and wrap my arms around him. He is my jailer, but he is often kind . . . and I am lonely.

The way he looks as he leans in to kiss me is new, and I think that I could make him love me enough to escape him. He is desperate, afraid of what will happen when he returns to his university, and I suspect that he means only to kiss me chastely. In all of these weeks, he's never been anything other than distantly affectionate. He is not a passionate man with me, and it is passion that I need in order to escape him.

I press my hips to his and wrap my arms tightly around his neck so my breasts are pushed against his chest. Leo has not parted his lips for me, but he has not pulled away yet.

Then words come between us, tugging Leo away as surely as a hand on his shoulder. A man asks, "Who's the tart?"

And Leo pulls away from me.

I look past him to the man standing on the beach between us and the house. He is an older version of Leo, still fit but with the marks of age and bad choices etched upon his face.

"Father," Leo says as he turns to face the man and tucks me behind him. He still holds on to my hand; even now, he does not let go of me.

"She's a pretty enough piece," the man says. "What's your name, darling?"

I don't know what I am to do, so I whisper, "Leo?"

"Go inside, Eden, and stay in your room." Leo sounds angrier than I'd known him capable of becoming. He leads me around the man before he releases my hand. "I'll be in soon."

"Afraid of a little competition?" Leo's father asks.

"She's *younger than me*, younger than your *son*." Leo steps closer to his father. "You should be ashamed of yourself."

He laughs. "You sound like your mother."

"I'm not afraid of you." Leo squares his shoulders. "Go ahead and hit me like you—"

"Don't," Leo's father interrupts.

They are quiet then, standing staring at each other like two animals about to clash. Neither man moves, creating the illusion of the present and the future remembering themselves. Leo is determined not to become his father; he'd said as much to me one afternoon. The servants swear he is nothing like the man…except when he is.

"Go to your room, Eden," the man repeats his son's order and then adds, "Lock the door."

And so I do.

When Leo comes to my door late that night, his eye is blackened, and his lip is split. He's never come to my room at night, but I know that he has thought about it. I've heard his steps stop there many nights, heard his hand on the knob, but he's always walked away. Until tonight.

He is not weeping, but he is shaking.

"I hate him," Leo whispers, the words feeling somehow more real here in the dark. "I won't be him."

I don't answer because I can't.

Leo clutches me to him. "That's why I picked you. If you know what I like, what I want, you won't make me angry. I won't ever have to hurt you like he did with my mother and me. You'll be perfect, and we'll be happy."

When I don't reply, his hands tighten on my arms, and I know I'll need to wear a long-sleeved shirt tomorrow. It is not the first time he's left his mark on my skin, and I know now that I shouldn't cry out yet. He doesn't want to hear my cries until his mood has passed.

"I *can't hurt you*," Leo says. "Those are the rules, Eden. A selchie maiden cannot leave unless you strike her three times in anger. That's the truth, isn't it?"

"Yes, Leo," I agree.

"I haven't," he says. In all fairness, he isn't lying: neither fist nor foot has touched me in anger. He is careful even when his temper is unsettled.

"I know." I don't bow my head or shudder. I want to cringe from him even as I consider feeding the rage that simmers so close to the surface tonight. I think I could make him strike me in anger, but I am afraid of the pain. "You have never struck me."

"I hurt her, though," Leo confesses. "She left me because of it, just like my mother left *him*." Leo pauses and stares at me. "If I hit you when I'm not angry with you, is it the same?"

I shiver. There is something in his voice that I've never heard before. It's colder than the seas in winter, and I am afraid. Gently, I touch his unbruised cheek. "Why would you ever need to? I'm yours, Leo. I'm not able to leave you."

He stares at me, and I try not to flinch away.

"I love you," he says, and this time it is a question and an order.

So I answer without looking away from him, "I love you."

He lifts his hands to the arms he just bruised and strokes. I hide my pain easier under a smile and ask, "Will you sleep in here tonight? I'd feel safer with you beside me."

Leo nods. "Only sleep, Eden. We're not married or even engaged yet. Until then, there are other girls I can…" His words fade, and then he caresses my face. "I like that you are pure, Eden. Our first night will be special."

Meekly, I look down, as if I am as shy and innocent as he believes.

"Maybe I'll get you a ring for Christmas. We could be married on Valentine's Day, then. Would that make you happy?"

"Yes, Leo," I lie.

The house is silent the next day. Leo's father took him to university. The visit had been a surprise, one the man thought would please his son. At Leo's insistence, I stayed in my room until after they'd gone.

I decide that afternoon that I will not wear a long-sleeved shirt. Leo isn't here to see my disobedience, and the staff all knows that he has his father's temper. They've whispered that I'm fortunate that he only grabs me. I smile and say nothing. Leo has ordered me not to speak to them, and I don't know how to do otherwise.

Days pass in a quiet blur. I spend most of my time reading or staring out the window. Leo has allowed me to paint, so I do that when the mood strikes me. I speak to him every day, although it is not so much speaking as it is listening.

It is night that is different now. Leo had said that I am not to cross the threshold alone, but he did not say I couldn't climb out of windows. I obey the orders he *spoke*, and this was not forbidden.

I walk along the water. Sometimes, I stretch my body on the

sand and let the waves wash over me. I take pleasure in the sand and salt, and I hope that the brine on my skin does not give me away when I return to my cage. I am sure the staff suspects, but they do not accuse me. They do not bar my window.

Nights here are growing colder, and I miss my other-self. The thick fur of my selchie form would allow me to be warm in the water. Without the skin that he has stolen from me, I am trapped in this human shape. Soon it will be too cold to enter the sea for even these few stolen hours.

Tonight, I think of what has been stolen from me, and I scream. My voice is almost lost under the crash of waves, but I hear other selchie-kin in the waves echo my cries. They know I am here, have known for months. I've seen them as they dart away, trying to hide themselves to spare me the pain. Tonight they answer, and I scream until my throat feels like it might bleed.

"Are you hurt?"

I open my eyes. A man, one I've seen walking on the beach when I was hidden inside the house, is bending over me. He looks so different from Leo—tan where Leo is pale, clothes tattered rather than pristine, gaze concerned instead of possessive.

"Do you need me to help you stand or...something?" He holds out a hand, but when I simply stare at him, he says, "Or I could call someone if you want." He pulls a phone out of one of his trouser pockets. "Here."

"No."

I stand up, and he looks away quickly. My clothes are wet and clinging. I laugh, and he glances back at me. His gaze is steadily fixed on my face.

"I don't need a phone," I say. "I was calling to them when you arrived, but they can't come to me. They can't help me."

He stares at me like he thinks I might be mad, and I know that he has no idea that I am selchie. He thinks I am a girl, one perhaps crazier than those he knows. He does not know I am Leo's.

And I decide then that I will not tell him.

"I do need some things," I say firmly, not needing to whisper or speak meekly since he is not Leo.

"What?"

"Your name, a friend, a kiss." I step back, forcing him to look at me. "Someone to talk to at night."

He swallows before saying, "Robert."

"And the rest?" I prompt.

When he simply stares at me, I decide that I am beyond tired of silence. Selchies have always come on land to lie down with human men. Leo may not know that, but I do. I am no more innocent than any other creature with appetites. I strip off my wet clothes as Robert stares at me.

"I am lonely here," I admit.

Robert looks around like he expects to see someone watching him or perhaps someone to tell him what to do. There is no one on the beach at this hour. Tonight is the first night I haven't been here alone, and I think this man is a gift of sorts, that the universe has decided that I deserve some happiness.

I step closer and say, "This is not a trick. We are alone, and I am sad."

"You want to..." His words fade as I step closer.

"Yes."

I don't expect the bliss I find. Maybe it's only because I've been so lonely. Maybe it's because I am not asked to be someone I'm not. Maybe it's simply because I am choosing this. I don't know. What I do know is that we meet in the dark most nights after that. He tells me about his plans. (He's going to Europe to "experience life" in the spring.) He tells me about his family. (They are wealthy and indulgent.) He tells me about his best friend. (A sad, messed-up man whose father has all but destroyed him.) He tells me that he's meeting his best friend's girl here in a few weeks. (She is sweet and innocent, and Leo is going to bring her here to propose.)

It is November now, the day before Leo returns. We are to be having a dinner for a holiday he calls Thanksgiving. Leo has called almost every night, and after he tires of talking, I climb out my window and meet Robert on the beach. Tomorrow, everything will change. I will lose Robert. If he doesn't keep our secret, I may be set free by Leo's anger. I would prefer Leo choose to give me my freedom, but I have thought much about inviting his anger.

He need only hit me three times. Then I am freed. I think I can endure three blows easier than the slow death of many years in this cage.

"Do you want to come to my friend's house with me tomorrow?" Robert asks that night as he's holding me in his arms. He's asked me to meet people so often that I can't help but feel sorrow for the way I've kept these secrets. He's a good person, and if not for my imprisonment, I would stay with him for the next few months. I might even meet him on European shores. I cannot offer either because Leo took those choices from me.

"I like you." I sit up and look into his eyes.

Robert grins. "That's good, since I think I love you."

I wish it could be simple. For a moment, I think I might love him. He's funny and kind, and he makes me feel happier than I have since I became a prisoner. He treats my body like it is rare and precious—and he treats my words the same. If I were free, I could love him. I tell him more of the truth than I have other nights.

"I could love you," I admit. "If I were free to do so, I could love you, and if you still want me after tomorrow...I would go on exactly as we are. I would meet your friends and walk at your side."

Robert kisses me before saying, "You're strange, Edy, but I like it. Is that a yes? Will you come meet Leo? We've been friends forever, before his mom disappeared. He's peculiar, but I think things are turning around. He met someone, and he sounds happy."

"I will be there." I brush the sand from my arms and bare chest, stalling before I confess. I do not meet his gaze as I dress and stand.

When Robert comes to his feet, I ask, "Will you walk me to the house tonight?"

"You're finally going to tell me where you live?" He's teasing, but there is a happiness in his voice that I can't miss.

"I don't live there by choice, Robert." I glance at him and don't try to hide my sorrow. "I'd leave if I could."

He hugs me closer to him as we walk. "My family could help you. We can go to them and—"

"They can't," I interrupt. "Not with this. He owns me."

"Edy, no one *owns* you." Robert shakes his head. "Is it like an immigration thing or does he have something he holds over you?" He steps in front of me. "Is it a legal thing? Did you do something illegal?"

"I can't explain." I shiver a little from both the cold air and the fear that presses against me. "I care for you, but he owns me. Unless he lets me go, I can't leave."

Robert continues arguing as we walk, but when we stop at the side of the house, his words stop. His mouth opens and closes once before he finds speech again. "Mr. Ponties owns you? I know his son, and—"

"Leo," I correct. "Leo owns me. He is not bringing his girl here. I am here, and I cannot leave." My anger spikes, and I gesture widely at the house. "It is my prison."

He says nothing.

His silence continues as I climb up the side of the house and into my room. When I look back, he stands below me staring up at the window, staring at me with confusion plain on his face. I tell him, "I will be here tomorrow when you come, and when he is gone back to university, I will come to you if you still want."

But he still says nothing. My lips are sore from his kisses, and my body relaxed from our pleasures, but he does not speak to me. I do not know what he will tell Leo.

As I stare out at the sea, I remind myself again that I can accept three blows in anger to be free of these land-dwellers.

I wait anxiously for the sound of Leo's arrival. The staff has made the house welcoming. Fresh flowers fill vases, and Leo's bed is made up with clean linens. I've been made ready too. My hair is brushed thoroughly, and my skin is scrubbed clean of the salt and sand that usually adorns it. It was when they suggested that I be sure to get the sand all off that I knew that they were all too aware of my secret. They might tell him. Robert might tell him.

And here I sit, awaiting my jailer.

My not-so-secret sojourns at night are the only freedom I have known since Leo imprisoned me. I am afraid that these hours with the sea and with Robert are ending. If Leo takes these away too, I am not sure how I will endure.

"Eden?" Leo's voice fills the house, and at the unhappy tone in it, I worry suddenly that he'd expected me to be waiting at the door.

I go to him and look past him. Dread creeps into my voice, but I blame it on the person he fears. "Are you alone or is he...?"

Relief unclouds his expression as he accepts my lie, as he chooses to believe I was not at the door because of fear.

"No, love. He's not here." He embraces me. "I should've told you. My father won't be here. It's just us."

"I'm glad," I murmur, reminding myself to be meek. I have almost forgotten that in the joy of the nights with Robert, when I am allowed to be myself, to speak as I please, to do as I want. I concentrate though. I can do this again. I can be the Eden Leo has been trying to mold me into being. I duck my head slightly. "I'm glad he's not here."

And just like that, Leo is happy.

He talks as is his increasing habit in our nightly calls, and I listen in silence as I am supposed to do. It is stifling, like restraints drawn tighter by his very words, but I stare at him with the affection I would give to the sea. I look on him and pretend he is Robert.

Come evening, I am tired. The burden of being around Leo is wearing, and I almost refuse when he asks if I'd like to go out. Then he adds, "The staff says that you do not even ask to go for walks." He smiles at me with a strange pride. "You're a good girl, Eden. I like that you obeyed so well."

He takes my hand and leads me to the door. "Take off our shoes, and we can go out."

He stands and waits for me to obey. This is not new, but it has been months since I've had to kneel before him. It takes more effort to do so now. I bow my head to hide my face. I can do that now that my hair is longer.

Leo's hand strokes my hair as I kneel and remove first his shoes and then my own. Then, as I had when he lived here with me before, I hold up my hand, so he can pull me up to stand beside him.

He does not release me.

We walk, and I try to remember that I am to be thrilled by this small gift, by this permission to touch the water that is my rightful home.

"Would you like to wade in?"

This is new, and even though I do so every night, I am still grateful. "Yes."

"You earned this, Eden." He releases my hand.

I wade out until the water swirls around my hips. My eyes close, and I tilt my face to the sky. For a moment, I am happy, but then Leo speaks my name. I open my eyes and stare at him.

"By spring, maybe we can go swimming, or"—he holds out a hand—"maybe you'll be pregnant by then."

When I reach his side, he takes my hand and squeezes it. Then he releases me and draws a small box from his pocket. "I know we said Valentine's Day, but I feel like we shouldn't wait. We can be married at Christmas instead."

He opens the box and withdraws a ring. I was taught about this human custom, so I would know what to do when this moment came. The ring is beautiful, but I have no use for shiny rocks. I know I am expected to be happy, so I smile at him and hold my hand out to him obediently. He doesn't ask if I want to be wed, but I couldn't answer freely even if he did.

"In a few weeks, you'll be my wife." Leo slides the ring onto my finger and then kisses me briefly, a brush of the lips and then gone. "I'll be twenty in the spring, and my trust will be all mine then. I'll find us a place near the university."

"You mean live away from the sea?" My heart pounds like waves crashing in a hurricane, and I'm afraid to meet Leo's eyes.

He laughs though. "We can't live here, but we'll still visit. The ocean gave me you. I can't stay away from it all the time."

"How long is Christmas?"

Leo misunderstands my fear for excitement. "Less than a month. I go back in a few days, but I'll return for you soon after. I'll take you to our new home, and we'll be together every day then. You can learn new things then, other ways to be good to me, and soon we'll have our first child." He brushes my hair back, stroking my cheeks with his thumbs as he does so. "They say that marriages made so young don't last, but *ours* will. You can't leave me; you can't disobey me . . . and I . . . won't ever need to hurt you."

I cannot speak around the pain inside me. Leo means to take me away from my sea in a few weeks. He means to make me with child. There are ways to prevent pregnancy. Robert and I have used them, but I cannot disobey Leo. I stare down at the ring weighing down my hand, and I feel warm tears on my face.

"I feel the same way, but"—Leo kisses my cheeks, swallowing my tears, before continuing—"but it's only a few more weeks that we'll be apart, and later if you want a big ceremony, we can renew our vows. It would be the third time really."

I look at him.

"The night I chose you, we were bound more than any church can tie two people," he clarifies. "The second time, we can go to a courthouse. The third, we can have a lavish cere-mony . . . maybe on our third anniversary. The *real* one, the third anniversary of the night we met."

Mutely, I let him lead me into the house and into his bedroom.

"I know I wanted to wait till we were married, but we're engaged now," he says.

I try to find comfort in his kisses, try not to wince when he holds my arms too tightly, try not to cry out in pain when he enters my body without tenderness. I almost succeed, but then he grips my throat. Each cry only makes him happier. All I can do is stay still as Leo ruts and roars on top of me. Afterward, when he is quiet beside me, I realize that I have done exactly what he wants.

"You're perfect, Eden," he whispers in a tone of near reverence. "Soon, we can be together every day. I'll teach you how to be a good wife."

I close my eyes and say, "Yes, Leo."

By the time Robert arrives to see Leo, I am dressed. I wear a cardigan sweater to cover the handprints that once more decorate my arms, and for the first time, I wear a high-necked shirt to hide the bruises low on my throat. When Robert comes into the room, led by one of the nameless members of the staff who do not speak to me even after all of these months, I look to Leo for instructions.

He takes my hand and tugs me to stand beside him. I barely hide my wince of pain as I stand, but Leo doesn't notice. He releases my hand and hugs Robert.

"Eden is tired," Leo says, "but I couldn't wait a minute longer." He lifts my hand to show Robert the ring. "I wasn't sure... hopeful, but you know how women can be..." His words drift away, and I think of the other girl, the one he's mentioned briefly. I wonder if she is the reason he chose not to take me to bed before we were engaged. It's odd to think that, knowing as we both do that I had to say yes, but Leo is—as Robert once told me—a very broken man.

I hear him still talking and force myself to listen as he says, "...but she said yes. Eden is going to be my wife in a few short weeks."

Leo smiles widely at me.

Robert looks at me, and I know that when Leo returns to university, Robert will not be waiting for me in the dark.

"I've met her," Robert says. "While you were away, I met her. I didn't know. You've got to believe me. If I had...I wouldn't have." Robert looks as heartsick as I feel. "I swear I wouldn't have fallen for her if I knew."

"Eden?" Leo asks. There are so many questions in those few letters, and I don't know which to answer.

"I didn't cross the threshold," I whisper. "Robert didn't know I was...yours."

The hand that was hanging at his side curls into a fist, and I brace myself. I think that it would be better if Robert left— almost as much as I hope he will stay. I know this is my path to freedom, but I am afraid.

"We had sex the first night," I say quietly. "I didn't know he was your friend then."

"And after?" Leo prompts. He's staring only at me now. "Did you stop when you knew?"

I lift my head a fraction and say, "No."

"I think you should leave," Leo says, and I know that he isn't talking to me even though I wish he were.

Robert steps forward and touches Leo's arm. "Leo—"

"Now." Leo is not looking at Robert. His gaze is only on me, and I see his father in him. There is fury here, more than I was expecting. I consider begging Robert to stay, but this is what must happen to set me free.

I start to walk away, as if I could go with Robert, and Leo grabs me. I yelp. He shakes me, and I wonder how many ways he can hurt me without striking me.

But I do not want to lose my nights of freedom. They were all I had left, and they are gone too. I have to do this. "I lay down with him every night," I say quietly.

He lifts a hand.

"Leo!" Robert yells.

And Leo punches him instead.

"No!" I step between them, and the second blow hits me. I've never been hit before, and the force of it is unlike my imaginings. I lift my hand to my cheek. "He didn't know. I seduced him, Leo. I crept out at night and seduced him. He is innocent."

Leo raises his hand again, but Robert grabs him. "Stop it! What are you doing?"

Trapped as he is, Leo can't swing at me, so he kicks me. That hurts even more than the punch. I fall to the floor and look up at him. I'm afraid, but I am more hopeful than afraid. *Twice*. He's struck me twice. There are rules, and we both know them.

I open my mouth, but before I speak words to incite that third blow, Leo says, "No." He shakes his head. The anger is not gone, but his control has returned. He meets my gaze, but does not offer to help me to my feet. He swears, "I won't do it a third time, Eden. You can't leave me."

Robert looks between us like we are both strangers to him. He might not understand, but he knows that there is more going on here than what he can see. "Edy, why don't you go outside while Leo calms down."

"May I, Leo?"

Leo bows his head, to hide either anger or sorrow, and Robert releases his hold. Leo steps forward, but he doesn't touch me. "I shouldn't have done that," he says. "You know I shouldn't, but I won't hit you a third time. I still love you."

"If you really love me, tell me I can go home," I half ask, half demand. I stand and take off the sweater. Both Robert and Leo look at the fresh bruises on my arms. "Tell me I don't need to stay in a cage."

"It's not a cage," Leo insists. "I'll take care of you. We can be happy; I know it. It's just that you were alone; I'll never leave you alone again. You were weak, but I *forgive* you." He stands and comes to me. He kisses me with the sort of tenderness he didn't show me in his bed and then he tells me, "I know what will happen if I hit you again. That's why I picked you, so I wouldn't be like that. I can be better."

"I want my freedom," I tell him, being honest as I haven't been before. It took this: his threat to take me farther from the sea, his fist, his foot, for us both to show our desperation.

"No. I'll be better." Leo looks at me, and I think of the night he came to me with a bruised face. I think he remembers that same night because he touches my face. "You're mine, Eden. I'm not going to let you go."

"You hurt me," I say.

"I *love* you," he swears. "I won't be like him. I swear it. We'll leave here, and we'll be together. Everything will be perfect."

All the while Robert stands watching us. He looks between us, and my heart hurts for them both. It hurts more for the freedom that felt so close. I cannot lose what little of the sea I still have. The thought of never touching it, of not hearing it, not seeing it, or smelling the brine—it destroys me.

If we were staying here, I could try to wait, try to find ways to make Leo hit me again, but even as I think it, I know that I do not want to feel the other pains he delivers. I do not want to wear these bruises. I do not want to kneel at his feet. I do not want my voice to be silent.

I could kill Leo; he's never ordered me not to hurt him. I'm not sure I can take a life, but I think of it now. If he were dead, I could take my other-skin from wherever it is hidden in the house. While he is alive, I cannot even search for it, but if he were to die, I could reclaim my soul.

I could let the sea take me. It is what my kind has often done. Without our souls, without the sea, many of us sink into a sorrow deep as the darkest caverns in the sea. This, I can do.

"May I go to the beach, Leo?" I ask quietly. "You tell me you are different. You say you are not like your father. You say this isn't a cage." I hold his gaze and challenge him. "Prove it."

He agrees, and I walk out the door.

"To the beach, Eden," Leo calls as I reach the deck. "I'm not setting you free."

Distantly, I hear Robert say, "You keep her a prisoner? Seriously? What are you thinking?"

I don't stop to hear the answer. I believe Leo when he says he won't hit me again. He knew he had to strike me three times, and even in his anger, he knew when to stop. There are other pains though, and even without the pain, I live in a cage like a pet. I cannot consign a child to this fate. I cannot live like this.

I glance back as Robert and Leo come outside. They're following me. I knew they would, but I have to believe they won't reach me in time.

I don't stop when I reach the edge of the water. I wade in.

The cold water rushes over my legs, and I look to the horizon. I don't see others of my kind, and I know they can't come to me when I am wearing only my human self.

"I have your skin; you can't leave without your skin!" Leo apparently realizes as he says it that there are other ways to leave, and he runs back toward the house.

At the same time, Robert runs toward me. "Edy!"

The water is wrapping around me as I start to swim, and when I glance behind me I see Robert wading in.

"I'm sorry, Edy! Wait!" Robert yells.

I don't stop; I can't. I go deeper, feeling the shock of the water starting to numb my body already. As I start to swim, I concentrate on going as far away from the shore as I can.

I tread water for a moment. The cold and my bruises are sapping my strength. I need to go farther though. I need to be unable to hear the words if Leo orders me to shore.

The moon spills light on the water like a path, and I concentrate on following it. The water feels strange against my clothes, and I realize that I've never swum with clothes. I never needed them.

I feel the pull of my other-skin as I start to go farther from it, farther from the prison where it remains. It will be nothing more than a pelt once I am gone. Without it, without the rest of myself, I will drown before I reach deep water. It is not the choice I thought I would make, but like so many women before me, I cannot survive in a cage.

Splashing and voices behind me tell me that Leo is in the water too.

I start to swim as fast as I'm able. I do not conserve any of my strength; I only need to be deep enough, far enough, that the currents will pull me out farther.

Leo's voice calls, "Eden—"

So I dive under the water where the rest of his words won't reach me. If he orders me back, I will have to obey, so I need not to hear them yet. I have to get farther away, to swim until I am so tired, so numb from the cold, that I cannot obey if he demands that I return to the shore.

When I surface for air, I hear that Robert is yelling too.

I dive again. The water doesn't feel as cold, and I think that shock shouldn't set in so soon—but I'm grateful all the same. No woman should live in a cage. I won't do so for another day longer.

This time, when I come up for air, I glance back at them, and I see that Robert hasn't come any deeper into the water. For all of his protestations of love, he does not risk the sea for me—or maybe he loves me enough to let me have the choice.

It is Leo who swims toward me, propelling his body through the water with one arm. He's forbidden me access to the water even as he swam in it every day, and aside from my few nights in it, I have not had a chance to keep myself strong enough. Leo has the strength I lack now, and he is catching up quickly.

I renew my efforts. If he reaches me, he can drag me back to shore.

"Come back with me. Please! This isn't what was supposed to happen," he says.

There are no words I know to make him understand. Selchies have been where I am now for centuries. We all know that to be captive is to die a little each day. There are good men, and there are broken men.

"Eden," he calls my name and then he orders, "Eden, stop!"

I obey; I obey completely: I stop fleeing, stop swimming, stop keeping myself above water. The human body can't stay under water as long as a seal can, and I count on that.

What I don't count on is Leo's determination. He dives under the waves and grabs me. I can't fight him as he pulls me above the water.

I stay limp in his grasp. I will not help him return me to the land, and he doesn't think to order me to do so.

"I don't want you to die." Leo kisses my head and murmurs, "I'm *not* like my father."

Then I feel something brush against me and realize why he was swimming with only one arm. He has brought my skin into the sea. He pushes it toward me, returning it to me of his own will. It clings to me, wrapping around me, and I forget Leo. I forget everything except for this: I am whole and free.

I let out a bellow of joy, and I hear the answers of my selchie-sisters. They call to me, echoing my happiness, rejoicing that I am home. I am tired, but they will help me. I have only to swim toward them, and they will take me to safety.

I hear splashing behind me, and I turn. A human boy is saying something. He speaks my name, and I think that there is something more I should do here, but I am exhausted. I can't recall if I am to help him or take him under the water where his land-dwelling lungs will fill with the sea until they burst. He is struggling in the water, but my selchie-sisters call out, letting me know that they are nearing.

This human is not my concern. I leave the splashing behind and enjoy the welcoming waves of my home. I am whole, and I am free. There is nothing else.

Author's Note ....

Before I was a writer, I was a teacher. One of my favorite novels to teach—both in American literature courses and women's literature courses—was Kate Chopin's *The Awakening*. The inevitable classroom discussion of women who walk into the sea or otherwise see death as superior to enslavement was met with the ever-foolish idea that "that was then, and we no longer need feminism because we're all equal." I didn't agree then, and I agree even less now as I watch state after state in my nation pass laws limiting women's ownership of their bodies. I don't think suicide is ever the answer, but I do think we live in a world where feminism is still essential.

Tangled into this Chopin-influenced short story is my love for selchies. I've been to Orkney three times in the past four years. I've walked among seals, and I've had them follow me in the water as I walked on the shore. It's easy to see a human face in the mist. It's easy to understand the origin of the mythology, and when I add that mythology to Chopin, I see a woman entrapped again, but this time with another option—one in which her need to enter the sea is more than seeking death. The sea still offers freedom.

New Chicago

KELLEY ARMSTRONG

As Cole hurried along River Street, the cries of the peddlers changed. One minute they were hawking mended shirts and worn boots and the next they were selling equally worn-out dreams and promises. "Peddlers of hope," people called them. "Predators," his brother, Tyler, said. Preying on hope, because that was the only thing the people of New Chicago had left.

If Tyler caught him here, Cole would get a lecture. There was no danger of that, though, because his brother wouldn't set foot on this part of River Street. He said it was because he didn't want to give the hope peddlers an audience, but Cole suspected Tyler feared temptation. Walk past the peddlers and he might hear a pitch that would make him dig into his pocket for coins they couldn't afford to spare, wagering them on the dream of a better life in New Chicago.

New Chicago. The name itself rang with promise. People from across the nation fought starvation and bandits and the infected to get to the great city. When they were finally admitted, after weeks in quarantine outside, they wept. But they did not weep for joy.

They'd heard that New Chicago was like the metropolises of old, clean and safe and bursting with promise. Instead they found a ravaged place with peddlers selling maps to the city they'd just left.

Tyler's dream wasn't to leave New Chicago. He knew there was nothing better for them out there. But there *was* something better in here: Garfield Park. Beyond its walls was a real city— safer, cleaner, better. To get in, though, you needed money. Lots of it.

As Cole passed through the hope peddlers, he noticed a group gathered in front of one booth.

"—guaranteed to ward off the infected," the young woman was saying.

She was about Tyler's age—twenty-two—and dressed in not nearly enough, given the bitter wind driving off the river. That, Cole decided, explained her crowd.

"—my friend Wally," she continued, waving at a barely upright drunk beside her. "He was out there, beyond the city walls, for three days and not a single one of the infected bothered him. Why? Because he was wearing this."

Cole pressed into the crowd, as if straining to see what she held. His fingers slid into a man's bulging jacket pocket. Out came a switchblade. Then he reached into a woman's shopping bag and nicked two bruised apples. While the crowd absently shoved him back, he tucked his winnings under his jacket. Then he backed out and continued on.

This part of the market was the best for lifting and picking. There were always crowds, and there were always distracted people, most who'd just finished their shopping farther up.

If Tyler found out what Cole was doing, he'd get another lecture, this one about empathy. If they started stealing from other people, they were no better than the infected. But life here was a battle, and only the strongest would survive. Tyler knew that. He worked for Russ McClintock, the most feared man in New Chicago. Tyler wanted better for Cole, though. He always had. So he pretended he slung boxes and cleaned warehouses for McClintock, and Cole pretended he spent all day reading the books Tyler brought home. And both brothers slowly added to the small fortune they'd need to buy their way into Garfield Park.

Cole was moving slowly past the peddlers' booths, as if reluctantly being pulled along by some other task. You had to act as if you were just passing through so you didn't catch the attention of the peddlers themselves, who hated anyone stealing from their marks before they could.

Cole came through every other day and picked only four or five pockets before moving on. It helped that he was small for his sixteen years, average looking and clean. The "clean" part counted for a lot in New Chicago. Good water was so hard to come by, but Russ McClintock liked his employees to be shaven and scrubbed—it lifted them above the riffraff. So he had plenty of reasonably clean water, and he let Tyler bring Cole around for baths, in expectation of recruiting him someday.

Cole was almost through the hope peddlers when he caught sight of something interesting. A man from Garfield Park. You could tell because his clothing didn't look like it had been mended more than a time or two. Cole's gaze slipped to the man's right jacket pocket. It gaped open, ready for the picking. Unfortunately, the man looked uncomfortable here, his gaze darting about. Not an easy mark.

The man finally found what he was looking for—an older man with a dragging leg, cheeks patchy with graying stubble, eyes dull with the "New Chicago look," that empty gaze, expecting nothing. When the old man saw the guy from Garfield Park, he lifted a hand in greeting. The rich man's eyes narrowed, as if thinking the old guy looked vaguely familiar. Then he nodded and approached. They exchanged a few words and headed toward an alley. Cole followed.

He knew his way through the alleys around the market. Now, seeing where the two men were going, he skirted down a side road and came out near the end of their alley.

"I remember you had an interest in special items, Mr. Murray," the older man was saying, his voice a hoarse rumble. "A scholarly interest."

"If you summoned me here to sell me some cheap bauble—"

"I wouldn't do that, Mr. Murray. I know you're a very busy man. This is something special. I'm told it's well known in certain circles."

"Everything is well known in certain circles," Murray snapped. "And almost all of it is as worthless as that crap they're hawking out there, so if—"

"It's a monkey's paw."

Silence. Cole inched toward the corner.

"A what?" Murray said finally.

Fabric rustled, as if the older man was pulling something from his pocket. Cole leaned around the corner. He could see the old man holding something, but he couldn't make out what it was.

"There's a legend—" the old man began.

Now it was Murray cutting him short. "I've heard it."

"Three wishes. They say the paw grants three wishes."

Murray snorted. "If it did, you wouldn't be here trying to sell it to me."

"I . . . made mistakes," the old man said. "I didn't know you need to be very, very careful what you ask for. The gentleman who gave me the paw tried to explain, but I heard only the part about the wishes. He was a wealthy man I'd helped, as I used to help you. He wanted to help me in return. So he gave me this. He told me to take care, but I didn't listen and I used up my wishes."

"And now you want to sell it to me?"

The old man shook his head. "Not sell. Give it away, as it was given to me. That's only right. You helped me, Mr. Murray, and I never thought I'd be able to properly thank you. But now I can."

"If you expect me to believe—"

"Then don't. It is, as I said, freely given. At worst, it would make an amusing addition to your collection."

Murray snorted again, but he dug into his pocket and pulled out a couple of bills. He took the paw. When the old man didn't reach for the bills, Murray let them drop. Then he walked away.

Cole ducked back as Murray passed, but the man was busy shoving the paw into his pocket.

Cole looked down the alley. The old man was walking away. He'd left the bills on the ground.

Cole slid soundlessly down the alley. When he reached the bills, the old man looked over his shoulder. Cole froze. He could easily scoop up the money and run, but too many of his brother's teachings had stuck and instead he pointed down.

"You dropped those, sir."

"Take them," the old man said.

Cole hesitated, but the man seemed serious. Cole supposed Tyler would say it was the principle of the thing. The old man had tried to repay a debt, and if Murray was too uncouth to accept the gift, that was his problem.

"Thanks," Cole said. "Here."

He tossed one of his apples. The old man caught it and nodded, unsmiling. Then he continued on, dragging his bad leg behind him. Cole scooped up the cash and took off after Murray.

Cole wanted that paw. He didn't believe it had any special properties. There was no magic in this world. He wanted it because it would amuse Tyler. He'd tease Cole about it every time his little brother complained. *You miss Pepsi and burgers, bud? Why don't you ask the paw? Just be sure to ask carefully, or you'll get rat and piss.*

Lately, making his brother laugh practically took magic. Hell, most people hadn't found much to laugh about in ten years. Not since H2N3.

H2N3. A boring name for what had, in the beginning, been a boring virus. People got it, they suffered through a mild flu, and they recovered. Then they'd get it again. And again and again. Traditional treatments didn't work and the rate of spread was insane. Soon it was putting a massive strain on health care and workplaces across the world. Something had to be done. A vaccine had to be found. And one was.

Later people would say that the vaccine testing process had been rushed, that the results were faked, that it was a conspiracy by the drug companies in collusion with the government. But Tyler said no—he remembered their parents nursing them through round after round of the flu, grumbling at the government to hurry up and approve the vaccine. Finally, people got it and everything seemed fine.

Then the reports started coming in. Gangs of ordinary people roaming the streets, attacking passersby for pocket change. People on the subway being murdered for a sandwich or a cup of coffee. The victims who survived reported that it was like being savaged by a wild animal—clawing and biting and ripping. Then those who'd been bitten began to change, to become like their attackers.

"It was a zombie apocalypse," people said, "just like in the movies." Which was crap. Cole had seen a zombie movie once, sneaking in when Tyler's friends brought one over. The infected were not zombies. They hadn't died; they weren't rotting. They'd just changed. They'd become feral—that's the word Tyler used. Whatever stops a hungry person from attacking a kid for an apple, that's what the infection robbed from its victims.

Ten years later, most of the population was infected. The rest had retreated to fortified cities like New Chicago. If there was any real hope left, it was that eventually the infected would annihilate themselves out there. But they sure weren't hurrying to do it. In the cities, things weren't much better, as the increasing shortage of food and clean water meant that you could still lose your life over an apple, murdered by a regular person who needed it to survive.

In a world like that, if you could do something to lighten someone's spirits, you did it. So Cole wanted that paw for Tyler.

When Cole caught up, Murray was holding it again, looking down on it with distaste, as if he wanted to be rid of the thing.

Just toss it in the trash, Cole thought. *Or in the gutter.*

Murray paused outside a soup shop. The smell made Cole's mouth water, but even with those bills in his pocket, he wasn't tempted. Before Tyler worked for McClintock, he'd run errands for these shops—killing rats down at the river and digging rotted vegetables out of the market trash. That's what you could expect from prepared food in New Chicago.

Murray didn't seem to know that. The rich scent of hot soup caught his attention, and he followed it to the shop door. Then he paused and fingered the paw.

It's dirty. Filthy, Cole thought. *You'll need to wash before you eat now. Just get rid of it.*

Murray shoved the paw into his pocket and walked inside.

In the old days, this place wouldn't have been considered a shop at all, much less a restaurant. Cole remembered restaurants. Fast food ones mostly. Sometimes, now, he'd wake thinking he smelled fries and it would set him in a lousy mood all day. Tyler would tease that, of all the things you could miss, fried potatoes should rank near the bottom. But they both knew it wasn't really the fries—it was the idea that you could walk into a big, gleaming restaurant, scrub your hands with free soap and water, and order hot, safe food for less than half the twenty bucks your dad gave your brother when he decided to take you to the park that morning.

This soup shop would have fit in one of those fast food restrooms. Hell, it probably *had* been the restroom for this place, once a big department store, the top two floors now destroyed in the bombings, the remainder divvied up into a score of tiny, dark "shops." There were certainly no tables or chairs. You pushed your way up to the counter, got your soup, and pushed your way to a spot to eat it, standing. You could take it outside, but with November winds blowing through threadbare clothes, Cole suspected most patrons didn't even really want the soup—it just gave them a chance to squeeze in someplace warm.

Murray would take his soup and go—Cole could tell that by the contemptuous gazes the man shot around him. He even seemed to be reconsidering whether he wanted to remain long enough to get a meal. Cole had to act fast. He slid up behind Murray and got into position. Then, when a man left the counter, jostling and elbowing through the crowd, Cole knocked into Murray.

Murray spun on him, scowling.

"Sorry," Cole said.

He offered a chagrined smile. Murray muttered something, turned, and pushed his own way through the crowd, stalking out.

Cole watched him go. Then he glanced down at the paw in his hand. He smiled, shoved it deep into his pocket, and made his way out.

Tyler was in a foul mood, which was rare. It was usually Cole who grumbled while Tyler soldiered through. Today was different. Cole knew that as soon as he saw the candle burning.

Tyler often joked that they had a penthouse apartment. Not only was it on the top floor, but they even had a second story. The roof had been blasted off, so their upper floor was four walls with no ceiling. Those walls, though, cut most of the wind and they could spend the daylight hours up there and save their candles and lantern oil. If Tyler was staying on the first floor and burning a candle mid-afternoon, something was wrong.

"Where were you?" Tyler demanded as Cole crawled in.

His brother was sitting on a chair—actually a crate, but they called them chairs. He was playing solitaire with a worn deck, slapping the cards down onto another crate, this one known as "the dining room table."

"Just walking. Getting some air."

"Did you finish your schoolwork?"

"I read three chapters in history and two of *Moby-Dick*. I also swept and emptied the piss bucket, as you can see—and smell."

Tyler sighed and gathered up the cards. "Sorry, bud. Rough day."

"I see that. Catch."

He tossed Tyler the remaining apple. The corners of his brother's mouth quirked. "Thanks." He started to take a bite and stopped. "Do you have one?"

"Already ate it."

"Are you sure? You need more fruits and vegetables. I—"

"I ate one, Ty. Go ahead."

His brother worried that poor diet was the reason Cole was so small. He doubted it. He remembered kindergarten—his only year of school before the world went to hell. He'd been the small-est kid there, too. But Tyler still worried. Some days, Cole thought that was the only thing keeping his brother going—worries and problems and the faint hope that he could fix them.

Tyler didn't ask where the apple came from. Cole was in charge of the money and the shopping. Tyler considered it a practical application of his math lessons, which made it easy for Cole to sneak extra cash into the kitty and put extra food on the table.

Tyler took a bite of the apple, snuffed out the candle, and waved for them to go upstairs, where they pulled pillows and thick old blankets out of a box. Cushioned and bundled against the cold, they rested, enjoying the faint warmth of the late-day sun.

"So what happened at work?" Cole asked.

"Same shit, different day." Tyler paused and then looked

over. "When you were out, did you hear anything? Rumors? News?"

"Like what?"

Another pause, longer now, until Cole pressed.

"They say one of the infected got in," Tyler said.

"Again? What's that? Third time this month?"

"Yeah. It's getting worse. They always catch them, but the fact that they're getting in..." Tyler shook his head. "Just...be careful, okay? When you're out?"

"I always am."

After a moment, Tyler asked, "So, how much money do we have so far?"

He said it casually, just an offhand question, but Cole knew it wasn't offhand at all. This was what was really bothering his brother—that the situation in New Chicago seemed to worsen so much faster than their stash grew.

"Four hundred and sixty-eight dollars to go," Cole said.

Tyler swore.

"We'll make it," Cole said. "Less than a year, I bet."

"I used to earn that much in a month, mowing lawns. Then I'd blow it on video games and movies."

"We'll get there."

Silence fell for at least five minutes. Then, without looking over, Tyler said, "We have enough to get you in."

"No."

"But we could—"

"No. We go together, or we stay together. If you want to make money faster, let me work. McClintock offered me a job—"

"No."

"But if I was working, we'd have enough by—"

"No."

And there was the impasse. Cole wouldn't go without Tyler, and Tyler wouldn't let him work for McClintock. Cole's "job" was studying. There were real careers in Garfield Park, like in the old days—doctors and businessmen and teachers. Most kids Cole's age couldn't even read and write. That would give him an advantage, Tyler said. Cole couldn't see how taking a few months off would make much difference, but he knew it wasn't really about that. It was about Cole staying away from McClintock and the life he offered.

"We'll get there," Cole said.

Tyler tried for a smile, pushed to his feet, and rumpled his brother's hair. "I know we will. I'm just in a mood. I need to go back to work. Big job tonight. It'll be late."

"I'll lock up."

Tyler laughed. "Yeah. You do that. And see if you can't get another couple of chapters read before the light's gone."

It was only after Tyler left that Cole remembered the paw. He was sitting there, trying to come up with other ways to make money, when he remembered it. Even then, he didn't think "I can wish for money!" He wasn't that stupid. Instead, he took it out, turned it over in his hands, and wondered how much he could get for it.

You could just wish for the money, he imagined Tyler saying.

His brother would laugh when he said it, but there'd be a little piece that wouldn't be laughing. A piece that would be hoping, even if he'd never admit it. Tyler would make that wish, just in case.

Cole chuckled softly to himself as he fingered the mangy fur. "All right, then. I wish—"

No, the old man said he had to be careful. Be specific.

Cole closed his eyes. "I wish for five hundred dollars."

He sat there, clutching the paw. It felt familiar, and it took him a moment to realize why. Because it reminded him of another paw he'd had once—a rabbit's foot that he'd insisted on buying on their last family road trip before H2N3 hit. His lucky rabbit's foot. He'd carried it everywhere for a month and then stuffed it away in a drawer. The last time he'd seen it, he'd been making a wish. Clutching it and praying that the bite on his mother's arm hadn't infected her. Praying she'd walk out of the quarantine ward and come home and see the rabbit's foot, laugh, and say, "Good god, Cole. Do you still have that flea-bitten old thing?"

Of course, she hadn't come out. She'd been infected, so they put her down.

Put down.

They had a dog once that had to be put down. It wasn't the same thing.

When Cole opened his eyes, he could feel tears prickling. He swiped them away with a scowl and then turned that scowl on the monkey's paw.

Yeah, you'll make me some money all right. As soon as I figure out how to sell you.

Cole scoured the commercial section of New Chicago—the market and the shops—trying to figure out where he could sell the paw. The old man had talked like people knew what it was, and Murray said he did. Was it a famous superstition, like a rabbit's foot? If it was, it had to be rarer—there were a whole lot more rabbits around than monkeys. But if it was *too* rare, could he sell it without someone realizing that he'd stolen it?

He was walking past the hope peddlers, when someone called, "You! Boy!" He glanced over his shoulder to see the old man, bearing down on him. Cole tensed to run, but he couldn't, not without causing a scene that would mean he'd be remembered here for weeks.

He waited for the man to catch up. "If you want that money back, you said I could have it."

"No, it's not that."

The old man waved him to the side. He looked agitated. Upset, not angry. Cole relaxed a little.

"If you need *some* of the money back, I could—" he began.

"No." The old man turned. "It's something else. There was a paw."

"A what?"

"A monkey's paw."

Cole fixed the man with his best look of confusion. "A paw from a monkey? I took that money, and only because you said I could. If you dropped anything else, I didn't see—"

"I gave the paw to a man."

Cole stiffened. "If you're accusing me of stealing—"

"I don't care if you filched it or found it." He met Cole's gaze imploringly. "This is very important, son. Do you have the paw?"

Cole felt a flicker of guilt. Maybe he could just give...No, it might be a trick, forcing him to admit to theft.

"I don't have anything like that." Cole opened his jacket. "Go ahead and check." He'd left the paw safely in their cubby.

The old man shook his head. "All right. I'm sorry, son. That's what the money was for, so I thought maybe you'd followed the man who got it. He says it was pinched from his pocket."

"He probably changed his mind and wants his money, without giving you the paw back. People do that kind of thing. They'll take whatever they can get here."

"I know." The old man's words came out on a sigh.

"I could look for it," Cole said. "I'm pretty good at finding things."

A faint smile. "No. With any luck, it's gone for good. I only hope that bastard got a chance to try it first."

"Try it?"

The old man clapped Cole on the back. "Nothing. Go on, son. I'm sorry to have bothered you."

As the old man started to walk away, Cole called, "Wait. If I do hear about it, should I tell you? Or does it go back to your friend?"

"Oh, he's not my friend. And I would most gladly see him take the accursed thing. In fact, I'd *pay* to give it to him again." He paused. "Let's say ten dollars. If you do hear of it . . ."

"I'll let you know."

"Thank you."

Cole had no idea what the old man had been talking about, but at least now he had a plan. He'd wait a day, and then say he'd scoured the alley where they'd first met and he'd found the paw there. Ten dollars was more than he'd hoped to get selling it.

Maybe the "accursed thing" did work, in its way. It was just like everything else in New Chicago. You had to lower your expectations. Significantly. Wish for five hundred bucks. Get ten instead.

Cole laughed softly as he approached his building. Then he stopped. There were three men outside. Two huge thugs and an older man in the middle. Russ McClintock.

When they heard him coming, they all turned. Cole couldn't see their expressions in the gathering dark, but he called a greeting.

"Is Tyler looking for me?" he asked, hooking his thumb toward the building.

"No, Cole." McClintock stepped away from his goons. "I came to talk to you."

"Me? If this is about a job—"

"It's about Tyler."

Cole's heart began to thump. "T-Tyler? Where—?"

"There was an accident on the job tonight. Tyler's team was scouting in one of the abandoned skyscrapers. The floor gave way. Your brother fell."

"Fell? Where is he? Is he okay?"

"No, Cole. He's . . . not okay. It was a long fall. He didn't make it. I'm sorry. I know how close you two were and, while it was an accident, I take care of my own." He reached into his pocket and pulled out a wad of bills. "This is five hundred dollars. For you."

Cole sat in the dark, shivering and alone. He'd already flown into a rage. He'd already broken things. He'd already cried. Now he sat on his crate with the pile of money in front of him. But he wasn't looking at the stack. He was looking at the crate where he'd hidden the paw.

That accursed thing.

Cole hadn't been specific enough—he hadn't said *how* he wanted the money. So the paw provided it, in the worst possible way. That's why the old man gave it to Murray. Cole had no idea what Murray had done to the old man, but it had been something, and that "gift" was revenge. That's why he hadn't taken the bills.

I killed my brother. I was foolish and I was greedy, and I thought maybe, just maybe, I could be lucky. I got my money and it cost me the only thing I cared about.

Unless…

Cole rose and made his way to the crate. He reached in and found it, down in the bottom.

The monkey's paw.

He could use it to bring Tyler back. He'd learned his lesson. He took the paw's powers seriously now and he knew to be very, very careful what he asked for. That was the trick. And if it failed? Well, it had already done its worst.

Still, he formulated his request with care.

"I wish my brother—"

Was alive again? Hell, no. That wasn't nearly specific enough. Tyler would probably rise from wherever McClintock dumped him, his broken body crawling back—

Cole shivered. No, he'd read too many horror novels to make that mistake.

"I wish my brother, Tyler, was alive and healed, just as he was before he fell, and I want him to be right outside our building, safely standing on the ground, in two minutes, with no memory of how he died or how he arrived there, just thinking that he's come home, tired, after a regular job."

There. You couldn't get any more specific than that.

Cole stuffed the monkey's paw back in the crate. He crawled out into the dark alley, looked one way and then the other. There was no sign of Tyler.

Had he done something wrong? He ran through the wish again. No, it was specific—

"Hey," said a voice behind him. "What are you doing out here? Locking up?"

He turned and saw Tyler. His brother managed a faint smile and then rubbed his eyes. He yawned and looked around, blinking as if confused.

Cole's heart thudded and he wanted to run over and hug Tyler like he hadn't since he was twelve. But he didn't dare, as if Tyler might evaporate the minute he threw his arms around him.

"You okay?" Cole asked finally.

"Yeah. Just a long day." Another tired smile as Tyler clapped Cole on the back. "Come on, bud. Let's get inside."

Tyler had conked out as soon as he lay down. It took hours for Cole to fall asleep. He kept crawling over and listening to make sure his brother was still breathing. He was. He seemed fine. He'd rubbed his right arm a few times, but there was nothing wrong with it that Cole could see. He must have knocked it before the fall and it still stung.

Finally Cole drifted off. He'd barely gotten to sleep when Tyler bolted awake, Cole jumping up, too.

"Jake," Tyler said. "Goddamn, Jake. That son of a bitch!"

Cole scrambled over, his heart thudding again. "What's wrong?"

"It's Jake. That bastard pushed me—" Tyler stopped and blinked. He looked around, as if getting his bearings. "Okay..."

"What?"

Tyler shook his head sharply, the anger gone from his voice. "I was dreaming that I was on the job last night. We were in a building, ten floors up. Jake pushed me over the edge."

"Well, obviously he didn't." Cole's laugh was strained, but Tyler didn't seem to notice.

"Yeah, obviously not." Tyler rubbed his arm again.

"Are you okay?" Cole asked, pointing at the arm.

"Yeah. Must have done something to it." Tyler clenched and unclenched his fist. "Seems fine, though. Sorry I woke you."

"No problem."

Cole lay down again. Jake was the leader of the gang Tyler worked with. Had he actually *pushed* Tyler? Had Tyler found something that Jake wanted? Or could it have been on McClintock's orders? Was that why he'd been so generous with the payout?

Cole hadn't decided yet what to tell Tyler about his death and resurrection. He'd need to say something. Tyler couldn't just walk back to work tomorrow. If McClintock had ordered Tyler's death, he *really* couldn't walk back to work.

He'd have to tell Tyler the truth, as crazy as it was.

"Cole? How much money do we have now?" Tyler asked in the darkness.

Cole stiffened. "Uh, five hundred and thirty-two dollars. Like I said this afternoon."

"Right." A pause. "Can I see it?"

"Now?"

"Sure. I just want to..." Tyler trailed off. "No. I don't... Why...?" A soft laugh. "Damn, I really am tired. I have no idea what I'm saying."

"Oh, I know what you're saying. You want to see where I'm hiding the money so you can slip some out and buy me more books. Uh-uh. That money is hidden for a reason. I do *not* want more books."

Tyler laughed again. It was true—he had a bad habit of raiding the kitty to buy things that he decided Cole absolutely must have, which was why it was hidden.

"Go back to sleep," Cole said. "Everything's fine."

"Where's the money?"

Cole jolted awake to see Tyler's face over his. His brother's eyes were wild and bloodshot, his face twisted, nearly unrecognizable.

"Wh-what?" Cole managed.

Tyler grabbed him by the shirtfront and yanked him up. "I want my money, you goddamn little punk. It's mine. I earned it."

I'm having a nightmare. I must be. This isn't Tyler.

"Can you hear me, brat? I said I want my money."

Something's wrong. Look at him. Something's really, really wrong.

"You're having another bad dream," Cole babbled. "Like earlier. With Jake. You're overtired. You're just—"

Tyler wrenched him up and threw him across the tiny room. Cole hit the wall and slumped to the floor, staring as Tyler advanced on him.

This is not my brother. Something went wrong. The monkey's paw. It tricked me. It did something to . . .

Cole's gaze dropped to Tyler's arm. The spot he'd been rubbing earlier was bright red now.

Cole remembered their father coming home one night, while they were still at home, while they still had a home, before the military began sending people into walled neighborhoods like Garfield Park and bombing the rest, trying to exterminate the infected.

Their father had come home, tired and dazed. In the middle of the night, he'd woken up. And he'd come after them.

You brats. You ungrateful brats. Spending my money. Eating my food.

As Tyler reached for him, Cole's gaze shot to his brother's arm. To that fevered red spot. To the white semicircles around it. The faint scars of a bite mark.

They say that one of the infected got in.

It's Jake. That bastard pushed me.

Because Tyler had been bitten. He'd gotten ambushed by one of the infected, and Jake saw it happen and pushed him over the edge because he knew what was coming. Because Jake was a friend and that's what you did if a friend got bitten. You gave him a quick and merciful death.

Then I brought him back. I asked for Tyler back as he was before the fall, whole and healed. So the bite healed, but his body was still infected.

Cole swung as hard as he could, plowing his brother in the jaw. Tyler stumbled back. Cole leaped up and raced to his dresser crate. He snatched the monkey's paw and tore out the door.

Cole didn't lead Tyler out onto the street. He might attack someone else. More important, though, he could be spotted. Cole had to solve this himself. So he stayed inside their bombed-out building, leapfrogging over small debris piles and hiding behind bigger ones, keeping one step ahead of Tyler as he tried to figure out what to do next.

He remembered the night their father got infected. Tyler had put Cole in the locked bathroom and told him to stay there, but Cole had snuck out. He'd followed as his brother led their father through the dark streets, steering him straight to a guard station. Tyler had shouted a warning and the guards came out and... And then there was a shot.

For weeks, Cole had hated his brother. He'd run away. He'd fought when Tyler came after him. He raged and shouted and called his brother every name a ten-year-old knew. He remembered Tyler explaining that this was what their father told him to do. Once you were bitten, even if you seemed normal for a while, something inside you had changed and no matter how good a person you were, you'd hide the bite, and you wouldn't warn anyone. So they had to kill you before you killed them.

Eventually, Cole had understood, and they'd come to a pact. If either of them was bitten, they'd do the same thing. Don't hope for a cure. Don't hope it would get better. They knew it wouldn't. A merciful death. That was the final gift they could give, as Jake had for Tyler.

Except this was different. Cole still had one wish left.

One cursed wish. One wish that would almost certainly go wrong.

The first time, he'd blamed himself for being careless. Yet he hadn't been careless with his second wish. He just didn't know all the facts, and there was no way around that, no way to account for every possibility.

Cole knew what Tyler would want him to wish for. Grant Tyler a merciful passing. Undo the second wish. Protect himself. Don't take a chance.

For six years, everything Tyler had done, he'd done for Cole. To give him a better life. Now that dream was within Cole's grasp. He had the money to get into Garfield Park and plenty of extra to help him lead a good life, a safe life, a hopeful life.

A life without Tyler.

What kind of future was that? His brother had already sacrificed everything for him and now he had to sacrifice his life, too? Tyler didn't deserve that. Goddamn it, Tyler *did not* deserve it. If the world was a just place, Cole would be the one infected and Tyler would put him down and get the kind of life he truly deserved.

But that wasn't happening. Cole had two choices: undo his second wish or pin his hopes on a third cursed one.

Cole rounded a chunk of wall and nearly ran into his brother. Tyler snarled and lunged at him. Cole stumbled, twisting and getting his footing just as Tyler caught his shirt.

"Give me that money, you ungrateful brat. It's mine. I worked for it while you sat on your ass and—"

Cole wrenched free. As Cole ran, Tyler continued shouting after him. Shouting insults and curses. Maybe that should help his decision. It didn't. Cole couldn't even tell himself that maybe this was what Tyler really felt, deep down, because he knew this was the infection talking. His brother had given him everything because it gave him a purpose, it made him happy.

And you know what he'd want to give you now. The best chance possible.

Which is exactly what I want to give him.

So once again, they were at an impasse. And Cole had to break it. He had to make a choice.

Cole saw a door ahead. It led into a rubble-filled room. When they'd first arrived here four years ago, they'd tried to clear that area—a room with four standing walls and a door was rare. But the ceiling was half caved in and the rubble too heavy to move.

Now that's where Cole ran. He raced through the door, banged it shut, and leaned against it. Then he took out the monkey's paw and gripped it tight.

Tyler slammed into the door. It jostled Cole but stayed closed. His brother pounded, as if his mind was too far gone to even try the handle.

Now Cole had to make a choice. Wish for a merciful death? Or wish for his brother back, uninfected and healthy, and pray, just pray, that it worked out this time, because if it didn't, he was out of wishes.

Was there a choice? Really? Was there? No. Not for him.

"I'm sorry," Cole whispered. "I know what you'd want me to do, and I know what I have to do, and if I make the wrong choice, I'm sorry."

He squeezed his eyes shut and very carefully, he made his wish. The words had barely left his lips before the door went still. Cole stood there, listening and hoping and praying. Then he took a deep breath, reached for the handle…and opened the door.

Author's Note . . . .

My first exposure to "The Monkey's Paw" was a television adaptation, which I watched when I was certainly too young. While I don't recall much of the actual show—not even enough to identify the version—I've never forgotten the horrifying final moments, when the desperate, grieving parents heard the knock at the door and realized their child had returned just as he had died, broken and mutilated.

When I finally read W. W. Jacobs's story years later, I'll admit to being disappointed. It didn't have the visceral impact I remembered. But I continued to return to it, coming to appreciate the slow escalation of dread, and the tale has stayed with me as a prime example of true horror. When I was asked to contribute to this anthology, there was little question of which story I wanted to reinterpret. It had to be "The Monkey's Paw."

The Wood Beyond the World (1894). William Morris was an amazing man. Among his many accomplishments, he was a designer of architecture and home furnishings (the Morris chair is still made today, and his wallpaper designs are still extremely popular), a painter (he was one of the founders of the Pre-Raphaelite Brotherhood), a pioneer socialist, a designer of type fonts, an illustrator, a translator, and a writer. It is in this later capacity that he produced the first great fantasy novel employing an invented world, constructed from his own imagination. It was, I think, Morris's outright rejection of the burgeoning industrial revolution that was so rapidly reshaping the English cities and landscapes around him that led him to develop a "fresh scrubbed world, done up in the bright, timeless light of Medieval tapestries" amid high castles and lush landscapes, through which his heroes move calmly in adventure after epic adventure. To enjoy any of Morris's novels, you are forced to put aside the rushing to and fro of modern life and relax into his lyrically described worlds of long ago and far away.

The Wood Beyond the World

The Soul Collector

Kami Garcia

I'll never forget the first person I killed. The world went silent, and there was nothing but the sound of my heart pounding and his body hitting the floor. I spent days picking the dried blood from underneath my fingernails afterward.

I was barely sixteen, but I only had one regret.

I should've done it sooner.

It was after midnight when I finally made it back from the Triangle—twelve blocks where the city's roughest neighborhoods converged, and a haven for drug dealers, hookers, and junkies. Not the kind of place most fathers sent their daughters, unless your father was a sick son of a bitch who took in foster kids to pay the rent and score him drugs.

I stared at the bare bulb above the front door. It flickered like it was as scared to burn out as I was to go inside.

"Petra?"

Will stepped out of the shadows, his lip cut and the skin around his dark eyes ringed in fresh bruises.

I came down the steps and reached out to touch his face. "What happened?"

He caught my hand and pulled it behind his back, drawing

me closer. "Jimmy and I got into it again. Same shit, different day."

I kissed the cut on his lip. "I wish you didn't have to let him do this to you."

Will shrugged, long hair hanging in his eyes. "Don't have a choice." Not while his little brother lived in Jimmy's house—that was the part he didn't say.

He leaned his head against mine. "Let's get outta here. Tonight. After Jimmy passes out, we can take Connor and go."

I closed my eyes and tried to imagine a life without dirty needles on the kitchen counter and puke all over the bathroom floor—a life without Jimmy.

"We don't have enough money yet," I said. "And we can't squat in abandoned buildings with your eight-year-old brother."

"Maybe it's better than this."

The words hung in the air.

Years later, they would still haunt me.

I looked up at the lightbulb again. "I should get inside. He'll only get worse if he doesn't get a fix."

Will nodded. "I'm gonna find somewhere to crash tonight."

I pressed my lips against his one last time.

Will walked down the sidewalk backward, smiling at me, until he disappeared into the night.

When I opened the door, Jimmy was waiting at the top of the stairs tweaking and sweating pomade, his rayon dress shirt buttoned on the wrong buttons. "Where the hell have you been? You got my shit?"

I handed him two cellophane bags, hoping he would lock himself in his room and speedball his way through what was enough coke and heroin to kill any normal person.

Instead he grabbed my arm, his dirty nails digging into my skin. "This won't even get me through the night."

I shrank away. "You only gave me a twenty."

Jimmy tightened his grip and dragged me down the hall. "Doesn't matter. Castillo's gonna hook me up after I hand you over."

My blood turned to ice in my veins.

I had heard about the girls who disappeared in the run-down houses Castillo controlled in the Triangle. Most of them went inside looking for drugs. Then there were the others—girls like me who were handed over like crumpled twenties.

By tomorrow night, I would be lying in a filthy bed in one of those houses, drugged out of my mind and offered up to any scumbag that walked in the door.

"Jimmy, please—"

His fist slammed into my jaw. A rush of pain shot up the side of my face, and I stumbled back.

He caught me around the waist, pinning my arms against my body. "I waited two years for you to hit sixteen." He slid something out of his pocket—a needle filled with enough of his poison to leave me unconscious, or at least compliant.

I twisted and squirmed until one of my arms slid free. The table where Jimmy kept his works was only a few feet away. I reached for the edge, trying to pull myself away from him.

Something rolled under my fingertips, and my hand closed around it.

I plunged it down over and over.

I didn't stop when I felt the pen slide into Jimmy's flesh. Or when he jerked away, screaming.

I didn't stop until the pen slid from my blood-soaked hand.

Killing a man is easier than you think. It happens fast—in the span of a few heartbeats.

I don't remember grabbing my backpack and leaving the house, or much of anything in the weeks that followed. I stayed in a shelter until they started asking questions. After that, I slept in Dumpsters and ate out of trash cans behind a Chinese restaurant.

Every night, I fell asleep picturing Will's beautiful face, promising myself I would go back for him. But those dreams morphed in the darkness, and every morning I awoke in a cold sweat with the memory of Jimmy's dead eyes staring back at me.

Whatever hope I had of seeing Will again was just that— hope. I was a murderer and possibly payment for one of Jimmy's drug debts to Francis Castillo.

There was no going back.

Three months later, I met Kate. She never told me much about herself, except that she had left home at fourteen and fig- ured out a way to make enough money to buy her meals instead of scavenging them. Turned out, I had a talent for stripping cars. If we picked the right ones, it paid well enough for the two of us to pool our money and sleep in cheap motel rooms.

Until the night everything changed again.

I was working the rims off an expensive SUV when I heard a voice behind me. "Need some help?"

I whipped around, wielding the wrench in my hand like a bat. The guy towering over me looked like he was in his thirties and had missed a few shaves.

The guy pointed at the rims. "You know the trick to that?"

"What?"

He flashed his badge. "Don't get caught."

I turned to run, but he caught my arm before I got more than a few feet.

"Please don't arrest me," I begged.

He hesitated and really looked at me. "How old are you?"

"Sixteen."

"Where are your parents?"

It was a question I had been asked a hundred times. The answer never got any easier. "I don't have any."

"You don't have any, or you don't like the ones you've got?"

For once, I had the truth on my side. "My mom was a junkie. I grew up in the system."

He loosened his grip on my arm without releasing me. "Criminals and cops have something in common. They both see the world in black and white. Only difference is their white is our black." His face softened.

"Maybe you're just on the wrong side of the line."

Four years later, his face is harder, from a combination of too many nights working undercover and too many bottles of whiskey, like the one on the table between us. But now we're on the same side of that line, and I'm a cop instead of a criminal.

Bobby saved my life that night. I'll never understand why he gave me a place to live and a chance to turn so many wrongs right.

I know something is bothering him because he's not talking, the thing Bobby does better than anyone.

He pours himself another shot and downs it. "We've got a chance to get someone on the inside. Castillo's triggerman turned up floating in the river the day before yesterday."

Castillo.

"Are they sending you in?" I ask.

"No. They need someone who knows the players and the

neighborhood." He takes a swig straight from the bottle. "Someone with a range score above ninety-two."

It feels like someone sucked all the oxygen out of the room. "I'm the only person with a range score that high."

He won't look at me. "I know."

It's too much.

Castillo and the Triangle. Kidnapping girls no one will miss and selling them like raw meat—and they were the lucky ones. The rest ended up in the high-rises, their veins full of junk, servicing Castillo's crew and anyone else willing to pay.

I was almost one of those girls.

"Wait." I hold up my hand. "Castillo won't trust somebody off the street. I'll have to prove myself."

Bobby raises his eyes to meet mine, hope and shame so tangled together that it makes my stomach turn. "I know."

I've only killed one person, and I can still hear him screaming.

I push my chair back, and it drags across the floor. The bartender glances over, and I lean closer. "You're asking me to execute people," I hiss under my breath.

His jaw sets, transforming him into the cop who can convince even the most hardened criminals that he's one of them. "You wouldn't be killing people. The guys Castillo works with are scum. Dealers. Rapists. Cop killers. The way I see it, you'll be doing the world a favor."

Bobby has to see it that way, or he won't be able to justify what he is asking me to do.

Twenty years on the street changes a person, especially a cop. Bobby had seen things that kept him walking the halls at night and swimming in a bottle during the day.

"What happened to all that shit you told me the night we

met about criminals just being on the 'wrong side of the line'?" I ask.

Bobby stands up and lights a cigarette, tossing a few bills on the table. "You don't believe that anymore, do you?"

Francis Castillo isn't what I expected. Clean-shaven and handsome, in a dark suit and pressed shirt, he looks more like a businessman than a psychopath. He's sitting in the back of Machiavelli's flanked by his lieutenants, sipping espresso and reviewing spreadsheets. The restaurant isn't open yet, chairs still flipped over on the tabletops while the staff bustles around in the kitchen.

He glances up at me and turns back to his paperwork. "A woman. I like that. No one expects a face that pretty to be the last one they see."

Castillo hands the guy to his left a folded slip of paper. "Set her up with whatever she needs."

I play the part—sugar laced with a little cyanide, that's what he's looking for. I let my eyes drift across my cleavage and down to the holster inside my leather jacket. "I've got everything I need right here, Mr. Castillo."

His expression changes and even in his two-thousand-dollar suit, I see the hunger in his eyes that led him here. "I bet you do."

I follow Castillo's lieutenants, aware that his eyes are still on me. Another one of his thugs comes in as we're leaving and holds the door open for us.

"Is he in the back?" the guy asks.

The voice slams into me like a fist. I look up slowly.

Will's dark eyes stare back at me from inside a man's body. The boy I never stopped loving.

Will can't hide his shock, and I look away, breaking the connection for both our sakes.

The lieutenant nods. "He's waiting on you."

I'm still reeling a few hours later, while I wait for my mark at a deserted construction site. I was right about Castillo. He's not a trusting guy, and my first job is only hours after our meeting.

I force myself to stop thinking about Will and concentrate on what I found out about the guy I'm supposed to kill. Torres owns a couple of the high-rises where Castillo houses his prostitution operation. A few days ago, one of the buildings was raided and the cops hauled this loser in for questioning. My guess is that Castillo either thinks Torres made a deal or is thinking about making one.

The office goes dark, and Torres comes out of the trailer.

I try to wrap my mind around what I'm about to do—shoot a man in cold blood.

Not a man. A monster.

The voice is so faint I barely hear it. I turn around and scan the area, but there's no one out here except Torres. He's on his cell, standing in front of the trailer like a bull's-eye.

Anyone with a passing range score could hit this guy from where I'm standing.

I take a deep breath and raise my gun.

Even in the dark, I can see my hand shaking.

If I don't do this, I'll blow my cover. I need to hear Castillo order a hit, or he'll keep hurting girls who aren't as lucky as I was.

I'm holding the grip so tight that my fingers go numb. I drop my arm and slip behind the Dumpster next to me. I close my eyes, the metal cold against my back.

"You don't have it in you."

My eyes fly open.

A guy stands a few feet in front of me. There's something in his hand.

Instinct takes over. "Drop it."

He cocks his head to the side and smiles as he raises his arm.

I squeeze the trigger. Even with a silencer, I can hear both shots. The bullets pierce his black V-neck sweater square in the chest. I wait for his body to fold from the impact, for him to stagger and fall.

None of those things happen.

He takes a penny out of his pocket and winks at me. "For your thoughts."

He must be wearing a vest.

But he didn't even flinch.

"Don't move," I say. "Or they'll be picking up pieces of you all over this parking lot."

He raises his hands, palms facing me. "You've got me."

Before I have time to fire off another shot, he yanks the sweater up so I can see his bare skin.

There's no vest.

And no blood—

I pull the clip out of my gun and check it to make sure I'm not losing my mind. Two rounds are missing.

"You shot me, Petra. I think we both know that." He lets his sweater fall and snakes his thumb through one of the bullet holes.

It's not possible.

I try to bridge the gap between logic and what I just saw. It has to be some kind of trick.

He brings a finger to his lips, signaling me to be quiet. "You don't want to disturb Mr. Torres over there. He's engaging in a very sensitive call with a tantalizing young lady, who is actually a young man in Ohio."

"Who the hell are you?" The words tumble out before I can stop them.

"I'm a businessman, but I like to think of myself as a problem solver. And you have a problem I can solve."

"What are you talking about?"

He gestures in Torres' direction. "You need him dead, and you can't kill an innocent man, though I'm using that term loosely. I can take care of him for you and no one has to know. But you have to give me something in return."

His voice is hypnotic, like waves breaking on the shore. "What do you want?"

"Nothing you'll miss." He smiles. "A kiss."

"Then what? I turn to stone or something?"

He laughs. "If past experience is any indication, you'll enjoy it. And you can earn the Blood Merchant's trust. Did you know that's what they call Castillo?"

I remember Jimmy dragging me down the hall. The needle in his hand...how close I came to being sold to the Blood Merchant.

I step forward and press my lips against the stranger's before I can stop myself. He slides his tongue in my mouth and I taste him—burnt toast and honey.

He steps back, with that Cheshire cat grin still on his lips, and crosses the parking lot.

Torres notices him right away and pulls his gun. He fires off three shots, but the stranger doesn't even break stride. Torres stares, dumbstruck.

"What the f—"

The stranger walks by and extends his arm, a single out-stretched finger pointing at Torres. He doesn't even glance up as a slit opens in Torres' neck and slices across his throat, following the path of the stranger's finger, like a laser.

Is he carrying some kind of military-grade weapon? What else could cut through a man's neck that way?

Torres clutches his throat and drops to the ground in a pool of blood.

The stranger looks back at me and blows me a kiss before he disappears into the darkness.

Castillo was impressed with the scene at the construction site. "Cutting a man's throat is a work of art, and it sends a message. Shows you're not afraid to get your hands dirty." I had only nodded, afraid to trust my own voice, and grateful I didn't have to face Will again.

I wasn't as lucky the next time Castillo summoned me.

It was two in the morning when my cell rang and three o'clock when the black sedan pulls up in front of the furnished apartment the department supplied for me.

Machiavelli's is closed, but the lights are still on in the back room, and "La Bohème" is playing loud enough to break glass. Castillo sits in the corner with his eyes shut. The owner of the restaurant has his sleeves rolled up and gestures as if he's con-ducting an orchestra.

"Can you feel it? The desperation? The sorrow?"

Castillo opens his eyes. "Yeah. It feels like shit." He nods and one of his men kills the music. The owner scurries past me like I'm contagious. I wonder if he knows who I am, at least who Cas-tillo thinks I am.

One of Castillo's lieutenants takes a piece of paper from the inside pocket of his jacket and hands it to me. It's folded four times like the love notes boys pass you in high school.

Castillo stands and walks to the front of the restaurant. He's the piper, and we all follow like rats. "You have style, Miss Nicov," he says. "I like that in a woman."

He lifts his hat off the bar and puts it on. When we step out onto the street, his car is waiting. The driver opens the door, and Castillo slips inside. He tips his hat to me, a ridiculous gesture. "Let's see if you can up your game."

The car glides down the street, and he leaves me standing in the dark. I don't want to unfold the paper and see the name of the next man I'm supposed to kill. I don't want to know what kind of evil this man has perpetrated or the number of lives he has destroyed.

"Petra?"

My breath catches at the sound of Will's voice. It's deeper, but it still sounds like anger and desperation. I can't turn around.

I feel him walk up behind me, sense the way his body fills the space between us.

"When I came back and the cops told me Jimmy was dead and you were gone, I thought...I don't know what I thought." He hesitates. "Did Jimmy hurt you?"

I don't want him to dig any deeper. "He tried, but I stopped him."

"Petra, will you look at me?" He's fumbling, trying to figure out how to have an impossible conversation. "You don't know how many times I imagined what it would be like to see you again."

He touches my arm, but I don't turn around. I don't even breathe.

Will comes around from behind me so I have to face him. "Just tell me why." He drops his head, embarrassed. "Why didn't you come back? I would've gone with you." He laughs, but it sounds lonely and faraway. "I would've followed you anywhere."

"I couldn't go back." I choke out the words. "Not after what happened."

Will reaches out and runs his thumb across my cheek. "Petra?" He swallows hard. "What did he do?"

"He was going to trade me."

Will doesn't ask me to elaborate. The details were written all over my bedroom ten years ago in Jimmy's blood.

He pulls me closer before I can stop him, and I'm in his arms. He feels exactly the same.

"There's never been anyone else," he whispers.

His lips are on mine. It's not like kissing the stranger who bartered for my affection. I don't have to give myself to Will. I already belong to him.

My hands tangle in his hair.

"Petra," he breathes, and I'm drowning in him.

I pull away, gasping.

He keeps his hands on my waist. "When I saw you with Castillo, it was like seeing a ghost."

Castillo.

Will works for Castillo. He thinks we both do.

"I have to go." I stumble away from him, off balance in every way.

"Stay." He reaches for my hand.

"I don't want you to get hurt." It's the truth even if he doesn't understand it.

Castillo will find out that I'm a cop eventually, even if he's in cuffs when it finally happens. If he thinks Will was in on any of this, he'll make sure Will is the next guy who turns up floating in the river.

When I'm safely in a cab, I unfold the paper with the name of the next man I'm supposed to kill. I recognize it immediately from the case files: Enzo Feretti, heroin supplier for half the dealers in the Triangle—the half Castillo doesn't control. At least he isn't some poor guy who can't afford his protection payments.

This hit is harder. Feretti isn't hanging out at a deserted construction site. He's at home with a harem of hookers, if the notes Castillo's lieutenants gave me are accurate.

Castillo mapped out the whole place for me. I'm supposed to take out the guy covering the back door and access the service stairs to the second floor of Feretti's house. One of the hookers is a plant, and she will text Castillo's men when Feretti passes out for the night and the other girls get kicked out.

From where I'm hiding in the trees, I can see Feretti's guy at the back door. I unlatch the safety on my Sig 9, and try to convince myself I can do this—that Bobby's right and it's all for a greater good.

Deep down, I don't believe it.

"I would be happy to take him off your hands."

I whip around. Standing right behind me is the stranger in the black sweater, the man who slit Torres' throat without touching him.

"Where the hell did you come from?"

He shrugs. "Around. I like to keep an eye on my investments." He glances at Feretti's man. "Are you really going to execute a poor idiot with nothing but a GED and a bad gambling habit?"

All I can think about is some poor kid getting sucked in by Feretti. A kid like Will.

"What do I have to give you?"

He tilts his head, considering. "A memory."

"A memory? That's it?" I laugh. "Take them all."

One corner of his mouth tilts up slightly. "I only want one, but I get to choose."

"If you don't kill the guy guarding the door."

The stranger crosses his arms, clearly irritated that I've added terms. "Deal."

He takes off in the direction of the house, keeping close to the tree line.

The stranger is behind Feretti's man before the thug realizes it, and his arm slides around the guy's throat. With one sharp pull, the stranger cuts off the guy's air supply, and he passes out.

He gestures for me. I move quietly, but unlike the stranger, I can't keep my footfalls silent.

I follow him up the back stairs to the second floor. He heads directly to Feretti's room with no guidance from me, as if he has a map of his own.

The lights are out in Feretti's bedroom, but the gold paint and white lacquer gleam in the darkness. The room smells like hard liquor and sweat, and my stomach churns. Feretti is sprawled on the bed passed out, his gut heaving with every breath.

My eyes meet the stranger's, and I offer him my gun.

He shakes his head. "Have you ever heard the expression 'There's more than one way to skin a cat'?" He unearths a silver lighter from his pocket, and the stranger's face contorts into a wicked smile. "There's more than one way to skin a man, too."

The lighter sparks, and he tosses it on the bed. The sheets ignite, and the flames accelerate at an unnatural rate.

Feretti bolts upright, thrashing and screaming as the fire wraps itself around his limbs. I gag and cover my mouth. The smell is worse than rotting flesh—like the smell of pain itself.

Feretti rolls onto the floor screaming, every inch of his body completely engulfed in flame.

I hear voices. A moment later, people bang on the door.

The stranger pushes me onto the balcony and leads me along a ledge that snakes around the second story. We reach the slanted roof of the garage below us. He grabs my hand.

I don't realize we've jumped until my feet hit the ground.

Smoke pours from the window we had climbed through only moments ago.

The stranger drags me into the woods.

When we finally stop running, I drop down on the ground and hug my knees, shuddering with every breath.

What have I done?

He's watching me, his pupils wide and hungry. "You owe me a memory."

"Which one do you want? My first kiss? Or the worst beating I ever took?"

He kneels down in front of me until we're only inches apart, his icy blue eyes ripe with anticipation. "Something a little more interesting." He runs his finger over my bottom lip. "Like how you ended up here."

I rub my hands over my face, and streaks of black ash come off on my fingertips. "I'm not telling you that."

"You don't have to." He leans closer and his mouth is on mine again.

I try to pull away. But we are bound by something more powerful than desire and I can't break free.

"Petra," he murmurs. "I want it all."

The memory crashes over me . . .

"Castillo's gonna hook me up after I hand you over."

The stench of sweat and crack.

"I waited two years for you to hit sixteen."

I try to pull myself out of the moment—the memory—but I'm drowning as the images pummel me and I can't find the surface . . .

The needle in Jimmy's hand.

My fingers closing around the pen.

His blood splattering all over me.

Silence.

The memory recedes slowly, like the tide drawing back from the beach. The stranger's lips are still on mine as he whispers, "My sweet Petra. What did he do to you?"

I'm in his lap clinging to him. Tears run down my face as he tugs on my lip one last time. He breaks the connection between us, staring at me as if he experienced the pain along with me.

"What are you?" I ask the question while the taste of him lingers on my lips—the one I should have asked after he slit a man's throat without even touching him.

"Some people call me a devil or a crossroads demon. But they all call me evil." His blue eyes blink back at me, looking deceptively human. "I'm a Soul Collector."

I untangle my body from his, struggling to catch my breath and desperate to get away. "You steal people's souls?"

He walks toward the woods, stopping before he recedes into the shadows. "I don't have to steal them. They give them to me."

*   *   *

When I arrived at my apartment, covered in dirt and ash, a car was waiting. Castillo's driver didn't even give me a chance to change my clothes. He drove directly to Machiavelli's and ushered me inside through the back door.

Castillo sits at a table in the back reading some papers and smoking a cigar. Will is nursing a drink at the bar. His dark hair curls around the collar of a shirt that looks like it cost more than Jimmy used to spend on a month's worth of food when we were kids.

But we aren't kids anymore.

Castillo sees me and rises from his chair clapping, the cigar still wedged between his thick fingers. "You burned the guy alive?"

Castillo and his men laugh—all except Will, who I'm too ashamed to face. My stomach roils. Castillo lifts the papers he was reading off the table and slips them back in the brown folder. I recognize them immediately.

My personnel jacket.

He drops it on the table between us, and a photo of me in uniform slides across the polished wood. "Now what kinda cop does something like that?"

Will's barstool clatters to the ground, but I don't turn around.

One of Castillo's men clamps a heavy hand on my shoulder and takes the gun from inside my jacket.

Castillo signals someone on the other side of the room. "Take them down to the basement. I want to know who they've been talking to."

My eyes find Will. Two of Castillo's men grab his arms from behind and slam Will's face against the bar, forcing him to look at Castillo.

"He doesn't have anything to do with this," I say.

Castillo moves closer and grabs my face roughly. "You think you're the only one who can dig around and find some bones? I know you both lived with that sleepwalker, Jimmy Rollins."

I glance in Will's direction. "I haven't seen him since we were kids."

Castillo shoves my chin away roughly and nods at his thugs.

They drag us down to the storage room. Cans of olive oil and tomatoes are stacked against the wall, across from two metal chairs bolted to the floor. Castillo's men zip-tie our ankles to the chair legs and our wrists behind the chair backs before they close the door and lock it from the other side.

Will stares at me, his eyes full of questions. "Why didn't you tell me you were a cop?"

I almost laugh. "You work for him. What would you have done?"

"I'd never do anything to hurt you." He says the words as if no one has ever spoken anything truer, and I can still see the boy I loved more than anything.

The one I left behind.

I want to tell him I never stopped thinking about him, but I can't.

"How did you end up working for Castillo?"

He looks down at the floor. "I took off with Connor after everything happened. There weren't a lot of jobs for a seventeen-year-old dropout."

The door scrapes against the concrete, and Castillo steps inside. His suit jacket is gone, the sleeves of his expensive dress shirt rolled up. He grabs Will by the throat, the tendons in his hands straining. "That's a sad story, William. Did you tell her how I hid you from the cops after they found that piece of shit foster father of yours stabbed to death?"

Will's body jerks in the chair.

"How I gave you a job so you could put your kid brother through school?" Castillo squeezes harder, and the color drains from Will's face.

"Stop it!" I shout. "He has nothing to do with this."

Castillo releases the iron grip, and Will gasps for air.

His expression hardens, and Castillo kicks Will in the chest. "I thought I taught you something about loyalty."

The chair falls back, and Will's head hits the concrete floor and lolls to one side.

Castillo walks over and stands in front of my chair, a sadistic smile on his face. "You're gonna tell me who you've been reporting to and exactly how much they know, or I'm gonna lock you up in the towers and let every junkie in the Triangle screw you."

Something moves in the corner of the room.

The Soul Collector steps forward without a sound and stands only a few feet behind Castillo. His eyes find mine, silently asking me the question I've answered twice before.

"I'll give you anything you want," I say.

Castillo thinks I'm talking to him. "I know you will."

The Soul Collector looks me in the eye. "You have to say it."

Castillo whips around. "What the hell?"

"My soul!" I scream. "You can have my soul."

Castillo goes for his gun, but the Soul Collector is faster. He reaches out, and his hand breaks through Castillo's rib cage like it's butter. Castillo's body sways and drops to the floor.

The Soul Collector stands before me, holding Castillo's

heart in his hand. He glances down at Castillo's crumpled form. "I'm taking this one for now."

He leans in and kisses me, Castillo's blood running down my neck where the Soul Collector's hand cradles my head. "I'll be back in one year to collect what you owe, Petra. Make sure you're ready."

Will and I disappeared together that night—the way we should have so many years ago. We left our guns and regrets behind and started over with nothing but each other. We didn't talk about what happened in the basement, and I didn't tell him about the stranger who saved our lives. I spent the next year trying to forget the Soul Collector, praying that another debt would outweigh mine. As the months went by, he started to fade like a dream you can't quite remember—a memory blurred around the edges just enough to forget.

It's still early when I come back from the farmers' market. Will usually sleeps late, which gives me time to make breakfast. I want everything to be perfect today—the day I tell him he's going to be a father.

When I open the door, I'm surprised to hear voices in the kitchen. We don't have many friends, and they never stop by unannounced. Realization tugs at the back of my mind, but it's eclipsed by anticipation of the news I can't wait to share.

When I see him, I drop the paper bag in my arms and a bottle of milk explodes on the floor. In a single moment, a day I never wanted to forget has turned into a day that I hoped would never come.

The Soul Collector sits across from Will at our kitchen table.

Will's face is a haunting mask of fear and pain. I wonder how much the Soul Collector told him.

"I'm sorry, Petra." The Soul Collector stands and extends his hand. "But it's time."

"Please—" I'm prepared to beg, but he shakes his head, silencing me.

"You owe a debt, and I have to collect. It's not something I can forgive."

Will stands and walks toward us, his every movement and expression an act of determination. He looks so broken, and I know I'm the one holding the bat.

"Can we have a minute?" he asks.

The Soul Collector nods and moves to the door, waiting inside the archway. There's something unfamiliar in the stranger's blue eyes. Is it sadness?

The tears fall before I can stop them. "Will, I'm so sorry. I should have told you."

"Shh. I understand why you did it." He takes my face in his hands and looks at me the way no one else ever has—as if I have real value. "Everything's going to be okay."

I stare at his beautiful face and wonder if he would have made a different decision if faced with the same choices.

"You're the only person I've ever loved" are the only words I can manage.

Tears run down his cheeks, and I realize it's the first time I've ever seen him cry. He presses his lips against mine, telling me all the things we don't have time to say.

Will pulls away and walks toward the stranger who killed for me, and ultimately saved both our lives. I know Will wants to find a way out of this, but I've seen enough to know that we're beyond that point.

I've made thousands of choices in my life that led me to this moment.

Killing Jimmy was the first.

"Will, there's nothing else—" I can't finish. It feels like my body has run out of breath and I'm already dead.

Soulless.

Will is standing next to the Soul Collector, whose hand is already on the front door, and suddenly I understand. I try to make my legs move, but I'm frozen in place.

Will walks across the threshold backward, smiling at me.

The Soul Collector stops and turns to me. "A sacrifice is worth far more than a trade, Petra."

"Will!" I tear across the room and reach the door just as it slams shut. The latch hasn't even clicked into place before I throw it open again.

The sidewalk stretches out in front of me.

Empty.

When I was a child, my great-grandmother spent hours reading to me from *Grimms' Fairy Tales*, not the sanitized American versions but the original stories in all their dark and terrifying glory. "Rumpelstiltskin" was always one of my favorites. It was only after I reread the story as an adult that I realized what else was hidden beneath the layers of folklore, wish fulfillment, and straw that turned to gold in the right hands.

At its core, "Rumpelstiltskin" is the story of a father who trades his daughter to a king, knowing the king will kill her when he finds out that the girl does not possess the magical skill the man has promised. As a result, the girl must trade with Rumpelstiltskin to save her own life.

Before I became a writer, I taught in the inner city. I watched poverty and drugs ravage families and communities, robbing people of their choices and often their lives. "The Soul Collector" revisits the classic fairy tale I loved so much as a child, juxtaposing my fascination with the paranormal against a backdrop of poverty and drugs, to explore other ways women are "traded"— and the ways we trade ourselves. The crossroads demon (or Soul Collector, as I call him in this story) is the Rumpelstiltskin of the urban fantasy world. He can solve your problems and even grant you wishes—for a price. The question is always the same: What are you willing to trade?

Without Faith, Without Law, Without Joy

Saladin Ahmed

> *There lies he now with foule dishonour dead,*
> *Who whiles he liu'de, was called proud Sans foy,*
> *The eldest of three brethren, all three bred*
> *Of one bad sire, whose youngest is Sans joy,*
> *And twixt them both was borne the bloudy bold Sans loy.*
> —The Faerie Queene, Book I

I.

> *Which of all earthly things he most did craue;*
> *And euer as he rode, his hart did earne*
> *To proue his puissance in battell braue*
> *Vpon his foe, and his new force to learne;*

Holiness has murdered my brave brother.

Holiness has mangled my mind and my name.

Holiness has stolen God's love from me.

I am walking a winding road of pale stone. Who am I? Where am I? I have answers, but they are forged falsehoods. For...days? Years? My brothers and I have been forced to live in this world that is not our world. And I have half forgotten my own.

The one who abducted us—the mailed man-thing called

Holiness—calls this place *Albion*. He calls it Faerie Lond. He calls it the Glorious Isle. The sunlight here is cold and lifeless, the trees are strange, and the birds have evil eyes.

He has brought us here to test himself. To prove himself a worthy knight.

To hunt us.

I do not know how he brought us to this land of blood and iron masks. I know only that I am a real man trapped in a mad landscape of living lessons.

My brothers and I were spirited here from my home in... Damascus? Yes, praise be to God that I can remember *that*. The sound of the street preachers, and the smells of the spice vendors' stalls. *Damascus.*

We were sipping tea in a room with green carpets, and I was laughing at a jest that... that *someone* was making. Who? The face, the voice, the name have been stolen from me. All I know is that my brothers and I suddenly found ourselves in this twisted place, each aware of the others' fates, but unable to find one another. Unable to find any escape.

Now my eldest brother has been slain. And my next eldest brother has disappeared.

Who am I? I do not know how he changed our names. But in this world of lions and giants and the blinding shine of armor, I am called Joyless, as if it were a name.

It was not my name. It *is* not my name. But this is *his* place, and it follows his commands.

And thus, now, here, Joyless is my name, and Joyless has always been my name. This place, this *Albion*, has scrawled its hateful sigils over even the past. Now, when I remember my mother's voice calling for me across the small souk, I can only hear her voice of rock and honey calling "Joyless! Joyless, come here at once!" Now my father's last whispered words to me as sunlight streamed in the wood-lattice window, his last words all those years ago, were "Joyless, my beloved, thanks be to God that you are such a smart boy." It is the only name I can find in my mind now. Whatever name I was once called, whatever name I once called *myself*, has been stolen.

Joyless.

A part of me knows it to be false. Some small, near-dead piece of my soul knows that I was once a joyful man. Sometimes God grants me...flashes of the man I once was. Of what *joy* was. The feel of the falconer's glove as I hunted with my beautiful birds. The jeweled light on the water the first time I saw the sea. The old poet at court granting my scribblings unfeigned praise. These are the sunbeams that break the murk for a moment here and there.

"Memories" is too weak a word. They are like lightning. Like the pain a marked thief or maimed soldier still feels in a hand that has been lost. But they are so fleeting that they do, in fact, become flashes of pain. And each day they fade. Fewer. Farther. Each day it becomes easier to succumb to the grim magic of this place that has claimed my kin.

To forget joy.

To forget who I am.

II.

> *Gentle Knight was pricking on the plaine,*
> *Y cladd in mightie armes and siluer shielde,*
> *Wherein old dints of deepe wounds did remaine,*
> *The cruell markes of many a bloudy fielde;*

I am walking along a road of pale stone.

I am hunted and I am growing mad, but at least I live.

My brave brother—ten years older, he was, and like my second father—is dead. My beatific brother, whom I can only call Faithless, though that should not be his name. He has been murdered by a madman who calls himself a knight. A butcher who is called Saint in this place.

What to call this killer? He has stolen our names and given us pissed-in husks as replacements. He calls us Sarazin. *Sans* and *Sans* and *Sans*. But he has kept names, so many names, for himself. He is called Redcrosse. He is called the Knight. He is called the Saint.

He is called Holiness.

It takes all my power to break the spell of this place and its false names for even a moment. To snatch the breath to call him not Knight, but abductor. To call him not Saint, but brother-killer.

I walk past a twisted thing of moss and bark, flesh and tears— a man? A tree? Redcrosse has filled this place with such horrors. To teach himself lessons. To teach himself what it is to be a Saint.

I keep to the road.

He is using this strange place to test himself. To prove himself to his God and his Queen. And killing us is part of his test, it seems. He has hunted us, or set his creatures on us. The lion. The dwarf. The arch-magi.

But it was Redcrosse himself that struck down my brother.

I was not there when they fought, but the vision came to me, emblazoned across the sickly sky of this place. Sent as a gruesome taunt, perhaps, by Redcrosse himself. I heard the sounds of plate and mail. I saw the Saint's hulking mass as he entered the dueling circle. His muscle and metal. His blood-seeking sword.

And I saw my poor brother, lean as a walking-stick. I watched him kneel to pray before the battle, watched his confused, terrified expression as he found that he had somehow lost the words. Faithless, this cruel knight had renamed him.

I could do nothing but watch as Faithless—may God forgive me for remembering that as his name—faced his foe bravely, knowing nothing of the dark spells that guided the Saint's arm.

I watched them salute and advance and exchange feints. I watched the heat of the fight overtake them both. I saw them dodge and parry and swing. Then Faithless's sword struck true—how my heart had swelled!—and it should have laid open the Saint's mail and rib cage alike.

But the Knight's magic had saved him. The cross on his armor had somehow turned an unturnable blow. That's when I knew that this was all a foul jape. A madman's mock world.

But my brother's death was real enough. In that one thing, the Mad Knight showed me reality. I saw it enameled in sky-fire but, as I watched, I *knew* its truth in my soul. Redcrosse raised his sword with that huge, inhuman arm, and brought it down on... on...no, it is no use—he brought it down on Faithless's head. My brother's helm was split in two, and I saw his brains glisten in the pale sun of cursed Albion.

My brother's faith had failed to protect him. It had left him with a ruined skull. And as I watched wise Faithless's body fall, I was struck by lightning again. Or I felt a pain in something cut off from me. I saw my eldest brother, rising for the early prayer while I mumbled wine-stained curses at the muezzin into my pillow. He wore a smile as he chided me, as if the old words "Prayer is better than sleep" were written across his face.

And then, as the vision faded from the sky, for the briefest of moments, as his shield lay there in the dust, I saw new letters etch themselves across it. Letters that spelled a name that was not Faithless. But they were too far away—or was it that they were too faint?—to see.

III.

> *So long they fight, and fell reuenge pursue,*
> *That fainting each, themselues to breathen let,*
> *And oft refreshed, battell oft renue:*
> *As when two Bores with rancling malice met,*

Still I follow the serpentine stone road. My beloved brother is dead. My only hope now is to find our father's second son. For the Saint has stolen him from me, too.

My second brother—who lives by law above all else—has also had his name mangled by Redcrosse. Now he is called Lawless. And he, too, is being hunted by the Saint and his beasts.

I can't hide the truth from God: Lawless and I share little love. Both my brothers shamed me for my love of wine, but Faithless did it with love. Lawless... Well, he lives his whole life by being mindful of what is permitted and what is forbidden. It is all he cares about. When we were children he was a tyrant of an older brother, and little has changed since then. He tells me I am too permissive with my own...

With my own...

It is no use. Some memory of mine has been stolen.

I cannot dwell on this now. I must focus on the matter at hand: Lawless is my brother. I know not what has happened to him, but I will walk this world until I find out. For, if ever I should find some way to escape, I cannot leave him here. I *must* find him.

And then the sky erupts in flame again. And I am granted another vision.

My brother, the tallest of us, the largest in limb, stands in a clearing, the weird trees of this place all around him. His sword is in his right hand. In his left he holds his shield, the word "LAW-LESS" glowing golden across it.

Suddenly—I can see it in the sky-fire as clearly as if I were there—monsters fly forth from the woods. Things that are half-beast and half-man. They dance on cloven hooves and play oaten pipes even as they try to rend my brother's flesh to bloody shreds. His eyes widen with terror above his neat-trimmed beard as he beats them back.

Do they fight of their own will? Do they do Redcrosse's bidding? I don't know. But they harry and drive him until he stands in another dueling circle. Two dozen paces from him, a fierce figure in green steel plate stands waiting.

Is this Redcrosse in another guise? Or some poor soul forced to play this brutal role by the same magic that has snatched us from our home? I no longer know whether it matters. My brother is going to die.

The knight in the green armor strides forth, bristling with sword and dagger. He is tall and cowled in a cloak of leaves. Though he wears a man's shape, there is something in the way he moves that tells me, as loud as if it were shouted from the mountaintops, that he is not a man.

Then he throws back the cowl. Two small horns adorn his forehead, and there is a goatlike glint in those eyes. Lawless's mouth curls down in disgust. They draw their swords, bellow angry words, and fly at each other.

As they fight, I feel I am watching my brother fight his reflection. Their swords meet, again and again and again and again. One warrior is knocked back by a blow on his shield, then the other is. The goat-knight draws blood, then my brother draws blood.

But no sooner do the cuts appear than they are gone. And now I see the truth of it—my brother will not die. Redcrosse and his accursed Albion have damned him to a crueler fate. This battle will *never* end. This creature that faces Lawless is part animal, and, in fighting it, Lawless has become part animal himself. This is worse than death for my brother. He has lost his law, his connection to God. He will be trapped in this battle, snarling, bestial, lusting for blood, forever.

I can watch no longer. As soon as I turn my gaze, the vision fades. It has done its work, I suppose. It has made certain no spark of hope—no spark of joy—might catch in my heart.

Unless…unless I can destroy the Redcrosse Knight. Unless I can kill Holiness.

IV.

Curse on that Crosse (quoth then the Sarazin)
That keepes thy body from the bitter fit;
Dead long ygoe I wote thou haddest bin,
Had not that charme from thee forwarned it:

I am the only one who really lives now. I am the only son of my mother and my father that this thing-in-armor has not slain in body or soul. But it is only a matter of time—of that I am certain.

I can think of only one way to escape this fate. I could slay *myself*.

The thought drifts to me, sweet and gentle as a breeze. Yes, I could destroy myself and be free of this place. My hand grasps my sword hilt. In my mind I see each of my brothers die again.

And I take three deep breaths. No.

No.

I cannot abandon faith so. I cannot abandon God's own law so. Not when I watched my most beloved brother die fighting. Not when I've seen my law-loving brother turned into a beast.

No, I cannot flee the Saint. And if I cannot flee from him, I must hunt him.

It does not take much to find him. He is singing songs of praise for his Queen, his voice like a trumpet as it blares across the plains.

I walk the pale stone road, following the sound of his songs. Past castle and cavern, past a sleeping giant and a woman with a mouth full of scorpions. How many of us has he brought here with his magic? How many have been twisted into monsters on which he might whet his sword-edge?

After a half day's journey, I finally spy his tent, like a great red war drum. He has stopped singing. I approach as quietly as I can, keeping to the trees, trying to remain unseen.

Outside the great scarlet tent of the Redcrosse Knight, I see my dead brother's battered shield propped against a tree stump. "FAITHLESS" is painted on it in gaudy gore. And beside it, another shield—

LAWLESS. He is dead, too, then? But still this false name shadows his soul.

In the old poems, enchantments often die with those who've cast them. If I can—somehow—kill the Knight, perhaps I can free my brothers' souls from this mad land. I call on God for strength, and I force myself to remember that my brothers lived by faith, and by law. My eyes must burn and water with the effort, and as I watch, the letters waver as if seen through smoke.

Has Almighty God rewarded me? Is the Saint's strange magic fading? I don't know. But as I step from the shadows and into the sun, I see the hooks and edges of FAITHLESS melt and dance and change into the flowing script of my mother tongue. The script of the language of God.

Abdullah, the Servant of God. *That* was my brother. Spending all of his time with the poor. Softly chiding me for my halfhearted fasting in that sweet, reedy voice.

And LAWLESS—those letters are gone. Now the name *Abdul Hakam*, the Servant of God the Judge, is painted across my second brother's shield. I see Abdul Hakam walking with Abdullah through the small souk, his big hand on his sword. Making it his duty to protect poor and rich, Muslim and Jew, from cheats and thieves.

But my memory shrivels as I peer past the shield and into the great red tent. I see *him*. I see Holiness. The man-shaped monster is before me again, but this time it is no vision.

My bravery fails me.

The great bulk of him. That great gleaming sword of his, as long as a man. That great cross on his tabard that no sword can pierce, as red as blood or hellfire. He has made himself great in this place, and he has made me weak. My knowledge is instant and utter—I cannot kill this creature.

He does not see me, he does not hear the grass crunch beneath my feet. Perhaps he is not even looking for me. He hunts greater monsters. Dragons and devils.

I could run and hide and bide my time. It would be the easiest thing in this world.

But again I think of my brothers. Of faith and of law. And of... something else, just beyond my grasp. Something that once brought me joy.

I can cower no longer. If I face him, I will die, and it will not be an easy death. But I can cower no longer. I, the youngest son, the would-be poet who sleeps too late, will stand for my brothers, and God will decide my fate. One way or another, I will have an escape from this place.

His back, a great mailed mountain, is still turned to me. I

could strike. But though this place has stolen God's love from me, I will not let it make me a devil. I will not let this *Albion* make me a backstabber. I will not let it make me a murderer.

I call out a challenge.

V.

Whereas an errant knight in armes ycled,
And heathnish shield, wherein with letters red
Was writ Sans joy, they new arriued find:
Enflam'd with fury and fiers hardy-hed,

The Knight of the bloody Redcrosse, the killer Saint, the hate that calls itself Holiness, turns slowly. His impossibly handsome face is radiant, an unforgiving sun. His ice-blue eyes are alight with bloodlust and madness.

He answers my challenge with haughty mock honor. He can afford this charade, for he knows that his grisly magic protects him. He has his chivalry and his cheat both. He wipes his gory hands on an unstained tabard.

Soon we stand twenty paces apart, in a circle of hard-packed earth. Each of us prepares our arms and our armor, our hearts and our souls. Each of us dreams of killing the other, though I know my dream is folly. Across the tanned leather of my buckler, JOY-LESS, the only name I know, is scrawled in lines like knife slashes.

Another flash. I am young, in the courtyard of a small mansion. I can see the old tree that I grew up reading beneath. An important man in yellow silk—my father—is training me to use the saber, though he knows I will never be the type who loves fighting.

"Always remember, Joyless, that you are fighting a man." Some part of me knows that my father did not call me Joyless.

And yet I can remember the smell of his breath as he did so. "It is the man you are fighting, not his sword or his dagger."

The lightning flash fades. A look up at my foe. This Redcrosse is no man. He is anger in a suit of armor. He is war made flesh.

We raise our blades and step toward one another.

His great sword swings. I deflect the blow with my saber and riposte. We each dodge death once, twice, thrice. But each blow I meet rings through my muscle and weakens me. I will not last long.

We match blow for blow for blow. Our swords meet in a storm of steel, and each of us staggers from the impact. For a long moment we can only stand there and stare at each other, as shocked as two rams that have just butted heads.

But I see in his snarl that this is all a mock to him. Sweat barely beads his brow, and his breath still comes easy. And my own body is sore and tired. Each breath I suck down is like drinking a bowl of fire. I will die soon.

Redcrosse attacks again. His great downward chop knocks my shield away, splitting the wood beneath the stretched hide. It comes close enough to killing me that I can smell the oil on his sword.

I will die soon, but I will not die hiding. I will die doing what is right. What law and faith demand. And…

And then the moments flow as slow as honey. And God takes mercy on a man about to die far from home. The Lord of the Universe—of the *true* Universe—grants me a boon.

Before my eyes, the letters on my lost shield slip and tumble and writhe. They squirm and wriggle like newborn babes until I can nearly read my name.

My name!

My name, not the name this murderer-Saint has given me. Not the evil name that he has forced me to falsely recall having painted there.

The man-thing Holiness, with his monstrous mock courtesy, waits for me to regain my feet.

I stand slowly, my eyes on the shield at Redcrosse's feet. And as the letters reweave themselves, stolen memories return to my barren mind, like cool water on parched lips.

My wise little daughter, sitting on her divan, mastering her letters at four.

My daughter, Aisha. When we learned my wife would never give birth again, I thought God had robbed me by not giving me a son. We had named her after the wife of the Prophet.

Aisha—*Alive.*

As she grew, I knew what true joy was. The clever tricks she pulled. My pride, in spite of her uncles' disapproval, as she wrote her first lines of poetry. *Her name is Aisha!* Redcrosse's spell stole that joyful sound from me, but now it is mine again! *Aisha,* who made me as proud as any son could have. I will never see her again, but I will not die having forgotten her.

Yes, I once knew joy.

"My daughter's name is Aisha," I say. My voice, her name, is sweet and strong to my own ears. Like an angel's war horn. This place had nearly made me forget that I can speak!

"My brothers were Abdullah and Abdul Hakam."

Redcrosse's eyes widen with shock and fury, and he bares his teeth.

Again I fix my eyes on my lost shield. *Ain. Ba. Dal.* The letters of my name weave themselves into words. *Lam. Waw.*

I am *not* Joyless. I have *never* been Joyless. "You have lost, creature. I am *Abdul Wadud!*" I shout at the Saint. "Abdul Wadud, the Servant of God the Loving!"

And as I raise my sword and go to my death, I am smiling.

Author's Note ....

Sir Edmund Spenser's *The Faerie Queene* is, in many ways, the unacknowledged urtext of the modern Anglophone epic fantasy novel. Everything we love about epic fantasy—sword fights, monsters, jaw-dropping scale, a cast of thousands, deliberate antiquarianism, the ability to make magic real to the "rational" reader—is there in *The Faerie Queene*. Book One, at least, is one of the masterpieces of English literature.

However, *The Faerie Queene* also prefigures many of epic fantasy's weaknesses: It rambles horribly in later books (and was in fact never finished). There's far too much description of clothing. More important, via a series of gruesome caricatures—of women, of Arabs, of Catholics—Spenser sets a sort of precedent for epic fantasy's all-too-common hatred of the Other. Despite this, or perhaps because of it, Book One's recurring Muslim villains—the "Saracen" brothers Sansfoy, Sansloy, and Sansjoy—have always spoken to me. What was it like for *them*, being trapped in this hateful allegory? That question led to this story...

"Goblin Market" (1862). The reclusive Christina Rossetti was already a very popular English poet before she published this long poem. Peopled as it is with two loyal sisters and a host of little goblin men offering their enticing wares, it was first thought to be merely a fairy tale intended for children. But the careful reader has only to ponder the "Hug me, kiss me, suck my juices, squeezed from goblin fruit for you" or "Eat me, drink me, love me; For your sake I have braved the glen, and had to do with goblin men" to see other levels to her enticing poem. This subtle, erotic subtext has, over the years, enticed many illustrators to draw from it. Christina's brother, Dante Gabriel Rossetti (the Pre-Raphaelite painter), was the first, followed by Laurence Housman and Arthur Rackham among many, many others.

·Goblin Market·

Uncaged

Gene Wolfe

I ought never to have read the letter. More signally, I ought never to have returned to the Ivory Coast. The letter found me at Cape Town. It was accompanied by another, from one Dubois. His went something like this:

> *For the present, monsieur, I have the honor to hold*
> *the position of your good friend M. Bercole, who*
> *is, alas, somewhat ill. This is to say, I am acting*
> *administrator general of this district. It is to be hoped*
> *that my term of office will be but short. The letter I*
> *enclose reached my hands only yesterday, though it has*
> *been weeks, it may be months, in the hands of others.*
> *Rest assured, monsieur, that it has been read not by*
> *M. Bercole nor by myself, and that those who placed*
> *it in our hands had not the capacity.*

> *My Dear Friend:*
> *Do not be offended, I beg you, by this salutation. When*
> *one drowns, any passerby is the dearest of friends.*

You may recall that the administrator general advised
Joseph to shoot me. For me to appeal to him now
would be hopeless. Your eyes were filled with a pity
which I then resented. Yes, I was such a fool! Joseph
is dead. He was killed by a leopard, the workers say.
There is no work for them and no chance of payment
should they work. They are fewer each day. I am
imprisoned in this cage. Sometimes I am fed. More
often I am not. Please help me! You look so kind!
Please help! Marthe Hecht

I went. What else could I do? A trading schooner returned me to the Ivory Coast, a voyage of thirty-two days that might easily have taken much longer. Bercole was clearly too ill to accompany me, though he wished to go. Dubois, the new man, flatly refused. To give him his due, he had nearly worried himself into a breakdown, crushed under the new responsibilities fate had heaped upon him; the trek up-country would have done him good. I tried to persuade him, but he was adamant. Seeing that argument was useless, I left as soon as possible, with four porters and a native gendarme called Jakada. He had brought the letter and so was a potential source of information about the Hecht plantation and specifically about the condition of the late owner's wife. I write "potential" because I really got few facts from him. She was *kai gaibou*, a leopard, meaning possessed by a panther spirit. When I inquired concerning her cage, he affirmed that she was locked inside it—but soon spoke of her roaming at night in search of prey. When I reminded him that he had told me she was caged, he shrugged.

I have written earlier of the baboons. They were as numerous as ever and seemed even more curious about us than before. They were, I believe, simply bolder in their curiosity because my party was smaller than Bercole's had been. Here I ought not, perhaps, record an experience that I still find uncanny and has no connection that I can see to what was to follow. Between one step and the next I found myself seeing myself and our party through the eyes of a baboon. It (or perhaps *she*) was normal, as were the rest of the troop, her friends and relations. I was utterly askew, a pale cripple forced to walk on my hind legs alone and covered with scabs. This took, as I have tried to say, no time at all. Then it was over, leaving me with the feeling that something intended for a baboon had been delivered to me by mistake. Before I had taken another ten strides, a young female ran up to me, felt the material of my shorts, and took my hand. For the next quarter hour or so we walked on in that manner, the young female reaching up to clasp my hand and walking easily on three legs. At length she released me and bounded away. I have no explanations to offer. Not even for a moment did I suppose that before a week had passed I would be shooting these same baboons.

Reaching the Cavally, we forded it and marched upriver for three long days, fording it again when we came in sight of the plantation that had been Hecht's. It appeared deserted, its fields returning to jungle. Seeing it, I felt quite sure his wife was dead.

We had come too far, however, to return to the coast without investigating, and it seemed at least possible that a few items of interest might be found in the bungalow. I told Jakada and the porters we would camp here for the night, and perhaps for two nights. When we had set up our camp, Jakada and I entered the bungalow.

We had no more than set foot in it when a woman's voice called, "Oku? Amoue?" Tired and sweating as I was, I ran toward it.

The cage was built against the side of the bungalow. A door of the kitchen gave easy access to it, and to the wide slot in its barred door through which trays were passed. I saw her then, her hands gripping the bars, and saw, too, the unmistakable joy she felt at the sight of me. It touched my heart, and touches it still. Yes, even after all that has happened.

I would have released her at once if I could, but the cage door was closed with a formidable padlock, and the key was nowhere in sight. When I asked Marthe whether she knew where it was kept, she replied, "Please do not call me by that name. It is not mine. Joseph used it because he wished the world to think me French. Though I loved him, I never loved the name he gave me."

I was tempted to question her then, but the chief business of the hour, as I then saw it, was to free her. Thus I asked again where I might find the key.

"Joseph always returned it to his pocket," she said. "He used to visit me in the evening. I feel quite certain you understand."

Of course I said I did, and went off looking for the key.

After an hour or so it occurred to me that if I had been in Hecht's position I would certainly have kept the key in my pocket, and not in a drawer of my desk or any other such place. Some of his employees might well have been minded to assault his wife or even to kill her. They might perhaps have accomplished her death by thrusting spears between the bars of the cage, but it would have been difficult and perhaps impossible. If they could enter her cage, however, one slash of a cane knife might easily have been enough. Those who had found Hecht's body might well have taken the key, but where were they now? Except for Hecht's widow, who could not leave, the plantation seemed utterly deserted.

And if they had not taken the key, it had presumably been interred with Hecht. The prospect of exhuming a corpse, one that had spent months in a shallow grave in central Africa, positively horrified me.

By that time I had discovered a workshop in one of the outbuildings. Such tools as remained there were few and simple, but I collected them and attacked the bars with a will.

Two hours of hard work availed nothing. My porters and I prepared a tray for the imprisoned woman. Her disappointment as she accepted it was as obvious as it was understandable.

I had washed and taken refuge beneath my mosquito net, sick with self-recrimination. I ought to have brought tools—no doubt they could have been purchased without difficulty in Abidjan. I ought to have brought skeleton keys, and asked a locksmith's advice, too. I ought to have learned the location of Hecht's grave. Though his widow could never have seen it, she might have known it. I could have sent Jakada and a couple of porters to look for it. Before I fell asleep, I decided that since all my labor on the bars had been fruitless, I would concentrate my efforts on the lock and the hinges in the morning.

And that is what I did. In a little over an hour I had drawn the pins of all three hinges and opened the door. But I have omitted too much by speaking of that humble triumph now. Not long after I had fallen asleep, I was awakened by a pistol shot. I called out, and one of the porters came. He told me that Jakada had shot at a leopard. He himself had not seen this leopard; Jakada had seen it and shot at it. I told him to send Jakada to me;

but if Jakada came it was only after I had returned to blissful sleep, and Jakada did not wake me.

That night I dreamed that a woman's naked body was stretched upon my own, and that she was kissing me. It was, I know, a dream of a kind only too common in men who have been long separated from the warm commerce of the sexes. Later this woman lay close beside me whispering, promising all the delights of marriage with none of its pains. I longed to tell her its pains would be my delight, if only we were wed; but I could not speak, only listen to her; and her voice might have been that of a breeze from the sea.

There has been another loss, a small boy this time. Sailors and volunteers are searching the ship. If we were ashore, I might buy handcuffs at some shop catering to the police. Then I could handcuff Kay to me and entrust the key to a friend. Nothing of the sort seems possible here. I would have the steward lock us in if that might be done; but the mechanism of our stateroom door prevents it, locking automatically when we go out but opening readily to those within.

How then, does Kay reenter? She must possess a key of her own. If I can find it and drop it over the side, she will be unable— no, what a fool I am! She takes my key from my pocket while I sleep. Thus the solution is simple. I must hide the key. She will not dare to leave unless she can reenter. I will hide it tonight, but I will most certainly not name its hiding place here.

Later. There, it is done! Kay has not returned; presumably she is still playing cards in the lounge. I will go out and rejoin her. When we return to this stateroom, I will tell her that I have left my key behind (which will in fact be sober truth) and get the steward to unlock the door and let us in. Clearly I cannot do the same thing tomorrow night, but I will have all day in which to think of a new plan. Or something better, I hope.

Morning. Kay was still sleeping when I left. My little ruse seems to have worked perfectly. The key was where I had hidden it, and I saw nothing to indicate that Kay had gone out. What I must do tonight, clearly, is return to our stateroom before her and conceal the key. When she returns, she will find me bathed and in my robe. In the morning I must rise before her and retrieve the key before she wakes.

But what am I to do when we reach New York?

Kay excused herself at dinner, I assumed to go to the ladies' room. She did not return. When she had been gone for half an hour, I enlisted the colonel's wife. She returned to say that Kay was not in there. She had looked in the booths, had looked everywhere, and there was no sign of her. Mrs. Van Cleef suggested that she might have been taken ill. It seemed unlikely—the South Atlantic was anything but rough—but I nodded, left, and toured the railing. She was not there.

Several people were out on deck, where the air was cooler. I described Kay, a beautiful woman, young, somewhat heavy, dark, black hair, yellow dress, and so on. No one had seen her, but one woman suggested that she might have gone back to our stateroom.

Unable to think of anything better (though the key was in my pocket), I went there. When I opened the door I got the shock of my life.

The stateroom was dark. The corridor in which I stood brightly lit. In our stateroom, emerald eyes glowed with reflected light!

I flipped the wall switch. Kay (Marthe?) lay on our bed, quite nude, propped up on one elbow and smiling. "I thought to arrange the small surprise for you."

I switched off the light and shut the door. "It was." I was gasping, and grasping at straws, too. "I couldn't imagine what had happened to you."

"You could not? You like our food, I think."

"It was good, as ship's food goes."

"This I do not think. It make me so ill I think to retire. The steward admit me."

I nodded. "I see."

"When I am undress, I am well again." Pouting. "You do not like my surprise? It may be I find the place for sleep elsewhere."

"Please don't." I was undressing too by this time. Without pondering the unintended irony I added, "It might be dangerous."

"For me you worry and worry." She laughed. "You pull up the pins. Is this what you they call? With the oil and so many tools you push them up. You must get them out! You work and work."

"You mean the hinge pins of your cage. Yes, I did."

"Perhaps I fool you. Perhaps I reach through my bars and pull them up." She sounded amused.

I refused the bait. "Perhaps you did." There had been three hinges and it had taken me almost an hour to remove the first. The other two had required at least twenty minutes each, even after I had learned how to do it.

"I worry also. About you I worry. That is bad, no? Most bad."

I was touched. "Foolish, at least."

"Not foolish, only bad. I worry that I may hurt you." She sounded genuinely concerned.

A thin line of fine, soft hair ran up from her pubic hair to her navel. I stroked it as I spoke. "I have been hurt before," I said. "I'm still here."

"Why is it you come to Africa?"

"To see it. I'd read a lot about it, and felt as though I should have a look myself while I was still young enough to do it." I recalled how difficult the decision had been, and the enormous relief I had felt when the ship was actually under way. Suddenly and delightfully, I had felt that I could fly—that I could do anything.

When she said nothing, I added, "I thought I might do a bit of big-game hunting, too. Elephants, rhinos, and hippos. Lions and leopards. Heads on my wall. All that nonsense."

She laughed. "Very long you would take to eat the elephant."

"You're right," I told her. "We should kill only to eat. I shot antelopes to feed my men. There were six of us coming, four porters, Jakada, and myself. Coming back, you made seven."

"You shoot the baboons. For this I am always grateful to you."

"They would have killed you," I told her.

And it was true—they would have killed her if they could. When they finally fled her, those nearest fled last. Torn and bleeding. Limping. Silent. The uninjured had chattered loudly. Not these. One's arm had been torn completely away. Neither my bullets nor Jakada's had done that.

"What is it you think? Always you think and think, always you are so silent."

"I suppose." We lay sweating in the dark, side by side.

"When you are old, old man, you will wish to speak but none will listen. He is old man, they will say. These old men know nothing."

Very well. I feel as old as a man can ever feel this night, older than you might believe, and I will say this. Old men know one thing. They know how little they know. Does Kay really harbor the spirit of a leopard? The soul of one? What is it, this thing we call the soul that it can—perhaps—be passed like a handkerchief from one hand to the next? Or does it pass itself, as a man leaves the house his parents left him and enters a new one?

Could Kay (who had been Marthe and how many others?) actually take the form of a leopard? Ridiculous on the face of it; but human eyes do not reflect the light. Only the eyes of an animal do that.

"Did you shoot the elephant? Give much meat to the men who help you?"

"No," I said. "I never shot one."

"For a tribe it is good, perhaps. There are so many hungry mouths there. The children crawl inside and come out. Then their little bellies are round with elephant meat." She laughed softly.

"I never shot one," I repeated.

"For you there will be vultures, jackals, hyenas. Feed us, *bawana*! We are your children."

So they would call, I thought, and they would be right. They are our children, the heirs of mankind.

"Leopards are cleaner than we," I said. This was not said to Kay; I was talking to myself as I sometimes do when I know I'm right. "They kill because they're hungry, and eat all they kill. We kill to create moth-eaten dust-catchers our human heirs will drop into the trash."

Kay murmured, "I am glad," apropos of what, I cannot say.

"The lions and leopards fear us as honest men fear criminals, and we fear them as criminals fear the police."

I fell silent until at length Kay said, "What it is you think?"

She was stroking me, but there were signs that it could not go on forever.

"I was thinking of the baboons. They chatter and chatter, and it doesn't mean a thing. Human beings must have chattered in the same way, with meaning gradually creeping in. Thus the origin of speech, which has puzzled so many."

"When I am a little girl, it is the same. My parents leave England and go to France. They send me to the French school. It is so I will be made ready for the school that come before school."

"Kindergarten," I said.

"That is German, garden of children. It is what we say in America?"

"I think so."

"I know only a few words English at that time, words I remember from England. I try and try to remember them all. At night in the bed I whisper them. It is like I pray."

"Because they had meaning," I said. "The French words you heard others say had meaning, too. But not to you, at that time."

"I love you," Kay whispered; and I wondered just what meaning, if any, those words held for her.

And for me.

Much later, after she had left me to go into the little bathroom down the corridor, and had returned to me (as I had greatly feared she would not); and after I had left her for much the same purpose, and had returned to a gently rocking bed I had feared would be empty, and had found her asleep there, she began to purr. It was a deep and vibrant purr, very soft.

I told myself over and over that I was dreaming, and at last I left our bed, dressed quietly, and went out. Her purr followed me until I cut it off by shutting the steel door of our compartment behind me.

Outside I found that the stars had come out before me.

Africa is an excellent place for seeing stars—I mean when one is out from under the trees, out on the veldt or in a field of some plantation. The sea is almost as good when the night is far advanced and the ship almost dark. The few running lights are invisible. The searchlight on the bridge probes the night, a shining pencil of light—and then goes dark. The night air is hot, and would be still if it were not for the motion of the ship. The stars do not twinkle but seem to be what they in fact are, distant fires.

"There is a big cat on board," a voice behind me said.

I turned to look, seeing only the pale blur of a face shadowed by a dark mustache. I wanted to say that he had certainly been mistaken. What I said instead was "It seems every ship has at least one cat."

"A much larger cat than that."

"You mean a big cat?" I asked. It sounded terribly stupid, but I could think of nothing else to say.

"Yes, exactly."

"Are you talking about a lion? Something of that sort?"

"Yes."

"A tiger, perhaps." I tried to sound amused.

He shook his head, the gesture scarcely visible though he was not two feet from me. "We just left Africa. There are no tigers in Africa. Tigers are found in India, China, and a few more Asian nations."

When I did not speak, he said, "Leopards are found in both Asia and Africa."

"So I understand."

"You yourself are interested in leopards, sir. Deeply interested. I hope you will forgive my touching on what is perhaps a personal matter."

"Certainly." I turned away, looking out to sea.

"We have had a death on this voyage. Two children appear to have vanished."

Without looking at him, I nodded. "So I understand."

"You have interested yourself in all three. You questioned Mrs. Bowen and the children's mothers."

"I believe I did," I said, "but you can hardly blame me. Those things have been the talk of the ship."

"While your interest in them has not been."

He had not asked a question, but I answered it anyway. "No. Or not to my knowledge. Why should it be?"

"You vouchsafed no information whatsoever to either woman."

"That is by no means true." I turned to face him. "You seem to know something about me, sir. I, on the other hand, know nothing whatever about you."

"I am Dr. Miles Radner. There is no ship's doctor aboard— perhaps you were aware of it."

I shrugged. "I haven't been ill."

"It is the case." Dr. Radner was almost whispering. "I am the only doctor on board. Passenger ships often carry a physician as a part of their crew. The post is a difficult one to keep filled, however."

No comment from me seemed to be called for.

"A married physician will rarely wish to spend so much time separated from his wife and family. Furthermore, a physician thus separated cannot refer his most difficult cases to a hospital. Too often his patients must die under his care, not because he lacks skill but because he lacks facilities."

"The dead man...?" I let the question hang.

"No. Bowen was dead when I was brought to see him. Nor could I have saved him if he had not been. He had been bitten in the back of the neck, a powerful bite that severed the spinal cord. It is the way in which big cats, and even lynxes and bobcats, kill."

I said, "You seem to know a great deal about these matters, Doctor."

"Thank you. Four years ago, I was called upon to treat a native who had been attacked by a leopard. Also to examine the bodies of some native children who had been killed, I would judge also by a leopard. Killed and partially eaten. Wolves and dogs tear the throat. The big cats bite the nape of the neck."

I did not turn away to face the sea again, but neither did I reply.

"Was this your first trip to Africa? I do not intend to pry."

"It was," I said, "but I stayed almost two years."

"You are independently wealthy. I am not, but I saved for more than twenty years in order that I might achieve my dream of hunting in Africa."

"I hope you enjoyed it."

"I did, though I hunted very little. Or killed very little, let us say. For one thing, I wanted to see the place every bit as much as I wanted to hunt. For another, every village had its sick—or so it seemed. I found I could not walk away and leave them."

"You had taken an oath," I suggested.

Dr. Radner shook his head. "It wasn't that. I did what I could, and quite often that was a lot. Infected wounds and broken limbs..."

"Did you ever get a trophy?"

"Nothing that would get me into the record book. One day Dan Harwood came to me with a new idea. Dan was my professional hunter, and he'd done his best for me. Record animals, even animals that just possibly might set a new record, are damned hard to find. Maybe a professional hunter sees a dozen, or half a dozen, in his entire career. But Dan had been listening to his shortwave and he'd heard something he thought might interest me. I hadn't gotten a leopard yet, and there was supposed to be a man-eater up in the Saraban. It might not be a record animal, he said, but it sounded like it had to be a big one."

You can guess how I felt when I heard the doctor say that. He can't have seen much of my face in the dark, and I wished with all my heart that he hadn't been able to see it at all.

"Record animals aren't the only ones that can get a hunter into the books. Kill a man-eater, and everybody who writes about big-game hunting will know your name. You'll be in a dozen books, in the papers, and in magazine articles a hundred years after you're dead. I told Dan I wanted to go after it, and I'd do whatever it took."

I said, "As interesting as this is, I think I'd better go. My wife will be getting worried."

For a moment I could see the doctor's teeth under that black mustache. "It gets more interesting to me—and I'd certainly think to you. If you'll take my advice, you'll stay and listen."

I did.

"We engaged a bush pilot to fly us up there. You can't land in that area, but there's overgrazed pasturage in the French Sudan not far from it. We hired a guide and a few porters, and ended up at a plantation owned by an immigrant named Joseph Hecht. I've heard he's dead now; did you know him?"

I shrugged. "I met him once."

"Not a friend, I take it."

I shook my head.

"He had sugarcane fields and coffee trees and so on, and

shipped his produce down the river. His plantation was about the only civilized place in the area. I met his wife as well, though he wouldn't let her out of her cage. I remember that I lit a cigarette for her. She smoked it with a good deal of pleasure and thanked me for it. Her husband didn't allow her matches—or at least, that was the impression I got." Dr. Radner took a cigarette from a gleaming case and lit it from the lighter built into the top, then offered me one, which I declined.

"Her name was Marthe, and although she was foreign she spoke understandable English. We left, and I never saw her again. Certainly I didn't expect to see her on this ship."

"Did you get the leopard?" I inquired.

"For a time I wondered if there was any. Have you heard of the leopard-men?"

I said I had not, but they sounded interesting.

"It's a sort of lodge." His teeth reappeared. "Something like the Masons. I'm a Mason myself."

There were deck chairs behind the promenade on which we stood. As he spoke I realized that something—a child, perhaps, or some sort of animal—was moving soundlessly among them.

"Many of them are witch doctors, or so I'm told. They wear leopard skins on their midnight raids, so that people who glimpse them will think they've seen a leopard. Have you ever worn brass knuckles?"

"No," I said, "but I know what they are."

"Their claws aren't quite like that, but the idea is much the same. The claws are iron and protrude between their fingers—that's what Dan told me. There's an iron handle inside that they grasp. They claw their victims, and the deaths are blamed on leopards."

"That's what you found in the Saraban?"

"It wasn't—that was what I half expected to find, based on tales I'd heard. Dan had warned me, you see. So had the bush pilot and some others. The best way to hunt a leopard is to construct a blind a hundred or a hundred and fifty feet away from his kill. In this case we couldn't do it, because the kills had been human beings. We staked out goats instead, and searched for pug marks in the morning with native trackers. It took ten days, but I got my leopard. By that time I had to go. I had already spent more time in Africa than I had intended or budgeted for. We thanked Hecht for his hospitality and radioed the bush pilot. The day after we left Hecht's plantation, we got word that another child had been killed by a leopard. It seemed that the leopard I had shot had not been the man-eater."

I asked whether he had gone back for that one.

"I didn't, nor did I want to. Now I've seen Hecht's wife on this ship, which was quite a surprise. I wasn't sure until I heard her talk, but now I have and that's her. What happened to Hecht?"

"He died," I said.

"Killed by a leopard?"

"So I'm told. I didn't see his body."

Dr. Radner nodded and flipped his cigarette over the railing and into the South Atlantic, where it died like a meteor.

"You told me Bowen had been bitten in the back of the neck," I said.

"I did." Dr. Radner nodded. "He was."

"What about the children?"

"I have no idea. But leopard-men kill their enemies, or at least that's what everybody says. I suppose they might kill their

enemies' children, too. Hatred of the family or revenge. Still..."
He let the sentence trail away.

"You must know the slanders that were directed against my wife."

"I do," Dr. Radner said. "I also know that it is utterly impossible for any human being to turn into a leopard, far less turn into a leopard for a few hours and return to human form. It is far from impossible, however, for a human being to *believe* that he or she does it. The witches of the Middle Ages believed they flew through the air on brooms. They believed that utterly and sincerely, and many like instances might be given. A man—or a woman—might believe that he or she became a leopard at times, and might use iron claws of the kind I had described to claw his or her victims to death. I told you what I did because it may be useful to you to distinguish between true and false leopard kills."

"There are no leopards in the United States." I made it as firm as I could.

"Correct, there are none—outside of those in zoos and circuses, and an unknown number in private hands. There are mountain lions, however, in almost every state in the union; jaguars are reported from time to time in the southernmost part of the Southwest."

When I said nothing in reply to that, Dr. Radner stepped back from the rail, touched his hat, and added, "Good night, sir. It is late, I've had my say, and I wish you pleasant dreams."

He left, and a few minutes later I heard a slight disturbance, a few confused noises followed by utter silence.

For an hour or more, I leaned against the rail, staring out to sea. It was not really cold, but a cold south wind had sprung up, and I had on only a lightweight tropical suit. I would have given a good deal for a drink then, but the ship's bar had been closed for hours. Eventually the colonel appeared, in search of a spot in which he could enjoy the last cigar of the day in peace. I welcomed him, he offered me a cigar, which I declined, and I chanced to lament the too-early closing of the bar. At that, he produced a silver flask, which he offered to me.

I accepted gladly and took it, limiting myself to two sips, though it tasted wonderful. It was gin, and I believe Bombay Gin; at the second sip I found myself visualizing the self-consciously old-fashioned label, with its portrait of Queen Victoria. I thanked him and returned his flask. We chatted for a few minutes, and I left.

I was perhaps halfway to the stateroom I shared with Kay when I found what I had expected to find rather nearer: the body of Dr. Miles Radner. For a minute or two I squatted beside it, examining the bite to the neck that had killed him. (Though he had been clawed as well.) From what I saw, it seemed obvious that the animal had shadowed him for a time, then sprung upon him from behind. Its claws would have held him for the necessary moment, and its bite had been fatal.

I rose and went on to our stateroom. Perhaps it was the gin, but I felt tired and very sleepy. Our cabin was dark; Kay was already back in bed and sound asleep. I undressed as quietly as I could and joined her without waking her.

Such is my story. There was some trouble about Kay's entering the country without a passport, but we explained that hers had been lost in Africa, and they soon let us in. She has applied for a new one, an American passport, since she is now the wife of an American citizen. Rather to my surprise she has asked that it carry her maiden name, which she gave as Kay Gaibou.

I see I have not mentioned that we are comfortably lodged now at my parents' place in upstate New York. To the best of my recollection it has been six years since I was last here. They are in Europe. I cabled them soon after we came ashore, telling them I was married and asking their permission to open the old place up and await them there. They agreed at once, as I expected.

Perhaps I ought to add that I have since received a letter from my mother; I must write to her as soon as I finish this. She says Germany is in chaos, with communists and National Socialists fighting quite openly in the streets. They will cut their stay there short and go on to Austria before returning home.

There was a piece in the paper this morning about the death of a fifteen-year-old girl (page A2). She was, the paper said, apparently killed by an animal. The article did not say whether parts of her body had been eaten. It was found lodged in a tree, about ten feet above the ground.

I showed the piece to Kay, who said she had already seen it. "Is it not terrible?"

Afterward I read the whole piece again. It is, of course—terrible and horrible, but what can I do?

What in hell can I do?

This story had two godmothers, if you will. The first was, obviously, that I love "The Caged White Werewolf of the Saraban" by William B. Seabrook, one of those wonderful short stories we have utterly forgotten; I wanted to draw attention to it. There are sins and there are *sins*. When I am gone, I do not want my prosecutor saying: "My Lord, Gene found this lovely story starving in a subcellar, climbed up, and forgot all about it."

Second, because it is a story that makes the reader say, "What happens next? Can one civilized man, alone at a plantation in Africa, imprison a woman for life and get away with it? Of course not! If he doesn't kill her, she's going to get out sooner or later—and probably sooner rather than later."

Contributor Biographies

SALADIN AHMED was born in Detroit. His short stories have been nominated for the Nebula and Campbell awards, reprinted in *The Year's Best Fantasy* and other anthologies, recorded for numerous podcasts, and translated into several foreign languages. His first novel, *Throne of the Crescent Moon*, which *Kirkus Reviews* called "an arresting, sumptuous and thoroughly satisfying debut," was recently published to wide acclaim. Saladin lives near Detroit with his wife and children.

KELLEY ARMSTRONG has been telling stories since before she could write. Her earliest written efforts were disastrous. If asked for a story about girls and dolls, hers would invariably feature undead girls and evil dolls, much to her teachers' dismay. Today, she continues to spin tales of ghosts and demons and werewolves, while safely locked away in her basement writing dungeon. She's the author of the #1 *New York Times*–bestselling Darkest Powers young adult trilogy as well as the Otherworld and Nadia Stafford adult series. Armstrong lives in Ontario with her family. You can find her online at www.kelleyarmstrong.com.

HOLLY BLACK is the author of bestselling contemporary fantasy books for kids and teens. Some of her titles include The Spiderwick

Chronicles (with Tony DiTerlizzi), the Modern Faerie Tale series, the Good Neighbors graphic novel trilogy (with Ted Naifeh), the Curse Workers series, her middle-grade novel, *Doll Bones*, and her vampire novel, *The Coldest Girl in Coldtown*. She has been a finalist for the Mythopoeic Award, a finalist for an Eisner Award, and the recipient of the Andre Norton Award. She currently lives in New England with her husband, Theo, in a house with a secret door. You can find her online at www.blackholly .com.

Neil Gaiman writes books for readers of all ages, including the Greenaway-shortlisted *Crazy Hair*, illustrated by Dave McKean; *Instructions*, illustrated by Charles Vess; *Coraline*, which won the British Science Fiction Association Award, the Hugo Award, the Nebula Award, the Bram Stoker Award, and the Elizabeth Burr/ Worzalla Award; the Hugo and Nebula Award–winning *American Gods*; *Anansi Boys*; and *Good Omens* (with Terry Pratchett); as well as the short story collections *Smoke and Mirrors* and *Fragile Things*. Most recently, Gaiman was both a contributor to and co-editor with Al Sarrantonio of *Stories*, and his own story in the volume, "The Truth Is a Cave in the Black Mountains," has been nominated for a number of awards. You can find him online at www.neilgaiman.com.

Kami Garcia is the *New York Times*– and internationally best-selling co-author of the Beautiful Creatures novels. *Beautiful Creatures* is being published in forty-eight countries and translated into thirty-seven languages. Academy Award nominee Richard LaGravenese directed the film adaptation of *Beautiful Creatures*. Kami is also the author of *Unbreakable*, the first book in her upcoming solo series, the Legion, which is currently being developed as a motion picture. When she is not writing, Kami can usually be found watching disaster movies or drinking Diet Coke. She lives in LA with her family and their dogs, Spike and Oz (named after characters from *Buffy the Vampire Slayer*). You can find her online at www.kamigarcia.com and @kamigarcia.

MELISSA MARR is the *New York Times*– and internationally best-selling author of the Wicked Lovely series, *Graveminder*, and *Carnival of Souls*. With Kelley Armstrong, she has edited two anthologies (*Enthralled* and *Shards & Ashes*) and co-authored the upcoming children's series the Blackwell Pages. Prior to writing, she taught university literature, including courses on the short story and in gender studies. You can find her online at www .melissa-marr.com.

GARTH NIX has worked as a literary agent, marketing consul-tant, book editor, book publicist, book sales representative, bookseller, and as a part-time soldier in the Australian Army Reserve. Garth's books include the award-winning fantasy nov-els *Sabriel*, *Lirael*, and *Abhorsen*; and the young adult science fic-tion novels *Shade's Children* and *A Confusion of Princes*. His fantasy novels for children include *The Ragwitch*, the six books of the Seventh Tower sequence, and the Keys to the Kingdom series. More than five million copies of his books have been sold around the world, his books have appeared on the bestseller lists of the *New York Times*, *Publishers Weekly*, the *Guardian*, and the *Australian*, and his work has been translated into forty languages. He lives in a Sydney beach suburb with his wife and two children.

Tim Pratt is a Hugo Award–winning science fiction and fantasy author whose works have been nominated for most of the major genre awards (including the Nebula Award, World Fantasy Award, Campbell Award for Best New Author, and Theodore Sturgeon Memorial Award, among others). His stories have been reprinted in numerous Year's Best anthologies, including *The Best American Short Stories*. He is a senior editor at *Locus*, the magazine of the science fiction and fantasy field, and edited the anthology *Sympathy for the Devil*.

Carrie Ryan is the *New York Times*–bestselling author of the critically acclaimed Forest of Hands and Teeth series, which has been translated into more than eighteen languages and is in development as a major motion picture. She is also the editor of the anthology *Foretold: 14 Tales of Prophecy and Prediction*, as well as author of *Infinity Ring: Divide and Conquer*, the second book in Scholastic's new multi-author/multi-platform series for middle-grade readers. A former litigator, Carrie now writes full-time and lives with her husband, two fat cats, and one large dog in Charlotte, North Carolina. You can find her online at www.carrieryan.com or @carrieryan.

Margaret Stohl is the *New York Times*– and internationally bestselling co-author (with Kami Garcia) of the Beautiful Creatures novels, as well as the forthcoming Icons novels, both from Little, Brown. *Beautiful Creatures*, which has sold more than one million copies, has been published in forty-eight countries and thirty-seven languages, and was released as a major motion picture from Alcon Entertainment and Warner Brothers in 2013. Alcon Entertainment is also developing *Icons* as a feature film. A graduate of Amherst College, with an MA from Stanford

University, Margaret made video games for sixteen years before turning to writing full-time. Margaret now spends most of her free time traveling to faraway places with her husband and three daughters, who are internationally ranked fencers. You can find her online at www.margaret-stohl.com or @mstohl.

CHARLES VESS has been drawing ever since he could hold a crayon and crawl to the nearest wall. Charles graduated with a BFA from Virginia Commonwealth University, and worked in commercial animation for Candy Apple Productions in Richmond, Virginia, before moving to New York City in 1976. It was there that he became a freelance illustrator, working for many companies and publications, including *Heavy Metal*, Klutz Press, Epic Comics, and *National Lampoon*. His award-winning work has graced the covers and interior pages of many comic book publishers including Marvel (*Spider-Man*, *The Raven Banner*) and DC (*Books of Magic*, *Swamp Thing*, *Sandman*). His work now is found more in book illustration, such as *The Ladies of Grace Adieu* (Bloomsbury), *The Coyote Road: Trickster Tales* (Viking), and *Peter Pan* (Starscape). Charles's art has been featured in several gallery and museum exhibitions across the nation, and in Spain, Portugal, the United Kingdom, and Italy. Charles's awards include the Inkpot, three World Fantasies, the Mythopoeic, two Spectrum Annuals—a Gold and a Silver—two Chesleys, Locus (Best Artist), and two Will Eisner Comic Industry Awards. He has resided on a small farm in the southwest corner of Virginia since 1991 and works diligently from his studio, Green Man Press.

GENE WOLFE is one of the most highly respected living authors of science fiction, best known for his ambitious and groundbreaking

Book of the New Sun series. He is a Science Fiction Hall of Fame inductee, a winner of the World Fantasy Award for Life Achievement, and a SFWA Grand Master, as well as the winner of two Nebula Awards and four World Fantasy Awards.

RICK YANCEY is the author of several novels and the memoir *Confessions of a Tax Collector*. His first young adult novel, *The Extraordinary Adventures of Alfred Kropp*, was a finalist for the Carnegie Medal and has been translated into seventeen languages. His novel *The Monstrumologist* received the Michael L. Printz Honor and was named a YALSA Best Book for Young Adults and a Booklist Editors' Choice for Youth. The sequel, *The Curse of the Wendigo*, was a finalist for the Los Angeles Times Book Prize. *The 5th Wave*, the first novel in an epic science fiction trilogy, will be published in the summer of 2013.